# THE JACARANDAS

A novel
*(Based on a true story)*

## Mark Whittle

ISBN:  978-0-578-99056-9

*To my dear friend Daniel, whose life story inspired this novel, and to Sebastian, my Argentine son*

## The facts

In the mid-1970s, Argentina was one of many Cold War proxy conflicts around the world that included Vietnam and others. The Soviet Union and Cuba pumped money, arms, and leftist terrorists into Latin America to destabilize fragile democracies supported by the United States. Angered by the escalating bombings and assassinations and by the growing armed guerillas, Argentina's military overthrew the Peronist government in March 1976. The new military regime promised to restore order and fix the crumbling economy. It embarked on a heavy-handed war on terrorism.

It went too far.

## The fiction...

We used to wonder where war lived, what it was
that made it so vile. And now we realize that we know where
it lives...inside ourselves.

–Albert Camus

# PART I

# CHAPTER 1 – LOS MONSTRUOS

## *The Monsters*

*Spring 1976*
*Buenos Aires, Argentina*

The call for the pickup came early. There was nothing odd in that, but it was an unfamiliar client and from Belgrano too, and the sum of these considerations made Daniel pause on his porch. These days one needed to be careful. It seemed the country now was full of monsters.

That's what his father told him anyway.

Daniel grunted. His father had too much imagination and not enough courage.

Daniel lit a cigarette. He wasn't in the habit of smoking, but he was angry at the interruption to his morning routine. "Antonio's not feeling well," his father had said, his hands wrapped around his *mate* tea gourd. "I need you to take this first trip for him before you go to the university." Daniel made the best of it by stealing a pack of cigarettes from his father's coat by the door. The dark blend *Particulares 30*, deceptive in their white packaging, were too strong for Daniel's liking and he would throw most of them away, but he thought perhaps taking them would make him feel better all the same.

The streets were empty at this hour. It took Daniel only twenty minutes before he slowed his brother's *remis* taxi in front of the Italian-style villa on Calle Aguilar and waited, the

9

engine idling. Neat rows of sycamores formed an arching canopy over the street. This part of Belgrano brimmed with mansions and ambassadors' residences, yet this particular house lay conspicuous on a rounded corner of two quiet streets. A wrought-iron fence crowned a stone wall curving around the entire front of the house. The spear-shaped spikes bristled, more menacing than protective.

Daniel debated whether to announce his presence. Houses like these always had staff on hand, and no doubt his arrival had been noticed. Big houses tended to contain big egos, and the longer he was made to wait, the more rushed and impatient was the client. The more gripes about the service, and the clearer the logic to explain why no tip could be given at all.

The front door opened, and a man stepped onto the portico. He wore a crisp naval uniform and the confidence of a senior officer. He looked irritated, and he shouted something back into the house. A woman appeared at the door. She was crying.

A white Argentine mastiff padded out by the man's side. Setting his soft leather briefcase on the landing, the officer rubbed the dog's head and spoke to him.

*An admiral.* He seemed quite young, and no doubt had been promoted quickly. After the military coup seeking to restore order to the streets, the government now had much demand for such officers. But to whom much was given, much was required, and this officer surely would not disappoint. There was a manly purposefulness about him, and Daniel sat up straighter in his seat.

When the Admiral collected his briefcase and began descending the stairs, Daniel jumped out and held the back door open.

"To the ESMA," the Admiral said. He had the clipped tone

of one accustomed to giving orders.

Daniel eased the remis through the tree-lined streets and turned north onto the broad Avenida Libertador. *The ESMA?* His father wouldn't like this man. He would say he was one of the monsters. *Why couldn't his father be more like Uncle Ricardo?*

Daniel looked in the rearview mirror. The Admiral gazed out the window, his elbow on the armrest and his hand under his chin.

"You stare?" said the Admiral. "Curious why I'm using a regular remis, no?"

Daniel's face reddened. He focused his eyes on the traffic.

"I fired my chauffeur this morning. *Un imbécil,*" said the Admiral. "This is your remis?"

"No, sir. It's my brother's. My father's, actually," said Daniel.

A pause.

"Your father has two sons. Of course he does," said the Admiral, and then more to himself than to Daniel, "What I would do to have a son. Or a daughter."

Daniel thought about the woman crying at the door.

They passed a church and Daniel glanced at the San Cristóbal swinging from the mirror. His father would have reached out and touched it.

"If I had children," said the Admiral, "I'd expect them to do something more significant with their lives. This is what you do, no? You drive for your father?"

"No, sir. I just help when needed. I'm at…at the university. At the UBA."

A muscle in the Admiral's jaw jumped. "Is that so?" he said.

Daniel suddenly wished he hadn't shared so much information.

"Why would you waste your time in that subversive hellhole?" said the Admiral. "I hope you're not one of those leftists contributing to the violence." He settled back in his seat and waved his hand as if clearing some invisible obstacle. "You don't seem the type."

"No, sir," said Daniel.

He stole a glance in the rearview mirror, which he positioned at an angle to see out the back window and keep an eye on the passengers. It was something he'd learned from his father, who used to drive a regular taxi. His father had stories. He had seen it all. The abusive drunks and the bloodied passengers. The crazies. Couplings in his back seat. His father knew when a passenger was about to bolt without paying, and when he was about to be robbed. He kept a screwdriver under his seat which he had used more times than he cared to remember. The remis, he had told Daniel, brought a better clientele.

"What do you study at the university?" said the Admiral.

"I'm at the medical school," said Daniel. "It's my father's dream for me, really," he added, feeling a need to justify himself before this man.

"Your country needs strong young men like you in the military," said the Admiral. "Men with medical training. You're due for your military service, no?"

"I've not received a draft notice," said Daniel.

"No doubt your lottery number will come up soon," said the Admiral. "Just hope you're not sent to fight the guerillas in the jungles of Tucumán, or some other *mierda* place like that. Use my name. Tell them Admiral Bertotti said to take care of you."

"It's most kind of you, sir," said Daniel. He wondered when he would get his notice and how he would feel about it. A small part of him *wanted* to be called up.

They arrived at the *Escuela Superior de Mecánica de la Armada*. Four naval guards stood by the barricade, but as the Admiral emerged from a regular remis taxi, they quickly broke attention and ran to assist him.

Daniel leaned over to accept the cash from one of the guards. He wondered if what he'd heard about this place was all true. Rumors of dark green Ford Falcons arriving here at night with their hooded occupants. The tortures and the disappearances. *Los desaparecidos.*

To be honest, he had never thought much about the subject at all and might not have believed it anyway, except that Uncle Ricardo had told him stories from the police force. "The only way to prevent a civil war and reestablish order," he had told Daniel, "is to meet violence with violence, *¿viste?* It's the only thing these bastards understand. *¿Entendés, Dani?"* His uncle always knew how to explain things in a way that made sense.

Daniel stared at this naval academy with its forty tidy acres anchored in the middle of the city, and he suddenly felt unmoored. Before him was order and discipline and purpose.

Daniel felt for the pack in his front pocket and lit a cigarette with a flick of his wrist. His hand rested on the steering wheel, and the smoke jittered out the open window.

He shoved the car into gear and darted back into the traffic of Avenida Libertador. His brother would need the remis back, and he needed to catch the bus for class.

# CHAPTER 2 – LA CARTA

## *The Letter*

Daniel slid the window farther open. It was always stuffy in the *colectivo* after his classes.

The bus was in Flores now. *Almost home.* He pulled the rope and stood up. *"Disculpá,"* he said, jostling his way through the crowd in the aisle. The bus slowed, never fully stopping, and Daniel hopped off.

He glanced up the street. His brother's remis was not there. *Good.* Antonio always brought out the worst in him.

*"Hola, Papi,"* said Daniel as he entered the back door. He found his father sitting at the kitchen table, his shoulders slumping.

*"Hola, hijo."* Emilio's eyebrows shot up and were lost in his gray hair. It seemed to Daniel his father had aged since the morning.

Daniel tossed his bag onto a chair. A letter perched on the edge of the table. Emilio looked away, and Daniel knew what it was. He rubbed his temples and then reached for it. He thought of the Admiral he met early that morning, and he imagined himself standing guard at the ESMA in a naval uniform.

Daniel slid out the contents of the envelope and read it.

"We knew it might come," said Emilio. He let out a long breath.

"I think I might like the military, actually," said Daniel, dropping the letter on the table.

"*Like* it?" said Emilio, his mouth open. "It's dangerous. Your brother hated it."

"Antonio's a coward," said Daniel.

His father sighed. "They're not even letting you finish out the semester's classes. You're to report in one month."

"University's a waste of time anyway, Papi," said Daniel, grabbing a cookie from the Bagley tin on the kitchen counter. "All the student protests and disruptions. It gets worse every day."

"I know, *hijo*." Emilio laid his newspaper on the kitchen table and folded his reading glasses in a deliberate way. "But what will you do if you don't finish your studies? Drive a *remis* like your old man and your brother, and waste this opportunity you have? Think of all the sacrifices we've made for you."

Daniel heard the outside gate creak. His pulse quickened. He leaned against the kitchen counter.

"Antonio never had the chance—," Emilio continued.

"Antonio *what*?" Antonio stood in the doorway. "I never *what*?"

"*No es nada, hijo,*" said Emilio. "It's nothing. Daniel is tired. We were just discussing his studies at the UBA."

"Is that it again?" said Antonio. "The one who has every opportunity and wastes them all? Just let him quit. Why do you continue defending him?" Antonio threw his keys onto the counter. "He's lazy. I'm the only one who's not a quitter. I work for you driving your *remis* twelve hours a day, and I never say anything."

"I know you do, son. You do a great job. It's your remis too, remember. And Daniel's not quitting. He's just talking. *Vos sabés.*"

"And, Papi," said Antonio, "you might be out there driving every day, but you've quit too. You quit when Mother died."

Daniel clenched his fists. "Don't ever talk about them like that," he said.

"Shut your mouth," said Antonio. "I would have thrown you out long ago. You've never done a single damned thing around here. You're a leech."

"Antonio, please," said Emilio, stepping between his sons. "Let's be civil. Let's calm down. *Por favor.*"

Antonio stormed down the hall and slammed a door. The shower turned on.

Daniel seethed. He had almost clocked his brother. It would not have been a fair fight. It never was. Antonio was taller, but Daniel was stronger, quicker, and good with his fists. He was proud of his physical strength and self-confidence, but he had a temper. It could get him into trouble.

A train rumbled by on the tracks behind the house. The walls shook, and the dishes rattled in the cabinet. Most days Daniel didn't even notice the trains, and at night, he slept right through them. One got used to a lot of things, like sleeping on the sofa. He still shared a room with Antonio, but Daniel's bed had not been slept in for over a year. Today the train grated on his nerves. He heard his brother finish his shower and shut the bedroom door. Damn it. It was his room too.

Daniel pulled out a chair and sat at the table. His father looked out the dirty window. They had never gotten past it. The truck had come out of nowhere. Daniel's mami lay crushed against the windshield, her mouth open in surprise. He remembered the San Cristóbal swinging on its chain from the rearview mirror. It swung for a long time and everything was quiet. He was ten years old. He had never cried.

He had a memory of the closet door opening and his father coming in. Papi had knelt and wrapped his arms around Daniel as he sat on the parquet floor, his mother's clothing strewn around him. He had his mother's red scarf pressed to his face, smelling.

One day Daniel had come home from school to find some women in the house. The brittle flower bouquets lay in a pile by the trash. His mother's clothes had been washed and dried, and the women were folding and sorting them. They put them in cardboard boxes and loaded them into the back of an old car that wheezed and clattered and took his mami away for good.

Antonio, showered and dressed, returned and sat at the small kitchen table. Emilio prepared a dinner of fried *milanesa* and mashed potatoes. The three ate in silence.

Antonio poured himself a cup of coffee. Daniel cut his breaded steak.

"How was the pickup this morning, Daniel?" said Emilio, "The one from Belgrano? Antonio, you should thank your brother."

"It was fine, Papi," said Daniel.

"Antonio," said Emilio, "Your brother received his military service letter today."

"Did he?" said Antonio, a sneer curling one side of his mouth. He pushed back his chair and stood. "That's wonderful news. Maybe it'll grow him the hell up."

Antonio picked up his keys and left the way he had come an hour ago.

Daniel stretched his legs under the table while Emilio cleaned up the dishes. He thought about the Admiral. He slid the letter toward him and tapped it on the edge of the table.

# CHAPTER 3 – EL TÍO RICARDO

## Uncle Ricardo

The weather turned cold and a fine rain fell from the lead sky. Daniel stood beside a pillar at the medical school building, testing the droplets with an open palm. He tightened up his jacket and slung his book bag over a shoulder.

It was fifteen blocks to meet Uncle Ricardo at the federal courthouse on Calle Carlos Pellegrini. The wet spoiled any enjoyment in the brisk walk. He barely noticed the iconic obelisk in the middle of Avenida 9 de Julio, which Daniel crossed in a single green light by sprinting across the twelve lanes of traffic.

He fingered the letter in his pocket. Uncle Ricardo would want to see it.

Since Daniel began attending the UBA, they met from time to time, usually near his uncle's police substation just a few blocks from campus. This morning when Daniel had called, his uncle told him to meet him at the federal labor courts. He was providing police security detail for a judge threatened by leftist subversives. "We do a lot of this shit now, Dani," his uncle had said as Daniel struggled to hear from the pay phone in a busy university corridor. "Boring as hell. Come find me. We'll walk to Broccolino and have a pizza, ¿si?" Daniel wondered if that's what he could expect from his military service, and he tried to imagine what security detail would look like.

The honking cars and grinding buses inched along the

glistening streets of the evening rush hour. Daniel dodged umbrella-carrying pedestrians hurrying along the sidewalks.

He wasn't exactly sure what he expected his uncle to say. Perhaps, Daniel thought, he just needed someone who would tell him his excitement about the military was okay. Uncle Ricardo would know what to say.

Ahead he saw the granite steps of the federal courthouse. A group of people descended toward the busy street, and Daniel thought he spotted several police officers. At that moment, there was a tremendous roar and Daniel felt himself lifted through the air. Fear shot through him like a stabbing knife. White smoke rose thick into the air and enveloped Daniel. It smelled of plastic. It was difficult to breathe. Daniel's ears rang, and he could hear his temple pounding. He became aware of people screaming. A young woman ran by with blood pouring from her hand, and a man limped, his face an open-mouthed horror.

*Uncle Ricardo!* Daniel sprinted toward the blast. *Dios Santo, don't let him be there!*

A woman held her baby and screamed, "Where's my baby? *¡Mi bebé!*"

"You're holding your baby, *señora,*" said Daniel, touching her arm.

"No, no! My other one. I have another one." She was hysterical.

The pavement crunched beneath Daniel's shoes and the sound traveled through his legs and registered in his inner ear. It was glass. Blood and glass everywhere. Something green and shiny caught his attention, and he picked it up. It was a medallion of St. Jude, the patron saint of policemen and of hopeless causes.

Three bodies lay in awkward positions against the granite steps. One man's chest was torn open, and he was making a ghastly sucking sound, his eyes fixated on Daniel, who realized in a horrible instant it was Uncle Ricardo. Daniel lunged toward him but slipped on the rain- and blood-slicked stairs and went down hard on his side.

"Uncle! ¡*Tío*! Someone help!" Daniel cried. "*Ayudá*, for the love of God!" He collapsed. Daniel lost track of everything. He heard ambulances wailing in the distance and felt people moving about him. His hand hurt badly, and he pried open his clenched fingers to find the medallion. He tried offering a prayer to St. Jude but couldn't come up with any words, and he let it slide from his hand.

Daniel sat in the front row of the small chapel, staring at the discolored whitewashed plaster behind the closed casket and the familiar icons on their lonely pedestals. Nothing had changed. It was exactly as he remembered when his mother's body lay in the same spot as Uncle Ricardo's, the funeral presided over by the same dateless and muttering Padre Andrés, a man so focused on heaven that he was of no earthly good.

Uncle Ricardo would hate this place, Daniel thought. He wouldn't want to be here where nothing happened, where the crumbling lot beside the chapel was still for sale and covered in graffiti and the tattered remnants of Peronist election posters. No, his uncle would want to be outside in the sun doing something. Daniel remembered Uncle Ricardo telling him about the motorcycle trip he took many years ago on the Pan-American Highway, just before he joined the police force. "The sun on my face and the wind in my hair, Dani, the open road ahead," he had told him. "It's the closest I've been to heaven."

Daniel's insides roiled. Joining the military now was

personal. He hoped the rumors about the torture of the *subversivos* were true and that he'd have a chance for revenge. Daniel looked over at the federal police honor guards sitting rigid and immaculate in their uniforms. After the ceremony, they would take the flag-draped casket out the same way they had brought it in. Daniel wondered about the other policeman killed and whether his family and friends were in another chapel at this very hour. He heard the funeral for the assassinated judge was to be held at the *Catedral Metropolitana* and led by the cardinal archbishop himself.

An idea suddenly crystallized in Daniel's mind like pieces snapping into place. He wasn't going to stick around at home and at the university for the next month waiting for his military service to start. The world had taken so much from him, and he was going to take some back. An electric thrill surged within him. He'd never felt more alive.

# CHAPTER 4 – LA ESCAPADA
## *The Escape*

The next morning, Daniel lay on the sofa facing the wall and waited. His heart pounded. He thought about the settlement money from the truck company. His father had never spent any of it. Years ago, his father had converted most of it into crisp $100 bills to protect against inflation. Yet the banks were not to be trusted either, and the money lay hidden under the loose parquet tiles in his father's bedroom.

Antonio left first in his taxi and then Emilio. Daniel heard his father's remis start up and idle for five full minutes. When it pulled away, Daniel got up and walked down the hall to the back bedroom. Sinking to his knees, he removed the tiles and looked at the wrapped bundle that contained his mother's blood money. He unrolled it and picked up the stack of money. *I'll just take a little bit.* A third of it was his anyway, he figured. He undid the rubber bands and peeled off some bills. His share might even be half since his father never spent any and likely would divide it between his sons. Daniel took a few more bills then carefully wrapped it all back up and replaced the tiles.

He packed a rucksack and then sat on the sofa, wondering when he would be back and under what circumstances he would find himself. He imagined himself in a smart, crisp uniform. A hero.

Locking the door behind him, Daniel boarded a bus and rested the rucksack between his feet. He touched the bills in his breast pocket.

Daniel got off downtown and made his way to Calle Florida. *"Cambio, cambio. Dólares."* The money changers were always there. He nodded to one of them and was directed to a cramped side street office where a man pounded on a calculator and whipped through a thick stack of pesos wrapped in rubber bands.

Daniel recounted the bills, his eyes big. His sudden wealth filled him with a sense of freedom and possibilities.

He stepped back onto the street.

*"Cambio, cambio. Dólares."*

Daniel wandered most of the day. In the afternoon, he sat at a bar drinking hot *mate* and cold beer. He thumbed through the vinyl records at a music store. He paused at the window of a motorcycle sales shop, but when the salesman appeared, Daniel left.

He had a sudden urge to see someone who could share in his excitement. Forty minutes later, Daniel stopped in front of an apartment building in Villa Crespo. Sweat dripped from his forehead and slid down his back. The coolness clung to his shirt as he shifted the weight of the rucksack to the other shoulder. He stood at the lobby door but then crossed the street and sat on a bench. Valentina was not home yet. Her classes finished later. It felt good to sit.

The *colectivos* chuffed and coughed their way past him in an endless parade. The *butaneros* clanged down the street, exchanging empty bright orange butane tanks for full ones, the maids and housewives making signals perceptible only to the *butanero* men. A brief appearance at a window or door. The movement of a curtain.

The musical whistle of a knife sharpener pierced the air, and Daniel watched the old man walk his ancient bicycle with the grinding wheel on the back.

Clouds appeared in the sky and the wind picked up. Light raindrops fell. Daniel stretched out on the bench and tilted his head toward the sky.

Valentina walked right past him, her black hair bouncing off her shoulders. She wore jeans and a navy blue sweater that made her curves look good.

He missed her smell.

Valentina prepared to cross the street to her apartment.

"Vale!" Daniel called out.

She whirled around. *"¡Dani!"*

They kissed on the cheek and embraced.

*"Che,* I'm so sorry about your uncle," Valentina said. "I came to the funeral. I didn't want to bother you and the family."

"Yeah, thanks," said Daniel. "Let's get coffee."

"Okay, yes. I can't stay long. I'm sorry."

"Stop being so sorry," said Daniel.

They found a café on Avenida Scalabrini and picked a table inside. Daniel leaned against the window and ordered two *solos*. He placed his bag on the floor beside him.

"You seem to be doing okay," Valentina said. "Are you okay? I've been a bit worried about you, really. But even before your uncle died, I've not seen you at the student plaza or at El Barrio. I saw you once, maybe a week ago, across the plaza, but you were walking so fast I couldn't catch up. The others have been asking about you too."

"Marry me, Vale," Daniel said. He just said it. It was the exuberance he was feeling about everything. And something made him want to kiss her right there and to tell her he loved her. To tell her Cristian was all wrong for her.

"What?" said Valentina. "Don't joke like that. You've never liked me that way." She slid a loose strand of hair behind her ear and looked out at the street. *"Idiota.* I can't

24

believe you said that."

Daniel cocked his head and grinned. He stood and moved from across the table and sat in the chair beside her. He leaned his head on Valentina's shoulder. He smelled her hair, and he closed his eyes.

"You know things could have been different," said Valentina. She pushed Daniel off. "Cristian and I are happy together, you know."

Daniel sat up. "I'm going to leave the city for a while."

"What?" said Valentina. Her eyes settled on his rucksack on the floor. "You're serious? Where will you go?"

"A vacation," said Daniel. "You know, get away somewhere for a while."

"But why?" said Valentina. "What about your classes?

"It's a waste of time," said Daniel. "I'm done."

"I thought you wanted to become a doctor."

"Bah. That's been what my father wants, but I've realized it's not what I want. Anyway, my military service is coming up, you know."

Valentina's eyes were wide. She leaned in close. "What do you mean, Dani? Is that why you're leaving? Leaving the country? I've heard of people doing that so they don't have to serve. Waiting for things to, you know, to get less dangerous. Isn't it terrible out there, what's happening?"

Daniel chortled. "Sounds like you have me confused for a subversive coward." He smiled and slouched in his seat, folding his thick arms. "To tell you the truth, I think I'll rather enjoy being in the military, *¿viste?* Getting revenge for my uncle. Restoring order to the streets. I can be part of the solution. Not cowering, buried under books and hoping the problem just goes away."

"Is that what you think I'm doing? Cowering?" said Valentina. She turned and sat sideways in her seat to face him.

"No, I mean, *mirá vos*. You know what I mean, Vale."

"No, Dani, I don't know," she said, her jaw set. "What the police are doing, with their crackdowns, they're riling up the students and causing the problems. You know most of the UBA students couldn't care less about communism. It's a fad. It's what students do. They protest."

"You just don't get it," said Daniel. "What about my uncle? What about all the terrorist bombs and the assassinations? What do you think the military coup was for? You need to stop reading the Marxist papers on campus. They've brainwashed you."

"I know what's going on," said Valentina. "It's a dangerous time, Dani. It's not a time to do something stupid and try to be a hero. Finish out the year at least, then come back after your military service."

"That's just it," said Daniel, "I don't want to lay low. I don't want to miss the action." He laughed. "And I *am* going to be a hero. My country needs me."

"You've always had that macho image, haven't you?" said Valentina. "You going to be a federal policeman like your uncle? Don't do it, Dani. No good will come from it."

Valentina looked at her watch. "I have to go. I can't stay."

She pushed her chair back and stood.

Daniel pulled out some bills to leave on the table. He picked up his rucksack and together they walked to her apartment.

"You won't leave, will you?" said Valentina. "Come on. Let's go out on Saturday, you and me and Cristian and Fede and Javi. Gabriela. ¿*Sí*?"

"No," said Daniel, shaking his head. "I'm going on vacation for a while before my sign-up date with the military. An adventure. In fact, I'm going to try to get someone to go with me. You think Cristian will go?"

Valentina looked at him like he was crazy.

He kissed her on the cheek.

"If you marry me, Vale, I'll give you a chance to drop your ridiculous Basque names, Valentina Amozorrutia Goyenechea!"

Valentina smiled. Daniel waited for her to enter the lobby. She turned and looked back at him through the glass and waved a hand.

He shouldered his bag and walked to a cheap hotel to spend the night. Tomorrow, he thought, it will be tomorrow. It took him a long time to fall asleep.

The next day Daniel fed coins into a pay phone and spun the numbers on the rotary plate. He called his close friends first. They all turned him down. No one wanted to go. *Are you crazy? I have no money. I have commitments.* Even his most directionless friends suddenly found a new purpose, preventing them from giving in to their natural tendencies.

The list expanded to more peripheral circles of friends.

"Gordo, this is Daniel."

There was a pause.

"Daniel Romandini."

*"Che, ¿que tal, Dani?"* came the voice on the other line.

"Look, I'm taking a motorcycle trip out of the city, to get away for a while. An adventure, Gordo. A Che Guevara experience. I want to know if you'll come with me."

Another pause.

*"Si, claro."*

"You will?"

"Yes."

"I want to leave soon, Gordo. Really soon," Daniel said.

"I have no money, Dani. And I have no motorcycle. I have

no motorcycle," he repeated.

Gonzalo was an old friend from school, but they had never been close. He had a slight speech impediment, especially when he was nervous or excited. There were problems at home. Everyone called him Gordo as he was overweight, even as a kid. His bulk seemed to drag down his ambitions, too. Gordo never tried for university and was allergic to work. Daniel didn't know what Gordo did with his time. Daniel didn't care. What mattered was that he would go.

"Look, I'll buy the motorcycles," said Daniel. "I have money. We'll sell them when we get back."

Daniel hung up the phone. Gordo will be a good companion, he told himself.

# CHAPTER 5 – LA AVENTURA

## *The Adventure*

They met at a motorcycle sales shop. Daniel and Gordo smiled and gave each other the customary kiss on the cheek and an embrace.

They admired the bikes. They smelled the new tires and the oil-gasoline mixtures. The tile floors reeked of bleach. The combination proved intoxicating, and their conversation grew animated as they dreamed of the opportunities these two-wheelers could provide. The salesman wished to join in their exuberance, and he was welcomed in. An hour later with heads held high, they rode out on a pair of used and matching 175cc Zanellas.

Later that afternoon, they met at a café near the Pan-American Highway, each with a rucksack. Daniel ordered them coffees. Gordo tacked on a sandwich.

*"Sos loco, che,"* said Daniel, looking at Gordo's bag. "It's way too big. It'll pull you off the bike."

*"Che*, the only crazy one here is you," replied Gordo. "This is your idea. *Acordá."*

Now that they fancied themselves following the same route as the revolutionary, the filler word *che* gained renewed importance.

"You think we can get to Córdoba?" said Gordo, his eyes big. "I've always wanted to go. My grandmother is from there, you know. My grandmother is from there."

They had discussed taking the Pan-American Highway and

following Che Guevara's famous route in 1952. It hadn't occurred to them to consider anything else. Neither of them had been much farther than an hour or so outside of Buenos Aires. They had no idea how far the distances were.

The Pan-American Highway stretched forty-eight thousand kilometers and across fourteen countries from Ushuaia in the extreme southern tip of Argentina to Prudhoe Bay, Alaska, a distance baffling even to the most experienced traveler. It was the longest road in the world.

"Did you bring a map?"

"No, did you?"

"No."

"I know Che first went to Córdoba," Daniel said. "We get on right here and go north. The sign there says *Norte*, but I know Córdoba is more like west, so I assume it will curve west."

"You mean we might be lost before we've even started?" said Gordo. "Maybe we should get on where it says *West*."

Gordo would be no help with navigating. Daniel hoped his partner brought other complementary abilities to the adventure. None came to mind.

*"Boludo*, it's either north or south," said Daniel. "We're going north."

"How far is it to Córdoba?" asked Gordo, looking across the street at the entrance ramp.

"I don't know," said Daniel. "A long way."

They got the attention of the waiter. "How far to Córdoba?"

"A long way," the waiter said.

The young men finally pulled out and rode northwest on the Pan-American. They passed endless fields of soy, sunflower, and wheat. The warm air rushed through Daniel's hair and whipped about his ears. Buenos Aires felt a million miles away.

That first heady afternoon they traveled two hundred fifty kilometers before pulling over to spend the night. Their entire bodies ached as if they had been hiking all day rather than riding.

Motorcycle riding is a solitary experience and, having spent so much time alone with their thoughts that day, they prattled like schoolboys as they set up camp and made a fire to heat water for *mate*.

They stretched out on their blankets that night.

*"Mirá,"* said Daniel, pointing at the night sky.

They rolled onto their backs and gazed up. Neither had seen anything like it. The majestic beauty of the star-filled sky left Daniel in awe, and he struggled to grasp the vastness of the heavens. Yet there was a palpable nearness to it all as if he could reach out his hand and touch the stars. At once nothingness and everythingness.

*"Sabés, Gordo,"* began Daniel, but his companion was asleep. Daniel wasn't sure what he was going to say anyway.


They awoke late in the morning to the rumbling and tire slapping of trucks on the highway. Daniel boiled water and made coffee. "Just think. Today we'll be in Córdoba."

Gordo shook his head. "No way. I don't think I can even get onto my motorcycle," he said, warming his hands around the coffee cup. "The last sign I saw on the highway says we're still four hundred kilometers from the city, and yesterday we only did two hundred."

"Yeah, but yesterday we didn't start riding until the afternoon," said Daniel. "We can make more stops if we need to." He wanted to make it to Córdoba that day, maybe just to feel they were making progress.

"Come on," Daniel added. "We'll take a long lunch break somewhere. I'll treat you to big *bife de chorizo* and a beer."

This had the intended effect upon Gordo, and they climbed stiffly onto their motorcycles and pulled onto the highway.

They rode for several hours and stopped for lunch at a restaurant crowded with truck drivers and families spilling out of small cars, roof racks piled high with baggage. The all-you-can-eat buffet suited Daniel and Gordo just fine.

They parked their bikes on the side of the restaurant close to the windows and caught a glimpse of the *parrilleros* out back grilling the meats on vertical spits. It smelled wonderful and they hurried inside.

They ordered Quilmes beers from the waiter and headed to the buffet. Ignoring the salad bar, they made for the empanadas, pizza, chorizos, and the cuts of beef. There was no room on their loaded plates for the French fries and bread. These would have to wait for the second helping.

After their fourth trip to the buffet, they asked the waiter again to refill their chimichurri sauce. He sniffed at them, and they soon saw him speaking with the manager and pointing in their direction.

Daniel smiled. "Is this where the manager comes over now and tells us that's it, that's all we can eat?"

"He can't do that!" said Gordo, squeezing the words around his mouthful of beef. "It's an all-you-can-eat. I'm getting my money's worth."

"Don't forget who's paying for this," said Daniel.

Gordo waved his fork in the air, trying to swallow. "Considering the quality of this *entraña*, I think the manager is preparing to apologize to us. Damn right he should."

"I can't eat another thing," said Daniel.

"Well, I can," said Gordo, "and I won't be taken advantage of." He wiped his greasy mouth with a napkin and wedged himself from the booth for another trip to the buffet.

Daniel stretched his legs on the booth. His full belly and the warmth of the sun through the window made him drowsy. He closed his eyes.

*"¡Dani, Dani! ¡Levantá!"* Gordo shook Daniel's shoulder. "Come on!"

Daniel opened his eyes. Beads of sweat poured from Gordo's face. His eyes were white and wild. He stuffed food into his rucksack.

"What the hell, Gordo?" said Daniel. He sat up. Gordo was scooting toward the front exit, clutching his jiggling chorizo-laden pants in an unsuccessful attempt to keep them above his pasty crack.

Daniel heard a shout. The manager and waiter moved to block the exit. Daniel sprinted and plowed into them. The manager crashed up against the wood-paneled wall with a groan. The waiter tried to swing a tray at Daniel, who rolled to his feet and dashed out the glass door. He caught up with Gordo, who was kick-starting his motorcycle. Daniel swung onto his bike and they roared out of the parking lot, drowning out the curses and raised fists behind them.

"Whoopee!" Daniel yelled. Gordo was such a lovely idiot.

They rode for several hours down the Pan-American. They needed gas and pulled into a service station.

*"Che, ¿viste?"* said Gordo, pointing toward the young woman cashier. "She's big in all the right places."

"Yes, she is, Gordo," said Daniel. "Just like you."

"You're an ass."

They mounted their bikes and got back onto the highway.

It began to rain. The pellets stung Daniel's face, and it all seemed part of the grand adventure. He couldn't recall a happier time in his life.

In the late afternoon, they pulled off at an overlook to

stretch their legs. It had stopped raining, but a residual mist hovered low around the depressions in the green valley spread below them.

"See that big rock over there? The one that looks like a table?" said Gordo. "Watch me land this stone on the top." It skipped off the rock.

"I can do it," said Daniel. He lobbed a stone and missed the rock altogether. Gordo laughed and bent over to pick up another stone. The sun glinted off something tucked into Gordo's belt.

"*Che, boludo.* You have a gun? You didn't tell me you had a gun."

"What? You've never seen one?" said Gordo. He pulled out a Colt .38, flipped it open, and spun the cylinder. It was loaded. "Took this from my old man a long time ago. He thinks it was stolen. He bought another one. It's for protection." Gordo jerked his head. "It's for protection."

"You ever used it?" said Daniel.

"What do you mean *used it*?" said Gordo, and a wry smile creased his face. "Used it as in *shot* somebody? As in *killed* somebody?"

Daniel shrugged. "Let me see it."

"No."

"Come on. Let's shoot something."

They found an old hubcap lying in the dirt and set it on the rock table. Backing up fifteen feet, Gordo aimed and shot. The sound reverberated across the valley below. He missed all four times.

Daniel had never held a gun before, and it felt heavy and snug in his hand. The barrel was hot to the touch. "Watch," he said to Gordo, "just like John Wayne."

He shot from the hip and the force of the recoil took him by surprise. The gun almost jumped from his hand. He took aim at the bottle again, this time with both hands, but missed again.

A gust of wind blew the hubcap off the rock.

Daniel wanted to shoot some more, but Gordo took the gun back. In just a few short weeks, Daniel thought, he would have his own gun. Perhaps the military would issue weapons on the first day of bootcamp. The thought thrilled him, and he imagined whipping out his gun and shooting his uncle's assassin.

That day they made it within eighty kilometers of Córdoba before pulling off to spend the night. Finding a broken wooden crate, they made a fire to brew *mate*. Gordo sharpened a stick and skewered the pilfered flank steaks that he dug from the bottom of his rucksack.

After dinner, they lay on their blankets. The starry sky again loomed large.

*"Che,"* said Gordo, "maybe Che Guevara lay right here, just like us, looking at the stars and drinking *mate*."

"I'm sure of it," said Daniel. "Except he was probably thinking about which democratic government was in need of a violent revolution or preparing the next firing squad for his political opponents. Or some other big thought."

"Yeah, he probably wasn't thinking about that girl back at the gas station with the big *melones*," said Gordo.

"That's what you're thinking about?"

"Yes."

"Me too," said Daniel.

He sipped his *mate*.

"I liked this girl at university during my first year there, and she was big too," Daniel said, smiling and cupping his hands at his chest. "I mean *muy grandes*. The only thing bigger was her love of Karl Marx. Really fanatical. She lent me some pages from some book of his. Was all secretive about it. I read them because I thought she might let me gain some carnal knowledge. It didn't make any sense to me. Why is a person who has something oppressing someone who doesn't have something?"

Daniel shifted his body to find a more comfortable position on the hard ground. "What I remember best is the smell of the mimeograph pages. I liked the purple ink."

"I just think the Communists and the military," said Gordo, "all this shit going on right now, they're all a bunch of bastards if you ask me. Especially the government."

"Well, no one's asking you, Gordo," said Daniel, "because you don't know shit. My uncle was killed by terrorists just ten days ago, *¿sabés?* The only bastards are the subversives ruining our country with their protests and bombs. If you were the government, what would you do? Damned right you'd send in the troops. Last week on the campus, the police came in riot gear and in those trucks with metal grids protecting the windows and the lights. They broke up a protest with billy clubs and tear gas. I would have helped them if I could."

The words flowed easily from Daniel's mouth, and he liked the sound of them. They seemed to come from a hardened place within him that he didn't know was there.

He got up and wrapped a shirt around his hand. He picked up the pot of water heating on the coals and poured it into the *mate* gourd.

"*Che*, I didn't know about your uncle," said Gordo. "I'm sorry."

"Let me tell you something," Daniel continued. "My uncle, Uncle Ricardo, a few months ago before he died, he told me how terrorists kidnapped an owner of a potato chip plant in Pacheco where a couple of his friends worked. Held the owner for ransom. They kept a hood over his head the whole time. A few weeks later they found him dead, even after the family paid. Had to shut the plant down and everyone lost their jobs. Ninety workers. My uncle said the Communists have never created jobs for anyone. They just destroy them. That these radical leftists are more interested in tearing down the rich than building up the poor. I hear stories like that, and I see the crazies on the UBA campus, and it makes me want to be a cop."

"Now *you're* the crazy one, Dani," Gordo said. "I think it's best just to keep one's head down, you know?"

"You're just like everyone else," said Daniel, shaking his head. "You don't see what's happening. That's your problem, Gordo. One of many, I might add."

But they were both tired of talking by now. They finished their *mate* and watched the glowing embers die out.

It took Daniel a while to fall asleep. He thought about Gordo and why they had never been great friends in school. It wasn't anything he could put his finger on. Gordo simply wore thin. Daniel suddenly remembered a time in high school when a teacher, fed up with the rowdy classroom, ordered, "That bench, back there, out of here!" Daniel and the others in the row promptly picked up the bench and took it out to the hallway, much to the teacher's consternation. Gordo had been there, but he was the only one who stood by, unwilling to participate in the fun show of solidarity.

They awoke late the next morning.

*"Despertá, vago.* Get up! Let's get to Córdoba," urged Daniel, and he delivered a sharp kick to Gordo's blanket-wrapped form lying near the smoldering fire.

*"¡Hijo de puta!"* came a muffled reply.

Daniel packed his things and sat on his motorcycle, revving the engine.

"How is it possible your stuff can be strewn all over the place?" Daniel said. He began riding circles around Gordo and kicking his things toward him, a wadded sweater, a shoe, and a cup.

Gordo stood up, rubbing his eyes and cursing.

Daniel grinned and barreled toward Gordo, who only escaped a collision by grabbing the bike handlebars and shuffling aside.

It was a beautiful day, and Daniel was in a good mood. He enjoyed the ride so much that by the time they rolled into Córdoba in the afternoon, he almost wished it had taken longer.

# CHAPTER 6 – CÓRDOBA

## *Córdoba*

Córdoba was bigger than they expected. Daniel and Gordo found a cheap motel. After settling their stiff legs and aching backs, they took a luxurious nap in the comforts of a bed.

When they awoke, there were long shadows on the street below, and the dying sun gloried the tops of the buildings. They walked toward the downtown and found themselves in the Jesuit Block, *La Manzana Jesuítica,* near the national university.

*"Che,* do you remember *El Cordobazo?"* asked Daniel. "Wasn't it right here at the university?" Gordo hadn't heard about the student and worker uprisings in 1969. Several students had died in violent clashes with the police.

They came across a lively plaza and stopped at a pizza bar, its blazing neon lights casting a green hue onto the cobblestones. Young people sat at metal tables outside and on the curb of the street. Others stood in groups drinking. The two travelers ordered beer and pizza slices, and stood against a wall to take it all in.

To Daniel, the university student culture was familiar. He knew their type. Malcontents, group thinkers, anti-establishment protesters. Leftists because it was trendy. It reminded Daniel of the UBA campus, and he was glad to be away from there.

Gordo looked out of place and uncomfortable. They finished eating and drained their bottles.

"*Vamos,*" said Daniel. "Let's leave."

Late the next morning, they awoke to insistent knocking on the door. Light streamed through the slats of the blinds. The motel wanted them out. The room needed to be cleaned.

"I thought we could stay today. We could stay today," Gordo stammered. "I wanted to visit my grandmother."

"Sure, go see your *abuela*. Why the hell not?" said Daniel. "But we're not staying another night, so pack up your stuff."

They checked out of their room and Daniel went next door to the café for coffee and *medialunas*. He read the papers and enjoyed some time by himself.

Gordo came back from his grandmother's several hours later. They mounted their motorcycles and made their way back to the highway, heading northwest again and paralleling the sparkling River Suquía.

Just outside the city, they slowed at a line of cars and trucks. They had to wait to get over the rise before seeing it was a police checkpoint. When their turn came, the motorcycles were waved aside for questioning.

"*Cédulas,*" said a policeman, turning to the riders. His salt-and-pepper hair was closely cropped and his well-cut uniform crisp despite the heat.

A second cop, muscular and sweaty, stood beside him, the business end of his FAL machine gun pointed casually at the young men's feet.

Daniel fished out his identification. Gordo fumbled inside his bag.

"Why are you in Córdoba?" asked the older cop, comparing Daniel's photograph to the face before him.

"We're taking a vacation," said Daniel, observing the man's manicured nails.

"Where are you going?"

"Mendoza. The Andes."

"You are students?"

"No," Daniel said. "I drive a remis."

"Where?"

"In Buenos Aires. In Flores."

"You drive a remis too?" asked the policeman, turning to Gordo, who by now had found his ID and held it out, trembling.

Gordo squirmed. "No, I don't. No, I don't," he repeated.

The policeman cocked his head. "What do you do then?"

"Nothing really. I…I help my father."

Gordo now had the policeman's full attention.

"What do you mean, 'nothing really, I help my father'? Do you do nothing, or do you help your father? Or does your father do nothing, and you help him do nothing?"

"I…"

"Shut your trap!" The policeman stepped within six inches of Gordo's face. "Do you think helping your father is doing nothing? You think what your father does is worthless? He wants your help, and you sit around loafing? What kind of son are you?"

"I just…"

"*¡Cerrá el pico, chancho!* Do I want you to talk? I'll tell you when I want an answer. I know your type. You're a student, aren't you?"

Gordo froze.

"Answer!" said the policeman.

"I, I am not a student." Gordo's head jerked repeatedly. "I am not a student."

It was at this point that Gordo decided to have an extended coughing fit.

"Give me your bag, *cabrón*." The policeman opened

Gordo's rucksack and shook the contents on the ground. He kicked through the strewn items and tossed the bag aside.

Daniel thought about the .38 tucked behind Gordo's belt and wondered what the police would do if they found it. But like the agent at the estancia, this man was tough but fair.

A car backfired and they all jumped, including the young policeman, who whirled back wildly, his gun now pointed at Daniel's head.

The older policeman hadn't flinched.

"Give me your bag, taxi driver," he said to Daniel.

After rummaging through it, he shoved it back at Daniel and let them go with a dismissive wave.

Daniel felt elated as if he had passed some test. He had handled himself well, he thought. He was on their side after all, and he wished he had found a way to show this. Daniel imagined himself with that kind of power and self-confidence, with an FAL of his own and responsible for uncovering subversives.

Daniel looked down at Gordo, who was on his hands and knees gathering his strewn articles from the ground, a shirt, a single sock, and a link of chorizo that had rolled off the asphalt and into the dirt.

Gordo looked up, unsure, as if seeking some confirmation from Daniel that everything was okay. But Daniel felt an ugly combination of disgust and embarrassment. *Gordo was a damned coward, just like the terrorists.*

Daniel mounted his motorcycle and roared down the road.

# CHAPTER 7 – A SOLAS

## *Alone*

They had planned to get to Mendoza, but Daniel's heart was no longer in it. Their plans had been big and the open country inviting, but the vistas were left mostly unseen and the destinations unvisited. Their unbounded experience began to fray at the edges.

After Córdoba, something in their relationship broke that couldn't be fixed. They began riding apart with Daniel out front and Gordo trailing some distance behind.

While Daniel found increasing enjoyment from riding, he knew Gordo found it difficult and tiresome. Instead of getting more accustomed to riding, Gordo regressed. Each hour on the road widened the difference between traveling hardships and the comforts of a cold beer. He needed longer recuperation time at the bar and was more reluctant to leave the motel bed. His complaining turned incessant. Daniel wanted to push on, and he grew exasperated with his partner. It was the little things, like Gordo's inability to hold a steady speed. Gordo's speedometer used the full range of its many numbers, visiting each of them often and in random order.

One day after a particularly sharp exchange, Daniel gunned his engine and left Gordo behind. It wasn't until two days later they reconnected in a small town. Daniel had decided to enjoy his solitude and splurge on a nice dinner. As he sat in a restaurant booth, he saw Gordo pull into the parking lot and his mood soured.

Gordo was hungry. He seemed to want to patch things up. After a few beers and full bellies, the differences could have been forgotten.

"Let me ask you something," Daniel said, his head buzzing from the alcohol. "Why did you come?"

"What?" said Gordo.

"I want to know," said Daniel, "what made you say yes? I mean, let's be honest. You don't like riding. You don't like traveling. Hell, you don't even like me."

"Come on, Dani." Gordo said.

"I'll bet you're regretting coming on this adventure, aren't you, Gordo?" said Daniel. He knew he should stop talking. "You're thinking that however bad your crappy life is in Buenos Aires, it's better than a sore butt. Better than sleeping on the ground and peeing your pants in front of the cops."

Gordo put his knife and fork down. He leaned back in the booth.

"You're an ass, Dani. Just shut up. Shut up." Gordo's neck jerked. "But *che*, you're right. I *do* regret coming with you. I'm not like you. I'm fat, *¿viste?*" A bitter smile cracked across Gordo's lips. "I don't want to be like you. And you don't know me." He sat up and drained his bottle. "You don't know anything about me."

"Come, on, come on. I do know something about you," said Daniel, and the words just gushed out. "I've heard the stories, Gordo. We all heard them. We have no secrets here, you and me. Your family about to get evicted again? Are you running away from your old man? Did he beat you up just one too many times, *chancho?* More bruises like at school? Beat your mom with a belt?"

Gordo shoved hard on the table, trying to pin Daniel against the wall. He stormed out of the restaurant. Daniel caught up with him as Gordo mounted his motorcycle.

"Come on, Gordo, I'm just messing with you. Don't be mad, *che.*"

Daniel knew he'd gone too far. He followed Gordo out to a spot off the highway by a river where they had planned to camp. They slept apart that night, and Daniel tossed and turned. He wasn't quite sure why he'd done it. Somehow Gordo brought out the worst in him. He had just been joking around. Why couldn't Gordo have just rolled with it?

But being a sucker was one defect Gordo didn't have.

Daniel's money dwindled, and one morning they awoke to find Daniel's motorcycle had been stolen. The tracks in the dirt showed where it had been pushed to the nearby Pan-American Highway then disappeared.

Daniel stomped around, cursing his bad luck. He was irritated at Gordo, who sat on a log and smoked.

They spent a dejected morning, each lost in his own thoughts. By late afternoon, Daniel decided there was no alternative but to give up the adventure. He didn't have much money left, and he wouldn't enjoy riding two-up with Gordo.

They squeezed themselves onto Gordo's motorcycle and drove to a small pueblo. Over Pepsis and *choripanes*, Daniel explained how they would sell the remaining motorcycle the next day and use the money to buy bus tickets back to Buenos Aires. That night they camped by a creek about twenty minutes from the town.

The argument started over something trivial. Daniel said something, and they got into a heated argument. Daniel flew into a rage and pushed Gordo over. Gordo came at him, but Daniel cold-cocked him and Gordo went down again, his face hitting the ground hard and his body going limp. Daniel turned away.

He heard a click. Turning, he found Gordo facing him, the revolver shaking in his hands and pointed at Daniel's chest. Gordo's cheekbone bled badly, and his face made strange contortions.

Daniel sucked in his breath and kept an eye on the end of the barrel, wondering how much it would hurt to get shot.

"Do you know," said Gordo slowly, his stutter gone, "I didn't actually steal this gun from my father. I took it from him. I came home one evening. Could hear my father yelling and my mother screaming. He was drunk again and pistol-whipping my mother."

Gordo jerked his head. "I wrestled the gun from him. I threatened to shoot him if he didn't leave. That was the night before you called me. You called me the next morning. Now you know, don't you, you bastard? I said yes to you because I was sure I was going to shoot my father. Do you know what that's like? I laid awake all night, raging. Worried that if he showed his face at the house again, I would shoot him. Shoot my own father."

The gun shook harder now. Gordo backed toward the motorcycle. "And now, you *hijo de puta*," he said, "I'm leaving because if I don't, I swear to God and to the Holy Virgin Mary, I'll shoot you."

Gordo reached his left hand into Daniel's jacket that was slung over the bike seat. He pulled out the wad of cash in the pocket and threw the jacket on the ground. Picking up his rucksack and swinging his leg over the bike, he kick-started the engine. He stuffed the revolver back in his belt and spun the back tire, kicking up gravel in Daniel's face.

Daniel stood watching Gordo disappear into the distance. He wanted to feel anger, but he knew he had been a complete ass.

That night Daniel huddled under his blanket and edged

closer to the base of a tree, trying to keep the branches between him and the mocking stars in the sky. Its vastness now seemed to him an abyss. Gordo has taken the last of his mother's blood money, and perhaps the curse along with it.

# CHAPTER 8 – LA ESTANCIA

## *The Country Estate*

Daniel awoke with the bright sun streaming through the trees. He no longer felt alone, and in fact he was relieved to be away from Gordo and on his own. He tried not to think about what had happened, but deep down there was a nagging feeling that Gordo had been right about him.

It took him ninety minutes to walk to the town, and with each step, Daniel felt more and more sorry for himself. He entered a café and picked out a table next to the window. He didn't have any plan. The idea of stealing food crossed his mind.

The place was empty aside from a man at the bar and a waitress leaning against the counter. She watched Daniel with her arms crossed over her chest.

"I have nothing," Daniel said when she came to take his order. "Will you please refill my canteen?"

She returned a few minutes later with the canteen as well as a cortado, two medialunas, an orange, and a knife and fork wrapped in a white paper napkin. She placed these on the small table in front of him and slid the dish of sugar packets next to the coffee.

"If it's work you're looking for," the woman said, "follow the north road to kilometer six. Just beyond the marker. The estancia of Don Alfonso. Ask for Amancio. He's looking for help with the plantings. Tell him Rosita sent you."

Daniel lowered his eyes. *"Gracias."* He cut the orange rind in one long, circular length and made up his mind.

At the six-kilometer stone marker, Daniel dropped his pack to rest. It was hot and still. The insects buzzed. He wiped his brow with the back of his hand and took a drink. The arched stone entrance to the estancia lay just ahead.

He passed through the arch and walked down a long dusty road bordered by giant sycamores. The shade was cool under the tall trees. A breeze caught their tops, and the leaves swayed and rustled. Only a breath of wind licked against Daniel's hot skin.

A chorus of dogs ran out to challenge the intruder. Daniel picked up a stick and continued toward the large house in the distance.

Two field hands sat on a log stump repairing a piece of equipment.

"I'm looking for Señor Amancio."

One of the men jerked his head behind him.

Daniel followed around to the left of the big house. The clanking of tools resumed only after he had turned the corner.

Outside a large barn, a man rubbed down a dun-colored criollo mare. Daniel stopped twenty feet away. If the man saw him, he paid no attention. The criollo shifted her weight and moved her head up and down.

"*¿Señor Amancio?*"

The foreman turned and contemplated Daniel. It was not an unkind look, but one well-practiced at judging the worth of men and beast alike.

"Rosita sent me," said Daniel.

Amancio's face was creased and seasoned by the sun.

"I want no trouble at this estancia."

"I bring no trouble," said Daniel. "I swear it."

Amancio returned to his work with the mare.

Daniel sensed he had been weighed on the scales and

found wanting. "I know nothing about animals or farming, but I'll do anything," he said.

Amancio gave a sharp whistle. A man emerged from the barn.

"Give this man some work," said Amancio.

The supervisor nodded and beckoned to Daniel.

They crossed a cobblestoned courtyard surrounded by work buildings and barracks. At a large stable, several men shoveled out stalls and loaded manure onto the bed of a trailer. Daniel had never been in a proper barn before, and the pungent smell was overpowering.

The supervisor grunted and handed Daniel a shovel.

Daniel worked alongside three other men who neither spoke nor acknowledged him. When the trailer bed was full, they all climbed up, feet dangling as the blue IAME Pampa tractor rumbled to the fields.


Daniel had entered a world he could not have known except through books and pictures. The Estancia Las Rosas, he learned, was one of the few surviving Spanish colonial land grants in Argentina. The 10,000-hectare estancia in the Mendoza Valley dated back to King Felipe IV in the 1600s.

It was a beautiful land, one of golden rolling hills and purple foothills. Cool water from the Andes Mountains tumbled into its creeks and streams, giving life to the trees along their wandering banks, to the *algarrobo*, the *caldén*, the poplar, and the acacia. The waters teemed with *bagre* catfish and wily brook trout. It was the country of the gray fox and the puma, and of the soaring condor.

The estancia was in the heart of Argentina's wine country near the Uco Valley and the Tunuyán River. On the rocky slopes of the Andes foothills were the high-altitude vineyards, where Malbec grapes grew at 3,700 feet and were prized for their riper tannins and their greater intensity than those from the valley below.

Most of the extensive ranch land was for cattle grazing, but 2,500 hectares was dedicated to soybean cultivation. It was to this area Daniel was assigned. He found himself in the lowest of all ranks, and his fellow workers included the new and inexperienced, the dim-witted, and the punished. Common ground existed only in the marginalization by others, but that proved a flimsy basis for camaraderie, and Daniel formed none. The locals within this group seemed to accept their lot quietly, but the migrants among them were resentful and brooding.

Above him were the experienced workers and the farmers, who tilled and graded the land for planting. At the top of the estancia pecking order were the proud gauchos, men at one with their horses, the cattle, and the land.

Daniel was fascinated by the gauchos. He stared at them as they ambled bowlegged with gear, riding their horses out to remote work areas. Compact and tanned, they were easy with a laugh and quick with a knife. Completely squared away.

He watched them herd cattle toward the pens and maneuver their horses among the animals to isolate a cow and her calf. How they lassoed the front legs of the bull calves and castrated them with a few quick strokes of their deer-horn handled knives, the gleaming white testicles tossed into the air to the waiting dogs.

Daniel wished to join them, but his only connection to the lofty gauchos was through the back ends of their horses and cattle.

He threw himself into his work, perhaps to shut out the shameful memories that squirmed past his attempts to push them away. The lifting of the parquet tiles in his father's bedroom and the shaking gun in Gordo's hand. He thought of his father and how once he had told Daniel, shortly after his mother died, that if anything should happen to his youngest son, the hole in his heart would never heal.

He shoveled and hauled at a furious pace, his broad shoulders and sturdy legs concentrated in his work. His muscles hurt as they absorbed the new demands placed upon them, but Daniel pushed himself all the more and accepted the punishment willingly. He worked as he never had before. The fresh air and the backbreaking labor were a tonic to his body and soul. Each screaming muscle felt like penance that he hoped would merit forgiveness for how he had treated Gordo. As he worked, a weight seemed to lift from his shoulders, and his mood would have brightened considerably had it not been for the other field hands who viewed him with suspicion and resentment. His hard work made them look bad. Worse, he was from the capital. A *porteño*.

Daniel kept his money in his belt and counted it each day. He figured he needed three thousand pesos to pay for the bus back to Buenos Aires, and another ten thousand pesos for food and other expenses once he got to the city. He had a small debt to the waitress, too, one he planned to pay back.

Working alone in a barn one day, Daniel smelled tobacco and spotted Amancio leaning against a post, watching him from under his wide-brimmed hat. The *capataz* dropped the butt onto the dirty straw and ground it under the toe of his boot. Turning on his heel, he left as silently as he had come.

Amancio wasn't the only one watching him.

It was Saturday evening and the mood light. Daniel sat alone at the end of a long table eating a bowl of *puchero* stew made with chicken, ox tail, potatoes, leeks, and onions. Rough logs supported a corrugated roof over the outdoor patio that served as the workers' mess hall. The women from the kitchen brought stew, baskets of bread, fruit, and pitchers of wine.

A girl, perhaps seventeen, lingered beside Daniel and ladled him a large piece of chicken. The folds of her dress brushed his arm. She smiled, and he knew he would wait for her after dinner.

The moon had risen above the trees when the clanking of pots and pans in the kitchen finally died down. She came out the backdoor, drying her hands on her plain dress.

*"Buenas tardes,"* Daniel said.

*"Buenas tardes,"* the girl said.

They walked together to the edge of a pond behind the main house and sat on a log bench. Daniel felt for her small hand with his large callused one. She let him find it, and he held it gently.

"I don't like *porteños,"* she said, setting a small bag beside her and staring out at the silvered pond.

Daniel tightened his grip on her hand. "I can't imagine what you do with people you like then. And how can you not like me? You don't even know me."

"You're different. Not like the others," she said. "You're Daniel."

He looked at her. She was a pretty girl with delicate indigenous features.

She picked at her tight bun and let down her black hair. She combed it out with the fingers of her free hand. It shone in the moonlight and added several comely years to her.

"What's your name?" Daniel asked.

"You have to guess." She squeezed his hand.

"Give me a hint. What letter does it start with?"

"It's the name of something God gives us."

*"¿Concepción?* I could give you that too," said Daniel. He stifled a laugh.

*"Sos grosero.* That's not it." She covered her mouth with her hand.

"Is it Milagro?"

"No, but you're closer," she said. "It starts with the same letter."

"M, mmm… Mercedes?"

The girl smiled.

"God's never given me a Mercedes," said Daniel. "He gave me a motorcycle, then he took it away."

"Very funny," said Mercedes. "I wasn't named after the car, *tonto.* "

"Either way," said Daniel. "it's a very prestigious but rather religious name for such a pretty young girl."

"Thank you." Mercedes turned her head away. "I'm not so young." She squeezed his hand again. "Are you not religious?" she asked.

"I think there's a God, yes," said Daniel. "But I don't suspect he thinks about us much unless maybe someone is really bad or really good. I don't see God doing anything, really. Like your name – Mercedes. I certainly don't think God hands out mercies just because."

A breeze blew off the pond and the bullfrogs croaked.

"What's your name in Guaraní?" said Daniel.

"I'm not Guaraní. *Bruto.* My mother and father are Mapuche."

"So what's your name in Mapuche?"

"It doesn't have a translation," said Mercedes.

"There's no word for *mercies*?"

"No."

"See, I told you that mercy doesn't really exist," said Daniel. "The Mapuche know."

"Maybe it's because the Mapuche aren't Catholic," said Mercedes. "At least they weren't. They believe in their own gods. Spirits and things. Once, my mother was ill and she almost died. My grandmother called the *machi* to come. There was a lot of chanting. I was just a kid, and they wouldn't let me go in. They told me the *machi* was trying to make the *wekufe* leave. Sometimes, I still wake up scared of the evil spirits."

Daniel leaned toward her and smelled her hair. He laid his head gently on her delicate shoulder.

"My parents always took me to mass," Mercedes said. "My priest told me once that my name was special because mercy means God forgives those who deserve punishment."

"So you're an expert in religion?" Daniel said.

"No, I'm not much good at anything," Mercedes said. She scuffed the ground with her foot. "My family is humble. Do you know why Mercedes doesn't have a translation? It's because my parents don't want me to remember I'm part Mapuche. Mapuche is poverty."

The girl was quiet for a moment. She pushed Daniel's head off her shoulder and reached into the bag beside her. "Look, I've brought something." Mercedes pulled out a bottle of wine.

Daniel worked out the cork stopper and offered the bottle to Mercedes. She took a sip and giggled. Daniel took a long swig.

"It's from our estancia," said Mercedes. "Do you think it's good?

Daniel grunted and tilted the bottle again.

"The grapes are grown in the foothills over there." She pointed west to the moonlit outline of the Andes mountains. "Do you know they put netting over the vines to protect them from hailstorms?"

"So you know everything about wine too?" said Daniel. "Religion and wine?"

"No," said Mercedes. "I heard the winemakers talk about it." She tucked her legs underneath her.

At that moment, Daniel felt happier than he could remember. It just seemed to be a combination of things, like his full belly and the good honest hard work at the Estancia. It was the unassuming pretty girl beside him who somehow made him want to be a better man.

Daniel sat up and put his arm around Mercedes' shoulder.

"Let me ask you something," he said. "Why don't you like *porteños?*"

"Because you ask too many questions." She giggled. "And because you let me chatter on and on."

Daniel touched her chin with his hand and turned her face toward his. He kissed her lips gently. She leaned in and Daniel kissed her more deeply. She was inexperienced and it was sloppy, but he taught her.

His hand crept under her blouse. She jerked away and slapped him hard on the cheek.

"That's another reason I don't like *porteños!*" she huffed, but a wry smile snuck across her face. She stood and walked away.

*"Adios, mi pequeña Mapuche,"* he called after her.

Daniel stayed by the pond. He listened to the bullfrogs and finished the bottle before making his way to the barracks.

Late that night, he awoke with a start.

In the dim light, two men rifled through the belongings of his bunkmates. He waited patiently, his rage building. They edged closer to his cot. He sprang up and delivered an uppercut that sent one of the thieves crashing against the wall. He jumped on the second one and beat the man's face with his fist. The nose crunched and the man screamed. A knife flashed and made cutting strokes at Daniel, backing him off.

"What the hell?" someone said. Others were waking up.

The thieves fled.

Daniel lay trembling on his rack and considered the rage that had erupted within. He was proud of what he had done. He had never felt more alive or more capable, and he imagined himself protecting all things right and innocent, like the dark eyes and soft lips of Mercedes.

# CHAPTER 9 – EL FALCON VERDE

## *The Green Falcon*

The next day was when the accident happened and when the police came.

Two Ford Falcons drove in on the long road leading to the main house. The trailing plumes of dust swirled into the tall sycamores and mixed with the riotous dogs challenging their approach.

The first vehicle carried two local policemen. It was painted blue and white and had a red light mounted on the roof. The second Falcon, a newer model, was painted dark green and had no particular markings. Behind its tinted windows were three men.

When the dust settled, the two local policemen eased themselves out of their car and smoothed their uniforms. Amancio stood waiting for them. Daniel and the supervisor stood behind the foreman. They had been called in from the fields as witnesses.

Amancio and the cops shook hands. *"Buen día,"* they said, and they inquired about their families. Daniel thought the local cops looked nervous.

"Tell us what happened," said the policemen. They glanced back at the dark car behind them.

Amancio nodded. He motioned behind him. "This is the supervisor in the field at the time of the accident," he said, "and this is one of our field hands." He pointed to Daniel. "He saw it all."

The supervisor stepped forward. "A worker was crushed this morning by a tractor in the planting fields," he began. "It was a combination of several untimely circumstances. The young man was new and inexperienced. He was in the wrong place and his foot slipped. The tractor driver was distracted with a stuck gear. There's not much else to tell."

Daniel knew there was more to tell, but these details were unnecessary for the police report. The man had not died quickly. His midsection was crushed, and his legs had writhed for some time while his torso was still. He had made no noise at all. There was nothing they could do for him, except to call the Escamilla family's personal priest to administer the last rites before the soul departed the body one hour after death.

"The Doña would like to see you," said Amancio to the local policemen.

He led them all up the steps of the great house. Inside the grand foyer, amidst the ancient dark cabinets and towering ancestral portraits, they held their hats in their hands and waited for Doña María Isabel Rodríguez Escamilla de la Roca. They didn't have to wait long. The clip of heels on the red-tiled hallway drew them all to attention.

"I'm sorry you *señores* had to come here under these circumstances," said the Doña to the policemen when she entered the foyer. "Next time I hope it will be for a happier occasion. Please know you are invited. We'll share a coffee together. Will you take a coffee now, please? How is Capitán Manzano?"

"Yes, Doña María, thank you, Doña María. And no thank you, ma'am. Very kind of you. El Capitán is well. He sends you and Don Alfonso his deepest regards."

"I'll let you do your work then. Don Alfonso is not here. He's dove hunting in the Macha Valley. A message has been sent to him."

Doña María Isabel accompanied the policemen to the spacious porch. She stood as they continued down the steps with Amancio, the supervisor, and Daniel. The Doña spotted the dark car and her face clouded. Stepping back into the house, she shut the great wooden door.

Three doors opened from the green Falcon with the tinted windows. The men were dressed in civilian clothes, dark pants and wide-collared white shirts unbuttoned to the middle of their wolfish chests. They wore black boots and mustaches. Each carried a shotgun, the business end jauntily pointed up.

*"Buen día,"* said Amancio as the three men swaggered toward him.

"Hmph," said one of the agents, but he didn't seem to mean it. He took off his mirrored sunglasses and fixed Amancio with a cold stare. He was stocky and seemed to be in charge.

Daniel sensed Amancio was waiting to see if the agent from Mendoza would add anything beyond his grunted response.

"I suggest we all ride out to the field together," said Amancio, finally. "The supervisor can drive us in the work truck," he said, motioning toward a battered flatbed. "He and this field hand here are witnesses."

"We're not interested in the accident," said the stocky man. He cocked his head to one side and narrowed his eyes at Amancio. "We have a few questions for you."

*What could they want then?* Daniel wondered, and suddenly it occurred to him perhaps these agents had come to investigate the two thieves from last night. They must have been subversives. *That must be it.* He felt a sense of importance and duty. He could be useful to this investigation.

The supervisor looked at Amancio, who gave a slight nod.

"Please come with me then," said the supervisor to the two

local policemen. The cops seemed ill at ease and grateful for an excuse to leave the agents with Amancio. Daniel was about to go with them but Amancio motioned slightly with his hand to stay put. Now he was convinced this had to do with last night. *Why else would Amancio need me?*

"We need a place to talk," said the agent.

Amancio nodded and led the way around the corner of the main house toward the work buildings. The barns and workshops around the courtyard were unusually quiet.

The other two agents trailed at some distance, looking around as they walked, and poking their heads into doors. They didn't appear to be in any hurry to keep up with Amancio and the stocky agent in charge.

Arriving at his office, Amancio offered a wooden folding chair but the man ignored it and remained standing. He sniffed at the small, cluttered office.

"He can stay outside," the agent said, pointing at Daniel.

"No. He stays here," said Amancio, and Daniel detected a firmness to the foreman's voice he hadn't heard before.

The agent shrugged.

*Maybe there's more going on here at the estancia than I realized.* Amancio was nice, but maybe he's unaware. He may not even know about last night. And the thought came to him that perhaps Amancio was up to something he shouldn't be. Daniel looked at Amancio. No, that couldn't be. The foreman was honest. He was sure of it. But the ideas bounced about Daniel's head nonetheless. One thing he knew though. He would help these agents with any information he could.

"Let's not waste my time," said the agent. "I would like to know about your workers here at the Estancia. I'm interested in the newer ones, those not from around here."

"*Señor*, I am the *capataz* and responsible for all of the men on this estancia. It's a large place. I suggest…"

"You'll not suggest anything," said the agent. He had a hard mouth that said hard things.

"What is it you would like to know?" said Amancio.

"I'll ask the questions!" snapped the agent. He slung the barrel of the Ithaca shotgun against his shoulder and stepped to the doorway to check on his colleagues. They were speaking to a worker in the courtyard. Daniel saw the worker shift his weight from one foot to another.

"Show me the list of the workers on your payroll," said the agent, whirling back to face Amancio.

The overseer lifted a leather-bound ledger from a drawer in his desk. He opened it to the tab marked *1976* and flipped a few more pages to the last entries. Amancio slid the book around for the agent to read.

"This includes all the field hands and maintenance workers," said Amancio. "It does not include the gauchos or the stable hands. They are on another list at the stables. Everyone has a start date on the left. The crossed-out names no longer work here."

The agent pulled the folding chair to the desk and sat, his 12-gauge across his lap. He reviewed the list of names, stopping at a few of them. He went back a few pages, and then forward again as if looking for something in particular. He stabbed a finger at one of the pages. "Tell me about these right here," he said. "They started on the same day, two weeks ago. Where did they come from?"

Amancio craned his head around to read the names. "Those men were lent to me from Las Lunas. They're leaving some fields fallow this year and have some spare men. I've had a dozen men from there in the past few weeks."

"I don't care about them," said the agent. "What about these two?" He stabbed again at the page. "They started some ten days ago. Their names don't sound like they are from *provincia.*"

Daniel wondered if they might be the two thieves from last night. *The subversives.* He was about to say something, but Amancio answered and he lost the opportunity.

"That may be," said the foreman. *"No lo sé.* I wouldn't know."

The agent gave Amancio a hard-boiled stare. He flipped back a few pages, looking at some of the crossed-out names. "You have a number of workers here that have lasted only a few days. Why?"

Amancio shrugged. "We get lots of workers during the planting season. They might come during peak season then move on. Others don't work out, or they get into fights and cause trouble. Some just leave abruptly. They don't say why."

"You seem to have all the answers, don't you, *viejo?"* said the agent, brushing something off his well-polished black boots. "You think I don't know you're harboring subversives here?"

Daniel's pulse raced. *Yes, this was it. There was something odd going on here.*

"I don't know what you are talking about," said Amancio. "We plant soy and wheat, and we raise cattle. We hire many men during the peak seasons for temporary work. We don't keep troublemakers if that's what you mean."

*Amancio simply just doesn't know.*

"Shut your trap, old man! You know exactly what I mean." The agent stood and kicked the folding chair backward. "I want to speak with all of your men."

The agent stepped back and sized up Amancio, his gaze settling on the overseer's muddy pants and dirty boots. "You just save the bullshit on your shit-kickers for your field hands."

Daniel studied Amancio, too, and he noticed things about

the foreman he had never noticed before. His leather boots were cracked at the creases and the heels worn down on their outer edge. There was a damaged spot in the weave of his brimmed hat where the straw was frayed and jagged.

At that moment Daniel caught Amancio looking at him. It seemed to Daniel a look of kindness, but it was a kindness that hurt, and Daniel dropped his gaze.

The agent whistled out the door, and his other two men joined them. Amancio led the way and the three agents walked abreast with their shotguns. Daniel trailed behind.

At the cattle pen, Amancio gathered the nearby crews. "These men have a few questions for you," he said, addressing the group. He didn't bother with introductions. None were needed.

The agent spat. He stared the men down, looking for any challenge or sign of nervousness. "Any of you not from around these parts, not a local, step forward." He waited as the men shifted their feet.

Daniel joined two others who stepped out.

For the moment, the agent ignored those who had stepped forward, and instead stalked among those who had remained back. This man, too, thought Daniel, was a practiced judge of character.

The agent pointed to a young man with wire-rimmed glasses and thinning hair. "You there. Step out. You other men can go back to work." Flanked by his two colleagues, the agent turned his attention to the four men who remained.

"*Cédulas.*"

Daniel and the other three men fished for their identification cards. Daniel found himself staring at the agent's sunglasses.

The agent began with the first man, holding up the ID to his face. "What is your full name? Where are you from? Oh, from Rosario? Why are you here? What university do you attend? No university? What does your father do?"

Daniel was third.

"You are from *capital*," said the agent in a tone that was neither a question nor a statement. He seemed not to acknowledge that Daniel had been with him in Amancio's office. *That's right. He's keeping it professional.*

"Yes, sir," replied Daniel.

"What are you doing here?"

"I am earning some money to get back to Buenos Aires," Daniel said. "I was on a vacation and ran out of money."

The agent asked a few more questions, and Daniel let it slip that he was about to start his military service. He could tell the man seemed pleased with his self-assured manner and direct answers. The agent knew his business, and there was no business here.

The fourth man, the one with glasses, however, had all the wrong answers and appearances. He had large hands and feet and seemed not to know where to put them. He stumbled and stammered, and the agent's questions came faster and angrier. The agent was a master at his craft, working himself into a calculated frenzy. Here was weakness, but of the sort that made a mockery of his capabilities. This sort of weakness would have to be paid for.

The young man's answers became hopelessly convoluted and contradictory. His guilt was obvious, and Daniel could see this plainly now that it had been revealed. This violent Marxist revolutionary stirring up the peasants here with his subversive ideas from the capital.

Daniel recalled his uncle telling him once that the leftist terrorists were all cowards who never stood and fought. They hid in the shadows and in plain sight. They looked innocent and you wouldn't pick them out of a crowd. *Don't be fooled,* his uncle had once warned him. *These are wolves in sheep's clothing*. It all made sense to Daniel now. He imagined this bespeckled man beside him as the terrorist bombmaker responsible for killing his uncle and the judge and maiming those innocent people on the streets of Buenos Aires. Yes, the agent had unmasked this subversive. He couldn't be fooled, and neither would Daniel. He backed several steps away from this terrorist.

The young man sniveled and quailed before the agent. A vicious kick tumbled him into the mud, spattering his glasses and leaving them bent grotesquely on his face.

"Are you here to insult me?" demanded the agent, his face red and neck muscles straining. He hovered over the cowering impetuous man who dared to be broken before the breaking time would begin.

The agent snapped his fingers, and the young man was led away by the men with the shotguns and into the back of the tinted Ford.

Daniel thought about what his military experience would be like, and if he, too, would be entrusted to root out subversives. This agent was tough, Daniel thought, but he was doing his job. He was serving his country. And the agent wouldn't be any good at it if he wasn't a jerk.

But something didn't quite sit right with Daniel the rest of the day.

In the evening when the work was done, he found himself staring across the courtyard at the door to Amancio's small office. The light was on inside, and he imagined Amancio sliding his finger along a column in his ledger, crossing out the name of the man who died mangled under the tractor. Daniel wondered if the Doña would be sending some money to the man's family. He recalled the young man with the wire-rimmed glasses, muddied and frightened, led away to the dark green Ford Falcon and its death-car horrors.

It was just another name to be crossed out, Daniel told himself.

During an afternoon break one day, Daniel found the *capataz* in one of the work buildings reviewing papers posted on the wall. Daniel held his hat in his hand.

"*Señor Amancio*, I have enough money now to return to Buenos Aires. I'm leaving."

Amancio paused but did not turn around. "I know," he said.

Mercedes knew too. She stood in front of him and cried by the backdoor of the kitchen.

"Stay, Daniel," she said. "Stay here with me. *Por favor.*"

Daniel shuffled his feet. Before him was something that represented goodness and purity and he wanted to hold her, but he stared at his dirty fingernails. He was sorry they both would have to remember this.

The girl sobbed and put her hands to her face. She bent over, and her little body shook.

It was for her own good, Daniel told himself. He didn't belong here. He belonged in Buenos Aires, in a place Mercedes couldn't understand. Daniel shut his eyes. He knew in the capital he could do something good for his country. He thought of the loud buses and the crowded cafés. The pulsing life of the city. He was wasting his time here. His military service awaited him.

He felt he should give Mercedes something. He unclasped the *San Cristóbal* around his neck and placed it into the girl's hand. The saint hadn't protected his mother, and it probably wouldn't do Mercedes any good either. He didn't need it.

"*Adios, mi pequeña Mapuche,*" said Daniel.

He turned and walked past the main house and down the long dusty dirt road lined by the 150-year-old sycamores and out the arched entrance that said *Estancia Las Rosas*. At the six-kilometer stone marker, Daniel stopped. The buzzing of insects filled the air. He took a sip of water from his bottle, adjusted the rucksack on his shoulder, and walked toward the town.

He arrived in the pueblo, hot and sweaty. He paused to read a bus schedule. At the public fountain in the plaza, he splashed his face and neck with cool water that tumbled down from the snowmelt of the Andes in the distance. He tossed his boots and socks next to his pack and sat on the ledge of the fountain to soak his feet. Donning a fresh shirt and clean socks, he shouldered his pack again and headed toward the south end of town and toward the sound of the lumbering trucks and slap slap of tires on the Pan-American that broke the intermittent silence.

Daniel entered the café and sat at the same table by the window. It was busier than before. He looked up.

"Rosita," he said.

Rosita smiled. "You remembered my name."

She waited for him to speak.

"I'll bring you a *cortado*," she said finally.

Daniel caught her wrist. "I want to thank you...I...I'll have a *solo*, not a *cortado*. And bring me a *milanesa*. Please. Your uncle, Amancio..." He fumbled for the words.

Rosita nodded. She turned and walked to the kitchen. A short time later, she returned with a plate of *milanesa* with French fries and two lemon wedges. From her apron she pulled out a knife and a fork wrapped in a white paper napkin. She set down the coffee and moved the dish of sugar packets closer to him.

Daniel ate quickly. He paid in small bills and exact change, which he left atop the handwritten tab. He slid five one-thousand peso notes under his plate, and he picked up his bag and slipped out the door. The overnight bus to Buenos Aires was due in ten minutes.

Daniel heard the bus before he saw it on the horizon. The brakes squealed and the doors jerked open. Daniel paid his fare and found an empty seat in the back. The vibrations and the late afternoon sun made him drowsy.

He startled awake some hours later and felt for his bag. It was almost dark out.

A lonely country church out the window caught Daniel's attention. A small funeral procession shuffled toward the cemetery, the parishioners carrying candles and a coffin. A dark-robed priest led the way, his hands holding aloft a bloodstained Jesus on a cross decorated with battery-powered electric lights.

# PART II

# CHAPTER 10 – EL CURA

## *The Priest*

The small church on Calle Piedras had been dwarfed long ago by the gray buildings competing for sunlight in an ever-crowded downtown. While only a short walk from the grand Plaza de Mayo, the neighborhood around the church was in decay. A few urban blocks made all the difference.

Gastón sat on his bed in the rectory and listened for the shuffle of old Father Ezequiel. The young priest had never wanted to see his mentor as badly as he did now. Sweat from his fingers smudged the letter in his hand. He set it beside him next to the envelope with the broken red wax seal of the Jesuit Father Provincial. Surely Ezequiel would know about the transfer orders, he thought. The din of the city traffic came muffled through the thick walls of the church. Gastón knew the Jesuit's work among the poor was no place for a new priest, especially now with subversives hiding in the slums.

He wondered if he could turn the transfer down.

Gastón smoothed an invisible rimple on his bedsheet. He worried he didn't have the stomach for it. In fact, he now questioned his worthiness to be priest at all. The sixteen weeks he had spent serving at this downtown parish church had not been easy.

Perhaps it was his awkwardness, Gastón thought. He was a gangly young man whose obliviousness to fashion had been providentially rendered harmless by the priest collar. His wire-rimmed glasses perched on a clean-shaven face, an appearance achieved with a few plucks of the tweezers rather than a razor. He was a private person, the kind who would lose himself in a crowd and come out with a book.

Gastón always had a passion for the church, eagerly serving as an altar boy and staying late after mass to help put things away. He loved the liturgy and the progression of the church calendar through the year. He liked the dimly lit recesses within the churches where the mysteries of God could be contemplated. The vertical architecture seemed to reach for the heavens and promise hope from above. It contrasted sharply with the cramped horizontal spaces people lived in.

He strived for purity in word and deed, and he mentally catalogued his sins of commission and omission. Yet his weekly confessions and penitent acts never seemed enough to release him from guilt, and the more he confessed, the more sins kept surfacing from some inexhaustible source within. He was painfully shy with the opposite sex, and lust was a demon to be exorcised, so a celibate life seemed a worthy object if not a duty.

"Gastón, where are you?" The voice of Father Ezequiel came from somewhere inside the church. *"Vení."*

*"Voy,"* replied Gastón, and he scooped up the letter and dashed down the narrow stairs. In the nave, two shafts of light pierced the darkness and beamed oblong rectangles onto the floor. The air smelled of old wood and mortar.

The elderly Ezequiel came by several times a week to provide instruction and mentoring to the young curates at the parishes, but mostly, Gastón was on his own.

It was his charge to nurture the spiritual life of this community. Years ago, this small church had thrived, but the neighborhood had long grown old and the parishioners along with it. There were more funerals than baptisms now and more widows than brides.

The only youthful energy within the parish, Gastón had learned, was embodied by the prostitutes and drug addicts. Their sins were obvious, surely reaching the place of judgement ahead of them. But these transgressors were nocturnal creatures whose lives didn't coincide with the church's daytime business hours. Church was a daytime luxury they could ill afford. The infrequent occasions when one of them darkened the church door resulted in its baptism with unholy water.

Gastón attempted to befriend the prostitutes. He encouraged them to come for mass and confession, but the scope of their sin made them immune to the powers of the cloth. Disvirtue was a permanent condition.

Gastón found Ezequiel seated at the desk in the small church office. The old priest was bald aside from the thin wisps of white hair combed across his head. He wore a built-up shoe on one foot on account of a childhood bout with polio.

*"Buenos días, querido,"* said Ezequiel.

*"Buenos días, Padre,"* said Gastón, bending down to greet his mentor with a kiss on the cheek.

"How are you doing with your sinner friends?" said Ezequiel. "Have any attended mass?"

"No, Padre," said Gastón, the sense of failure again weighing heavy on his heart.

"Well, how about my old church lady friends?" Ezequiel's eyes twinkled. "How are they?"

"Same as always, Padre," said Gastón.

The core of the sparse congregation was comprised of the elderly women who attended the thrice-weekly mass. This faithful remnant, however, was similarly not in need of his confessional services yet for reasons quite different from their sinful nocturnal neighbors. These godly women were, by definition, unencumbered by the burden of sin.

The young priest had a lot to learn.

Gastón felt most inadequate, but Ezequiel seemed happy with his progress. Gastón thought about the transfer again and a new worry entered his mind. If he transferred to the Jesuits, would he lose his mentor? It was another reason to turn the offer down.

During his training Gastón had sought answers of an old priest named Mariano who had been assigned to instruct this incoming group of new priests. But Father Mariano's answers were unsatisfactory. Frequently the old priest had remained silent, making Gastón wonder if he had heard him at all, or if perhaps his question had been too impertinent to warrant an answer. Sometimes Father Mariano simply waived away the question with a remark such as "Have faith, my child" or "Pray that God will reveal this to you, my son." Perhaps there were important truths hidden there, but Gastón could not find them.

Father Mariano was one of those useless individuals that the church didn't quite know what to do with and couldn't get rid of. Over his long and drifting career, he'd been shuffled from one unhappy parish to another, accumulating little experience and much animosity. He was incurably addicted to bungling, and he simply refused to die.

But Father Ezequiel was not like Mariano. Ezequiel was wise and insightful. And Gastón needed his mentor's wisdom right now.

"Father, I received this letter this morning," he blurted, and he held it out to Ezequiel.

"I know," said the old priest, waving it off.

"And you didn't tell me?" said Gastón.

"It's not my place," said Ezequiel. "The Church decides on

the rotations of its young curates. And wasn't it your wish to work with the Jesuits?" The old priest leaned back heavily in his chair.

"But," Gastón said, his voice unsure, "I'm not ready. I've failed here." A disturbing thought crossed his mind. "Is this why I'm being transferred, Father?"

The old priest laughed. "If I told you stories of my first months as a curate, you would be surprised I'm still here. Come. Sit." Ezequiel motioned toward the empty chair in front of the desk.

"To be honest, Padre, I'm afraid," said Gastón. "I'm afraid I don't have the words. Even worse, I'm afraid I might be a coward and won't honor our Lord if I'm faced with persecution."

Father Ezequiel's snowy eyebrows shot up.

"This week I visited two women at their homes," Gastón began. "One is caring for her sister who was injured by a terrorist bomb. The other woman has a son who's gone missing. She's sure the *militares* took him. The government won't tell her anything. She grabbed my hands. Wouldn't let them go. She was desperate. Pleaded for me to do something. I was scared, Father. I pried her fingers off and ran back to my room in the rectory. I had no words for them. I tried to pray but didn't know what to say."

Ezequiel nodded. "It's natural for us to be afraid," said the old mentor. "Remember what the disciples did when Jesus was crucified? They ran away. The Apostle Peter denied our Christ three times. My son, you must remember that God chooses the weak of this world precisely to show his power. Saint Timothy writes that God has not given us a spirit of fear but of power and of love."

Father Ezequiel leaned forward. "You are frightened about serving with the Jesuits in Bajo Flores, no? I understand. It's a dangerous place right now. A confusing place. The poor have welcomed the subversives and their revolutionary messages, and the government has been heavy-handed there. That slum is a spiritual battlefield too. The Jesuit priests find it hard to serve the poor and maintain a moral and spiritual compass amidst the tensions. But this is where God is calling you, my son. The Lord will give you the strength and wisdom you need."

Gastón felt comforted by his mentor's words as if a burden was lifted from his shoulders.

Two weeks later on Gastón's last day before the transfer to Bajo Flores, he and Ezequiel walked back to the old chapel after visiting several infirmed parishioners at their homes. Ezequiel limped with his polio leg, and Gastón plodded along deep in thought. They stopped for a coffee so the old priest could rest his hurting leg.

"Some people go through life never asking any questions at all," Ezequiel told Gastón across the bar table.

"But when the *why* questions come up – and they do eventually – when the crises come, the personal tragedies – like illnesses and death, like injuries and disappearances. When the world doesn't make sense and there are no words, they search for clarity and meaning in a world that offers neither."

"This is our job, my dear Gastón," Ezequiel continued. "To lead them to the truth. We don't have all the answers, but as one theologian said, *the riddles of God are more satisfying than the solutions of man.*"

They left the café and wound their way back to the church. When they arrived, Ezequiel rested his hand on the doorframe. "My son, we all are fellow travelers in this world searching for truth. People search for it in all sorts of things, some in revolutions and some in traditions. There are elements of truth in many things, and some people are closer to it than others. But don't forget that their search for truth is a thirst for God."

An hour later, it was time for Ezequiel to leave. The old man placed his hands on Gastón's head and prayed for him.

When Ezequiel had finished, Gastón asked him, "The Jesuit rector there, in Bajo Flores – Alejandro Pausini. Do you know him?"

Gastón saw something flicker across the old man's face.

"Rector Pausini is highly thought of within the diocese," his mentor said.

At the heavy door of the chapel, Old Ezequiel prepared to lift his polio leg over the high wooden threshold, but he turned back toward Gastón, who stood with his hands clasped in front of him. "Be careful, my son," said the old priest, his face grave. "There are some priests who have let their passions cloud their judgement. Their theology has been dangerously confused."

"What does that mean?" Gastón asked.

But Ezequiel wagged a bony finger. "Just remember what our Lord told his disciples. *Be wise as serpents and innocent as doves.*"

And with that, the old priest stepped into the bright sunlight and shuffled away.

# CHAPTER 11 – LOS JESUITAS

## *The Jesuits*

Gastón arrived early at the Jesuit compound in Bajo Flores, and it seemed to him a garden oasis amidst the poverty. He crossed the courtyard and entered the small chapel to wait. He was glad to have a few minutes to absorb this new environment and calm his nerves before meeting the rector.

Leaving his bag on a pew, Gastón wandered the church that was to become his new home. A painting caught his eye. In a variation of Leonardo da Vinci's *Last Supper*, the traditional unleavened bread on the table had been replaced with a basket of empanadas and a plate of chorizo. But it was another detail that held Gastón's attention. The traitorous Judas was a fat, smug Spanish conquistador, half-dressed in armor and a sword at his side. He fingered a purse with the thirty pieces of silver and was the only disciple not looking at Jesus. His battle helmet lay on the table beside him, and a menacing halberd stood propped against the wall behind his red velvet chair.

"The Rector hates that painting."

Gastón jumped. He turned to find a young priest smiling, his hands folded behind his cassock.

The priest stuck out his hand. "I'm Father Ferrer. You're Father Gastón, I presume?"

"*Un gusto,*" Gastón said, grasping his hand. "A pleasure to meet you. Sorry. I came a bit early—"

"Don't be sorry," Father Ferrer interrupted. "This is your

new home. Rector Alejandro asked me to welcome you. He sends his apologies. He'll meet you after lunch, at 3 p.m. In the meantime, I'm to show you around and introduce you to the brothers. Did you bring your things?"

"I left them on the pew," said Gastón. "But, may I ask you what you meant?"

"About what?" said Ferrer.

"What you said about the Rector hating this painting," said Gastón, turning to face the canvas.

"Well," said Father Ferrer, taking a step closer to Gastón, who by now had decided he liked this priest very much, and he felt much less nervous than before.

"This painting is a curious symbol of rebellion," continued Ferrer. "It's a part of our Jesuit history the rector feels needlessly draws attention to us today." He raised his eyebrows, contemplating the conquistador. "This painting was commissioned in 1813 at the height of the battle for independence from Spain. The people in Argentina at that time didn't think too highly of the Old World, especially by Rome's siding with Spain and by the power of the Church. The painting caused an immediate controversy. The archbishop demanded its destruction, but the Jesuits refused and hid it. The Holy See was furious and persuaded the Spanish army to find it and destroy it."

"I don't understand," said Gastón, "what does it have to do with today?"

"Everything," said Ferrer, taking Gastón by the arm. "We're under scrutiny again today, *¿viste?* Our Jesuit community here in Bajo Flores is having new tensions and rebellions that have rekindled old animosities with the Mother Church and the government. Don't worry though," said Father Ferrer, smiling now and patting Gastón on the shoulder, "our rector, Rector Alejandro, he's keeping us out of trouble. He's only thirty-one years old, but he's smart. We're lucky to have him. His star is rising fast, you know. It's rumored his name is on a short list of high potential priests kept in the cardinal's offices. Come, get your bag. I'll show you to your room and introduce you around."

Fetching his bag, Gastón followed Father Ferrer through the sacristy and across an open bridge connecting the church to an apartment building. Ferrer opened a door at the far end and led the way up the stairs.

"We've put you in the room with Father Brizzio. His roommate moved to Rosario, so there's a place for you there. I hope you'll like it here. All our priests in this parish live in the compound. Right now, we have, let's see, eleven of us. Six rooms, plus the rector's, which is upstairs on the third floor."

They reached the second-floor landing, and Gastón followed Ferrer through a hallway. Laughter spilled from some of the rooms, their doors ajar.

"Today is one of the few days the brothers have time to relax," said Ferrer. "It's a good time to meet them."

Stopping at a door, Ferrer knocked. He pushed it open and motioned to Gastón.

"Looks like Father Brizzio is out," Ferrer said. "Come in. You'll like him. He's been here seven years, and we all look up to him. He leads mass at one of our churches and teaches theology at the school. Brizzio can help orient you in your first weeks here, but the rector will tell you all about that after lunch."

The room was simple and neat. It had the same venetian red-tiled floor as the hallway and stairs. Twin beds shared a nightstand and lamp, and two desks lay beneath an open window. On one side of the room, a closet held a coat and several monochromatic shirts and slacks, all hung neatly on one side. Gastón looked out the window onto a small garden within the walled complex.

"We eat upstairs in the dining room on the third floor," said Ferrer. "Everyone takes his turn cooking, but I must tell you, some are better than others." His eyes twinkled. "I hope your mother taught you to cook. Drop your things on the bed. Let's see who's around."

Ferrer knocked on a door down the hall and it opened wide.

"Oh, Father Brizzio," said Ferrer, "you *are* here. When I didn't see you in your room, I thought you were out. Gastón, meet your new roommate, Father Nicolás Brizzio. And this is Father Cristóbal, there on the bed."

Everyone shook hands.

"Gastón comes from the *centro*," Ferrer said, leaning against the door frame. "He's new to the Society. I've already taught him the secret handshake."

They all laughed. Gastón picked at the hem of his pants.

"Have a seat." Father Cristóbal got off his bed and slid him a chair. Plopping back onto his bed, Cristóbal rapped twice on the wall. "There are a few others around," he said, "but most are taking the day off and will be back late, after dinner."

A door opened down the hallway, and a moment later two more young men entered the room. "We're in the room next door. We heard you were coming today. ¡*Bienvenido!*"

Gastón shook hands with them too.

"*Un gusto.*"

"Tell us about the *centro*," said Father Cristóbal.

Gastón described the downtown parish and his mentor Ezequiel. They laughed as Gastón described his bumbling efforts with the old women parishioners and his contact with the prostitutes and drug addicts.

"You will find the neighborhood here is a bit different,"

said Brizzio, his black hair flopping over his pale face. "The poverty and desperation you saw downtown is peripheral, on the margins. But here in Bajo Flores, it's endemic. It's the kind of mission we Jesuits like."

Brizzio eased himself out of his chair. "Gentlemen, forgive me. I need to get a few things done before lunch."

"Come get settled," Brizzio said to Gastón on the way out.

In their room, Brizzio made small talk, but Gastón sensed his roommate wanted to be alone. From the other priests, Gastón learned later that his new roommate was from the same Bajo Flores neighborhood where they now lived and worked. Brizzio's father had been killed because of his involvement in the trade unions and the Peronist resistance against the previous government. The young Brizzio had been sent to a Jesuit orphanage and somehow never left the church's orbit. "What other occupation would make use of your excellent Latin?" one of the curates had asked the precocious boy. And that was that.

It was rumored Brizzio had a sister and that she had also been sent away to an orphanage run by nuns. But no one knew anything for sure, and Gastón didn't want to pry. There was something interesting and complex about Brizzio that drew Gastón in.

Gastón finished unpacking his things and found a quiet corner in the library to read. He would like it here, he thought. It was nice to be in the company of other young priests.

A few minutes before 1 p.m., Father Ferrer fetched Gastón for lunch.

The dining room on the third floor was light and cheerful. Each priest stood behind his chair, his hands folded in front of him. In unison they prayed,

> *In a world where so many are hungry,*
> *may we eat this food with humble hearts;*
> *in a world where so many are lonely,*
> *May we share this friendship with joyful hearts.*

There was a pause for quiet reflection. And then,

> *May this food restore our strength, giving new energy to*
> *tired limbs,*
> *new thoughts to weary minds.*
> *May this drink restore our souls, giving new vision to dry*
> *spirits,*
> *new warmth to cold hearts.*
> *Amen.*

At three o'clock, Gastón knocked on the door to the rector's office. Now that he had settled in, he thought he would feel less nervous at meeting him, but his heart raced. He hoped he wouldn't disappoint the rector and his new brothers.

"*Pasá,*" came the rector's voice from within.

Opening the door, Gastón faced a man with thinning blond hair and piercing blue eyes that contrasted with his black cassock.

"Rector," Gastón said, grasping his outstretched hand, "it's a pleasure to meet you, sir."

"Call me Father, please," said Rector Alejandro. He smiled and motioned for Gastón to sit. "We are excited you have joined our work here. Sit."

"You will find, Father Gastón," said the rector after he was settled, "that the life of the Jesuit is highly structured, more so than your position in the *centro*, I'm sure. We take three vows – of poverty, chastity and obedience," the rector continued. "Our work is with the poor, and we care for the whole person – body, mind and soul."

Gastón nodded. He understood the vows and wondered if he could put them into practice.

"Here in our Bajo Flores parish," Alejandro said, "we conduct mass at three churches, including this one. We visit the sick and the shut-ins, and we seek opportunities to further social justice among the poor. We teach catechism. Some of our priests here, like your roommate Brizzio, teach theology at the *Escuela Jesuita* a few blocks away."

Gastón nodded again. He was ready for instruction and discipline. At the downtown parish, aside from the periodic visits from Old Ezequiel, he had been largely left on his own.

"I want you to stick close to Father Brizzio. Assist him with mass and learn from him," said Alejandro. "Sit in on his theology classes." Alejandro leaned back in his chair. "Brizzio is very passionate about what he does. About ministering to the poor. We all are, of course. Just sometimes his passions run a bit hot." The rector laughed, and it struck Gastón as awkward and forced.

"Thank you, Rector. I will work hard," said Gastón.

"Call me Father, please."

"Yes, Father. *Disculpá.*"

The rector spread his hands on the table before him and cocked his head. "You are joining at a complicated time," he said.

Gastón thought about the painting in the chapel and what Ferrer had said.

"But we Jesuits are used to troubles. To persecution," said the rector. "Father Gastón, have you been to the Iguazú

Waterfalls? To see the waterfalls and the ruins of the old Jesuit missions?"

"No, Father," said Gastón, feeling he'd let the rector down.

"It's a magical place," said Alejandro, and a broad smile broke across his face. "Imagine three hundred waterfalls breaking out of the dense jungle along a five kilometer stretch of the Iguazú River. Toucans squawking over the canopy, and jaguars prowling the dark undergrowth. You must go."

"I would like to, Father," said Gastón, drawn in by the rector's story. It seemed to Gastón as if a curtain had lifted and he'd glimpsed a different side of Alejandro.

"Perhaps you will," said Alejandro, and just as quickly, his eyes lost their brightness. "Well, the hoped-for utopia didn't last. The Catholic Church felt that the Jesuits – with their colonizing missions among the Tupi-Guaraní – had become too independent, too successful, and powerful. Too *native*."

Alejandro paused as if to let this last word sink in.

"When the Jesuits were expelled," the rector continued, "the jungle vines reclaimed the abandoned missions, and like the waterfalls, they were lost to western civilization for one hundred fifty years. The Vatican rescinded the order much later, of course, and its relationship with the Jesuits much improved. You see, Father Gastón, the Church has helped us see the limitations of social justice."

Alejandro sighed. "We are just one small piece of our great Mother Church. We are to live in harmony with it despite these complicated times. The subversives enjoy much support among the people in this poor part of the city. We must focus on our mission to serve the poor. We are not to be political. *¿Entendés?*"

"Yes, Father," said Gastón, feeling unsure what this all meant but understanding the rector was communicating something important. He wanted to ask a question but thought it better to remain silent. Maybe he could ask Brizzio or the others once he got to know them better. Maybe this would all make sense.

Gastón couldn't shake a disconcerting feeling about his new rector as if he were holding back. Rector Alejandro was a rising star. Was something here in Bajo Flores threatening Alejandro's trajectory? The words of his mentor Ezequiel came back to him. *Be wise as serpents and innocent as doves.*

The rector stood and Gastón snapped out of his retrospection, embarrassed.

"Tomorrow, in our small chapel," said Alejandro, "you will stand before your new brothers and take your vows."

And with that, he shook Gastón's hand and showed him out.

# CHAPTER 12 – EL RECLUTA
## *The Recruit*

The overnight bus pulled into the *Terminal de Ómnibus de Retiro* in Buenos Aires at 5:12 a.m. Daniel was surprised to see so many buses and passengers at this early hour. The scene reminded him of another early morning subculture, the Almagro flower market, when his father had taken him and Antonio one dark morning to watch the trucks unload carts piled high with flowers and to listen to the florists haggling over prices and buying their day's supplies.

Daniel scanned the huge terminal and spotted a weathered sign listing routes and schedules for the local buses. An oversized woman with proportionate bags arranged around her sat on a bench and watched him.

"Don't bother reading that, *joven*. It's wrong," the woman said. "Hasn't been updated in years. Perón, he cared about us people. The buses were new. Buses had schedules. Now the buses do whatever they want. We all miss El Pocho. Don't you? Where are you going?"

"Núñez. Libertador."

"Núñez? That's north. The north *colectivos* are over there," the woman said, pointing across her bovine body. "But you'll have to wait. They don't run this early. Why are you going north? People come south in the morning."

Daniel found the bay for his bus, but it was empty.

He laid his pack beside the shiny brass spigot of a public fountain and pulled out a small bar of soap and a black comb.

He washed his face and armpits and dried them with a T-shirt. He wet his hair and combed it out. He brushed his teeth. From the bottom of his rucksack, he found a clean pair of pants and a button-down shirt. Daniel wondered if he should wait and get a haircut first. He pulled out his toothbrush and realized he'd already used it.

Línea 130 was still empty, but here and there passengers queued. Occasionally a bus started its grumbling engine and pulled out with a noisy grinding of gears.

Daniel bought a cup of *mate* from an old man with a *cafetero* cart and found a park bench where he stretched his legs. Clutching his bag to his chest, he dozed off.

When he awoke, the sun was bright. Daniel sat up and felt for his bag. People were boarding línea 130, and Daniel hopped up the steps. "To the ESMA." The driver took his money and flipped out the change from the bottom of the coin dispenser.

Twenty-five minutes later, the bus passed the entrance to the *Escuela Superior de Mecánica de la Armada*. Daniel pulled on the rope. He thought about the last time he had been here when he had dropped off the Admiral in the remis. It seemed like ages ago. His nervousness now was different.

The *colectivo* slowed at the next stop, and he hopped off.

The naval academy covered forty-two manicured acres and was surrounded by a wrought-iron fence, each section decorated with a silhouetted emblem of a full-rigged sailing ship. Daniel smoothed his shirt and tucked it in.

Outside the gated entrance, four guards in dress whites stood with FAL machine guns slung over their shoulders.

*"Pará.* Put your pack on the ground." One of the guards stepped toward him, his weapon pointed at Daniel's belly. "Stay right there."

"What's your business?"

"I'm here to see Admiral Bertotti."

The guard snorted. "Nobody sees the Admiral. He's not here. *Cédula.*"

Daniel fished for his identification.

"I was told to ask for him," Daniel said. "A... a personal connection. To come and apply with him. My military service starts in a week."

The guard studied the ID card. "Wait here," he said, and he disappeared into one of the guardhouses. He returned with a paper in his hand.

"Come back tomorrow. Bring this completed form."

Daniel's heart surged. He had waited for this day for almost a month.

The boot camp was held at an empty warehouse in Pacheco, north of the city. Daniel had been assigned to the federal police, but under the current regime, the military and the police had coalesced to become organs of the same tightly controlled government body.

Daniel was proud. He had passed a battery of physical and psychological tests to get here. He had done this completely on his own. He looked at the sixty-two young men beside him with a sense of camaraderie. Almost all were working class, and despite the low pay and unfavorable working conditions connected with police work, joining the force was an advancement and a bright career path for them. Some had fathers or relatives who were policemen or military. Others, like Daniel, had found a way into this duty to avoid posting guard in some remote base or, worse, fighting guerilla armies in the jungles of Tucumán.

The first day, the new recruits were stripped of all clothing and personal belongings. They were led naked out onto a cracked cement slab outside the brick warehouse to be hosed down. The sun was hot on Daniel's head, and his feet burned until they were sprayed with the water.

"Cover your eyes!" a sergeant yelled, and they were sprinkled with delousing powder. In newly issued army fatigues and T-shirts, they ran and did calisthenics, and performed tests of strength and endurance.

The training was led by a hard man named Lieutenant Cazorla, a military man who made it clear that enthusiasm was mandatory. Over the years, the lieutenant had lost colleagues and men to leftist terrorists. His passion against subversives was personal, and he would make it personal for his new charges too.

The young men were taught to fire handguns, carbines, and machine guns. They learned to scan crowds and to detect odd and suspicious behavior. How to take down a man and subdue him quickly. They handled grenades and learned chains of command.

It wasn't for everyone, and the group of sixty-two dwindled.

"Some say I'm too harsh," said Lieutenant Cazorla one morning to the lines formed before him. "That my methods keep our police force from being fully staffed." The lieutenant paced in front of them. "They tell me my training is too hard. What do you think?"

"*¡No, teniente!*" they yelled in unison.

"Anyone here think the training is too hard? Come on. Step out."

He stopped pacing, his hands folded patiently behind his back. "They tell me not to let excellent be the enemy of good," Cazorla continued. "That may be true. But I can assure you that thick donkey crap also is the enemy of good."

Some realized right away they were donkey crap. Others

had to be shown.

Daniel thrived in this testosterone-filled environment. Something unleashed within him, something restrained until now. He found that anything involving extreme pain and suffering he endured better than anyone else. He swelled with pride.

Daniel determined not to fail. He couldn't. There was nothing else. No going back. He thought of his father and the stolen money, and he pushed the shame to the farthest recesses of his mind.

One night Daniel awoke in a cold sweat. In his nightmare, the thick blackness of a night sky suffocated him, and he groped for something to cling to, but there was only a dark abyss.

*"¿Qué te pasa, boludo?"* whispered Cacho, a fellow recruit, who shook him awake. Daniel had clicked with Cacho, and they had become fast friends. Both were among the most competitive of the new recruits, and they stood out in the exercises and tasks.

One early morning, Lieutenant Cazorla again paced in front of his men, now a diminished group of forty-one standing at attention. He held a single sheet of paper and waved it at them.

"Do you know what this is?" he barked. "A list of policemen and civilians killed and kidnapped just in the past week. You think this is just a game?"

Holding up the paper, he began reading, "February 13, Capitán Miguel Ángel Barahona. Shot in the street while walking to the Army War College where he was a student. February 15, a bombing at the office of the state police deputy chief in La Plata. The ERP planted five kilograms of explosives filled with hundreds of nails. Officer Colonel Toledo lost an arm. Colonel Farias and three commissaries were severely wounded. The same day, February 15, Mr. Ricardo Sáenz, manager of Compañía Posadas in provincia, murdered. Last Wednesday, February 16, Mr. Alberto Gallardo, executive manager of the Fiat Company. Gunned down in his car on the way to work in Córdoba."

"If you are not paranoid, you will die," Cazorla continued. "The bullet of the subversive is waiting for you, the surprise bomb on the street. These terrorists deal in the business of death, and they desire death as much as you desire life."

He paused while the recruits internalized this information.

"Your minds are currently filled with *mierda*," he said. "We're going to clear all that out and fill it back up with fear and hate. These will empower you to protect your nation and democracy. Fear and hate for the Communists and the Jews."

But it didn't end there, and Daniel found it was a long list to be learned. They were taught to hate the armed guerillas – the *Montoneros* and the ERP army. They were taught to suspect the university students, professors, journalists, union leaders. But hatred needed to be created, and it needed to be stoked because men will not fight unless they despise the enemy. The propaganda of hate was an unforgiving mistress, and it was something at which this military regime was particularly gifted.

The weeks of training turned into months. Daniel noticed a man observing them from time to time. Always dressed in civilian clothes, a wide-collared shirt, and a plaid sport coat, he would stand some distance away. He was not introduced, and he spoke with no one. He stood with his hands at his side, coming and leaving like a shadow. Once Daniel caught Cazorla looking in the man's direction and scowling.

One morning the recruits awoke to the pleasant news of a change in their routine. After the morning exercises, Cazorla addressed the assembled men. "Today you will have an opportunity to put into practice some of what you have learned over the last sixteen weeks. Today you get some on-the-job training. We will travel downtown and provide police security at the Plaza de Mayo. You will protect the Casa Rosada."

"It may seem like a peaceful demonstration," Cazorla continued. "It's a group of subversive women making illegal demonstrations in the plaza. Call themselves the *Madres de Plaza de Mayo*, but don't be fooled by their matronly shapes and their neatly tied white scarves. They are wolves in sheep's clothing. Sons and daughters are damned killers."

Cazorla spat.

He walked up and down the straight lines in front of him.

"You will be outfitted with police uniforms and issued riot gear. You will do exactly what I say. I will be watching each of you."

The young men were soon to learn that besides fitness and hate, the military regime required loyalty, batons, and electric prods. And Daniel was willing to commit to it all.

# CHAPTER 13 – EL AGENTE

## *The Agent*

"Sit," said Lieutenant Cazorla. He pointed Daniel to a chair in his office. The training was almost completed, but Daniel had never been to the lieutenant's office, and he looked about to see if he could learn anything personal about him. But the office was as austere and singularly focused as the man before him.

The lieutenant pulled a cigarette from a pack wedged into the front pocket of his crisp shirt. He lit it with a flick of the wrist and tossed the lighter onto the desk. Putting his feet up, he took a long drag and cocked his head at Daniel. The smoke blew out the corners of his mouth and curled toward the ceiling fan.

"You've done well, Romandini. I've seen many recruits. Some fine recruits. You're among the best. I congratulate you on your training and your success."

"*Gracias, teniente,*" said Daniel. The smoke smelled good, blonde leaf. Jockey Club. Much better than his father's strong *Particulares*.

"Fortunately or unfortunately for you, and definitely unfortunate for me, you've been noticed by others too." Cazorla took another drag on his cigarette, looked up at the ceiling and exhaled, watching the smoke scurry around the blades of the slow-moving fan. "They always take the best ones," he mumbled. "*Siempre nos dejan con la mierda.*"

"*¿Cómo, teniente?* What?"

Cazorla ignored the question and handed Daniel a folded paper. "Tomorrow at 9:30 a.m. sharp, you will report to this address. Tell no one about where you are going. *¿Entendés?*"

"*Sí, teniente.*"

The lieutenant swung his legs off the desk, stood stiffly, and extended his hand. Caught off guard by the personal gesture, Daniel stopped himself in mid salute and grabbed for the hand just as it was about to lose hope and be withdrawn.

"Watch yourself," Cazorla said, and he waved him out of his office.


Daniel stepped off the bus and onto the sidewalk of the busy Avenida Leandro Alem. The air smelled of roasted candied peanuts and exhaust fumes. He had been curious all night about the address and had fought the temptation to share it with Cacho. He was pretty sure what this meeting was about, and he felt his pocket for the paper the lieutenant had given him. Ahead of him was the magnificent pink sandstone Casa Rosada, and Daniel's heart swelled to think his business brought him to the very center of government power. He wished his father could see him now.

At the presidential palace he turned onto the Plaza de Mayo. The first cross street was Calle 25 de Mayo, and turning right, he followed the imposing building to its entrance.

Across the street, eight federal policemen stood beside a police van, their fingers resting on the triggers of their FALs. Daniel pushed open the heavy door.

In the middle of the foyer was a wooden desk, and behind it sat a mousy man with big ears and oversized glasses. Two men in dark pants and white shirts stood against the wall holding Ithaca shotguns.

"You have something for me?" asked the man, pushing up his glasses. Daniel produced the folded paper from Lieutenant Cazorla.

"*Cédula.*"

Daniel handed over his identification. The man licked the end of his pencil and copied into his ledger Daniel's name and identification number, along with the date and time of entry. He handed Daniel back his ID but held the paper out for one of the men standing behind him.

"*Puede pasar, joven.*"

Daniel was frisked and motioned to follow. Walking past the elevator, they climbed three flights of stairs to a reception hall. A sign read *Secretaría de Inteligencia del Estado.* The red oval logo, outlined by the white and blue colors of the national flag, included two clasped arms and two simple initials *S.I.*

Daniel had heard about the intelligence service, SIDE. Everyone had, of course. As a kid, SIDE was about spies and adventure. Today the agency seemed to have taken on a less varnished reputation, and rumors were talked about in hushed voices. Daniel was sure most of it was untrue. He thought of the estancia and the men in the green Falcon.

The receptionist smiled. "*Buen día.* Take a seat, please. ¿*Café?*"

"*Si, gracias.*"

Daniel sat. The woman returned with a cup of coffee. Three men with shotguns waited for an elevator. The men shared a laugh. They were so sure of themselves, so cocky and brash. So jaunty in their civilian clothes with weapons resting easily over their shoulders.

"Romandini?" A man appeared from behind the partition. "*Vení.*"

Daniel was led through a maze of cubicles, many cluttered

with papers, articles of clothing, and military equipment. Bulletproof vests, batons, helmets, boots, FALs, and Ithaca 12-gauges. He imagined himself here with his own gear.

At the far end near a large corner office, a secretary greeted Daniel. *"Aguarde un momento, por favor,"* she said. The escort left and Daniel waited.

A loud voice erupted from behind the closed office door. "Get me that phone number. Last week that business manager, whatever his name. Vázquez. Ransomed for nine hundred thousand dollars. And now this? Four million dollars?"

Daniel recognized the voice. He struggled to remember, and then it hit him. Yes. It was the Admiral he had picked up in Belgrano. Daniel suddenly felt nervous. *Would the Admiral remember me?*

Another voice, quieter, said something that Daniel couldn't make out. The Admiral's booming voice responded, "What do these companies think the subversives do with this kind of money? You call Mercedes-Benz today. Read them the list of bombings and assassinations in the past few days. How many people die because companies like them pay…"

The other voice interrupted.

"I don't care who the hell he is," the Admiral replied, and there was a loud thumping like papers slamming onto a desk. "Tell him it's an order."

The secretary looked at Daniel and smiled. Daniel wished he was back at the barracks.

The secretary rapped on the office door and pushed it open. "Daniel Romandini," she announced. She turned to Daniel. *"Entre, por favor."*

Admiral Bertotti was seated behind an enormous desk on one side of the office. Daniel sensed an energy from this man that filled the spacious office.

The desk was surprisingly empty, only a few neat piles of

papers and folders. A picture of a large white dog sat on one corner. No family pictures. There was a sofa and two armchairs. The navy blue curtains had been pulled aside from the windows, and the morning sun streamed into the office. A row of metal filing cabinets lay against a wall, and near the door stood a floor-to-ceiling bookcase.

By the window stood the man Daniel recognized as the one watching his trainings.

"I'm Sebastian," the man said. "I work for the Admiral. *Sentá.*" He motioned Daniel toward the sofa.

The Admiral stood, holding a folder in his hand and looking at Daniel as if trying to place him. *He doesn't remember me. Of course, he doesn't.*

The Admiral glided across the floor and settled himself into a leather armchair across from his visitor. Sebastian took a seat in another armchair beside his boss.

"Do you know what we do here at SIDE?" said the Admiral, his eyes piercing.

"Yes, sir," said Daniel. "I think – "

"Shut up," said the Admiral. "You know nothing. *Sabés nada.* Whatever you may have heard is wrong. Not that we try to correct it. Rumors have a way of keeping everyone guessing. People have no idea what we do here, and we mean to keep it that way."

The Admiral folded his hands together. "You have a police connection, don't you? You want to tell me about your Uncle Ricardo? Killed by terrorists, I understand. Died in the line of duty trying to protect Judge Calva. Tragic. But let's be honest. Your Uncle Ricardo, he was a real piece of work, no? A cop for twenty-five years and never promoted. Makes you wonder. Suspended multiple times. A violent drunk, that's what he was. I think he was on the take. Do you want to be on the take, Romandini?"

"No, sir." Daniel's neck was hot. He struggled to process this barrage of information. *Was this all true?*

"Of course, you do," said the Admiral. "You have that corruption in your blood, don't you?"

"My uncle was not corrupt," said Daniel scrambling to his feet. *It wasn't true.*

"You know nothing, remember?" said the Admiral, motioning for Daniel to sit back onto the sofa. *"Nada.* But *we* know something, Romandini. We know a lot. Like you dropped out of university. Too hard for your blue-collar background? You never really fit in? Did you get suspended for fighting, like you did in high school?"

Daniel tried to control his anger. They were just trying to get under his skin, he reminded himself. It was just a test. Lieutenant Cazorla said they liked him. He relaxed. He wanted to like the Admiral like he had before.

The Admiral leaned forward in his chair. "Can you keep secrets?"

"Yes, sir. Yes, I can," said Daniel, and he hoped this was an opening and that his stammering didn't reveal how much he wanted to work for this man. There was nothing he wanted more.

"Yes, yes," said the Admiral, "you *do* keep secrets, don't you, Romandini?" and he tapped the folder in his hand against his knee. "But I have a problem with your kind of secrets. You see, you come highly recommended. In fact, Sebastian here likes you. At least he did initially." In the other armchair, the aide scowled.

"We've been reviewing your file," he continued, "and some things are troubling. We like you a lot less now. Do you want to tell us about these secrets of yours?"

"Excuse me?" said Daniel. *What secrets?* He rubbed his clammy hands against his pants, and the action made him feel this opportunity was slipping away.

"Why are you an admirer of Che?" said the Admiral.

"Sir?"

"I said, why do you love Che Guevara so much?"

"I don't, sir. I don't know what you mean. I'm not political."

"You don't love Che." It was neither a question nor a statement.

"No, sir," said Daniel.

The Admiral frowned and looked at the paper in his hand. "You're a medical student at the UBA. The same one where Che attended, no? You have a communist girlfriend. You took a motorcycle trip following Che Guevara's route. You spent time training at a leftist camp in Mendoza by the foothills of the Andes. You are a subversive."

Daniel's heart beat wildly. His mouth was dry.

"What do you think, Sebastian?" said the Admiral, but his aide said nothing.

The Admiral turned back to Daniel. "Do you know why you are here, Romandini?"

"No, sir." He thought it was to be recruited as an agent, but now he wondered if he would be detained.

"It is because you are all of these things and none of these things," said the Admiral. A handsome grin stretched across his mouth. "You now work for me. For SIDE. Congratulations."

Again, Daniel tried to process what he heard. *Was this some sort of joke?* But the Admiral was serious, and Daniel quickly recovered. *They're just messing with me. I'm in.* Daniel felt a thrill surge inside and then, just as quickly, he felt that somehow he was being used, and he wasn't sure if that was a bad thing or just a neutral thing.

The Admiral didn't give him any time to decide.

"I hear they call you *El Inglés*," said the Admiral. "Nickname you picked up at training because of your dirty blond hair? Maybe you smoke a pipe like the English?" The Admiral chuckled. "Let me explain what we do here at SIDE, Inglés. We are not the army. The army is busy fighting the Montoneros and the ERP, fighting guerillas in the jungles of Tucumán and in the province of Córdoba. And we are not the police battling the guerillas and subversives on the streets here in Buenos Aires and in Rosario. In La Plata. Trying to contain the violence. This is where most of your fellow recruits are headed. No, Inglés. At SIDE we do something else."

The Admiral stood and walked to a tall window. The morning rays shone so brightly on him that he seemed to glow like an angel. "No, my young warrior, we don't fight the subversive. We're here to make him see the error of his ways and to help him fail. Our interests at SIDE are personal. They are the union leader agitator, the leftist professor promoting armed rebellion, the journalist with dreams of a Marxist revolution. The radicalized university student duped into carrying out terrorist plots. The infiltrated Cuban. It's one big chessboard. We capture high-value pieces one by one."

The Admiral returned to his chair across from Daniel.

"You've been chosen because you are strong and because you have something useful to me. Useful to your nation. Do you wish to serve your country, Inglés?"

"Yes, sir," said Daniel, wondering what this meant and sinking farther down into the couch.

The Admiral continued. "You are a student at the university. You can get access where others cannot. Your objective will be to infiltrate the terrorists at the UBA. Officially, however, you'll be assigned to the *Cuerpo Guardia de Infantería*. You'll carry out your duties with the *Guardia*, like everyone else. But when we require it, you will be detailed to one of our special teams."

The Admiral leaned in toward Daniel. "You will tell no one in the *Guardia* you are part of the Intelligence Service. They mustn't know about that nor about your activities at the university. *¿Entendés?"*

"Yes, sir."

"You will learn *our* methods, *¿viste?"* said the Admiral. He smiled. "You see, the subversive becomes much more reasonable when his head is detached from his body, and thus subdued, he's less able to resist and more willing to learn the lessons the government wishes to teach him."

The Admiral stood. "Sebastian here will get you started. "And you'll need a nom de guerre, of course. *Inglés* will do just fine."

The meeting was over. The Admiral walked him to the door. Daniel glanced at the titles on the bookcase.

"I'm an avid reader," the Admiral said. "History and literature mainly, and yet I'm suspicious of all writers and readers. Are you a reader, Inglés?"

Daniel wasn't sure how to respond. He was sure it was another test.

"I like to read some," he said. "Not much, to tell the truth."

The Admiral ran his hand along a row of books. "Many of the great literary works of this century have profoundly leftist themes. But not all of them." He pulled out a volume. "Have you read *Animal Farm?"*

"No, sir."

Daniel caught Sebastian rolling his eyes.

"George Orwell was inspired by the Bolshevik revolution and its aftermath," said the Admiral. "The novel is about a group of animals that overthrow the farmer. *Animalism* is what they call their new philosophy. All goes well at first, but then the power struggles begin and the scheming. The purges are carried out."

The Admiral looked across the office and out the window at the traffic below. His face darkened. "It's the story of Stalin's Soviet Union and Mao's Communist China. It's the story of Castro's Cuba. Devastations wreaked by the pursuit of utopia."

He put his hand on Daniel's shoulder. "When you leave here and step onto the street, you're going to hear people speak against what we're doing. You're going to read about it in some of the newspapers – although certainly fewer newspapers now, isn't that right, Sebastian?" The Admiral grinned again. "Some people are just naïve. They don't know what we are saving Argentina *from*. They don't know what true repression is. The only people who advocate for socialism are those who have never lived under it. There's only one way to stop animalism. It's what we do at SIDE. It's what you do now."

Sebastian took Daniel across the hall to a conference room. The aide picked up a telephone and dialed. *"Veni,"* he said simply into the mouthpiece.

"You'll report to me," Sebastian told Daniel. "You're not to come to this office unless instructed. You're not to contact the Admiral unless told to do so. You're not to contact me unless told. Is that clear?"

"Yes, sir."

"Don't call me sir."

Daniel nodded, not at all sure how he should address him.

The door opened and a tall thin man in his late twenties entered. He carried a cardboard box. "I'm Canario," he said. He set his load on the table and extended a hand to Daniel.

"Canario will train you," said Sebastian, standing by the

door to leave. "An apartment has been rented for you in the city center."

Canario was all business. He walked Daniel through a few details that didn't last more than five minutes. He handed Daniel a piece of paper and a key. "This is the address of your apartment. You have another new agent for a roommate. Get settled today. You'll get a call tomorrow morning. Early. When you get the call, come out and walk two blocks north. I'll be waiting in a car."

Turning to the box on the table, the veteran agent opened it. He handed Daniel a well-worn 9mm Browning Hi Power with a dark wood stock. It felt good and well-balanced in his hand. He found himself wondering about its previous owner, and whether he had ever used it to kill someone and where he was now.

"Keep it with you at all times," said Canario. "Loaded. The worst part about it is always having to wear a jacket to hide it, even in the hot summer months. Here's a side holster."

Canario reached into the box again and slid him an extra magazine and two boxes of bullets. Daniel stuffed the 9mm into the side holster and left it on the table. He tucked the magazine and the ammunition into his jacket pockets.

"You have your police ID, right?" Canario said.

Daniel nodded and patted his breast pocket. It was issued after graduation from the academy. He'd rarely used it, but it was always there.

"You'll identify yourself mostly with that one," said Canario.

Canario held up a black leather wallet then slid it across to Daniel. "Keep this one with you, too, but hidden. You'll know when you need to use it."

Inside there was no name and no picture. Only the shiny SIDE emblem.

The agent stood and Daniel did too. "Don't forget about tomorrow morning, Inglés. Don't screw up. You'll be on probation for the first few weeks. You show up on time, you do what you're told, you learn quick. *¿Entendés?"*

Canario led the way back through the maze of cubicles to the reception area where he shook Daniel's hand and left him. Cacho was seated where Daniel had been earlier that morning. He looked up, and they both grinned.

When Cacho exited the building onto Calle 25 de Mayo, Daniel was waiting. He gave a sharp whistle from across the street. "Let's get a beer," said Daniel.

Pichín Bar y Sandwichería was nearly empty. The lunch crowd wouldn't come for another hour or so.

*"Dos cervezas de litro, bien frías,"* Daniel ordered from the bartender.

Cacho raised his glass to Daniel. "Here's to graduation from our training and to new adventures with SIDE. *Salud,* roommate!"

Daniel felt on top of the world.

"I think about our training group," said Daniel. "Poor bastards. You know, I used to think I'd be happy just having a police badge." He glanced around at the other patrons and lowered his voice. "But this SIDE thing tops it all!"

"Yeah," said Cacho, "we'll be kicking ass, getting respect everywhere we go. We were meant to be here, Inglés."

"To be honest, I can't believe they let you in," said Daniel.

"Yeah," said Cacho, "well, you're a damned doctor. What are you doing here? But who knows? Maybe you'll come in handy someday."

"The Admiral is an arrogant bastard," said Daniel. "He insulted my uncle. And Sebastian is slippery as a snake. I'm telling you, I'm watching my back all the time."

"You can trust me, Inglés. I'll watch your back."

Daniel smiled. "You're a good friend, Cacho."

They ordered the gnocchi and more beer. They spent the afternoon strolling the streets downtown, stopping for drinks, and feeling cocky and self-important. They had achieved something. They liked the hard feel of their new 9mms and the shiny badges.

Stumbling back to their new apartment, they fell into bed. Daniel closed his eyes. He would make something of himself. Something to make his father proud.

# CHAPTER 14 – EL REPORTERO

## *The Reporter*

The telephone rang early the next morning.

Daniel and Cacho dressed quickly. They tucked the Brownings into their side holsters and slid the badges into their jacket pockets. Daniel's head hurt from the drinking the night before.

Two blocks north, Canario waited in a car. He offered no pleasantries. Onboarding new guys likely was not his favorite job, thought Daniel. Maybe Canario was good at it. He needed to be. It was an occupation that ate its young.

"Pay attention today," said Canario, who proved quite chatty but not amiable. "You don't pay attention, and you get killed. Worse, you get *me* killed. I don't know why they bring you new recruits directly into SIDE. No experience at all. But I guess getting experience today often requires getting killed in the process. Makes it damned hard to learn when you're dead."

Canario turned the ignition of the Falcon.

"We're going to pay a friendly visit to an unfriendly journalist this morning," he said. "He's a foreigner. An American. Damn Jew too. Name is Robert Goldman of the *Buenos Aires Herald*. Been writing biased articles, works hard to get leftists freed from prison, and tries to help the Madres de Plaza de Mayo find people they say are disappeared. He's become good friends of the Madres, in fact. Made himself a general nuisance. Married to an Argentine, but even her family wants nothing to do with him. They cross the street so as not to pass him. So leftist he can't even work in his own damn country. Now he's causing trouble here. At least he only writes in English. But Jacobo Hautzig – you guys heard of him?"

Daniel and Cacho shook their heads. Daniel rubbed his temples, trying to absorb Canario's rapid-fire wisdom.

"Hautzig is a leftist, an Argentine journalist for *La Opinión*," continued Canario. "He's a Jew too. Sometimes he translates and reprints Goldman's articles. Creates big problems for us. But not anymore."

The SIDE squad leader smiled and eased the car into the early morning traffic. "Hautzig doesn't write anymore. He's in jail. Now we have friendlies running the paper. Opinions have changed at *La Opinión*." He snorted like a horse. "Now let's pay Goldman a visit."

The drive to the upscale bohemian neighborhood of Palermo took twenty-five minutes, and in that time Daniel and Cacho learned about anti-Semitism. Neither of them had thought much about the Jews before their training, and they were inexcusably unaware that the *judíos* were responsible for so many of the social ills in Argentina.

They pulled over to the curb on Calle Fitz Roy.

"Second floor, the windows with the green curtains." Canario pointed across the street at an apartment building.

"Won't he see us?" said Cacho.

"That's the whole point, rookie," Canario said, lighting a cigarette. "He knows about Hautzig, so he's going to be extra nervy today. He received a death threat a few days ago."

"You've waited here before?" said Daniel, trying to understand exactly what they were doing here.

"Of course. He's a regular on our circuit. You'll be assigned these duties too. Last week we faked an attempted kidnapping of his wife just to scare him. If he hasn't left the country by next week, we're going to pick him up and take him in. He won't like it. Just sit tight. He usually leaves for the office about now."

They sat behind the tinted windows and waited. Canario took the opportunity to enlighten the new agents about the dangers journalists posed to society. They simply had too much influence to be trusted, he explained, too much power to mislead the public. Reporters abused their independence and took too many liberties with their freedoms of the press. They were truculent and unaccommodating. They asked for trouble, and SIDE fulfilled their requests, particularly with this journalist, Goldman, who was Jewish to boot.

It all made a lot of sense to Daniel, whose learning process was helped by the squad leader's animated hand waving. His curiosity was peaked. He couldn't wait to see such a dangerous subversive, especially a Semitic journalist.

The curtain parted on the second-floor window, and a figure appeared for a brief moment.

"Here he comes," said Canario, flicking his cigarette butt out the driver's window. Daniel and Cacho craned their necks.

A balding man emerged from the apartment entrance, squinted across the street at the car, and began walking. Canario opened his door. He crossed the street and followed Goldman. Daniel and Cacho jogged to keep up.

The journalist glanced behind him and picked up his pace. He arrived at a bus stop and worked his way into the middle of the crowd waiting for the bus. Canario sidled up and bumped him.

*"Disculpá."* He jostled the man again, "Excuse me." Canario let the man feel his gun poking him in the side.

A bus arrived, and Goldman hurried to get on with the other riders. Canario, with Daniel and Cacho beside him, watched him get on and shuffle to the back. He stood, holding onto a handrail in the crowded bus, his back to the three men on the sidewalk. Canario glared at him and so did the trainees. The bus ground its gears and moved away in a cloud of exhaust.

Daniel was proud of his contribution toward keeping Argentina safe from outside influences. *How dare a foreigner like Goldman poke his nose into our business!* Daniel was a real intelligence officer now, dealing with foreign spies and parsing nuances about their powerful United States ally in this war against Communism. In just a matter of weeks his provincial perspective had now expanded to the world stage.

The training with Canario continued. Over the next few weeks, Daniel and Cacho studied the art of intimidation. They learned to communicate by snapping their fingers to avoid having to speak and giving away their voices. They met other agents. They familiarized themselves with the many detention centers hidden in the middle of the bustling downtown, like the dingy office of a parking garage on Calle Piedras and the handsome apartment overlooking Plaza Colón.

One day they accompanied Canario to revisit some old business. With Cacho now driving the sedan, the three agents pulled up just before 7 p.m. across from the offices of the *Buenos Aires Herald*, just a few blocks south of the Plaza de Mayo.

It was dusk when Robert Goldman left his office and stepped onto Calle Azopardo. Daniel and Canario exited the car and crossed the street. As the Ford Falcon swung around, they grabbed the startled journalist by the arms and shoved him into the back seat between them. They whisked Goldman to the police department in Belgrano where he was detained overnight and forced to endure loud music pumped into his cell.

The next afternoon he was released, shaken and bleary-eyed. The attempted kidnapping of his wife, the intimidations, it was all too much for him. A week later a death threat arrived, one with detailed information about his thirteen-year-old son. It was the last straw. The following week the Goldmans left Argentina for the peaceful suburbs of Northern Virginia.

The Goldman's departure was a big win in shutting down a mouthpiece for international audiences. For their work, Daniel and Cacho received an invitation to SIDE's headquarters to shake hands with the Admiral himself.

"Sebastian, pour us a drink," the Admiral ordered his aide, who scowled and rummaged in a cabinet for tumblers and a bottle of Johnny Walker.

Daniel felt proud. He thought of the last time he had been in this office, nervous as hell and wondering from the Admiral's sharp questioning if he'd even be accepted at all. But now, with this quick win and the confidence-building scotch burning down his throat, Daniel's initiation was complete. He was doing good. He was serving his country.

Winking at Cacho, Daniel tapped his glass in Sebastian's direction. The Admiral smiled and held out his glass too, and the aide's face darkened while the celebrants' lightened.

# CHAPTER 15 – EL CUERPO DE INFANTERÍA

## *The Infantry Corps*

To hide their SIDE affiliation, Daniel and Cacho were assigned as regular federal police. The *Cuerpo Guardia de Infantería* was comprised of three thousand policemen and headquartered at the massive Departamento Central de Policía that took up an entire city block downtown. Across Calle Moreno, a hospital and morgue completed the triumvirate.

Daniel and Cacho were detailed to specialized assault teams known as *grupos de tarea* that excelled in snatch-and-grab operations. Sometimes they formed into larger teams of twelve, the *grupos de combate*. When the police needed to break up demonstrators on the city streets or university campuses, several of these *grupos de combate* combined to make a great show of force.

Daniel absorbed everything with an enthusiasm not dampened by the slow fading of fall into winter. He loved the adrenaline rush accompanying the daily action and the opportunities to prove himself.

One evening he went out for drinks with Cacho and another friend, Luis, who was an unhappy *guardia* serving out his compulsory service. They occasionally met up after work when they could persuade Luis to ignore his family responsibilities.

"This military service will be the end of me, you'll see,"

said Luis when they settled at a table in the crowded bar.

"You mean you're staying until you retire with full pension?" said Daniel, winking at Cacho.

*"No, idiota,"* said Luis. "If it weren't for the military coup extending my service, I'd have been done with my commitment."

"Yeah, but then you wouldn't have met your two best friends," said Cacho, slapping Luis on the arm.

"And what would you be doing, Family Man?" Daniel said, getting in on the fun. "Working full-time as a rent-a-cop?"

"Go ahead and laugh," said Luis. He moonlighted several days a week as a security guard to make ends meet for his wife and two children. "You're both gung-ho and excited, but I'm telling you," he said, "I've been in longer than you. You'll want out too."

Luis scowled. He tilted back his beer and his face suddenly brightened. "Mónica has invited you for lunch tomorrow," he said. "We'll have an *asado*. She makes the best tiramisu. Can you come? You'll meet my family."

The next day was cold and blustery when Daniel and Cacho took the short train ride out to Florida. Daniel was pensive and quiet. It was the line toward his childhood home.

The train passed the church where he had taken First Communion and where two years later he sat at his mother's funeral wearing a stiff black suit. When Uncle Ricardo had died, there had been a lot of policemen in uniform, but now it was empty. The train passed a dirt lot where Daniel had played soccer. He recalled his first fistfight. The train neared his father's house, and he thought about his father and his gray head, and the money under the parquet tiles. No, he told himself, he would go back when he was ready. He'd make up for everything

*"Bienvenidos,"* Luis said when Daniel and Cacho arrived, and he embraced them. "This is my wife, Mónica."

*"Un gusto."*

Each planted a kiss on Mónica's cheek. Luis's wife was petite and fetchingly self-assured, and Daniel found himself wondering how Luis managed such an attractive woman.

The guests were shown into the small apartment and relieved of their coats. Sitting on the sofa, they found two wide-eyed children staring at them.

"Can you imagine doing what we do every day," whispered Daniel to Cacho, "and then coming home to a family?"

Cacho shook his head. "But climbing into bed with Mónica every night couldn't be so bad, could it?" he said.

They looked up to find the hostess holding glasses of wine. Cacho took his glass and coat and headed downstairs to the apartment complex courtyard to find Luis, leaving Daniel to fumble an awkward thank-you before dashing after his roommate.

The smoke rose from the *parrilla*, and the aroma of grilled meat made their mouths water.

*"Tomá,"* said Luis, offering them *chinchulines* from his tongs.

They ate the sweetbreads and the chorizo sandwich *choripanes*. Luis sprinkled salt onto the meat and rotated the handle to lower the grill closer to the coals. The meat sizzled and cooked. The three stood bundled in their coats.

Upstairs, when their bellies were full, they pushed their chairs back. Mónica served coffee and tiramisu.

*"¡Espectacular!"* they all agreed.

Daniel and Cacho rode the local train back to headquarters. As they neared downtown, a sense of unease settled on Daniel's shoulders. Maybe it was the normalcy of Luis's family life, Daniel thought. It felt like something he would never have.

He heard sirens. Outside the window, people congregated and talked in an animated manner.

Something was wrong.

They arrived to find the streets around the Departamento Central de Policía in chaos. Bricks and concrete pieces littered the street outside the cafeteria. Police milled about in shock. Fire fighters stood amidst the smoldering building, and paramedics wheeled stretchers with dead and wounded.

The air smelled plasticky. Daniel remembered the last time he had smelled this, the blast that killed his uncle. But this was bigger, much bigger. He found himself gingerly stepping forward as if bracing himself for another blast that would lift him off his feet.

Daniel and Cacho joined several officers standing nearby and began piecing together what had happened. While they had been enjoying their lunch, a terrorist had been at work at the police cafeteria downtown. On this cold winter day, an infiltrator from the *Montonero* guerillas had entered the crowded cafeteria with a police badge and a duffel bag containing twenty pounds of TNT and cans filled with steel balls. He had placed the bag on an empty chair near the middle of the large room, activated a timer, and put his coat over it. Pretending to go in search of a food tray, the coatless terrorist exited the cafeteria into the brisk air of Calle Moreno.

The bomb went off a few minutes later. The explosion ripped through the crowded lunchroom, the shrapnel penetrating the soft flesh of its victims and ripping them apart. It was horrific. Twenty officers died at the scene and sixty-three were wounded.

Daniel was enraged. He paced outside the supervisor's office with his colleagues. Someone read a statement the

Montoneros issued.

*"...This act of resistance demonstrates that there is no safe place for those that kidnap, torture, and assassinate the workers of Argentina. ¡Viva la patria! ¡Hasta la Victoria final!"*

The next day the government issued a statement too – a message of sorrow, but more, a promise of reprisal.

Daniel and Cacho volunteered immediately. They knew some of the victims personally and they wanted revenge. Over the next few days, Daniel and Cacho were involved in snatch-and-grab operations taking place all over the city. They brought the suspects to various detention centers and dropped them off.

One evening, the supervisor called Daniel into his office. He motioned for him to sit.

The supervisor cracked his knuckes. "How are you doing, Inglés?" he said.

"*Bien,*" said Daniel.

"*More* than good, actually," said the supervisor. He smiled.

The supervisor tapped a paper on his desk with the pencil in his hand. "Do you know the city morgue typically gets about one or two violent deaths per day? But since the bombing, what, five days ago, the *Morgue Judicial* has received forty-six cadavers. Forty-six!"

The supervisor leaned in toward Daniel and lowered his voice, "And this doesn't include other cadavers, ones that never made it to the morgue at all. *Chupados.* Detainees that are disappeared without the nuisance of a paper trail if you know what I mean. *¿Viste?* It gives us more options when they aren't officially registered."

The supervisor cocked his head, and Daniel could tell his reaction was being gauged. Daniel knew about the *chupados. Why is the super telling me this?* Then it struck him that he was being trusted with secret information. It felt good. He smiled back at the super and nodded his head.

The supervisor leaned back in his chair and put his arms behind his head. "So you see, we're doing good. These operations have done wonders for our grieving department, and you've been a part of this, Inglés. I'm promoting you. Tomorrow you lead your own operation. You ready for this?"

"Yes, sir," Daniel said.

Walking out of the supervisor's office, Daniel felt on top of the world. He was proud of his role in helping the department get payback and in getting some retribution for his uncle.

*"Che, Inglés."*

Daniel turned. It was Luis.

"I have to tell you," said Daniel, his face flushed with excitement and happy to share it with a friend. "I'm leading my own operations now."

Luis didn't seem enthused. "That's great," he said, his voice flat.

*"¿Qué te pasa, che?"* said Daniel. "What's the matter with you? Oh, I see. You've been missing out on all the fun. You're jealous."

"No, no. None of that," said Luis. "But I *would* like to know what's going on. I've been hearing stuff, you know. Here, I'll walk out with you."

Daniel grabbed his things. They walked toward the stairs, and Daniel told Luis about some of the operations he'd been on. It wasn't until they were out on the street that Luis spoke again.

"Do you know Fátima?" Luis asked in a hushed voice. "It's sixty kilometers northwest of here. Thirty bodies were found – if you can call them that. I wasn't there. I was just part of the clean-up crew. It was still dark. But the pieces of flesh no larger than *choripanes*. They were everywhere."

Daniel stopped and faced Luis.

"Why the hell are you telling me this?" said Daniel.

"It's true, Inglés. One of my colleagues was there. Told me the men and women were blindfolded and their wrists tied behind their backs before being shot and their bodies dynamited. Said they were told not to say anything. You know, they're calling it the *Masacre de Fátima*. It seems the government has gone too far, no?"

Daniel snorted. "Do you think Pedro Camacho's family would think it was going too far?" he said. "He had a wife and two small kids, just like you, Luis, and now he's dead. Blown to pieces while he was eating lunch in the cafeteria. You ever had a family member assassinated by these people like I have? Don't forget we didn't start this war. But we're going to end it. And like it or not, what happened in Fátima is what it's going to look like."

"But blindfolded and shot?" said Luis, his voice strained. "It's all over the papers."

"I've read those articles too," said Daniel, waving his hand in the air, "and they're shit, Luis. *Mierda.* Who do you think writes them? Leftist journalists, that's who. Trust me, Cacho and I know all about these journalists. They're so in bed with the subversives they can't think straight. Only one paper got it right. *La Opinión.* Says Fátima was an important battle where the military convoy was ambushed. Ambushed! I bet your colleague didn't tell you that, did he?"

"I don't know, Inglés," said Luis. "Why not arrest them? You know, make sure first."

"Because fighting terrorism is an ugly business," said Daniel. "It's not for a family man like you, ¿*viste?*"

Daniel was annoyed. He wished Luis hadn't told him all this. He wished Luis wouldn't look at him the way he was right then.

"I've got to go," Daniel said. "I've got an operation to lead tomorrow. Don't forget whose side you're on, Luis."

Daniel made his way to the bus stop. He should be feeling proud, he told himself, but dammit if Luis hadn't dampened the feeling. The bus was nowhere in sight, and he likely just missed one. He hated wasting time. He paced up and down the sidewalk. What Luis said bothered him, as if he had revealed a crack in the surface. Daniel suddenly felt that somehow the war had changed. Something hard and cruel was coming, and this bombing was the ominous warning.

Daniel shook it off and looked impatiently at his watch. *Luis knows nothing.* He's only a *guardia*. Besides, getting promoted felt good. He needed to focus. Tomorrow he had his own snatch-and-grab operation to lead. He would have more control. He would ensure things were done right.

# CHAPTER 16 – EL OSO

## *The Bear*

Daniel checked his weapon and nodded to the team to climb the steps to the landing. The night air was warm for the first time that spring, and the perfumed breeze filled Daniel's nostrils. Yet an uneasiness settled within him as if infiltrating with the last drag of his cigarette. It felt like one of those days that starts all wrong and sours everything into a ruinous spiral. And it wasn't the late-night operation. That was routine. He had led many of these since he'd been promoted a month ago. It was what would happen later.

The target was a union leader at the Ford Motor plant named Eduardo Ramón "Dito" Burgos. Dito was a person of interest in the assassination of Judge José María Calva Serna, a crusty anti-unionist advocate and government ally in the war against the subversives. These details didn't matter to the other two policemen outside the apartment, but they mattered to Daniel. Judge Calva had died beside Uncle Ricardo on rain-slicked steps of the courthouse. Uncle Ricardo had died trying to protect this judge.

"Let's get this bastard," Daniel said under his breath. He snapped his fingers, and they kicked in the door.

Passing the cramped living room, the men advanced into the hallway to search the bedrooms, their Ithaca shotguns in assault position. Daniel moved to the farthest door.

"*¡Policía, Policía! ¡No te movás!* Don't move!"

The startled couple was in the process of sitting up when

Daniel struck the man across the jaw with the butt of his shotgun. Dito grunted and thudded off the side of the bed. The woman screamed.

One of the cops dragged the woman to the living room. Pushing her onto the sofa, he pressed the gun muzzle against her forehead. *"Gritá y te mato.* Scream and I'll kill you."

In the back bedroom, Daniel pulled Dito from the floor and threw him facedown on the bed. The room reeked of sleep exhale. "Tell her to get him some clothes," Daniel ordered the other cop as he handcuffed the man. *"Apurá."*

The woman returned, shaking and crying. She opened a drawer and fumbled with some pairs of pants and shirts.

"Please take this sweater, and these shoes. *Tomá los zapatos,"* she pleaded. "He needs shoes! *Por amor de Dios, tené compasión."*

Dito was coming to. They yanked him to his feet, and he stood, wobbly, his pajama top torn. A hood was pulled over his head and the clothes stuffed into his cuffed hands.

*"¡Dito! ¡No se lo lleven!"* the woman sobbed as her husband was pushed through the hallway. "Please, don't kill him!"

In the small living room, one of the men carried a turntable and hi-fi receiver against his chest. "I found no weapons, *jefe,"* he said, winking at Daniel. "But I found this subversive equipment. I'll submit it as evidence."

Daniel shoved the cop, who stumbled and banged against the wall, his grin gone. "Put that shit back, you imbecile," said Daniel, realizing that perhaps he was trying to assuage his guilt from hitting the unfortunate Dito with the shotgun.

A dog barked. Lights were coming on in other apartments as the three men dragged Dito down the stairs to the street. A car screeched to the curb to collect them, and the driver gunned the engine.

Twenty minutes later, the car stopped on Calle Virrey Cevallos at a side entrance of the *Departamento Central de la Policía Federal*. The policemen hauled Dito out, his blindfolded head twisted in fright. He could not see the nineteenth-century white-stoned building that covered an entire city block. The wind had kicked up and the tops of the trees cast dancing black shadows against the pale façade of the building.

Daniel's uneasiness returned. His duties normally ended after delivering an arrested subversive to handlers at whatever location he was ordered – El Departamento Central, El Campito, El Vesubio, El Olimpo, La ESMA. There were others.

Tonight his orders were different because he'd made a personal appeal to Sebastian at SIDE. He wanted to witness the interrogation. He wanted to see this man suffer. That maybe it would help heal the wound of Uncle Ricardo's death. Sebastian had looked at him for a few seconds before agreeing. "Fine," Sebastian said. "Listen to the interrogation. Find out the other names in the trade union. I never trust the intel those bastards extract anyway."

Daniel knocked on a side door. They entered a hallway where two guards took the detained man still in his torn pajamas and clutching his clothes in his cuffed hands. Daniel dismissed his team and followed the guards, who pushed the hapless Dito along.

They descended two flights of stairs to the old building's basement where the air was warm and stale, and where the diurnal rhythms did not penetrate. Low-wattage bulbs hung from the ceilings, some pulsating intermittently and some missing altogether. Dito was locked in a cell, and a guard motioned for Daniel to follow him.

The guard's name was Palito, a thin, nervous fellow with

ill-fitting pants and a rumpled shirt. His jet-black hair was stringy and greasy and fell unevenly about his shoulders. Palito showed Daniel to a room furnished with several green plastic chairs. Old magazines and newspapers lay in a jumbled mess on a small table.

*"Esperá,"* said the thin guard. "Wait here."

Daniel sat in a chair and propped his feet on another. A fluorescent bulb buzzed above him. He closed his eyes and wished for sleep. It was late, and he had been having trouble sleeping. Sleep often came fitfully. He would lie restless for an hour or so before jolting wide awake, his thoughts racing. He would fall asleep once more, but the pattern continued all night.

Daniel opened his eyes. Kicking the plastic chair back, he let his feet fall heavily onto the cement slab floor. He sat up and rubbed his face.

Footsteps.

Palito appeared and gave Daniel a toothy grin. "El Oso is ready," he said.

The torture room smelled of urine, and the dingy paint peeled from the bare walls. A single light bulb hung from a wire in the ceiling. The kidnapped Dito, stripped naked save for a blindfold and gag, was tied spread-eagle to a metal bedframe.

A meaty man stood beside the bed. He was shirtless, and his bleached belly and bald pate glistened with sweat in the stark light. He had an unfinished look, and he grinned at Daniel. The heavy door clanked shut, and Palito stood inside and grinned now too. The fleshy man batted the hanging wire and the light caromed about the room. He never took his eyes off Daniel.

The reputation of El Oso, Daniel knew, was well-deserved. He belonged to a class of men willing to inflict horrendous suffering upon the vulnerable. Men otherwise shunned as sociopaths, but who in the dark pages of history find their skills in demand and are able to rise to positions of considerable power. Plumbers who operated the septic systems beneath the government seats of power. A necessary function but best kept unseen. Men such as El Oso, El Turco Julián, El Tigre, and others. Students of suffering, all who found gainful employment with a government that valued torture over the arts of interrogation. The regime needed operators like El Oso, and El Oso needed the regime.

The torturer leaned over the blindfolded man on the bedframe and inhaled his fear. "How do you like the *parrilla*, Eduardo Ramón?" he said close to the man's ear.

Dito jerked in horror and made a noise through the gag.

"I think he said something about his paperwork," said El Oso, grinning at Daniel and Palito. He turned back to the detained man. "I'm sorry. We don't do paperwork here. You see, Dito, if you were signed in, you'd be a *blanqueado* instead of a *chupado*, and then me and my friends here would have nothing to do. We wouldn't have this fun time together with you. You see, we're just the therapists. See? No paperwork to mess with at all."

El Oso rubbed his hands together. "Ready for some therapy, Dito?" He threw his bald head back and laughed. Palito snorted and bobbed his head up and down like a horse.

"*¿Cerveza?*" He uncapped a beer from a Quilmes crate and offered it in Daniel's direction.

Daniel waved it away. He wanted as little connection to this man as possible.

El Oso shrugged and took a swig. He set the beer on the floor beside a stack of empty bottles.

"Dito," said El Oso, turning his attention back to the man on the bedframe, "we have a special guest with us today. You should feel privileged. It means you're getting our best treatment."

El Oso chuckled. "Agent, would you like to say something? As our guest of honor?"

Daniel said nothing. He wished he hadn't come.

"Well, Dito, it's your turn now," said El Oso. "I'm sure you have a few things you wish to tell us. Things you need to get off your chest," and the meaty man ran his hand through Dito's gray chest hair. "We've created the perfect environment for you to tell the truth."

Dito strained at the ropes and made noises through the gag.

"No, don't try to talk," continued El Oso. "Shh. I need to tell you something first. Your pretty wife, she's next door, waiting her turn. We're going to treat her real nice too unless of course you don't want us to. Unless you decide you're not going to play nice with us, and that you would rather we treat her badly. And I really want to treat her badly, Dito."

Dito strained again at the ropes and snorted through the gag. El Oso drummed his fingers on the man's head. "Maybe you would like to call your wife? Here, I have a telephone for you."

El Oso produced a modified electric prod with a wire on either end. He placed one of the wires inside the man's mouth, around the wet gag, and the other he attached to the ear. Dito cried out and swung his head, trying to rid himself of the wires. El Oso nodded and Palito threw a switch.

Dito thrashed in agony, and his straining jostled the bedframe so that it scraped a few inches across the floor. El Oso removed the device and tore out the man's gag with a practiced hand.

Dito coughed and shuddered, his eyes wide with fright. "Leave my wife alone," he said. "She's done nothing. What do you want to know, you *hijo de puta*? I've done nothing!"

"Not so fast, my friend," said El Oso with a soft voice. "We aren't ready yet to hear what you have to say. Are we, gentlemen?"

He looked at Daniel and Palito in turn and smiled.

El Oso nodded to Palito, and his assistant pulled out a length of black cable connected to the back wall. The last twelve inches were exposed copper wire.

El Oso proceeded to shock the wretched Dito in the most sensitive parts of his anatomy, the fingertips, gums, genitals, and the feet. Dito screamed. A wet rag intensified the effect and made the applied part feel it was being torn from the body. Control of bodily functions was lost. Daniel turned his head away from the bedframe and toward the metal door. He tried to focus on remembering his uncle bleeding out on the steps of the courthouse.

Each time the cable was applied, the light bulb in the room dimmed. The room filled with smoke and screams. It smelled of burnt flesh. Dito's face and the soles of his feet turned black.

Time stopped. Daniel focused on the door. Sweat trickled down his back. He wanted to beat El Oso's face with his fist. Hurry up and get it over with. He wanted Dito to just shut up.

At last the screaming ceased and the sobbing began. In the end, Dito did talk, and he talked a lot. Yet it was clear this man had nothing to do with the assassination of the judge. But innocence was no match for El Oso.

Daniel noticed a trembling in his own hand. *What was this?* He tried to focus on what he was supposed to do. Maybe Dito wasn't directly involved, but he must have done *something* wrong. SIDE wouldn't have sent Daniel to pick him up if he wasn't mixed up with the terrorists somehow. SIDE did its homework. Sebastian missed nothing. Dito was a union leader after all, and organized labor was behind all of this, inciting workers against their managers. Destabilizing the country. These union leaders were enriching themselves too. Parasites. They took bribes from business owners desperate to end the strikes and the personal threats. The same ones who kidnapped the owner of that potato chip factory. All those workers lost their jobs.

Daniel turned back toward the bedframe. Dito was not innocent, and whatever he got today, he deserved it. Wolves in sheep's clothing, he reminded himself.

Daniel suddenly felt sick.

*"Abrí la puerta,"* he shouted. He pounded on the door.

The metal door swung open and Daniel stumbled from the room, his legs stiff from standing so long. He found the stairwell and exited through the same side entrance on Calle Virrey Cevallos. Daniel vomited.

Daniel wiped his mouth on his sleeve and tried to compose himself.

It was morning and the sun was bright. The ground doves cooed, and the creamy-bellied thrushes sang in the crisp morning air. Buses belched their way through the busy streets. Pedestrians hurried along sidewalks. Friends sipped coffee in cafes and discussed whether Menotti would add the young Diego Maradona to the national squad for next year's World Cup tournament to be hosted in Argentina.

Yes, Daniel thought, looking around. This is what we are preserving here. It's what makes all the ugliness worthwhile.

# CHAPTER 17 – LA MISA

## *The Mass*

It was Friday and the 7 p.m. mass was about to begin. To Gastón's surprise, the church was full, and still people continued to arrive, old and young, men and women, and children. They squeezed into the pews and stood along the side aisles. Many lived on the tricky edges of poverty where survival required resourcefulness and community.

Bajo Flores was a neighborhood of dirty tire shops and auto reupholsterers, of street vendors and knife sharpeners. It was a place where unemployment knocked first and sickness struck hardest. It was a place where dreams were stillborn and hope grew shallow in its rocky soil, choked out by the thorns of despair.

"This is so different to my parish in the *centro*," said Gastón to Father Ferrer.

"*¿Que decís?*" said Ferrer, yelling over the din. "What?"

"I said that our mass in the *centro* is quite different," Gastón said again. "Very quiet. Only old women mostly. Almost empty. This is just so…exciting. Like the people have come expecting something."

"Yes, they have," said Ferrer, looking out at the crowd. "They come for a blessing and for hope. You won't find this in the rich neighborhoods up north. People here come to plead with God because the only thing they have is suffering. And the church." He paused. "It's also one of the few safe places for crowds to gather."

"What do you mean?" asked Gastón.

"Well, the curfew and the restrictions on public gatherings. There are other things going on here too. It's complicated."

Gastón wanted to ask something else but Father Ferrer waved him off. "Let's take our seats. It's about to start." He took Gastón's arm and led him to the reserved chairs in the chancel beside the altar.

Ferrer leaned over to Gastón. "The Friday evening mass at this church, it's the end of the week and people come. It's something to see. You won't hear a word in Latin. Only Spanish. These people come too because of Brizzio. They want to hear Father Brizzio."

A hush came over the crowd. Several hundred faces turned their attention toward the front as Father Brizzio raised his hand to make the form of the cross. In a powerful voice, he invoked God's blessing on the people. Ferrer and Gastón led the introductory rites and the readings.

When it was time, Father Brizzio sprang up the three steps to the side pulpit. It was a simple wooden piece, and the thick varnish peeled around the edges where Brizzio gripped it.

"The Holy Scriptures read in Psalm 11,

*The wicked bend their bows;*
*they set their arrows against the strings to shoot from the*
*shadows*
*at the upright in heart.*
*But on the wicked the Lord will rain fiery coals and*
*burning sulfur.*
*For the Lord is righteous, he loves justice;*
*the upright will see his face."*

Father Brizzio paused and the faces peered expectantly from the pews and from the side aisles. "I ask you," he said, "when can we expect to see the Lord's face? When, Lord, will you rain fiery coals and burning sulphur on the wicked and the violent?" He raised his eyes upward as if expecting God to answer him right then.

"Jesus quoted the prophet Isaiah when preaching to the poor in Israel, *He has sent me to bring glad tidings to the poor, to proclaim liberty to captives.* I ask you," Brizzio's voice was quieter now, the question almost a plea, "when will this promised liberty come?"

There was a murmur in the crowd. Scattered voices shouted, "Now!" Feet shuffled. Bodies shifted in their seats.

"And you are right, my brothers and my sisters," said Brizzio. "We need look no farther for the answer than in the next Psalm. *Because the poor are plundered and the needy groan, I will now arise, says the Lord, I will protect them.*"

Father Brizzio waited for silence.

"There are those who wish for you to be patient," he said, his voice rising. "There are those who wish for you to be meek, to wait for the next life when you are in the heavenly kingdom. That justice and freedom from oppression will come then. They tell you it has not been promised for now."

"No," came the cry from the people, and the roar reverberated in the crowded room.

Gastón looked out at the crowd. People were leaning forward in the pews, faces attentive. A movement in the back corner caught his eye. The shadows were dark on either side of the open doors bathed in the glare of the streetlight. *Was that the rector, Father Alejandro?*

Gastón felt a stab of fear. He recalled the rector's words when he first met him in his office, *we are not to be political. Father Brizzio must know what he's doing, right?* Gastón clasped his hands between his knees.

Brizzio rocked back and forth on his heels. He started

again, the momentum building. "We believe our God is a God of action," he said. "He cares about the poor and the oppressed. He cares about us. And he cares about us not tomorrow, but *now!*"

"There are those who find it convenient," Brizzio said, "to have you identify with a dead and mute Jesus. To have you quietly accept a society that crucifies you. To blindly accept injustices because God will come *some* day and make all things right." Brizzio continued, now in a thundering voice. "My friends, that's not how I read the scriptures. My friends, that's not the Jesus I know."

The church bells announced the arrival of 8 p.m., and the priest raised his hand and gave a final blessing.

*"Blessed be the Lord, my rock, who trains my hands for war, and my fingers for battle."*

The church erupted.

Gastón looked to the back corner. The figure was gone.

Gastón watched the crowds shuffling out. They passed a large wooden Jesus hanging on the cross, his thorn-crowned head resting on his chest. Blood oozed from the wound in his side and from the nails that pierced his outstretched hands and overlapping feet. From Jesus's waist down to his bare legs and feet, the body color was almost black from the hands of worshipers seeking a final blessing before exiting the church. Black stains of guilt transferred onto their crucified savior. The poor and humble asked once more to identify with a savior beaten, dead, and mute. Lingering doubts. *How long, Lord, must we wait?*

# CHAPTER 18 – EL CARDENAL

## *The Cardinal*

The high-level meeting took place in the Cardinal's private offices above the Metropolitan Cathedral. One by one, the eleven bishops of the archdiocese arrived at a private door and were escorted through a passageway.

The Metropolitan Cathedral of Buenos Aires was like no other church building in Latin America. Built in 1580, it sat on the Plaza de Mayo beside the Casa Rosada, the presidential seat of power. The first thing the visitor noticed, however, was that it didn't look like a church at all. Twelve massive Corinthian columns and a triangular pediment graced the front of the building, making it look surprisingly like an ancient pagan temple.

Leaving the severe neoclassical façade and walking inside the cathedral, the visitor was back in familiar, albeit imposing, territory. Immense marble pillars supported a three-nave structure that led to the high altar chancel and the semidomed ceiling apse. The entire expanse of the church floor was covered with exquisite Venetian mosaics. Gold gilding covered the ceiling and the chancel, and above the choir loft was an 1871 German Walcker organ with 3,500 pipes.

The lavish interior did not, however, trickle down to the church pews, which were where the worshiper most intimately connected with the grandiose church. Upon closer inspection, one came to appreciate that this feature was designed not to glorify God but to instruct men.

The pews had been commissioned to a sadistic Italian artisan impossibly named Severino Sadisticceri. These spare eighteenth-century benches in the center nave safeguarded the parishioner from any temptation to believe that his seat might offer more comfort than the forbidding cushionless kneelers in front of him. Quickly learning that he was indifferent to sitting or kneeling, the worshiper found an easier time accepting that full attention at all times is required. And toward this noble purpose, the pews had been brilliantly conceived to instruct both young and old alike.

Far beyond the reaches of the parishioners and the visitors below, the Cardinal entered the opulent conference room from his adjoining offices. The eleven bishops rose in unison.

*"Buenas tardes, Su Eminencia."*

The pontiff ignored their greeting and was helped into his seat by his personal secretary, Ignacio. The bishops followed, easing themselves into the thick leather chairs. The Cardinal cast his calcified eyes onto each of his bishops in turn as if searching for something in their faces.

Archbishop Cardinal José Carlos Aburuzaga was an austere man. He possessed a long face and wore thick horn-rimmed glasses, which he constantly flipped up and down and on and off. His full head of gray hair was trimmed short and slicked straight back. He used the Castilian *th* pronunciations of the letters *z* and soft *c* lest anyone forget his proximity to the Old World and to the Holy See itself.

The Cardinal was a superior being as befits one selected by God for special duty. This man of the cloth had a heightened sense of sin in others, and no offense was too small for the Cardinal to ignore. A man more sinned against than sinning.

Aburuzaga was a man of tremendous energy. He awoke daily at 4 a.m. and spent sixty minutes in grandiloquent prayer on behalf of sinners. Few on his staff could match his pace or meet his expectations, and demotions and firings were common. Occasionally, Rome countermanded his decisions, and these interventions were deeply resented and not forgotten.

He was named Archbishop of Buenos Aires in 1975 and was elevated to cardinal by the pope a year later, giving him command over an archdiocese of 182 parishes and three million souls. And from his lofty perch, Aburuzaga had little use now for God but much use for religion.

"I have invited each of you here," began the Cardinal in a measured voice, "to address some rumors and instances of insubordination by some of our priests. I expect your full and confidential cooperation. You have my trust as I well know I have yours."

Eleven heads nodded.

The Cardinal unwound the button string of a manila folder and extracted some papers. He fumbled for his reading glasses until Ignacio slid them toward him. "Gentlemen, I have here a list of priests who are...," he chose his words with care, "misguided and misinformed. A few are much worse than that."

A dark cloud fleeted across the Cardinal's face, perceptible only to his watchful secretary Ignacio.

"Fellow bishops," the Cardinal continued, "I need not remind you that we live in a difficult time. As chosen representatives of Christ, we serve the spiritual needs within our archdiocese. We do not get involved with matters of the State. It's your responsibility to ensure our priests and laypeople understand this."

Flipping his glasses onto his nose, he studied the list and ran his finger down the page. "This priest, for example," he said, stopping at a line. "Says he visited a woman in his parish who tells of her son disappearing for two weeks, but now he's back. Wrote a report and gave it to his rector."

The Cardinal flung his reading glasses onto the glassy Honduran mahogany table. "Who the hell knows why her son disappeared! He's back!"

A few bishops chuckled and leaned back in their plush chairs.

"And this will happen to the other sons of those poor mothers in the plaza below," said Aburuzaga. "This priest, he's twenty-four-years-old. What does he know?"

A newer bishop raised his hand, his courage betraying his inexperience.

"Forgive my interruption, *Su Eminencia,*" he said, "but I, too, have priests in my parishes who have communicated similar disappearances, and none have reappeared. For some of them it's been several months. To be honest, it's a growing concern in our communities. We're getting many requests for help."

Several bishops nodded.

The young bishop continued, "People are asking for our intervention with the government."

The room grew silent, and everyone looked to the Cardinal.

The pontiff was pleased with himself. This was the very thing he wished to happen. It was a perfect segue. Still, he was irritated at the comeuppance, and he made a mental note. Ignacio scribbled on his notepad.

Aburuzaga pulled out a Vatican diplomatic envelope from the folder and stabbed at it with a long thin finger. "I have proof that a significant number of these supposed *disappeared* have recently *reappeared* in Bolivia, Cuba, and even Europe. All are leftist guerillas. Of course they disappear when the government forces start pressuring them! They flee across the borders and reappear to cause problems elsewhere."

A few snickers burst out around the table.

The pontiff resumed. "People in society disappear all the time. Runaway teens, suicides, unsolved murders, kidnappings, lawbreakers evading the authorities, women escaping abusive relationships. And, dammit, people simply move!" He snapped his fingers in the air. *"Desaparecidos. They eventually turn up."*

The Cardinal considered. Events now had forced this circling of the wagons and he must be careful. There were some fast-moving elements, powerful undercurrents. *Are they present here, at this level?* His bushy eyebrows swept the room. He knew his opening needed to be followed now by persuasive logic, a logic rooted in Church doctrine and the Holy Scriptures, that would remove any wavering of these bishops and steel their conviction. He must arm them with proper messaging to cascade throughout the archdiocese. It wouldn't do to show any emotion now. Cardinal Aburuzaga closed his eyes and willed his blood to drain from his flushed face and return to icier parts where it could be controlled.

"Gentlemen, we possess years of experience that our priests do not. These are complicated and confusing times for young people and for our priests. We must help them interpret these times, to understand the whole context. As men of God, we must bring them clarity and understanding. I need not remind you we are in a spiritual battle, a battle for the minds and souls of all Argentines. And this spiritual battle now manifests itself as a physical battle. The forces against us, the subversives, the communists, are anti-God. They are atheists."

The Cardinal patted his head and pocket and then snapped his fingers at Ignacio, who already was scrambling to retrieve the pontiff's reading glasses from where they had skidded halfway down the long table.

"Let me remind you that God himself used violence against the gentile nations arrayed against Israel for his purposes. The armies of God destroyed the Philistines and the Amorites. His righteous anger burned against the heathens."

The Cardinal leaned forward in his chair and peered at the bishops over the horned rims. "Our nation's military is not perfect, of course. Don't I know that! But make no mistake, my bishops. The military is God's hand of righteousness against today's forces of evil. Who are we to question God's chosen instrument to punish his enemies?"

He let this question hang in the air for a moment. It was having an effect. The bishops murmured and nodded their heads. It made sense to them.

"We are not politicians," continued Aburuzaga, "Leave them to do their job. We are not God. Let God use whom he will. You must do *your* job, which is to nurture and comfort the souls of our flocks in these troubled times. Take these messages back to your priests."

A side door opened, and four waiters stood in the doorway holding silver platters with coffee and medialunas. Ignacio nodded them in. It was a good time to take a break in the conversation. *"¿Café? ¿Solo o con leche?"* the waiters asked each bishop.

The Cardinal took his black. He sipped it and admired the logo of the Holy See. The china had been a special gift from Rome to his mentor, the late Cardinal Califano. Rome hadn't given him a damned thing, he thought. Only annoyances.

The waiters left, and the eleven bishops resumed attention.

"We now come to a most disturbing issue I must bring before you," said the Cardinal. "We have a Judas in our midst. Wolves threatening to tear our flock apart. A heresy. A threat to the Church from within not seen perhaps since the eternally damned Martin Luther."

The Cardinal crossed himself.

"I am talking about the insidious so-called *liberation*

*theology,*" he continued. "You've heard about it in other dioceses and in other countries. Colombia, Brazil, El Salvador. But now it is here too. A cancer within. It has infected our archdiocese and we must cut it out."

He flipped his glasses up onto his slicked-back hair. "I know some of you have priests engaged in it who are sympathetic to it. Priests who are ever learning but never able to arrive at a knowledge of the truth. They delude themselves and lead the faithful astray. They ask them 'What would Jesus do if he were here among us? He would march with us against the capitalist imperialists.' Hogwash. Pure nonsense!"

"It may be popular to be a socially active priest. Sounds nice to the young people. Gets them excited, all fired up. Packaged to make it impossible to resist. But it's dangerous. It's heresy." The Cardinal slammed his fist on the table. "Heresy!" he shouted.

Several of the bishops shifted in their chairs.

"Communism and Marxism reject God in favor of humanist atheism. How many examples have we already seen of these ruinous ideologies and the atrocities that accompany them? The Soviet Union. Maoist China. The Viet Cong. Cuba! Name one revolution in history that's been beneficial for the people. Perhaps the American Revolutionary War. And though not godless, it was Protestant." The Cardinal crossed himself again.

Worked into a fervor now, Aburuzaga rose, and Ignacio scrambled to pull back the pontiff's chair. "My fellow bishops, make no mistake. We will deal swiftly with priests who are involved with this liberation theology, this Marxist movement masquerading as Christianity. It will send a clear message to all the others."

The Cardinal paused again, and his eyes suddenly betrayed a defeated weariness and deep-rooted bitterness that long ago had robbed him of the ability to dream. "What these priests are doing is dangerous," he added. "If they persist in it, we will not be able to protect them."

With that, the meeting adjourned, and the bishops rose in unison. Archbishop Cardinal Aburuzaga held up the palm of his hand. "God's peace be with you," he said and then retired to his private offices.

The bishops were escorted back to the private entrance and to their chauffeured cars.

For the younger bishops, they had learned that cynicism was not something freely given. It would have to be earned.

# CHAPTER 19 – LAS MADRES DE PLAZA DE MAYO

## The Mothers of the Plaza de Mayo

While the Cardinal and his bishops were meeting, there was tension in the grand plaza below. The Mothers of the Plaza de Mayo had gathered again for their silent protest.

*Where are our children?*

The Madres stood because no one else could, their white scarves now a symbol of opposition to the military regime. Many held pictures of their disappeared sons or daughters. They unfurled white banners and stood quietly, facing the pink presidential palace.

*"Que Aparezcan Con Vida los Detenidos Desaparecidos"*
(We demand that the disappeared detainees reappear alive)

*"Niños Desaparecidos"*
(Missing children)

*"Solo Queremos La Verdad"*
(We only want the truth)

Daniel stood on the bottom step of the Casa Rosada, dressed in riot gear and forming part of the police wall confronting the protesters. Each policeman carried a Marcati rifle and a baton on his belt. Their superiors forbade them to smile or talk.

"Stand there and look tough. *Poné una cara de mierda,"* the men were told.

Behind Daniel and the phalanx of cops stood the senior policemen and military officers. They jeered at the women and yelled encouragement at the recruits. "Crack the old bags over the head! Maybe that will help them remember where their sons are!"

Daniel looked at the faces of these middle-aged women. There was pain and outrage. He thought about his snatch-and-grabs. Had he helped disappear any of these women's sons? Most of the detained were committed leftists, he knew, guilty of taking up arms against the government and hurting civilians to pursue their ends. *Even Stalin had a mother,* Daniel recalled Canario once telling him during SIDE training. He shifted his feet and looked at the cobbles on the plaza.

The officers behind him continued to hurl insults at the mothers. "Here, we'll give you shovels so you can go find your sons!" It was a hilarious affair. *Las locas* they called them, the madwomen.

But Daniel came to understand it was not a humorous affair at all. Sometime later he read in the newspaper that three of the founders of the Madres de Plaza de Mayo had disappeared and made an inanimate and decomposed reappearance – not in another country – but on a sandy beach in the resort town of Santa Teresita, three hundred fifty kilometers south of the capital.

Daniel stared at the photographs accompanying the article. He recognized one of the women. She had been in front of him on the plaza that day, holding a picture of her son. Daniel dropped the paper. He wished he hadn't seen the photo. He knew these murders would do nothing to stem the swelling tide of white scarves at the Plaza de Mayo.

# CHAPTER 20 – LA INFILTRACIÓN

## *The Infiltration*

*"Sí."* A pause. "Yes. I'm coming."

Daniel had expected such a call for some time. It was early. His pulse quickened. He pulled himself out of bed and dressed. He looked in the mirror and brushed his hair. After straightening his shirt, he took it off and put on another one. He spat onto each shoe then rubbed it with a wadded undershirt from the floor.

Exiting the bus onto Avenida Leandro Alem, Daniel walked past the Casa Rosada, turned onto Calle 25 de Mayo, and arrived at Number 11. It had been a month since he'd first visited the SIDE office, and it looked much more inviting in the burst of spring. There was nothing like the purple bloom of the jacarandas in Buenos Aires, but Daniel, who had lived among these trees, knew that such beauty could be messy. And in one of those oddities of nature, jacarandas bloomed twice a year and thus brought plenty of both.

The mousy man with big glasses was there as before, sitting behind the wooden desk in the foyer and twirling his pencil. Daniel showed him his badge and stated his business, all of which was carefully handwritten into the ledger along with the date and time of entrance. Daniel was frisked, and a guard led him up the three flights of stairs.

In the reception area, the guard motioned for Daniel to sit. He whispered something to the secretary who looked up and nodded at Daniel. He hoped she would offer him coffee like last time, but Sebastian appeared.

*"Inglés. Vení."* He led Daniel through the maze of cubicles and ushered him into the corner office.

The Admiral sat behind his oversized desk. *"Sentá,"* he said, motioning with an open palm to one of the chairs facing the desk. "Let's get right down to business, *¿sí?"*

Daniel needed coffee and had almost worked up the nerve to ask for it when the waiter came in.

"It's time to put you into play, Inglés," said the Admiral. "You remember the case of Judge Calva?"

*Remember?* He only thought about it almost every day.

"Of course you do," said the Admiral. "Your uncle died in that same blast. I understand you saw it all. Well, this means you're going to like what we have for you now. It will have particular meaning for you. A chance to do some good. A chance to redeem your uncle's legacy."

The Admiral cracked his knuckles.

"I'm getting a lot of pressure on this," the Admiral said. "For God's sake, he was a judge. Never mind that. The bigger issue is that Calva was related to General Zelaya. Calls me almost every day. Damned general. Damned judge too. Caused me problems when he was alive and he's causing me more problems now that he's dead. *¡Maldito condenado!* Get me my aspirin," he ordered Sebastian.

Sebastian quietly did what he was told. The Admiral popped the pills and tilted his head back.

"The leftist unions have been our prime suspects. We've chased all the leads we can. In fact, I believe you led a few snatch-and-grabs, no?"

Daniel nodded. He thought of El Oso and of the unfortunate Dito handcuffed to the metal bedframe. He wondered where the Admiral was going with all of this.

"We've finally gotten a break in this judge case," the

Admiral said. "Sebastian, give him the details."

The aide took out a thin folder from a bag at his side. "We know from the witness that the assassin jumped into a small white car driven by a young woman," said Sebastian. "Just last week, a 1964 white Fiat 600 was found abandoned in Tigre. It had been reported stolen the day of the assassination. The Fiat was clean, but now comes the interesting part," continued Sebastian with no change in inflection. "The car was stolen from a street by the university, next to the medical school. Whoever did this is operating from there. We know about the campus terrorist cells there, particularly at the Facultad de Medicina and the Facultad de Filosofía y Letras. They've been responsible for several bombings and assassinations. We believe they're planning more. We just haven't been able to get close."

"This is where you come in, Inglés," said the Admiral, waving Sebastian off. "You're going undercover. You will infiltrate the campus. We have several other assets at the Universidad de Buenos Aires but none at the medical school."

The Admiral paused. "Are you as good as they say you are?"

Daniel stared at his shoes. They needed more spit. He thought about the campus and about his friends, trying to imagine how this would this play out.

"You'll infiltrate this group," the Admiral continued. "You will focus on finding the judge's killers. It's the best lead we've had."

Daniel considered this information, and the more he thought about it, the more he liked it. He'd be a spy and lead a double life. He wondered what he'd do to fit in with the leftists. Maybe he'd grow out his beard.

"I'll do it," he said, speaking for the first time since he had arrived.

"Damned right you'll do it," said the Admiral. He took a sip of coffee and leaned back in his chair. "You'll do it, Inglés, because it's about law and order. And these cowards that hide among the students and the crowds, they represent the opposite. Disruption, chaos, anarchy. They throw rocks and they tear down. How easy it is to destroy. Any coward can do that. But to build – to build something – that is hard. And we can only do that if we first clear out the rot."

With a quick movement, the Admiral pounded his fist onto the desk. "Penetrate that cell at the UBA and find Judge Calva's killers. Find that termite colony so we can tear out the rot. ¿Entendés?"

"Yes, Admiral," said Daniel, and he filled with pride. He was tired of detaining suspects. This was a chance to really do something important and to work on his own terms.

The telephone on the Admiral's desk buzzed.

The Admiral sighed. "Put her through," he said.

Daniel could hear a tinny voice through the earpiece.

"Yes, I know you have an appointment," said the Admiral into the phone. "And no, I won't send the driver right now. Drive yourself. Or don't go. What do I care? You think the doctor will tell you something new? If he cures you of whatever is your problem, then I'll care."

The Admiral hung up the phone and rubbed his face with both hands. He seemed to snap out of whatever he was thinking and focused again on Daniel.

"Sebastian will set you up with some training," said the Admiral. "You'll give him an update once a week on your progress. I know you won't let us down. Not like my wife anyway."

And he smiled. A perfect white-toothed smile.

# CHAPTER 21 – SOLEDAD
## *Soledad*

"It's called cervical stenosis. The passageway through your cervix is unusually narrow."

The Admiral's wife had expected bad news, but it caught her unprepared nonetheless. She put her hands to her face and cried.

"There seems to be some blockage too," continued the gynecologist. "We'll need to do some more tests. I'm sorry. I wish I had better news for you."

The doctor offered her a box of tissues.

María Soledad Salaverri de Bertotti got into her car and left the fertility clinic. Her mind was in a deep fog, like the one that had rolled into the city that morning. She drove slowly, oblivious to the cars swerving around her. A baby would have solved everything, she cried to herself. His cheating and his fits of anger. A stab of fear shot through her. She felt trapped.

She rolled down the window to get some fresh air. One thought suddenly became clear.

It was not the first time she had contemplated suicide, but now she let her mind wander to specifics. She was surprised at how calmly she considered the subject of killing herself. *Could I?*

Some methods she rejected right away. She had a friend whose teenage son had hung himself in the closet. She imagined slitting her wrists, her lifeblood easing out in a hot bath. No. Sleeping pills and a bottle of wine. Yes. She knew just the place. There was a spot on the bank of the Río de la Plata in Martínez, a quiet place away from the bikers and the strollers and the picnickers. She knew just the wine.

A horn blast startled Soledad, and in her rearview mirror a bus barreled down on her, its lights flashing. She pulled over and stopped the car. Her chest heaved as she sucked giant gulps of air. She slumped over the steering wheel and sobbed.

Her husband had been so wonderful, thought Soledad, so strong and rakishly handsome. What a lavish wedding, a reception at the Alvear. It was talked about all year. She was a good catch herself, yes. It had happened so fast. Her father had been so pleased, so taken by the dashing young admiral too.

Soledad smiled, and a tear slid down her cheek and dropped onto her knee.

She had been so ordinary before, and the attentions of the Admiral had made her feel special and important. Her rare allure and a measure of luck had pulled her out of her middle-class roots and catapulted her into the upper crust of society. Power and money and beauty seem always to find a way to end up together.

All she wanted was to please him. A baby. He wanted a son. He's not even interested in me anymore, she cried. It's all my fault.

There had been signs before and signs after. That morning she had sat in his closet and smelled *her* on his clothes. She had pressed his suit to her face and breathed in, imagining the conversation, the attentions, and the love. How would it feel to receive that, to receive that from him? To have him smile at *me* like that? Hot tears had welled up in her eyes. She had sunk onto the rich carpet in the closet and sobbed.

*"Señora,* is everything alright?"

"Yes, I'm fine. Please leave me."

The maid had padded out of the bedroom.

Soledad worked up the nerve to start the car again and head home. She passed by Lucía's house and almost stopped. She missed Lucía. He didn't like many of her friends, and she had stopped seeing them. Some of them had stopped seeing her. She knew they whispered about her. She had acquired new friends, friends of his. They were different.

Almost without thinking, Soledad stopped at the curb in front of the Parroquia de la Inmaculada Concepción on the Plaza Manuel Belgrano. The church was just a few blocks from her house.

Inside, she sat on a pew near the front of the rotunda. She stared above her at the life-sized figure of Virgin Mary holding her immaculately conceived son. Mary and baby Jesus had their eyes closed, their heads bowed toward each other.

"O blessed Mary, Most Holy Virgin Mary, *Madre de Dios,"* prayed Soledad. "Please grant me a miracle." She wept. "I want to conceive. Remember me, *María Santísima,* and help me. *Ayudáme.* I believe. Help my unbelief!"

She heard footsteps and the swish of robes approaching, and she ran from the church.

# CHAPTER 22 – VALENTINA

## *Valentina*


Daniel stepped off the bus at the campus and checked his watch. His new daily commute from his apartment to the university in the urban center took twenty-five minutes. He picked his way to the far side of the sidewalk on Avenida Córdoba to get out of the way of the pedestrian traffic.

He lit a cigarette to collect his thoughts.

Infiltrating the terrorist cells on the campus would not be as easy as the Secretaría de Inteligencia de Estado wanted him to believe. Likely it would be more dangerous too. The revolutionary elements in the city operated in the shadows and with good reason, Daniel knew. These were not the uniformed ERP and Montonero guerilla forces that controlled rural towns and operated from the Tucumán jungles. In Buenos Aires, they hid within the sprawling slums where they found support among the poor and disenfranchised. They hid, too, in the universities where leftist professors and students sympathized with their violent plotting and provided easy cover. The Universidad de Buenos Aires was the center of the hornet's nest.

For all its sophistication and resources, Daniel found SIDE rather ignorant about UBA. Its data was old or wrong, often both. The list of professors hadn't been updated in years, and their campus maps failed to show the newer buildings. SIDE's guidance, too, was preposterous. All professors, Daniel's handlers claimed, were radicalized leftists moonlighting as terrorists. Students' fathers were all labor agitators. Tall pretty blondes most certainly were KGB agents. SIDE's jaundiced-eyed hammer found nails everywhere.

Daniel flicked the butt to the street and made his way toward the medical school. *How do I act like a normal student?* He considered going to his morning class but decided against it. He wasn't ready. Instead, he wandered to less familiar parts of the campus with some general idea of intelligence gathering, but he knew it was mostly from a desire to avoid seeing anyone he knew.

He found himself second-guessing how he walked and his mannerisms, and he tried mimicking the behavior of the students around him. Sebastian's infiltration training sessions had been useless. Daniel was on his own.

He found a café and bought a sandwich. In the late afternoon he sat on a patch of grass near the School of Philosophy, wondering how he would make contact with subversives.

The first subversive he met on the campus, Daniel mused wryly, was his friend Valentina. He spotted her crossing the quad and hurried to catch her.

*"¡Dani! ¿Cómo estás, querido?"* said Valentina, embracing him and kissing his cheek. "Where have you been? We've missed you!"

"I took a vacation, remember?"

"Yes, I knew that. *Che,* there's a rumor you bought a motorcycle and went to Chile and Bolivia. Is it true?"

"Yeah, I did take that vacation. But I'm back now. Back on campus, I mean."

Valentina screwed up her face. "I thought you were doing your military service?"

Daniel took a breath. "The military wants me to finish my medical training first," he said. "They need more medics apparently, so I've been deferred." The lie rolled off his tongue more easily that he expected. He took Valentina's arm and led her to a bench, out of the way of students going to and from class.

"You've changed, Dani," she said once they had settled themselves. The heat of the day was gone, and a breeze blew.

Daniel caught himself. *What could she tell?* He thought of the 9mm Browning hidden in his belt. "What do you mean?" he said.

"I mean you've changed. You look different."

He felt her eyes searching him. The back of his neck grew hot.

"I'm more focused now, perhaps," he said. "I just want to get back to classes and graduate. Last semester I was distracted. I didn't know what I wanted."

"What is it you want?" Valentina asked, her voice soft.

It caught Daniel off guard. It seemed a long time since he'd had a conversation with a female friend, with someone who cared for him. He'd been keyed up for so long. His hands shook, and he lit a cigarette.

"What's happened to you, Dani? You don't smoke." Valentina put a hand on his shoulder. "Give me one," she said.

"No."

"*¿Y por qué no?*"

"Because it's not good for you," said Daniel. "You don't smoke."

"Neither do you."

Valentina squeezed his shoulders and leaned her face toward his. "Tell me what's happened. *¿Si?*"

Daniel was guarded. He'd never felt this way with Valentina before, not when they were good friends and not after they had broken up and resumed friendship. His secret burned like a stomach ulcer.

"What's happened?" he said. "I'll tell you what's happened. I'm angry. I'm angry at the government, at what they are doing. I've seen things."

"So you're a communist now?" said Valentina, wrinkling her nose. "*You?* You've always made fun of the activists."

Daniel paused. He knew he needed to be careful. "I've seen things," he said. "It's not so black and white, you know." Daniel was sure it sounded contrived. "What about you?" he asked her, trying to shift the conversation. "Are you a communist?"

"Of course. Isn't everyone?" Valentina laughed. "Everyone here at the university anyway."

"You mean you're only a *campus* communist?" said Daniel, laughing now too, and he wondered at how brazenly students embraced leftist philosophies. Didn't they know how dangerous it was now?

"So," Daniel continued, "you're not a communist when you wake up in your parents' nice house in Villa Crespo, and your maid makes you breakfast. That's convenient, Vale. It's easy to be part of the oppressed masses when you have a nice place to go home to every night."

"*No seas boludo,*" she said. "Everyone's a communist. Why not? My father is a Peronist. But I can't be a Peronist. It's too confusing. I don't understand it. I can't support the military regime either, of course. I don't know anyone who does. My father does. And I thought you did too. At least before. What the government is doing is terrible." She grabbed his cigarette and took a puff. "I guess communism is the only thing left for me."

Daniel didn't know what to say and was worried he'd somehow mess things up. "How are you and Cristian?" he said.

"I'm fine. Cristian is fine."

He looked out at the quad. "What about the *and* part?" he said. He couldn't hide his jealousy. A part of him always thought of her as his girlfriend.

Valentina shifted herself on the bench to square up on him, one leg tucked up under her thigh. "That part's fine too, Dani."

"How's Fede?" he asked, turning back toward her.

"Fede's changed."

"Changed?"

"Yes, changed," said Valentina. "Like you."

"What do you mean?"

"I don't know. He's angry now too. He considers himself a real communist. He joins the protests and the marches. Tries to get us to go with him."

"And do you go?" said Daniel. He never would have cared for this conversation before.

"I've been," said Valentina. "It's kind of fun. Everyone's out there. It feels like we're doing something good. It scares me though. The federal police and the military sometimes come onto the campus and arrest students, even professors. One of my professors is gone. Just disappeared. They say he was detained for being a subversive. You must know what's going on, Dani. You said it yourself."

The cool breeze kicked up, and the shadows of the trees lengthened across the quad. The stream of students had thinned out. Daniel was unsure what to say. He heard of several professors who'd been arrested, and they deserved it as far as he could tell. They were real agitators and members of the Communist party.

Daniel wondered what Valentina would think if he told her the truth about himself. That he was a federal policeman. An SIDE agent even. She wouldn't understand. She wouldn't understand that he was protecting her. He was protecting everyone.

He wondered if Valentina was in any danger. She just didn't know how bad things could be. She would be fine if she didn't get mixed up in anything. He thought of the Madres at the plaza. Did they know their sons were mixed up in a bad way? That they were killers?

"Vale, it *is* dangerous," Daniel said. "Don't go to these marches. It's stupid. Just mind your own business."

Valentina's eyes narrowed. It made Daniel nervous. *Did she suspect anything?* He cursed to himself. He was second-guessing everything.

"I just want you to be safe," said Daniel. "Che, maybe we can all get together soon? I'd like to see everyone. I'd like to see Fede." As soon as he said the words, he felt like a fake.

"Sure, I'll arrange it," said Valentina. "By the way, Fede has a new girlfriend," she added with a smile.

"Who?" said Daniel, happy that Valentina seemed to relax. "Anyone I know?"

Valentina shook her head. "Her name is Eva. A real radical too. Fede told me she even helps organize some of the marches. He told me not to tell anyone. We don't see her much. She doesn't hang out with us, and we don't see Fede as much as before. She met us at El Barrio once for beers. She and Fede talked politics and about books they were reading. Communist stuff mostly. I was bored, to tell you the truth. Actually, I think she's at the medical school here. Maybe you'll recognize her."

*This was interesting.* How involved was Fede's new girlfriend? Perhaps she had contacts within the campus terrorist cell – if it existed.

"I don't like her," said Valentina, and she folded her hands together and rubbed them against her legs to warm them.

"*¿Por qué no?*" said Daniel.

"She's bad for Fede," said Valentina. "Maybe I'm being selfish. I miss Julieta. They made such a great couple, and now we don't see her anymore."

"I liked Julieta too," said Daniel.

"Yeah, but Fede has fallen for this woman, Eva. He's like a puppy dog with her."

"Love will do that," said Daniel.

"And what do *you* know about love, Dani?" She squared up again and faced him.

Daniel felt his face redden. It was all still there, just under the surface.

"Dani, I have to share a secret with you," said Valentina, and Daniel was glad for the redirection.

"What?"

"She's pregnant."

"Who? Eva?"

"*Sí.*"

Daniel considered this news. "What imbeciles," he said.

"I'm sure they didn't mean to, Dani."

"Don't ever get pregnant, Vale."

"Why not? I want babies someday."

"With Cristian?"

"Don't be an idiot. *Tonto.*" Valentina shook her head and ran a hand through her hair.

"You would make a good mother," said Daniel. He suddenly wanted to kiss her, to protect her forever. To take Valentina and go somewhere. The mountains, the campo. He would tell her everything so that she could understand.

"Look, let's get together soon," Daniel stammered. "All of us. *¿Sí?*"

"Yes, let's."

Valentina rested her hand on his shoulder. "How's your

father? How's Emilio?"

"I don't know," Daniel said, and he knew she could feel him tremble. "We had sort of a falling out." He stood and grabbed his rucksack. "I have to go," he said, and he cleared his throat. "This Thursday then?"

"I'll let everyone know."

Daniel slung the bag on his shoulder.

"Dani?" called Valentina. "Don't say anything. About Fede and all that. Nothing, okay? It's so good to see you."

Daniel nodded. He turned but stopped. "Vale, you can be a communist, but…just don't *be* a communist."

"What?" said Valentina. "Sometimes you don't make any sense at all. *Sos loco.*"

"I just mean be careful. It's dangerous. Just like you said."

"I'm a big girl, Dani. And since when do you care about my safety anyway?"

"Since always, Valentina," said Daniel, and he suddenly felt angry at himself for the emotions that welled up. He had a job to do now, dammit.

He walked away as fast as he could.

# CHAPTER 23 –LA CLASE DE BIOLOGÍA
## *The Biology Class*

The professor was speaking when Daniel entered the classroom late and found a seat in the back. He hoped he wouldn't see many familiar faces.

To explain his absence, he had thought up a simple story. It was mostly true, and that would make it easier to remember and more convincing. He hated the thought of engaging in the chitchat and the probing questions from friends, but it must be done.

Daniel's ears tuned into the professor's voice. "...discussed this past Tuesday. We will focus on the chemical processes within cells, and how molecules control a cell's activities and growth."

Daniel felt overwhelmed, but he remembered that this semester he wasn't here for the grade. Besides, if last year was any indication, the class would never get halfway through the course material anyway. The campus was a powder keg of anti-government sentiment, often exploding into protests that disrupted classes and snarled traffic all the way to Avenida 9 de Julio. The ghost of Che Guevara still lurked among the black marble pillars of the Facultad de Medicina and cast its shadow on the white granite steps descending to Calle Paraguay.

The police were reluctant to enter the campus unless they came in force, and at times they would, as Daniel knew well. The violent clashes with the tear gas and the rubber bullets were ugly.

Within the classrooms themselves, disruptions were constant. Anything and everything set off heated debates, usually off-topic. Professors had difficulty controlling them. They watched helplessly as learning migrated from the head to the arms and legs and from the classroom to the streets. Last year Daniel had been annoyed at the interruptions and politicizing of the campus. Today he found himself curiously looking forward to it all. The disruption in today's biology class started with a question from a student sitting near the front.

"Professor," a female student began. "It just all seems so perfect."

"What do you mean?" asked the professor.

"Well," the student continued, "I was at the engineering school before switching to medicine. It seems that cells, with all their molecular functions, they are beautifully intricate machines doing complex functions. They're remarkably like the complex machines humans build."

"Yes, aren't they?" said the professor, and she stepped closer to the young woman.

"Things like flagellum," continued the student, "that act like propellers and molecular rotors. They look like they've been designed by an engineer."

"Ah," sighed the professor, "Darwinism was a whole lot easier to believe when we knew a whole lot less about the cell, wasn't it?"

"What do you mean, professor?" asked another student. "What are you saying?"

"Well," said the professor, "some scientists today question whether natural selection acting on random mutations can truly account for the complexities and elegance we see in life. Quite frankly, the science increasingly has gone against the theory. Just ask those looking farthest out, like astronomers, and those looking closest in, like my own field of biology. We find ourselves oddly defending a mid-nineteenth-century scientific understanding."

From the back a student asked, "So, professor, you really believe in God and religion then?"

The class erupted in laughter. Someone yelled an obscenity about the pope. All the students leaned in. This was infinitely more interesting than chemical processes.

"There is no God!" yelled another student over the voices of the others. "My god is Marx and Engels. And Che of course!" The class burst into laughter again, and there were scattered applause and whistles.

"I'm not a religious person," said the professor smiling, "but the religious angle is interesting since you brought it up. If we hold to a material explanation for life, there can be no moral restraints, and life must have no meaning. There are no principles or causes worth fighting for, like all the passions raging out there," she said, gesturing with her arm toward the door. "A Darwinist has difficulty reconciling the most central aspects of human life. Like love and honor, dignity, beauty and justice. And kindness and compassion."

There were loud catcalls and whistles. A wadded paper sailed from the back of the class and hit the chalkboard behind the professor's head. "Nonsense!" someone yelled. "Everyone knows religion has been responsible for all wars throughout history." The students banged on the tables.

"Let's calm down, please," the professor pleaded, but the voices of violence were louder than the voices of reason.

Daniel sat in his back seat thinking. The professor was right, he mused. These students didn't know what they were fighting for and why. Did they really know what Communism was and its dangers? That Che Guevara personally murdered hundreds of people? The military government may have a lot of faults, Daniel thought, but the threats to the country were real, and the regime was trying to stop it. These students had no idea.

The atmosphere had changed a lot since last semester. Something was happening. There was an edge that wasn't here before. Maybe, he thought, *he* was the one who had changed. Maybe this contempt and arrogance was just normal university behavior. Perhaps, before, he might have chimed right in. No, something *had* changed. But weren't these the same students he had known at the university for the past two years? Could they be capable of the things he had seen and of the things he had been warned about?

His thoughts turned to his friends and the students he knew. For most of them, all the ideology and the protests, it was just talk. They were people who wanted to do something, who wanted to stand for something, and to belong to something. And perhaps with the influence of their professors, they were hopeful men and women for whom the promises of socialism made sense and for whom the ills of capitalism could be cured only through its violent demise. Young people convinced that centralized power is a force for progress and who were impatient to import what Fidel Castro was exporting. The revolution, this wise island sage pronounced, is a dictatorship of the exploited against the exploiters. Such propaganda proved irresistible and impervious to logic.

Yet Daniel knew that for some, it was more than just talk. Some were willing to go further than that. Much further. He recalled the terrorist bomb that killed his uncle and the one at the police cafeteria. Yes, there were evil elements here on the campus, agitators and provocateurs poisoning young minds toward violence. He would find them. He would find the powder keg itself.

This Eva that Valentina talked about, maybe she would be a good place to start.

# CHAPTER 24 – EVA

## *Eva*

*"Hola, Dani.* You're late!" said Valentina, giving Daniel a warm embrace and a kiss on the cheek. "We're already on our second round."

The bar was popular with students, and this Thursday evening it was crowded and loud. "Don't go breaking my heart," came Elton John's voice through the ceiling speakers. Kiki Dee's chirpy voice followed.

*"Che, ¿cómo están?* It's been so long," said Daniel, leaning over the table to embrace Cristian and Fede.

"We thought we'd lost our friend, and the world a budding doctor," said Fede, cool in his mangy hairstyle and ragged beard. "So what, now you're back at the university? Aren't you doing your military service?"

Daniel felt everyone's stares. He took a deep breath.

"Yeah, I'm back on campus," Daniel said. "I did my basic training, but the military wants me to finish my medical studies first."

Again, the lie flowed easily from his lips, and it boosted his confidence. "And I'm glad of it because I've missed all of you," Daniel continued. "And all of this," he added, sweeping an arm grandly about the familiar bar before taking his seat.

"Valentina says you really did go on a road trip," said Fede. "Good for you. I just can't believe you did it."

"And you went with Gordo? Gordo Pedraza?" said Cristian.

"None of you cowards would go with me. I might still have been gone even now," said Daniel. He grinned, but inside he wondered if he could do this.

A waiter set a beer in front of him. Fede lit a cigarette, and Daniel bummed one from him.

"What, you smoke now too?" asked Cristian.

"A bad habit he picked up in Chile," said Valentina. "Shame on you too, Fede."

"Any other bad habits you picked up, Daniel?" Fede said. "Do tell." He smiled and held the lighter for him.

*"Che, Fede,"* said Daniel, wanting to change the subject, "Vale tells me you have a new girlfriend. Isn't she joining us?"

"Yes," said Fede. "Eva promised to come."

"He has his hands full with Eva," said Valentina, smiling. "She gives the orders, and he follows. Not quite the role you're used to having, is it, Fede? Probably does you some good."

They all laughed.

"We're in love," said Fede, crossing his arms. "What can I say?"

Daniel slipped a hand under the table to grasp the cold metal leg. The company of old friends and conversation made him uncomfortable. He had gone so long without it. There was something he missed in the easy banter, but now it seemed something impossible for him and a sadness washed over him. He felt like a fraud.

He watched Valentina toss her head and laugh. He followed her arm as she placed it around Cristian. He pressed against the back of his chair to feel the hardness of the gun under his shirttail. The Eagles belted out a tune, and he recalled Cacho cranking it up in their squad car a few nights ago, a hooded subversive in the back seat.

*"¿Qué?"*

"I asked if you wanted another beer, *sordo*," said Fede.

*"Sí, otra cerveza,"* replied Daniel, but his response was drowned out by the scraping of Fede's chair.

A young woman appeared at the table. Everyone stood and welcomed her with the kind of airy kiss reserved for acquaintances. Daniel grabbed a chair from an adjoining table to make space for a fifth.

Eva was petite with long black hair that fell about a pretty pale face from which smiles seemed not easily extracted. Her lips were thin and drawn tight. Daniel thought he recognized her from one of his classes at the medical school. He found himself staring at her belly. He caught himself and looked away. She didn't look pregnant.

"And tell me, Daniel," said Eva after she settled next to him, turning to give him her full attention. "What are you all about?"

"You don't need to ask him that, *mi amor*," said Fede. "Just ask me. Daniel and I grew up on the same street. We've been friends since kindergarten. He even owes me his life, don't you, Daniel? Didn't I ever tell you about when he was in a fight with some bigger kids…"

*"Callâte, Fede,"* Eva interrupted, placing a hand on Fede's arm. "Let him speak."

"Well," said Daniel, turning in his chair to face her and taking a deep breath, "I'm a classmate of yours for starters. You're in my biology class, I think."

*"¿Ah, si?"* said Eva. She raised her eyebrows.

The waitress deposited more beers at their table. Eva ordered juice.

"Tell us more about your Che Guevara experience," said Fede. "You haven't told us anything."

"Yes, tell," added Cristian, and Daniel noticed his arm

around Valentina's chair and how he played with her hair.

They all nodded and smiled. Eva turned her head and looked at him.

Setting his beer on the table, Daniel took another deep breath. He had rehearsed his story in front of the small mirror in his bathroom, but his stomach churned and he steepled his fingers together to keep them from shaking. He began.

His voice rose and fell, and his emotions were real. He told them about the motorcycles and the wind in his face, and about the vistas and magical nighttime stars. He recalled the police roadblock and Gordo's stammering, which made the friends at the table laugh. How the motorcycles had been stolen and he and Gordo had separated. He talked about the estancia, and the agents who had come after the accident searching for subversives. He described witnessing the police taunting the Madres at the Plaza de Mayo when he had returned to Buenos Aires, and Daniel pursed his lips, just like he had practiced, before explaining how this all had made his blood boil.

"I don't know. I just feel different now. I want to do something," Daniel said finally, directing these last words toward Eva.

For a few moments, no one said anything.

"Bravo!" said Fede, "Bravo, Daniel! I would have never guessed it, but I think you are ready to become a radical. Who would've thought?"

Valentina reached her hand across the table to him. "I'm so sorry, Daniel. I'm so sorry."

Eva said nothing. Her juice was untouched.


The next week, Daniel watched Eva from his seat in the back of biology class. She sat by herself.

He had found himself thinking about her over the weekend, and as class time drew near, she had intruded so much on his mind he could hardly wait. He arrived fifteen minutes early to class.

Eva paid close attention to the professor, taking notes and seemingly unaware of the other students. At one point in the middle of class, she turned in her seat and caught Daniel staring at her. His face flushed, and he quickly turned away.

After class, Eva had somehow slipped out without Daniel noticing. He hurried out the door and looked both ways in the hallway. She was gone.

"Did you lose something?"

Daniel turned. It was Eva.

"No, no, I didn't," he stammered.

"You look like you were looking for something," said Eva. "I've seen people look for things before, and you were definitely looking."

Daniel felt his face redden. He shifted his weight to the other leg.

"Do you know *El Planeta*?" said Eva.

"Yes."

"Meet me there at 9 p.m., *¿si?*"


Bodegón El Planeta was an old bar on a sunless side street downtown. Daniel arrived early and sat at a table with his back to the wall. Two old men sat at the bar and a foursome played cards.

He saw Eva peer in the window before coming inside and making her way to his table. The old men paid no attention, but the card players looked up and ogled.

Daniel stood and kissed her cheek, inhaling as he did. She smelled of shampoo. He pulled out a chair and helped her sit.

"Are you hungry?" Daniel asked.

"I'm starving, to tell the truth," Eva said.

"Good. The sorrentinos here are superb."

"I'm surprised you know this place so well," said Eva.

Daniel pressed his hands together in his lap. He felt his breath quicken. Something in Eva's question seemed like she was testing him.

"Insomnia," said Daniel. "I know all the places downtown."

"Where do you live?"

"Here. Not far."

"You don't live with your father? In Flores? Fede told me."

"No, I live in an apartment with a friend. Shall we order?"

He caught the waiter's attention and ordered the sorrentinos and beer.

Daniel watched Eva butter a bread roll. She ate one and reached for another. Aware of his gaze, Eva smiled. "I'm hungry," she said.

"You said that."

The beers came and Daniel held his up to Eva. He felt he should toast something, but he felt paralyzed. *What should I say?*

"To new friends," said Eva finally.

"To new friends," said Daniel.

"Last week you only drank juice," said Daniel. "You left it untouched."

Eva looked at him from above the rim of her glass. "If you want to ask me if I'm pregnant just ask."

Daniel's toes curled up in his shoes.

"Are you pregnant?"

"Yes."

"Well, then, ¡*salud!*" said Daniel, raising his glass. "You shouldn't drink," he added.

"Don't tell me what to do," Eva said.

They said nothing for a few minutes. The faint horn of the late-night ferry announced its arrival from Montevideo, Uruguay across the delta. The sorrentinos arrived from the kitchen.

"You know, I liked what you said the other night," Eva said. "At the bar." She spooned parmesan cheese over her pasta.

"What?"

"About your motorcycle adventure. About your experiences with the police." Eva leaned in close and put her elbows on the table. "Are you still angry at what they've done? At what they're doing?"

Daniel reached into his mind to remember his murdered uncle and tried to conjure up a sense of rage. "Yes, in fact, I'm even angrier than I was before."

"Tell me," said Eva. Her deep eyes drew Daniel in like the mysteries of the dark River Plate just down the hill.

Daniel took a breath, and still holding his fork, he began telling her things he hadn't shared at the campus bar when they had first met. A lot of it he made up, and he was careful to keep everything consistent. He had practiced, and once he got started, the words came faster and easier. He told new stories that had happened to his friends. He added vivid details and tried hard to make his hate real.

Eva stopped eating. Daniel thought one of the card players had turned around and stared at them.

"Are you with a resistance group, Daniel?" Eva said. Her voice was soft.

Daniel cut into a sorrentino and took a bite. "No."

"Are you an ideologue?"

"You mean a communist?" said Daniel, his mouth full. "Of course. Aren't we all? All the students, I mean?"

"You know that's not what I mean."

A loud crash startled them. A waiter had dropped a plate.

Daniel put his elbows on the table. "I just want all of this madness to stop."

"Are you willing to do something about it?" she said. "Are you, Daniel?"

"Yes," said Daniel. "Are you involved in...in activities?"

Eva laughed, and it was the first time he had heard her laugh. She tossed her hair and Daniel caught the scent of shampoo again.

"I want you to meet a few people," she said. "I like your anger. You are strong. Fede thinks the world of you, you know."

Daniel finished his plate and pushed it away. Eva did the same. She fumbled in her purse and pulled out a cigarette.

"You shouldn't smoke either," said Daniel.

Eva frowned. "Yes, you're right of course. It's just been hard. The beer too. It tastes so good."

Daniel ordered coffees.

"It was a mistake to get pregnant," said Eva. "My friends, those who know. They all tell me to, you know, to get rid of it."

"So why don't you?"

"I don't know. It's not so easy. Everyone is telling me what to do. Maybe I feel something, something that's a part of me. My own flesh and blood. I don't have much family at all. It's probably my Catholic upbringing too."

"You?" said Daniel. "Valentina told me you're an atheist."

"Did she?" Eva's lips drew thin and tight. "I once was a good Catholic girl. I went to a boarding school run by nuns. I hated it."

Daniel looked her with curiosity. "Your parents sent you off to boarding school?"

Eva took a long draw on her cigarette and tilted her head to blow the smoke away. The front door of the bar opened, and Daniel watched Eva glance at the newcomers.

She turned back toward him. "You really want to know who I am, Daniel?" she said. "I'm all mixed-up. That's what. My father was murdered by the government. I was eight years old. My mother went crazy, and they locked her up. The judge ordered us to be raised as orphans, my brother and me, in the care of the Church. I was sent to be raised by nuns. My brother was sent to an orphanage. He was twelve. I didn't see him again for many years."

"It was hard," she continued. Eva looked toward the men playing cards. "I hated the nuns. I hated the government. I hated God. And I hated my mother, to tell the truth." She looked at Daniel and smiled faintly. "You see, communism is perfect for me. It so deliciously mixes all my hates into a tasty *puchero* stew."

Eva ground out the half-smoked cigarette into the ash tray. "I'm not so angry now, but I am more determined. More determined to fight against a corrupt government and a corrupt Church. I'm doing something. I'm trying to help fix the world."

"I'd like to fix the world too," said Daniel, and wishing with all his heart that things could be different, and he could show Eva how *her* side was the one causing the problems that required fixing.

"Do you see your mother?" Daniel said.

"Very little. I blamed her for a long time. I learned to live without her."

"And your brother?"

"Oh, he's a priest."

"What? A priest?" Daniel laughed. "So, you hate your brother as well since he loves God? He probably loves nuns too."

"God, no! I don't hate him," said Eva. "I love him. He's a priest, yes, but it's just complicated. He's complicated."

Eva glanced at her watch. "I have to go."

"Why did you tell me all this?" said Daniel.

Eva sighed. "Because you wanted to know, Daniel. Fede has told me a lot. I know about your mother and I'm sorry. You're smart. You see what's going on and you want to do something. To count for something. You're not alone."

She took his hands and squeezed them. "I like you. You could be of some good to us."

She got up and walked between the tables and chairs and past the men playing cards who stopped and stared until the door closed behind her.

# CHAPTER 25 – LA MANIFESTACIÓN
## *The Street Protest*

Daniel fidgeted in class. His knee bounced under the desk as if it had a mind of its own.

He hadn't expected to see Eva. She had missed the last few classes, but here she was today in her usual seat. He felt a sense of relief. He had begun worrying that his cover might be blown, and it kept him up some nights with his mind thrashing out all the ways he could have been compromised. The days when he didn't see Eva dialed up his worry.

He glanced over at her again and noticed she wore a loose-fitting blouse. *Was she beginning to show?*

After class, he resisted the temptation to find her. Their meetings would always be on her terms, Daniel decided. That's how he would play it.

"*Pará.* Wait."

Daniel stopped and turned. It was Eva.

"Do you always walk so fast?" she said, her voice ragged.

"I walk quickly wherever I go." Daniel smiled. "I always have."

"There's a student protest this afternoon," she said. "You've seen the leaflets."

He nodded.

"You should come," said Eva. "Your friends – Fede and the others – they will be there too."

"What's it for?" he said.

Eva brushed his question away with a flick of her hair.

"Today's protest is really big," she said. "The police will almost certainly come and bust it up."

Daniel held her arm and leaned in close, letting her hair brush his face. "Why would you want to be around for it? It seems dangerous, no?"

"We're doing our part, Daniel. Resisting and waving the flag." She lowered her voice. "We like to see what happens."

"You're not worried about...," Daniel stammered, "you know. About the baby?"

"I'm not an invalid," Eva said. She put her hands on her hips. "This is important, Daniel. You want to do something, then *do* something. We'll meet on Avenida Córdoba. At the corner with Junín."

The light was fading when Daniel made his way across the campus. The towering medical school cast a greedy shadow over Calle Paraguay and by now had stretched almost to Avenida Córdoba.

He could hear the noise long before he got there, and he fell in with a stream of students heading that way. Eva had been right. This was going to be big.

The courage of these students was something to be considered, Daniel thought, though it could well be stupidity. He imagined the scene at the central police station at that moment, the *Guardia* donning riot gear. Captains shouting orders. At the military barracks at Campo de Mayo the tanks and the personnel trucks would be idling their throaty diesel engines, and the adrenaline would be flowing. These men believed in what they were doing too, and they had orders to follow.

Daniel arrived at the crowded corner. Students were everywhere. They stood in groups and hung on lampposts.

They climbed the trees lining the street. Students linked arms and danced, and they blew horns and beat drums. In the apartment buildings on either side of Córdoba, curious onlookers leaned out of windows and peered over balconies. The charged air coursed across youthful faces reflecting a nervous anticipation as if they might get shocked at any moment.

Students unfurled large white banners made from sheets.

*Nos quitaron tanto que nos quitaron el miedo.*
They've taken so much that they've taken our fear.

*Perón o Muerte*
Perón or Death

*Estudiantes Desaparecidos*
Missing Students

Daniel pushed his way to the corner of Calle Junín and found Valentina and Cristian. Eva and Fede stood a short distance away. They nodded to him. Daniel smiled. He was still getting used to being among friends again. It felt good.

A chant started nearby that was joined by hundreds across the avenue and the side streets. A bullhorn squawked, but Daniel could make out nothing the speaker said. Cheers erupted, and the drums beat with more urgency. The bullhorn crackled again, and a fresh excitement rippled through the student protesters. The riotous noise reverberated against the buildings.

Daniel sensed it first in the pregnant air and then in his feet. A low rumbling, an almost imperceptible trembling in the ground. He scanned Calle Junín in both directions and the side streets a block away. Nothing. Yet he knew what was coming and where they were coming from.

The chanting changed, but the crowd's roar dropped

several decibels, and a murmur rippled through the protesters. Up in the buildings, windows closed, and balconies emptied as people retreated behind the safety of their curtains. A few students began leaving, but the cheering resumed as if they were encouraging each other, and the chanting got louder. Drums beat out rhythms to accompany the raucous singing.

Daniel wished his friends hadn't come. He visualized the soldiers and police lined up a few blocks to the east on Avenida Córdoba, their drab green uniforms tucked smartly into polished black boots, their batons and rifles held at the ready. A simple show of force, Daniel knew, would cause most of the students to disperse. Leave them a few exit options and begin moving forward. But there were always some who were determined to make them work for it, those willing to throw rocks to incite a violent response. Here the danger lay, as the soldiers' orders were somewhat opaque, with room for confusion.

A loudspeaker boomed from atop an armored truck appearing around the corner, followed by a phalanx of soldiers. "This is an illegal gathering. Disperse immediately. Go home. We are here for your safety."

Tear gas hurtled into the crowds and circles of empty space opened around the smoking canisters. A student bolted forward and hurled one back at the soldiers. A great cheer went up. The chanting and the banging got louder. The uniformed lines moved forward. The loudspeaker issued more warnings, and the student bullhorn replied with a string of insults and with a set of its own demands. The protesters hooted and whistled.

Daniel noticed a new line of soldiers on the far side of Junín. He nudged Valentina. "Leave, Vale. Leave now. *Mirá.*" He pointed.

Valentina grabbed Cristian's arm and pointed too. She was

frightened. Cristian said something that Daniel couldn't hear. Valentina shook her head and tugged at him. *"¡Vení, Cristian!"* she said. *"¡Apurá, Dani!"*

The couple joined the stream of students searching for an exit. Daniel scanned the crowd for Eva, but he couldn't see her. He needed her to see him, to see his commitment to the cause.

Shouts erupted near him, and he saw the soldiers moving toward them. Tear gas stung his eyes. He covered his face with his shirt and bent low to the ground. He moved toward the other side of the corner where he had last seen Eva and Fede. Students panicked. Feet shuffled and pounded in confusion. He stepped over several students who had been knocked down. He heard the crunch of batons and the crack of rifle butts. People screamed.

A man rushed by with bright red blood streaming down his face.

Daniel jumped onto a large cement planter to escape the rush of people crazed with fear and desperate for oxygen. The air zipped and popped, and a hot distorted rubber bullet bounced on the ground and came to rest on the planter beside his foot. Near him, a student shrieked and held his ear, blood seeping between his fingers. Another nursed a welt from a rubber bullet that skipped off the ground and hit his leg.

Daniel saw Eva. Their eyes locked. She huddled with a group of students backing away from a line of swinging batons. On the ground below him, Daniel saw a soldier beating a man. Daniel launched himself off his ledge and tackled the soldier, wrestling away the baton and striking the uniformed man across the face. Daniel's blood was up. It didn't matter these were cops just like him. Nothing mattered to him anymore except meeting this immediate threat.

Looking up, Daniel saw a soldier bolt toward Eva, but a

protester stepped in the way and took a hard crack to the head. He collapsed with a thud. The soldier raised his baton at Eva, and she held one hand over her head and with the other she protected her belly. Daniel lunged at the soldier's arm in mid swing and spun him around. He smashed the surprised soldier on the jaw, and he went limp.

The soldiers now surged forward to swarm this aggressor. Daniel didn't hesitate. He piled into the oncoming line, bowling over several soldiers and taking heavy blows across his body and knees. He went down. He looked back and noticed Eva on the ground. Daniel crawled forward and knelt over her, taking kicks and blows from the swarming jackboots. A crack to his head turned everything black.

Daniel awoke on the floor of a moving truck. His head throbbed. Boots dug into his back and legs. He struggled to get up, but the feet pushed him back and a kick to his shoulder blades collapsed him. He was blindfolded and his hands tied behind his back. There were others on the truck floor, and Daniel could feel them against his head and against his legs. Someone moaned.

The truck came to a halt, and Daniel was dragged by the legs and allowed to fall to the asphalt. With his hands tied behind him, he had no way to protect himself, but he managed to roll so his side hit the ground first and not his head. Other bodies thudded to the ground and cried out. Daniel was jerked up. He was pushed forward into a building where his blindfold was ripped off.

Daniel found himself in a cell with eight men, one whom he remembered seeing talking to Eva at the protest. In the wee hours of the night, guards came and pulled the men out one or two at a time. He heard other doors open and close too. The sound of moving feet, the murmur of voices. Four guards came for Daniel. He was shoved along a hallway and into a brightly lit room.

"This is the one," said one of the guards, speaking to a captain seated at a desk. "He has no identification."

Daniel scanned the room, worried someone of these might recognize him as a fellow policeman.

"Name?" The captain stared at his pad of paper, his pencil ready. "Name," he repeated. This time it was not a question.

Daniel met the captain's upturned gaze and knew that the officer could see no progress would be made here.

"Take him out, make him talk," the captain said with a flick of his head. The guards pulled Daniel to his feet. An uneven smile creased the officer's face. "I understand you like violence," he said to Daniel. "You've come to the right place then."

Daniel absorbed the pain for precisely twenty minutes, enough time, he knew, to make the torture marks convincing but before the precision instruments could be employed. By focusing his eyes on his torturer's wristwatch, he tracked the slow travel of the minute hand. He thought of El Oso.

When the time arrived, he announced he was ready to speak. He was given water and hauled before the captain with the pad and pencil. This time he was permitted to sit in a chair. One of Daniel's eyes was puffed shut and he reeked of burnt flesh.

The captain lit a cigarette and blew the smoke over Daniel as if to mask the smell.

"*¿Cigarrillo?*" he offered.

"*Gracias,*" said Daniel. "My hands. Will you please untie my hands?"

The captain shook his head, but he took his lit cigarette and put it into Daniel's mouth. Daniel took several puffs and the captain removed it and ground it out in the ashtray. He lit another for himself and sat back, observing Daniel. He scooted his chair closer to the desk and picked up his pencil.

"Name."

"Call the office of Admiral Juan Carlos Bertotti at SIDE," said Daniel. "Ask for his chief aide, Sebastian. Tell him El Inglés is here."

The captain's mouth fell open, closing only when he took such a hard pull on his cigarette that his sucked-in cheeks appeared almost cartoon-like. He nodded at one of the guards before exhaling like the sound of a long train whistle.

Sebastian came within thirty minutes. He asked for a private room, and the two were left alone. The Admiral's aide sipped stale coffee from a paper cup and contemplated Daniel's damaged body with wonder.

Daniel closed his eyes. He hurt all over, and his swollen eye was best left shut. He needed to think.

"I need a favor," Daniel said, rousing himself. "A woman, Eva, she is... I need you to get her out. I need you to ensure she is not...harmed. She's pregnant. Please get her released. There is another man too. Federico. He's a friend."

Sebastian listened.

"Don't make it obvious," continued Daniel. "Maybe you can make it look like a paperwork error or as part of a release along with others. Get me out a day later. It must appear I was mistreated."

"I can assure you none will appear more so," said Sebastian. He reached over and patted Daniel on the arm. "You're doing good, Inglés. *Muy bien.*"

Daniel needed to hear that. He closed his eyes again and tried not to think. His head hurt, and he felt gingerly for the spot where he had taken the crack from the baton.

Sebastian stood to go. "They told me about you," he said,

pausing at the door. "The soldiers you messed up on Avenida Córdoba. You know you wouldn't have lasted the night here."

# CHAPTER 26 – LA CEIBA

## *The Ceiba*

It was several days later that Eva rewarded him with a kiss on the cheek. It was not the airy kiss of an introduction nor the warm greeting of a friend. It was a different sort.

"I want to say thank you," Eva said. "For protecting me. On the street."

They sat on a patch of grass on the campus under the shade of a *ceiba*. The spikes on the bottle-shaped trunk had long worn off, but beyond a standing person's reach and along the spreading limbs above, the tree's sharp defenses bristled.

She held out her hands and let him hold them, hers delicate and pale in his own large and bruised ones. *What had these hands done?* Daniel wondered. *What are my own capable of?*

"Fede thanks you too," she said. "The others saw what you did. Friends of mine. They're calling you *El Gorila*. They were quite impressed."

Eva pulled her hands away and wrapped her arms about her knees. Daniel tried to act disinterested. He wanted to hear more about the friends she mentioned. He took a deep breath.

"They say we must be more careful," she continued. "We can't risk getting arrested. They think we were lucky. I've been arrested before, and you just never know what might happen, what mood they are in. What they might have on you." She turned to look at him. "What you did was stupid, Daniel. I'm surprised you were released. It must have been some mistake."

She seemed small and frail with her knees drawn up about her on the grass, but her stare burned a hole through him. Daniel rubbed his face. *Does she suspect something? Did I play it right?*

# CHAPTER 27 – LA CÉLULA

## *The Cell Group*

It was a week before Daniel saw Eva again. She found him after class one day. "I want you to meet someone," she said, putting a hand on his arm. "He's the one who nicknamed you *El Gorila* after what you did at the protest."

Later that afternoon Daniel met Bagre for the first time. He had been introduced simply as a friend, but he seemed to have a lot of unfriendly questions for Daniel. Bagre was a man to whom nature had not been kind. Ugly and sinister looking, he was deserving of his catfish *nom de guerre*. His crooked yellow teeth flashed with surprising frequency for a man who never smiled. The noble qualities of manliness had been beaten out of him, leaving an impulsive stump that revealed itself from a disconcerting, wandering eye that Daniel had unwisely followed.

Daniel worried he'd made a poor impression, and as nothing seemed to come of the meeting, his fears seemed justified.

He was on the steps of the medical building one day when Eva stopped him.

"Will you do it?" She studied him closely.

Daniel demurred, not wanting to appear too eager.

"You don't have to of course," Eva continued. She looked away. "Bagre was just asking, that's all."

Daniel's carotid artery pulsed like a bass drum and he turned his head in case Eva noticed. He had no idea what he was being asked to do, but he was sure it was a test of his commitment.

*"Claro,"* Daniel said. "Why not? What's it about anyway?"

"Bagre wants to plant a little surprise for someone," Eva said after pausing to look around her. She smiled. "It's not a big deal. Most of the time these things don't even go off."

*How could Eva smile?* Daniel remembered the bombs that killed his uncle and the one in the police cafeteria. *Did she participate in them?* He shook the thought from his head. He knew she was no bomb expert.

At 10 p.m. that evening Daniel stood outside Pizzería Domani. After waiting forty-five minutes, he wondered if he had heard correctly. Just wait outside. That's what Eva had told him. He poked his head into the restaurant and ordered a slice of napolitana.

He had just taken a bite when a car pulled up. Eva was driving, and she motioned him to get in. Dumping the pizza into the trash, he slid into the back seat. Bagre turned from the passenger seat and nodded as Daniel settled himself. Beside Daniel in the back seat, a man waved his hand.

"El Turco," the man said simply.

Eva's perfume filled the car. Daniel had never smelled the scent on her before, and he stared at her slender neck and shoulders in front of him.

They drove onto Avenida General Paz and north on the Pan-American. In San Fernando, Eva pulled over, the headlights illuminating a sign for the Yacht Club Argentino.

Bagre turned again to Daniel. "Gorila, you come with me and El Turco. We'll take care of the *guardia*. We don't want him alerting the soldiers."

"The soldiers?" said Daniel.

"They'll be guarding the *lancha*. Eva will distract them."

Daniel thought about the perfume.

They got out and left Eva sitting behind the wheel. The yacht club's decorative masthead rose brightly lit before them, the blue and white Argentine flag limp. Daniel remembered fishing near the club with Uncle Ricardo, staring wide-eyed with boyish wonder at the sleek boats and the manicured lawns. The Yacht Club Argentino was an unreachable world as elusive as the fighting Golden Dorado that captured the anglers' imagination but delivered only bottom-feeding catfish.

Now following Bagre and El Turco toward the entrance, Daniel felt only nervous anticipation. The briny Luján River saturated the air and his clothes clung heavily to his body.

After that everything happened so quickly, and Daniel later remembered it as a blur. And he would try later to keep it that way.

The night watchman stepped out to get a better look at the odd-hour visitors, and sensing something was not right, he dashed back to his guardhouse. Without thinking, Daniel rushed forward and grabbed the man from the back and covered his mouth. Daniel saw the flash of Bagre's knife before it plunged into the guard's stomach, sounding like the squelch of Uncle Ricardo's blade gutting a fish.

The man moaned. Daniel thought only of how quickly the fish's eyes turned glassy, and he wondered if this man's were turning too, the life in them transferred to Bagre who stood glint-eyed and smiling. Horrified, Daniel eased the wounded watchman onto the floor.

"You've got good instincts, Gorila," said Bagre. "Stay here. Keep watch."

He heard Eva pull up in the car and pass through the gate.

Daniel was suddenly alone with this dying man in the booth. He found a rag and applied pressure to the watchman's wet abdomen. He convinced himself it was too late to call for help, that no one would get there in time anyway.

He stumbled out to get some air. Up ahead, Eva stood beside her car and chatted with a pair of soldiers. Daniel knew Bagre and El Turco were planting a bomb on a yacht, one that likely belonged to someone important, perhaps a general. He didn't want to know. The less he knew, the less he would feel obligated to say anything about it to Sebastian. Besides, chances were high no one would get hurt anyway. Eva had said that. SIDE wanted him to get inside, and that's what he was trying to do. But dammit if this didn't all feel wrong.

Daniel's hands shook. Nothing had prepared him for this. He wanted a cigarette but didn't have any. He thought of the guardhouse and how there probably was a pack on the desk just inside, but he suddenly shivered uncontrollably until he had to sit down.

He didn't see Eva for another week. He filled the time by trying to forget what had happened and trying to remember every detail to justify what he had done.

Eva found him again on the campus, something Daniel now expected. Daniel couldn't help himself.

"What happened?" he said.

"With what?" Eva said. "You mean the thing last week?"

"Of course," said Daniel. "You know. With the yacht."

Eva sighed. "It went off," she said, "but no one was on it. Probably better that way. Sometimes the wrong people get hurt, *¿sabés?*"

And Daniel *did* know, and he grasped at this straw to justify what he felt for her.

"Daniel, are you alright?" Eva looked at him curiously.

"*Sí*," said Daniel. He felt his face flush. *"Sí, todo bien."*

*"Mirá,"* Eva said. "Bagre's invited you to a meeting. A planning meeting. It's all part of the process, *¿viste?* It's a big deal you've been invited. Bagre likes you."

*Well I hate him,* Daniel wanted to yell. He wondered how Eva could put up with Bagre, and he imagined Eva with some sort of magical power that kept her unsullied by all the ugliness.

That evening, Eva waited for Daniel by the steps of the medical building. She gave him a slight nod and led the way across the quad. The night air was cool for late spring. The few remaining late evening classes had just let out, and students were pulling on sweaters for their commutes home.

Daniel felt a bead of sweat trickle down the small of his back. *Could they have found out about my identity? Maybe this is all a trap.*

At the Filosofía y Letras building, Daniel followed Eva around to a side door. She paused. She put a hand on his arm, and he liked her touch and how it lingered there longer than expected.

"You must distinguish yourself for my sake," she said. "Some in the cell group believe my judgment of you to be clouded since you're a friend of Fede's. That I'm blinded by love."

"And *are* you?" Daniel said.

"I don't know, Daniel, am I?" Eva said, and she turned her porcelain face toward him with a jaunty smile. He wanted to kiss her right there.

"Well, what about Fede?" Daniel stammered. "Will he be at the meeting too?"

"No," Eva said, and she looked away. "Fede, he's not involved in this way. And he mustn't know," she said.

Daniel nodded. "So blind, but not love?" he said.

"Don't play with me, Daniel," she replied, her lips pursed.

"You know Fede better than I. He...at this level. Look, Fede keeps me rooted in normalcy, okay? *Dejálo ya.* Leave it there."

Eva opened the side door. "We're here," she said.

They entered the building and descended to the boiler level. They passed dusty storage rooms. Eva knocked on a door and ushered Daniel into a room with discarded furniture and rusted locker cabinets.

In a cleared space, a group sat in a semicircle. They turned and stared. Bagre grunted and motioned to the empty chairs beside him.

Daniel recognized none save Bagre and El Turco. Several looked too old to be university students. Perhaps they were graduate students or even professors, he thought, but some didn't seem to fit these categories either.

"Welcome, comrades," said Bagre, his yellow teeth flashing. "The leadership thanks you for volunteering for this new operation."

There were throat clearings and a scraping of chairs in anticipation.

Bagre held up his hand. "But first, we welcome our new comrade, *El Gorila.*"

All eyes turned toward Daniel. He wasn't sure if he should say something, so he remained silent. In fact, nothing more was said about Daniel, and no introductions were made. Personal information among the subversives was a liability, Eva had explained to him. The less one knew about a fellow guerilla, the less likely an arrest would yield useful information for the government. How could you confess to something you didn't know? It was a matter of practicality.

"New comrades are our lifeblood," said Bagre. "We must continue to fill our ranks."

One of the group interrupted. "*Camarada,* allow me to

speak."

The speaker's accent was musical, and he slurred together the last syllables of his words. *He's Cuban,* Daniel concluded. Lieutenant Cazorla had been right. Cuba was exporting agitators and provocateurs throughout the continent.

Daniel glanced at Eva. *Did she think it right that foreigners were interfering with Argentina?*

"Camaradas!" the unlikely student continued, not waiting for Bagre's acknowledgement. He stood. "I, too, wish to remind you that your heroism is serving *La Revolución.* That your sacrifice is bringing about a day when the people can join hands from the north of Latin America, from my paradise island, to the southernmost tip of this glorious continent. We're fighting the Imperialists, and we are overthrowing the military governments one by one. In El Salvador and in Bolivia, in Chile and Brazil. And here in Argentina."

The Cuban stepped toward Daniel. "New comrades join us every day, like this one," he said, putting his hand on his shoulder. "Remember that you, you here in this room, will be noted. You will have positions of power in the *Revolución.*" He took his seat again. "I thank you, Camarada Bagre, for giving me a moment to share these personal words from *El Comandante.*"

It would have been humorous to Daniel had it not been for the grave nods around the room. He was trying to wrap his head around what the operation and his initiation might be. He remembered the impassioned speeches by Lieutenant Cazorla at his police boot camp and the dedicated fervor of Admiral Bertotti. *So this was it.* He was on the other side, and it was equally committed to its cause.

Bagre nodded to the Cuban. "We will attack the police station in San Isidro," the cell leader said simply.

It took a few seconds for Daniel to process what Bagre had

said. He realized he had never thought of what exactly he might be asked to do as a new member of the cell group. He crossed his legs. His mind raced to consider all sorts of scenarios and outcomes.

"We'll attack at night, kill as many as we can," continued Bagre, "but our main objective is the cache of weapons stored there. They won't expect us. It's a small station. There won't be much trouble getting in and out quickly."

Bagre stood and fiddled with a locker behind him. Reaching his hand inside, he suddenly spun around and levelled an FAL machine gun at Daniel. Daniel froze. His legs turned rubbery. He thought of his Browning he had left in the bedroom dresser of his apartment. It wouldn't have done him any good now anyway.

"You know how to handle one of these?" said Bagre, a sneer crossing his face and the others snickered.

*They're just messing with the new guy*, Daniel told himself. *Mierda.* He breathed out slow and steady.

Bagre turned the weapon sideways and offered it to Daniel. Daniel grasped the FAL like an old friend, and reflexively checked it. It was unloaded. The room grew still. Daniel realized his mistake.

"Maybe he's a cop," said a burly man in the group. Someone laughed nervously.

"I served my obligatory time in the military," said Daniel, shrugging his shoulders.

Bagre raised his eyebrows and everyone waited. He suddenly broke into a smile, and he waved his hand as if to signal it was all okay. Daniel began breathing again.

"It will be Monday night. We'll use three cars," said Bagre, returning to business. "The drivers will keep their engines running."

Daniel met Sebastian at the Plaza San Martín and sat on a park bench under the shade of a giant rubber tree. The Admiral's aide listened as Daniel told him about his progress with the infiltration. He nodded when Daniel explained that this cell was part of a larger Montoneros group that provided strategic and logistical support. Sebastian nodded again when Daniel told him about the planned operation against the San Isidro police station. It was the first time Sebastian had been pleased with anything.

*"Bien.* We'll be ready," Sebastian said. "Inglés, don't forget about Judge Calva. The killers behind his assassination are your main objective. I needn't remind you the Admiral expects quick results." The aide stood and disappeared through the trees.

Daniel felt uneasy. His hands clenched the edge of the park bench. He should never have done it this way, to use his friends to infiltrate like this. It was stupid. It could have been done a different way, he thought. *It'll turn out okay.* But he would be more careful from now on.

# CHAPTER 28 – LA BOCA

## *La Boca*

It was a risky move for many reasons. He saw her light from the street, and he knocked on the door of the third-floor apartment. Eva stood in the doorway in a nightgown.

"You are…alone?"

She nodded.

"Put on a dress."

"What are you doing here, Daniel?" said Eva. "How did you know where I lived?" She shifted her weight and a bare leg revealed itself from a slit in the fabric, luminous against the shadows.

"It's past midnight," she said.

"Come with me."

Daniel felt her eyes take in his clean-shaven face and slicked-back hair, his carefully ironed pants, and the leather jacket. The cologne was too strong.

She closed the door and reemerged fifteen minutes later wearing a long narrow black skirt and black top. Her hair was pulled back into a tight bun. It was the first time he had seen her with makeup. She looked beautiful.

Daniel had a borrowed Renault parked below. He held the door for her. They drove south on an empty Avenida 9 de Julio and turned east on Avenida 25 de Mayo toward the River Plate. Neither said anything. Daniel glanced at the young woman beside him and smiled. Eva smiled back, and Daniel felt a sudden thrill burst from within, a joy of being young and in the company of a pretty girl. Of forgetting everything for just one night.

A light drizzle fell, and the dark streets glistened under the orange glow of the streetlights. They circled the port and drove past the hulking rusted cranes in the shipyards.

La Boca had always been a gritty section of the sprawling city, distinctive for its cacophony of primary colors on corrugated metal houses. Decades ago, brothels had found a niche here servicing the waves of Spanish and Italian male immigrants. But the brothels stayed long after the gender balance was restored on the simple premise that men always want more sex than women are willing to freely give them.

La Boca was known, too, as the birthplace of tango. But the great *milongas* had been closed and their doors shuttered. Suspicious of crowds, the military regime had forbidden public gatherings of more than three people. Strict night curfews had been imposed. Songwriters had become dangerous voices of resistance and were silenced through imprisonment or exile, their songs banned. The famous Argentine culture of late-night dancing went underground, accessible only to those willing to risk arrest for a night of abandon.

And to those who had connections.

Daniel slowed the car in front of a crumbling warehouse under the shadow of the Club Atlético Boca Juniors stadium where a young Diego Maradona dazzled the blue-collar crowds.

Daniel eased his vehicle into the narrow alley beside the warehouse and onto a dirt lot. He opened the door for Eva. He knew he shouldn't be here. This was stupid. There would be policemen here who might recognize him. He had almost made up his mind to close Eva's door and drive her back, but she was already out of the car, eager and holding onto the crook of his arm.

They walked across the uneven ground. Daniel spoke quietly to the bouncers standing beside a rusted door. They nodded and accepted the bills pressed into their hands. He reached for Eva's elbow and glanced at her sideways. *What is she thinking?*

Once inside Daniel kept his head down, but his eyes scanned the club as he led her to a private table to sit. He didn't immediately recognize anyone, and he was glad for the dimly lit ambiance and the screen of cigarette smoke. He shifted his attention to Eva. She was focused on the packed floor, her eyes following the dancers. He saw the pulse on her white neck. He watched her breasts rise and fall with her quick breaths.

The *tanda* ended and the *cortina* began. Leaders led their partners back to the tables and searched for new ones, trying to catch their eye. The *cabeceo,* head nods, signaling an agreement to dance for the next three songs. A tanda.

Eva turned back toward Daniel and caught his unblinking stare. She smiled and nodded her head, keeping her eyes fixed on him until he held out his hand for hers. They crossed the dance floor as the first song began, their bodies moving together and their feet following in a crisp snapping to the on- and off-beat rhythms of the two bandoneons, the piano, the violin, and the string bass. They kept their steps small and their feet on the floor as they glided across the crowded room.

Eva was a gifted dancer. After several tandas, Daniel begged off and encouraged her to take up the offers of more accomplished leaders wishing to partner with this exquisite ballerina.

Daniel watched as Eva danced, her face flushed and happy. His heart skipped a beat when a policeman acquaintance took a turn with the young subversive lady, the two dancing cheek to cheek and creating a strong emotional and creative connection, which is the deepest secret of tango.

The milonga reached the final wee hour of the morning, and the mood changed. Daniel approached Eva on the dance floor again. The quintet struck a *tanda* of slower, more intimate music. The strains of Pugliese drifted into the smoke-filled air and settled lightly on the enchanted dancers locked together, their eyes closed, each imagining a joy and a hope and a dream that existed only at that moment and soon would be gone forever.

"That was magical. Thank you," she said on the doorstep of her apartment. She reached up and kissed him on the lips. She touched his ear and traced a finger across his cheek. "Tomorrow we will forget all of this," she said, and she went inside and closed the door.

# CHAPTER 29 – EL TOPO

## *The Mole*

It was after midnight, and the neighborhoods of San Isidro were quiet. Daniel sat behind Eva, who drove the lead car with Bagre in the passenger seat.

Daniel was tense. Eva was all business, quiet and gripping the steering wheel in front of him. The night at the tango club seemed so long ago, the memory inaccessible.

In the back seat beside Daniel, a cell member fidgeted with the strap of his machine gun.

They cruised past the front of the police station and all looked normal. Outside the front entrance, a cop on a smoke break gave the cars a glance as he flicked the butt onto the pavement to go back inside.

Turning onto a dark residential street, Daniel and the others exited their cars. He could almost hear his heart thumping in his chest. *Did Sebastian get my message and pass it along?* If not, Daniel thought grimly, policemen were going to die tonight.

Three terrorists circled behind the police station while Daniel and the others rounded the corner to approach the front.

Bagre held up his hand. Something was not right.

The interior lights were off now. A floodlight clicked on, illuminating the front entrance and betraying several cars across the street parked at odd angles. Their operation had been compromised.

*"Mierda,"* Bagre cursed and frantically waved the abort signal.

Engines roared to life from across the street, and headlights pierced the darkness. The guerillas ran back to their waiting cars.

Daniel felt the adrenaline rush through him. Eva popped the clutch and screeched from the curb, taking the lead. Out the rear window, Daniel saw the last car peel off at the corner to collect the other three terrorists around the back.

The pop-pop-pop of gunfire erupted from the next street over.

Only the skill of Eva's driving saved two of the cars and their occupants. It was not until late morning that details trickled in regarding the fate of the third vehicle. Its driver had found the back street blocked and a gun battle erupted. One terrorist had been shot and killed, and another was wounded but managed to make it to the car and escape. The third was still missing.

Two weeks later there was another failed operation. Daniel learned it from El Turco.

*"Che, Gorila, ¿oíste?* Did you hear?"

Daniel found himself beside El Turco as they stood in line at a sandwich shop on Calle Junín.

"We've had this army colonel under surveillance for ten days," said El Turco, keeping his voice down. "We knew his daily routines. But yesterday, when we had decided to carry out the hit on this colonel, the house was completely empty. People are saying we have a mole in our cell, *¿viste?"*

Daniel felt his heart skip a beat. He tried to read El Turco's face. *Does he suspect me?* Daniel hadn't known anything about this operation, so he certainly hadn't warned anyone. It angered him that there might be other operatives at the UBA that were complicating matters for him.

"I'm telling you, Gorila. Everyone's paranoid. Nobody trusts anybody."

The next afternoon, Eva slipped a paper into Daniel's hands. The note was from Bagre. "Meet me tonight. Come alone."

Eva disappeared into the crowd of students. Daniel held the note and a chill swept over him. He knew what this meant. For a moment Daniel allowed the thought to cross his mind. He could just blow the cover off everything now. He was so tired. He shook off the idea. He would not give the Admiral the satisfaction.

Since beginning his work as an infiltrator, Daniel had adopted elaborate routines to ensure he wasn't followed. He would board a bus and observe who got on with him. Sometimes, at the last second when the doors were closing, he would jump off. He would take a bus in one direction and catch another coming right back. He would turn a corner and duck into the nearest doorway, watching for followers. He knew every street and alley in downtown Buenos Aires.

But this evening as he returned home for a few hours before the meeting with Bagre, he didn't follow any of these routines. It no longer mattered.

The note from Eva changed everything.

Daniel found Cacho at their apartment. They saw each other less now and rarely spent time together. His roommate had a new girlfriend and wasn't around much anymore. A few weeks earlier, Daniel had come back to the apartment one afternoon and found the young woman alone in the apartment, waiting for Cacho. They had greeted each other but it hadn't stopped with the kiss on the cheek, and fifteen minutes later, she had smoothed down her skirt and left. It had happened so fast. Somehow, with Cacho not around, the two of them had needed something, something provided by his absence.

*"Che, Inglés, ¿qué tal?"*

Cacho was speaking to him. Daniel collected his thoughts and brought them back to the present.

"Good, and you?" said Daniel, his betrayal manifesting itself as an imaginary itch on his face.

*"Bien."* Cacho studied him and Daniel lowered his eyes.

"I never see you anymore," Daniel said.

Cacho shrugged. "It's my girlfriend, Inglés. You should try it. A girlfriend would do you a lot of good too."

"I've tried it," said Daniel, crumpling onto the sofa and running his hand through his hair. "But I have bad luck. Every woman I get close to...you know. It ends badly."

"I know what you mean, *¿viste?*" said Cacho. "Something always screws it up, no? Look, *disculpá*, sorry. I'm on my way out."

Cacho left to collect some things from his room. Daniel stretched on the sofa and closed his eyes. Cacho knew little about Daniel's role as an infiltrator, enough not to ask questions. Daniel couldn't think of anyone he trusted more. *I betrayed his trust.* He decided he would tell Cacho everything right now. He'd ask him to come and back him up in confronting Bagre.

Daniel needed his friend.

Cacho returned and paused at the front door. *"Che, cuidate,"* his roommate said. "Take care."

"Cacho," said Daniel, sitting up.

*"¿Qué?"*

*"No, nada.* Nothing," said Daniel. He rubbed his knees. "Hey, tell Luis hello for me. You see him much?"

Cacho nodded. "He asked about you the other day. Said maybe he'd invite us over again for an asado."

"I'd really like that," said Daniel, and he would have given anything to take back what he had done to his best friend.

After Cacho left, Daniel sat for a long time. He would face this meeting with Bagre alone.

Long after the evening had faded, Daniel showered, trimmed his beard, and changed into clean clothes. He checked his weapon and tucked it in his leg holster. He hooked a grenade onto his belt. If things got ugly, he would be prepared.

He found his police badge in a drawer and studied it before slipping it into his jacket. He thought about his uncle. He would make him proud.

Sitting at the desk, he pulled out a sheet of paper and a pen.

*Querido Papi*, he wrote, but he suddenly crumpled the paper and stood. He looked in the mirror and straightened his jacket. There was nothing else to be done.

Daniel drifted down the stairs and stepped into the cool night. The knot in his stomach tightened on the ride to campus on the *colectivo*. As the bus turned onto Calle Paraguay, the pain eased, and he felt a calm brought on not by peace but by resignation.

When he entered the basement room of the Facultad de Letras, Daniel was surprised to find only Bagre and Eva. He knew what was coming though. How they wanted to do it didn't really matter.

He searched Eva's face for some final confirmation, but she gave away nothing.

He took a seat in a chair across from them.

"You weren't followed, Gorila?" asked Bagre. The cell leader was fidgety. Sweat beaded on his forehead and glistened under the overhead light.

"No," said Daniel. The lie came easily. He had been sloppy because it no longer mattered.

Bagre stopped fidgeting, and his wandering eye snapped back. "We have a mole in our cell," he said. His yellow teeth clicked.

Daniel's stomach felt like a bag of rocks. It would not do to show nervousness. He tensed and listened for sounds at the door. Any moment now. He leaned back against his chair to feel the hardness of his grenade. He would start with this hideous man in front of him. Daniel clasped his hands together to keep them from trembling. He took a deep breath.

"You suspect me?" he asked. *Of course they suspect me!*

He tried to read Bagre's face. Eva stared at the ground.

"New guy shows up and all this shit starts happening," said Bagre. "What do you think?"

The room went still.

Eva coughed. "It's been a problem for a while," she said.

"Shut up," said Bagre.

Daniel felt a wave of relief wash over him. *They don't have proof yet. They don't really know.*

He glanced at Eva. She still stared at the floor.

"Eva keeps saying you're clean," said Bagre. "That you've shown your loyalty. But you're just a bit too slick, aren't you? Things don't add up for me, Inglés. I saw how you flinched when I knifed the watchman."

Daniel felt Bagre's stare, like a clairvoyant searching for any telltale sign. But it was proof to Daniel they had nothing on him.

"Bah," he said, stretching out his legs. "If you want to catch the *real* mole, you should set a trap."

"A trap?" said Bagre.

"Yeah," said Daniel, his mind going into overdrive. He'd thought about this before. "You run some tests," he continued, "like you invite and disinvite the likeliest suspects to various operations to try to isolate the common problem. If a suspect involved is indeed the mole, then those operations likely will be compromised, the targets tipped off."

Bagre cocked his head and chewed on a fingernail. His right foot jiggled.

"Maybe Inglés can help us," said Eva quietly. "He's new, yes, but that could be a good thing. He doesn't have the complicated past and uncertain networks the others have. He's quiet and discreet. We can trust him."

"Shut up," said Bagre again.

There was another awkward silence.

Daniel waited. He knew by orchestrating his own tipping off the police – or not –, he could manipulate whom fell under suspicion.

"Don't think this changes anything, Inglés," said Bagre finally. His upper lip curled. "And who knows?" he said. "Maybe we have our own informant, someone buried deep within the Departamento Central de Policía. Someone else working on this mole problem for us."

Daniel's body stiffened and his skin tingled. *An informant Bagre has within the department? Someone who's looking for me?*

"So maybe you *can* help us," continued Bagre with a yellow grin. "By burning both ends, we'll find out who it is soon enough."

"We like to cover our bases," said Eva. "And who knows, maybe *you* are the mole, Daniel." Her eyes shone, and she tucked a lock of hair behind her ear.

# CHAPTER 30 – LA AMENAZA

## *The Threat*

The soft red glow of dawn pushed through the narrow slats of the thick roller blinds and cast a geometric pattern on the wall. Daniel hadn't slept at all that night. He spent most of it wandering the downtown streets and sitting on the living room sofa staring at the wall.

Daniel got up and reached for the phone.

It was midmorning by the time Sebastian settled himself on the park bench beside Daniel at the Plaza San Martín.

"An informant," the Admiral's aide said.

"Yes," said Daniel, "in the federal police department."

Sebastian opened a bag of sunflower seeds and cracked one with his front teeth. "I wouldn't worry about it," he said, dropping the shells at his feet.

"Not worry about it?" said Daniel. He suddenly felt very tired. He had been wrong to think Sebastian could help.

"I'm very exposed here," Daniel continued. "You know what they said? They said their informant, this federal policeman, is working on uncovering their infiltrator. He's working on uncovering *me*."

"*Alleged* infiltrator," said Sebastian. "You need to get a hold of yourself, Inglés, ¿viste? Look, this cell group doesn't know if it's an infiltrator, or if one of their own is passing information for a bribe, right?"

A couple walked by and Sebastian paused. He watched them and then lowered his voice. "Besides, do you know how many policemen leak information? Lots. Happens all the time. And what information could they possibly have? These are low-level police. They have nothing. Even if it's someone higher up, no one knows about you, Inglés."

"No one knows about me," Daniel repeated as if testing out the idea to convince himself this was true. He thought about Cacho. *Could my roommate compromise me?* His mind reeled.

Sebastian cracked several sunflower seeds in quick succession and rubbed his fingers to wipe off the salt dusting. "See?" he said, "the worry is gone. It's a remote possibility. The only thing you need to worry about is Judge Calva."

Sebastian stood. "You look like shit, by the way. Get yourself together."

The Admiral's aide left, and Daniel wandered over to the statue of San Martín. He climbed the steps and leaned against the granite block base. The plaza converged with Retiro Park, which stretched down the hill, across Avenida Libertador. He knew Sebastian would continue pestering him about uncovering Judge Calva's killers. *Well he would just damned have to wait.*

Daniel stepped back onto the plaza pavers and stumbled. He steadied himself. He believed Sebastian was wrong about the informant threat within the federal police department. Daniel suspected only Bagre and Eva knew the informant's identify, and likely, they would keep it that way. Asking questions would only raise suspicions.

It was clear he was on his own again. He would find this informant before he – or she – found *him.*

Daniel returned to his apartment. As he unlocked the door, he was gripped by a sudden panic, and again, he questioned Cacho's loyalty. *Could Cacho be the informant?* He felt he was going crazy. Maybe Sebastian was right. He just needed to calm down.

Cacho wasn't there.

Under the hot shower, Daniel began thinking more clearly. He could work with Bagre and show how loyal he was. He could deflect any possible suspicions they might have of him and cast them instead on others. It would also buy him some time to figure out a plan for finding the police informant.

Over the next few weeks, Daniel met with Bagre and Eve regularly. He would sit with Bagre and Eva, comparing notes and gravely considering the probabilities that a certain cell member was the mole, and then he would introduce the possibility of two independent moles or a mole working with an informant from the second circle. In the next operation, Daniel would tip off the police and thereby confound the previous analysis, casting doubt now on a new terrorist whose actions until then had been completely aboveboard and his conduct impeccable.

"It's not working," said Bagre one day. The cell leader paced the room in the basement of the medicine school. He flicked his Bic lighter on and off and held the flame close to his face to reveal his twitching mouth. "These tests are creating all sorts of fireworks within the group. They say I'm playing favorites."

What Bagre said was all true. The guerillas resented being invited to some operations and not others. They suspected they were being excluded for some unknown reason, that they were no longer part of the inner circle. Old animosities resurfaced, and new ones formed.

Daniel sighed loudly, hoping to diffuse the tension.

"You want to know what I think?" said Bagre, coming close to Daniel and flicking the lighter flame between their faces. "I think *you* are the mole."

Tendrils of fear probed the edges of Daniel's heart. He could see Bagre searching his face to detect anything.

"You know what the problem is, Bagre? It's you," said Daniel, meeting the cell leader's stare and opting for a bluster tactic. "You're screwing this up. You're incapable of hiding your suspicions, and the cell members sense this and become angry and morose."

Bagre ground his teeth but Daniel could see his mind processing this information. "It doesn't really matter," Bagre said, "because we're going to find out very soon anyway."

And with that, the terrorist stomped toward the door and slammed it behind him.

"Don't worry about him," said Eva, coming behind Daniel to touch his arm. He hoped Eva couldn't feel him trembling. "You know how he is," she said. *"Relajá."*


Daniel began using the tensions within the cell group to his advantage. Because of the petty jealousies and infighting, most of the terrorists were eager to find an ally and confidant in this worthy new subversive. Daniel had an established reputation as a fierce fighter, and his cool, quiet magnetism made them want to talk.

But as he got close to finding out those responsible for the bombing deaths of Judge Calva and Uncle Ricardo, he found himself now not wanting to know, even afraid to know, because he suspected Eva was involved. He tried convincing himself he didn't really care anymore because it was all in the past, and that even if Eva had been involved, she had never meant for any harm to come to Uncle Ricardo. It had all been an unfortunate accident. The only target had been the judge, who was probably a pompous ass anyway.

A guilty thought entered his head that maybe the Admiral was right about Uncle Ricardo being a drunk and a failure, and perhaps his heroic death was the best thing that could have happened to him and his family. The sum of all of this was that by the time Daniel positively confirmed that Eva was the driver for the bombing, he was not shocked at all. In fact, he felt relief. She only played an ancillary part, he told himself. But most of all, it gave Daniel a mental justification for what he already had long decided: he would never give Eva up.

What he could not find out, however, was the identity of the actual assassin who rode with her. No one seemed to know. But that would have to wait.

Daniel's attention turned to the more urgent and worrisome information gap. He needed to find the terrorists' mole within the Departamento Central de Policía.

# CHAPTER 31 – EL DESCUBRIMIENTO

## *The Discovery*

It was after midnight, and an office light was on in the Departamento Central de Policía. A man stood beside a large filing cabinet, riffling through personnel records. Paper coffee cups littered the top of the desk behind him. The heavy glass ashtray overflowed with orange butts protruding from a mound of gray cinders.

The man's elbow knocked over a stack of papers. Cursing to himself, he stooped to pick them up but was overcome by a bout of wheezing. He slumped into his chair to recover. It was late and he was tired, but he also was on edge. His ears strained for any sound of anyone else on the floor. It was unlikely, and he could fumble an excuse for being in his office at this hour if needed, but he'd rather not raise any suspicions.

His finger traced a handwritten paper before him. It contained a list of a dozen or so names to be checked out. To be honest, the list scared him. He couldn't wait to finish up and get rid of it, just like the ugly Bagre had instructed. He picked up the pencil and looked at the first name. Turning to the stack of employment files, he thumbed through them trying to find a match.

The man cursed again. Had no one thought of filing the police records alphabetically? But they are filed chronologically by date of first employment. Should he start with the older records or the newer records? And then there was the issue of the deceased. These were supposed to be pulled out and separated, but recently there were just so many of them. It was all very inconvenient.

The possibility of a police mole hidden within the terrorist cell was unsettling, to say the least. He went to get another cup of coffee to help him stay focused. They were pressuring him to get this done quickly. *Damn them!* They had no idea how long this would take, and the risks he was taking.

Many of the records didn't check out, and he could tell none of the names fit. There were all kinds of reasons why this might be. Records were missing because they were misfiled, lost, or never created in the first place. Sometimes they were filed under aliases. He rubbed his temples. He would need to try a different angle – the SIDE angle, one he was hoping to avoid because it would take more work.

He reached into his briefcase and extracted some fifteen pages of handwritten names. It was a list of visitors to the SIDE offices. It hadn't been hard to get, but now he cursed at how poorly it had been copied and at the mousy man who had greedily taken his money.

The man tapped out the last cigarette from the pack. The informants, he thought. Could they be so dumb? Yes, they could be, and they were. Most informants had little information of value, and the agents couldn't be bothered to guard their identities, so the informants simply showed up or were asked to come directly to the white granite office on 25 de Mayo. He would spot them if he found them on the two lists. But he knew there was a different kind of agent too. The one he was looking for. A mole who was playing both sides. This was the kind he turned his attention to now.

Maybe he could do this a faster way. He ran down the list of the SIDE visitors to see if he recognized any from the first handwritten list from the terrorist Bagre. He paused at a name.

He kept scanning and found the name again, a visit some weeks later. He looked at the original list again. The spelling was slightly different. Maybe it was the sloppy handwriting. Damned Italian surnames. But at least they were easier than the Basque ones.

An idea came to him. He walked across to another cabinet on the other side of the floor. Payroll Records. Thankfully these files were in alphabetical order. He opened a few files and found the section labeled "R." There was little information in these files other than a name and current salary. No pictures, no other data. He found a name and put his finger on it. *Daniel Romandini.* So many of these SIDE agents started out as cops. Yes, and this name, Romandini, was on the list of the dozen names that Bagre had given him. He congratulated himself on being so smart. He pulled the payroll file and stuffed it into a manila envelope.

He leaned back in the desk chair and closed his eyes. The terrorists would be happy now. They would get the name they were looking for. What they did with it was none of his business. This was the last thing he would do for them, he thought. He would just collect his envelope of cash for this work and be done. They always scared him anyway, especially that damned terrorist with the yellow teeth. He had enough now to help cushion his crappy pension from the government. Retirement sounded so good. He thought about his family house in the pueblo in Entre Ríos. He would fix it up real nice. He would repair the *quincho* with fresh mortar and a new set of hardware, and he would grill his meats and drink his wine, and never come back to the capital again.

# CHAPTER 32 – El Moto Boy

## *The Courier*

Daniel had no idea where to start rooting out this informant in the police department, this traitor using his police access to try to find *him*. He couldn't sit still, and he couldn't sleep more than three or four hours. Eva would never say anything, he knew, and it would be too suspicious if he asked. Sebastian, too, was useless. The Admiral's aide didn't even think it a problem and only stepped up the pressure to find the judge's killer.

Daniel was completely on his own, and he felt he was barely hanging on. *How am I supposed to juggle being a student, a cop, an SIDE agent, and a terrorist?*

He bought a pack of cigarettes and smoked two of them before he decided on a plan.

That night he staked out the Facultad de Medicina and the Facultad de Filosofía y Letras, hiding in the shadows and watching the side doors he himself had used so many times. He didn't quite know what he was looking for, or what he might find. Maybe his patience would be rewarded with something to help discover the informant and, more importantly, prevent his own discovery. He felt completely vulnerable.

"What would you do?" Daniel asked Cacho the next day on a rare afternoon they had crossed paths. "If, let's say, you were a policeman passing information to the subversives? How would you do it?"

"That's messed up," said Daniel's roommate.

"Yeah," said Daniel. "So, hypothetically, what would you do? How would you communicate?"

Cacho plopped into a chair. "I wouldn't use a phone, that's for sure. Lines can be tapped, and pay phones are too hard to coordinate. Too impractical. I might just meet them in person. Somewhere secret, or maybe out in public. I might use a courier."

Daniel listened. Somehow the cell was getting good intelligence on police movements. How was the informant communicating with the cell?

"Maybe I would use a drop zone," continued Cacho, his eyes brightening.

"What do you mean?"

"You know, like hiding spots," said Cacho. "I saw this movie once where spies left messages for each other under park benches and behind the water tanks of the toilets. Are you okay, Inglés?"

"Yeah, I'm fine," said Daniel. He wasn't fine, but it felt good talking with Cacho.

That night, Daniel resumed his stakeout. Some nights little happened, and the cigarette butts would pile at his feet. At other times there were multiple late-night visitors entering and exiting. Three days a week the late-night classes let out, and every evening there was the odd professor or graduate student working late. Students gathered to talk. Couples lounged on the front steps of the buildings or the few grassy areas.

He was exhausted and constantly worried it wasn't enough. *How can I possibly keep track of everyone? What if what I'm looking for is too well hidden or hiding in plain sight?*

One night Daniel was struggling to stay alert. He caught the sound of a scooter engine cutting in and out as it labored in the distance and drew nearer. Scooters were not unusual.

Many students used them. But it was odd for this time of night during the enforced curfew.

The sound grew louder and came to an abrupt stop beyond the Facultad de Letras. A figure emerged with a hurrying sort of walk. Someone with a purpose. Crossing the front of the building, the man entered the side door and emerged several minutes later. The scooter started up again, and its engine whine slowly faded.

Several nights later, Daniel observed the same man arrive and depart as before. The third time he came, Daniel was ready.

When the man reemerged from the side door and headed to his scooter, Daniel waited in a taxi. The taxi followed the motorist as he wound his way through the city in a southeast direction. The red scooter parked on a sidewalk beside other motorcycles, and the rider disappeared into an apartment building.

Daniel was tired and just wanted to sleep. He knew if he went home, he'd worry about losing the progress he'd made with this lead. He shoved some bills into the taxi driver's hand and told him to wait. He found a pay phone and dialed a cop friend.

"You want to borrow it now?" said Tuerto.

Daniel knew he should be more delicate, but he was past caring what his friend thought.

"Yes, dammit," Daniel said. "Just do me this favor."

"Tonight? What's wrong with you, Inglés?"

In the end, Tuerto agreed to let him borrow the scooter. Daniel jumped into the waiting cab and it took ten minutes to arrive at Tuerto's house. He drove the scooter back to the apartment building. After checking the red scooter was still there, he found a piece of cardboard and a nook on the side of the building to curl up in.

He woke up with a start when something wet touched his face. A dog walker muttered something and yanked her dog away. Daniel rubbed his eyes and sat up. The red scooter was still there.

It was another hour before the young man exited the apartment lobby. Daniel waited with his borrowed scooter. Daniel followed him as he picked up and delivered parcels, which he carried in a rucksack. Sometimes he made calls from a pay phone. He spent a lot of time at a convenience store which, Daniel discovered, also operated as a small courier service.

The hardest part of the surveillance was maneuvering a scooter through the traffic of Buenos Aires at high speeds, chasing the courier who rode like an Olympic champion. It was all Daniel could do to keep him within sights. At the lights the courier deftly eased through the parked cars to the front of the line, and Daniel followed, at times scraping mirrors. Once, seeing his path blocked, Daniel jumped the sidewalk, ignoring the curses of the pedestrians. He bounced back onto the street as the light turned green and narrowly missed colliding into a car. The courier glanced over, and Daniel worried his cover might be blown.

The young courier was not a diligent worker. He was fond of breaks and did a whole lot of nothing. How he could keep himself occupied for so long just sitting was a wonder to Daniel, who observed from a safe distance. The courier would sit on a doorstep or spend an hour nursing a beer and staring. Twice the young man met up with a friend who seemed to share the same zeal for boredom.

What Daniel hated most was dozing one minute, and then with no warning at all, frantically chasing the courier through traffic at death-defying speeds.

On the afternoon of the second day while waiting at a light

and keeping the courier several cars in front of him, Daniel's motor coughed. He feared he was out of gas and might lose his target. An irrational terror gripped him that this very moment might determine whether he would be killed or would live, and he almost cried out. A bead of sweat trickled down his eyebrow and stung his eye.

A breeze suddenly kicked up and rustled the sycamores lining the street. It gusted through the rows of parked cars and carried away the exhaust fumes and Daniel's fears. He closed his eyes and felt the warm wind on his face and the rumble of his motorcycle through his boots, an open expanse of highway before him. He smelled the fresh cut hay in the fields of Córdoba. A butterfly wing fluttered on the hand brake.

He wiped the sweat from his face.

The light turned green.

After the third day of this, Daniel considered simply confronting the moto boy and finding out what he needed to know. He had missed a shift with the Guardia already, and his supervisor was not an understanding man. Worse, Eva might start asking questions about where he was. Perhaps Bagre had by now figured out his identify. Daniel tried to calm down. There were many reasons why confronting the courier now was a bad idea. He might tip his hand for one. It could ruin everything.

No, it was best to be patient and hope his luck wouldn't run out while he waited.

It was on the fourth morning that Daniel followed the red scooter to the Departamento Central de Policía. He breathed a big sigh of relief. He had begun doubting himself. *Maybe this was not the same scooter, or did the scooters on the campus each have different couriers? Maybe there was no connection after all?* But he had stayed with it, and it seemed his hunch might prove correct after all.

The courier dismounted on the sidewalk across the street from the police department and waited beside it. He lit a cigarette. Daniel parked his own scooter among the rows of other bikes beside the building. Staying out of sight, he crossed the street and watched from under the shade of a jacaranda.

It was almost noon at the police headquarters, and Daniel knew the employees were on their third cup of coffee and beginning to consider lunch. The traffic in and out of the building was light compared to what it would be in one hour. Daniel tried to imagine what this informant would look like if indeed it *was* the informant. It had to be.

Daniel alternated his attention between the courier and the front door of the station across the street.

At that moment, an overweight police veteran exited and stood blinking and wheezing on the bright steps. He wiped his forehead with a handkerchief and adjusted a leather pouch he clutched against his body. Daniel watched as the veteran descended the steps and prepared to jaywalk across the street.

Pulling a cap over his head and adjusting his sunglasses, Daniel swung into motion. The courier had never seen him, but he couldn't take any risks, especially here. As the man walked across, Daniel set out, trying to time his approach. He paused near the two men as they greeted each other, pretending to wait for traffic to clear before crossing the street himself. Daniel saw a manila envelope exchanged. He strained to catch any words of their conversation.

Daniel was surprised the exchange took place in the bright sunlight in plain view. But then again, couriers were used for everything at the police department, and that in and of itself avoided suspicion. Since the courier likely had no idea what the messages contained, it would be suspicious if the informant tried to engage the courier outside of normal routines anyway. *But what if this was a routine handoff after all? Maybe this cop was not the informant at all?*

No, Daniel told himself. This must be the informant. He knew his own name could very well be in that manila folder, ready to pass to Bagre. Daniel's mouth went dry.

The fat man prepared to cross the street again as the courier returned to his scooter. Daniel followed the policeman. He couldn't afford to lose him. He would have a hard time finding him again in such a vast building with so many entrances. He could only hope the courier would deliver on the usual night schedule.

*Can I hold all this together?*

The policeman eased his way up the front stairs of the station, and Daniel's mind clicked into action. Yes, it had to be him, Daniel convinced himself.

He took a deep breath. He would have to play this up to the hilt. He knew he was treading on thin ice, but he didn't care. In fact, no one else would care either – except, perhaps, this fat traitorous cop.

# CHAPTER 33 – Lunati

## *Lunati*

Daniel flashed his badge and followed his subject through lobby security and up the stairs to the third floor. He stayed on the opposite side of the corridor, paralleling the veteran cop and keeping the sea of cubicles between them. Daniel pretended to look at some papers and have business on the floor. His pulse seemed to leap out of his neck. He took a deep breath.

He'd been on this administrative floor only a few times before. It contained the back-office functions that greased the complicated gears of the vast federal police department. While the staff had ballooned since the military regime had declared war on the subversives, the physical office space had not. The floor was overcrowded, and every corner filled with boxes and papers. It was noisy, too, and this suited Daniel just fine for what he was about to do.

The man entered an office and closed the door.

Daniel picked his way through the orderly mess, glancing at the offices and cubicles he passed. A sign above the area read *Payroll and Benefits*. The nameplate of the office read *Lic. Ignacio Lunati Barrios*.

Without knocking, Daniel stepped into the office and closed the door behind him. A surprised Lunati looked up from behind his desk.

"Excuse you. May I help you?" Lunati demanded. His face was flushed from the exertion of climbing the stairs. Sweat trickled down his thick head of hair and collected in his bushy eyebrows.

"Yes, I do hope you can help me." Daniel eased himself into one of the chairs in front of the desk. "I have a problem," he continued. "In fact, it's your problem too. *¿Viste?* We might be able to help each other."

"Help *me*?

"That's what I said."

"With what? Who the hell are you?" Lunati yanked off his reading glasses and threw them onto his cluttered desk. "Get the hell out of my office! If you need something, make an appointment."

Daniel put his feet on the man's desk and folded his arms so his muscles bulged. The gun strapped to his leg made an unmistakable clunk on the wooden surface, and Daniel saw the first hint of doubt creep across Lunati's face. This human resources manager surely had dealt with many an angry policeman about some injustice to his paycheck, perhaps an overlooked promotion or an error in the employment status. Lots of things. He'd probably been confronted at times by unstable policemen with coping troubles. Work issues bleeding into domestic problems at home. Mental problems. Undoubtedly there were many of those lately.

Reaching inside his jacket pocket, Daniel placed his SIDE badge on the desk.

Lunati gave a start.

"You see, Lunati, we're conducting an investigation."

"An investigation?" said Lunati.

"More of a cleansing operation within the police department."

"A cleansing?"

"Dirty cops," said Daniel. "Informants. Traitors giving information to the subversives."

Lunati coughed and reached for his handkerchief.

"Well," said the policeman, regaining his bluster, "I don't see how that involves me." He rolled his eyes and pretended to return to the papers before him.

"I think we both know how this involves you."

"You, you," Lunati stammered, "maybe you think I have some information for you? I don't have anything."

"Look," continued Daniel, removing his feet from the desk. "I'm going to do you a favor. Do you have your sidearm?"

"No," said Lunati. An eye began to twitch. "I mean, yes. There's one locked in the cabinet. I've never used it."

"Get it out."

"Get it out?"

*"Get it out."*

Lunati opened a drawer and fumbled about for a key to unlock the cabinet. He pulled out a 9mm Browning and placed it gingerly on the desk in front of him.

"Is it loaded?"

"No. Of course not."

"Load it."

"They don't give me any bullets. I never have used this thing, not even in training. *Por favor*. You can understand."

"It's okay, Lunati. I'm going to give you one," said Daniel. He reached down his leg and drawing his own weapon. Lunati's eyes widened. "You're lucky I have one for you," said Daniel as he ejected the magazine and slid out one of the bullets. "As you can imagine, we use a lot of these at SIDE. We often run out."

Daniel reached across the desk and set the bullet carefully on its end in front of the HR manager. Lunati licked his lips and stared at it.

"You see, you're going to want to use this bullet. And you're going to want to use it sooner rather than later. I know you'll agree with me in a minute."

"Look, maybe I can get someone to help you," said Lunati. "If you wait just a minute…" He stood and made for the door, but Daniel reached over and shoved him back into his chair.

"You're making me nervous," stammered Lunati, his voice cracking. "I still don't know what exactly you want with me. I just work in payroll."

"You *should* be nervous because I know everything," said Daniel, and he slapped his hand hard on the desk, making the man jump. Lunati's wide eyes fixed on the bullet, which quivered but remained upright.

"I'll pay you, if that's what you want," said Lunati, his eyes wide. He licked his lips again and looked at Daniel, desperate for any sign of interest.

Daniel shook his head. "I don't want money," he said. "But you're right. There is something you can do for me. I want the list of names and photos you've collected for Bagre. Where is it?"

"The list?" asked Lunati, spacing each word as if they were not connected. "Bagre?"

Daniel picked up Lunati's 9mm laying on the desk and ejected the empty magazine. He plucked up the bullet and loaded it. Shoving the magazine back into place, he pulled back the slide to chamber the round. Lunati drew back in horror.

"Yes, yes," Lunati began, "It's just... I told him it would take a few weeks. Nasty person. He was very insistent."

"Where is it? I want that list of names."

"It's not, it's just that…"

"Get it out."

Lunati's hands shook, and he dropped the key. He

unlocked another drawer beside him and extracted a sheaf of handwritten pages from a manila envelope. Daniel recognized them immediately.

"Ah," said Daniel. "I see we have a mutual friend in common. The little man at SIDE. The funny-looking elf that sits in the front entrance and records everyone who comes in and out of the building. He does a good job, wouldn't you agree?"

Sweat poured from Lunati's forehead. He reached for a handkerchief and dabbed his brow.

"So you've been paying this little man to give you a copy of his ledger every week," continued Daniel. "Very smart, Lunati. Allows you to get a good idea who is undercover. Useful for comparing it to police payroll and personnel records, right? And you can access their files, look up their photos, where they live, the names of their wives and kids. I'll bet your terrorist friend at the university finds the information very useful."

Lunati squirmed in his chair and dabbed again at his brow.

Daniel leaned forward. "What else do you have in that drawer, Lunati?" he said, and he shoved the HR manager aside. Daniel pulled out some payroll printouts of officers whose last names started with the letter *R*.

"Are we good now?" stammered Lunati. "Would you please leave? It's all I have. I will think no more about this. I will cut off communications. I'm through. I'm about to retire, you know. Collect my pension. My wife and I are going to our pueblo in Entre Rios. Do you know La Paz? Right on the Río Paraná. A beautiful spot, walking on the cliffs. You have done me a big favor, you know that? You are right. This burden is off of –"

"*Cerrá el pico!*" Daniel said.

But Lunati couldn't shut up, and he couldn't help himself

anymore.

"If you would please tell me your name…"

"You know damned well who I am!" thundered Daniel. He stood and towered over the cowering man. "When did you send this information? When?"

"Today, this morning, just a little while ago. They made me do it."

Daniel stared at the man shaking in his chair.

"To the courier who was downstairs just a few minutes ago?"

"Yes."

"To Bagre?"

"Either Bagre or the young lady. I don't know her name. Please. The courier always leaves it with whomever he finds first."

Daniel flopped into his chair. He looked out the window. He thought of Eva. *Does she know already? Does Bagre know?* No, they don't. He would stop this. It was all going to work. He clasped his hands together to keep them from shaking. Lunati knew too much.

"Before I leave," Daniel said slowly, focusing his eyes back on Lunati. "There is something you haven't yet finished."

"What is that?" said Lunati in a tentative voice that struggled with accepting that the worst might not be over after all.

"You need to make a choice," said Daniel.

"A choice?"

"A choice between dying now or dying later," said Daniel, gesturing toward the Lunati's loaded gun still on the desk

"I think later might be best," said Lunati, his eyes wide as if surprised by the sight of the gun lying on the desk. He stood and backed away from it.

"Ah, I think you'll choose differently," said Daniel. "You see, I have done a bit of research myself. I know that it was you who created a police badge for the terrorist who entered the police cafeteria last winter. Twenty pounds of TNT. You were able to do that quite easily weren't you, right here in the payroll office? Your office badges officers all the time, doesn't it? Just think what the cops in this building will do when they find out you were responsible for this atrocity, for the twenty dead policemen that worked in this very building and all the wounded? You might not die right away but die you will. And they have ways of making death a most unpleasant experience. SIDE will make sure of it."

Lunati had been standing near the shelves, but now his knees buckled, and he stumbled back and collapsed into his chair.

"As I said, I'm going to leave," said Daniel. He slid the man's Browning to the center of the desk. "Think of your family, Lunati. You'll be stripped of your pension. How will they live? You'll be a shame to them. Your friends will learn what you've done. Do the manly thing, Lunati. Do it now. See how I'm doing you a favor?"

Daniel stood. "You have two minutes before I tell everyone in the entire department here what you've done."

He opened the door and stepped into the hallway. Closing the door behind him, he walked through the crowded office holding the manila folder in his hands.

A muffled shot rang out.

Daniel felt numb. He thought he would feel sorry for the man and perhaps have a sense of guilt, but there was nothing. By the time he reached the stairwell, he began feeling rather good about himself. With each step down toward the lobby, his confidence grew.

He could do anything he wanted.

# CHAPTER 34 – LA INTERCEPTACIÓN
## *The Interception*


Daniel blinked in the sunlight on the front steps of the police department. The bothersome courier was a loose end that needed to be tied up.

He walked around the corner of the building toward the rows of motorbikes parked behind the department. He tried to spin the lock combination to his scooter, but his hands shook so badly that he had to stop. He took a deep breath and tried again.

When Daniel arrived at the courier's apartment, the red scooter was not there. He gunned the small engine, weaving in and out of traffic. He slowed by the corner convenience store and other likely spots. The courier wasn't there either. Every red scooter and motorcycle caught his attention. Sweat stung his eyes and his shirt sleeve was wet from the constant wiping.

He returned to the courier's apartment. He had to urinate. The cigarette pack in his pocket was empty. *Maybe the courier already made the delivery of Lunati's file?* Daniel had only seen him make deliveries at night. But maybe Lunati had told him it was urgent and to make an off-schedule delivery. *What if Bagre and Eva already know?* Damn it. Too late to ask Lunati now.

At a café nearby, Daniel used the bathroom. He bummed a cigarette from a passerby and waited.

By 8 p.m., Daniel was exhausted. He had lingered there six

hours now, his ears straining at the sound of any scooter or motorcycle, his body tense. He sensed the neighbors watching him.

He knew if he went home, he wouldn't be able to sleep.

The red scooter appeared suddenly and parked. The courier bounded into the apartment. Daniel cursed his indecisiveness. He could have followed the courier into his apartment. Confronted him right there, found out what he needed to know and taken the package.

Instead, he waited.

It wasn't until almost 11 p.m. that the courier finally reappeared from the apartment, carrying his familiar rucksack. The streets were quiet, and Daniel kept his distance as he followed on his own scooter. Daniel was moving. He was doing something. Staying awake. More importantly, they were headed in the right direction toward the UBA.

Wanting to beat the courier, Daniel cut across the campus, risking the attentions of any security.

The scooter parked in the same place on the far side of the Facultad de Letras, and Daniel was there to meet him. He tried to slow his heavy breathing.

*"Hola."*

The courier looked up, surprised.

*"Tranquilo, che,* I didn't want to scare you," said Daniel. "Look, Bagre can't meet today. Something came up. He asked me to wait for you and take delivery of the package for him. He says it's important."

The young man hesitated.

*"Mirá,* I don't have time for this. *¿Viste?"* said Daniel. "Bagre told me you would be here an hour ago. You're late. I'm tired of waiting around. Do you have something for him or not?"

The courier shrugged and slipped off his rucksack. He

pulled out a manila envelope and handed it to Daniel.

Daniel waited a moment for the courier to head back before tearing open the pouch. There was his name, circled in red. *Daniel Romandini.* He squinted at Lunati's scrawled note beside his name. *I don't have a photo yet but will get one soon.*

Daniel glanced around, his heart pounding. He might be spotted by one of the cell group, maybe even Bagre or Eva. He hurried to another part of the campus where he applied his lighter to the edge of the paper. His trembling fingers fanned the flames until there was nothing left but ash.

Back at his apartment, Daniel stood under the shower and let the hot water pour over his head. When the butane tank ran out and the water turned cold, he finally got out and flopped into bed.


Daniel awoke late. A thick fog enveloped the city that morning. He heard the drone of a distant prop plane. Military, most likely. The Ezeiza International Airport would be closed on days like these, and inbound commercial flights diverted to Montevideo and Rosario.

The phone rang, and Daniel jumped. *Who could be calling?* He wondered if it was connected to last night.

No, no one had his number.

Sebastian had his number.

"Meet me in one hour," the aide's voice came through the earpiece.

When Daniel arrived, their usual bench was occupied. Sebastian sat at another bench, rubbing his hands. He brought no sunflower seeds this time.

"You've provided no updates for a week."

"I've been busy," said Daniel.

"Busy with what?" said Sebastian. "Sleeping until twelve p.m.?"

"I've been handling the mole problem," said Daniel. "The one you said not to worry about."

"You've wasted time," said Sebastian, "like I warned you. What's your progress on the judge?"

*Nothing*, Daniel wanted to say. Finding the mole had taken time and left him no closer to discovering the identity of Judge Calva's killers. He brought it up once to Eva when he heard of another judge in the crosshairs, but she had cut him off and told him it was none of his business, that his business was rooting out the mole in the cell group.

He knew Sebastian was getting pressure from the Admiral for results. Daniel would have to start delivering. Well, he wasn't going to give up Eva. She may have been the driver in the assassination, but he would never reveal this. SIDE was only interested in the assassin. She wouldn't need to be fingered at all. He would just have to play his cards right.

"Look," Daniel said, "I'm getting close. I need a few more weeks."

*"No es posible,"* said Sebastian. "We can't wait weeks."

"Then why don't we just move in now, blow things wide open," said Daniel. "Arrest everyone. Interrogate them. I can set it up." He was surprised he hadn't thought of this earlier. It would be so easy. He could warn Eva and get her safely out of the way.

But Sebastian shook his head.

"Your undercover operation is too valuable," the aide said. "Besides, we might not get the assassin and only drive him further underground. You have one week to get me something, Inglés. I'm setting up a meeting with the Admiral in one week. You better have something, and it better be good. It had better match up with the other corroborating information we have."

"Other corroborating information?" Daniel said. *What other info? What did they have?*

Sebastian waved an annoyed hand. "You worry about your task, Inglés. And hurry it the hell up. *Apurá.* You're lucky I've gotten the Admiral to give you one more week. You make sure you have something for him. "

# PART III

# CHAPTER 35 – EL PARQUE RECOLETA
## *Recoleta Park*

The summer squall from the evening before had left everything bright and clear in the morning. It was a lovely day, and the lawns below Recoleta Cemetery swelled with picnickers and strollers. The artisans' market was busy. The sweet scent of roasted candied peanuts filled the air. The familiar strains of a concertina drifted from the direction of the giant rubber tree just outside the cemetery gate.

The Gran Gomeros, the great *ficus elasticas* in Recoleta Park, were 220 years old. Their huge buttress roots and massive branches supported a majestic crown measuring fifty meters across. Iron posts braced the great weight of its sprawling boughs, and under its shade, tango dancers performed just outside the famous cemetery where Evita Perón was buried, the tourists entertained by the quick and the dead.

Old Ezequiel had suggested the spot, and Gastón found his mentor already set up with two wooden folding chairs, a thermos, and a bag of *mate* tea accoutrements. A green parrot perched in a cage next to the aged priest.

"How are you, Padre?" said Gastón. "No, please don't get up. See? I am coming to greet you right there in your chair. It's good to see you."

Gastón kissed Ezequiel's cheek and sat in the folding chair that the old priest tapped with his bony hand.

"What a beautiful parrot!" said Gastón. He reached to

scratch the bird's head but jerked back as the animal almost took a chunk of his finger.

"Be careful with Pancho," said Ezequiel. "He's a sinner."

Ezequiel reached into his bag and brought out a gourd and a paper envelope with the *mate* leaves. He packed the gourd with the dried tea leaves, his wrinkled and experienced hands arranging them artfully, almost to the lip of the hollow cup.

"So tell me, how are you, *querido?"* said Ezequiel.

Gastón wavered. *Should I tell him I'm worried my roommate is mixing politics with theology? That Brizzio is in danger with the government and the Church?*

"To tell you the truth, I'm finding the work with the Jesuits difficult and sometimes confusing," said Gastón. "Our Savior seems at times so powerless and irrelevant. Things are happening, and the Church is acting in His name, yet He seems to be absent. Forgive me."

Gastón rubbed his temples. "I have doubts and fears. I feel so inadequate." *Should I tell him I'm scared of standing with Brizzio on the side of the poor?*

The old cebador picked up the thermos and slowly poured the hot water into the gourd. "Did you know," Ezequiel began, "when the Jesuits began their missions among the Guaraní, they worried about the addictive properties of the *yerba mate* plant. They tried to stamp out the practice, but they failed." He rummaged through his bag again and produced a tarnished silver bombilla, which he inserted into the gourd before handing it to Gastón. "In fact, the Jesuits began cultivating *mate* on their missions, and today our nation is one of the largest tea producers in the world. Imagine that!"

Gastón drained the gourd and handed it back to Ezequiel. The old man filled it back up with hot water and leaned against his creaking chair to drink.

"You see, *mi hijo*, the history of the Church is a story of mistakes and errors, of doubts and corrections. The church is run by humans, and we are prone to such things. Look at Jesus's early followers – all uneducated and fearful men. The incredible thing is that God chooses to work through flawed individuals to bring people hope for a world free from sin and suffering."

"But why can't God reveal his direction more clearly?" said Gastón.

Ezequiel sipped the gourd. He looked out across the lawn at the children playing happily and shouting, and up toward the cemetery wall. "You know, children often have no idea what their parents are up to, and often the children conclude they are unreasonable and unkind. The Lord's wisdom is not the world's wisdom. How He chooses to act and reveal himself is hard for us to understand."

They enjoyed the afternoon and drank their *mate*. Gastón felt better just being with him. He had a lot to think about. He was glad, too, that he hadn't asked his direct questions. To be honest, he didn't know anything for sure yet. He would feel silly if it all turned out to be nothing. No, he would find out more on his own first.

A car honked.

"Ah, there is my niece. I admire your honesty, Gastón. God loves doubters and skeptics. He wants us to wrestle with our faith because it leads to real belief."

Gastón helped the old priest to his feet and helped him fold the wooden chairs.

"You see," said Ezequiel, "God is not distant, and He cannot be ignored. And when He is silent, He is not absent."

It seemed to Gastón a bad time for God to be silent, and he wished he could feel God's presence more. He needed clarity.

Maybe it would help to speak directly with Brizzio.

# CHAPTER 36 – LA CONEXIÓN

## *The Connection*

At an outside café a few blocks from the church, Gastón sat across from his roommate. He was glad Brizzio had accepted his invitation, but now he wondered if he was doing the right thing. *How would Brizzio react?*

The waiter took their order of ham and cheese empanadas and coffee. "It's my treat," said Gastón to his roommate.

"What is it you want to talk about?" Brizzio rubbed his hands together. Gastón knew he would get right to the point.

"I guess I'm just worried." Gastón rearranged the salt shaker on the small table.

His roommate raised his eyebrows.

"About you, Brizzio, to tell the truth," said Gastón. "I watch the people at Friday mass. They hang on every word you say. It's a true gift, this magnetism you have. I wish I could speak like you."

The waiter brought the coffees and empanadas.

Gastón paused for the waiter to leave. He lowered his voice. "Please don't take this the wrong way, but what you say is dangerous."

"So that's it," said Brizzio, smiling.

Gastón leaned forward. "You're encouraging the people toward violence. You're playing into the hands of the leftists. They would like nothing more than for the people to believe that God is on the side of Marxists."

Brizzio stirred sugar into his coffee and let out a long

breath. He seemed unconcerned.

"You're drawing attention to yourself," said Gastón, flustered and hoping to convey the seriousness he felt. "I'm sure we're being watched."

The words just fell out, and Gastón wondered if he sounded afraid. And in that moment, he came to the sinking realization that he *was* afraid, and a terrible feeling washed over him that his whole motivation for this conversation was not out of love and concern for Brizzio but because he was scared for himself, scared of getting mixed up in something and getting hurt.

"My brother," said Brizzio, selecting an empanada from the plate, "you're mixing issues. There are two here – a theological one and a political one. My biggest concern is the first. I don't care about the second, and I don't care about it because I can't be faithful to my priestly calling without some measure of personal danger."

Brizzio took a bite of empanada and tugged a thin paper napkin from the holder.

"Help me understand," Gastón said, "because I...."

Brizzio raised a finger as he finished swallowing so he could continue. "The theological question here is what we as Christians should do on this earth when confronted with evil. Bear our sufferings meekly? No, we have a duty to resist evil. To be a light in whatever dark corner of the world the Good Lord has placed us. For us, it's right here, right now, Gastón. I must speak for those who can't speak for themselves."

Brizzio's eyes burned brightly and his face glowed. It was the same look Gastón saw on his face during mass.

Gastón reached across the table and took Brizzio's hands in his, praying that God would guide the motivations of his heart. "Yes," Gastón said, "we must resist evil but not encourage violence. Violence was not the way of our Lord.

He said love your enemies and pray for those who persecute you. Do Jesus's words mean nothing? Let's not forget the real predicament of man is his soul. It's a change of the heart that's needed, not a sword."

"And how can a change of heart occur," cried Brizzio, "when one's physical needs are so great? No, we must fight the structures that oppress the poor. It's the only way I know how to fulfill Jesus's command to feed the hungry and clothe the naked."

"But, Brizzio, it will lead to trouble for you," said Gastón with a sideways glance, "trouble with the government and even with the Church."

"It doesn't matter," said Brizzio, pulling away his hands away, "I don't want to be caught on the wrong side of history again."

"What do you mean?"

"I mean," said Brizzio, lowering his voice, "I mean that the Church here...the Nazis, Gastón. There was something rotten in the Church back then, and there's something rotten in it today."

"You want to talk about rotten, do you?" said Gastón, his voice strained as he tried to whisper. "What about the terrorists? They're violent killers. Militant atheists. How can you possibly support such a cause? Communism has only ever led to oppression."

Brizzio sighed. "Let me ask you, Gastón. Did Rector Alejandro tell you the story of the Church shutting down the Jesuit missions and expelling them from the Americas? Well, it wasn't because the Jesuits were getting too powerful. No. It was because the Church was in cahoots with the Spanish kings to protect the valuable slave trading by Spain and Portugal. The Jesuits were protecting the Guaraní Indians from them. The Church is not always right, my dear Gastón.

Don't forget that."

Brizzio glanced at his watch. "I have to go. I appreciate your concern, I really do."

"Be careful, please," said Gastón.

"It's too late for that, I'm afraid," said Brizzio, and it seemed to Gastón that his roommate's burning eyes went dark.

Brizzio stood and fished for some coins, but Gastón stayed his hand. Brizzio grunted and picked his way through the tables and chairs.

Gastón watched until his roommate was out of sight among the crowd and traffic. He thought of the books he had found hidden under his roommate's mattress. Camilo Torres, Gustavo Gutiérrez, Hélder Câmara. Controversial Marxist clerics.

"Father, forgive him," he prayed silently.

He was convinced more than ever his roommate had secrets.

Gastón decided to find out that very night.

*Father, forgive me.*


It was past 10 p.m. when Gastón observed Brizzio crossing the dormitory hall toward the stairs. He saw just how easy it was for his roommate to slip away when all the other priests were lounging in their rooms and winding up their day.

At the end of the hall, Gastón glanced over his shoulder before bounding down the stairs. In the courtyard, he opened the side door and saw Brizzio at the end of the block, crossing the street.

Gastón followed him down to the *subte* station. He boarded the subway car next to Brizzio's. After changing lines, his roommate exited at the Córdoba station, and Gastón followed for three blocks and onto the UBA campus. At one of the buildings, Brizzio suddenly stopped and turned around, scanning the plaza.

Gastón froze.

Brizzio opened a side door and entered. Gastón jogged to the door but hesitated, his hand on the handle. *What if I run into him?*

He walked back toward the front of the building as a group of students suddenly burst through the main doors, talking and laughing as they descended the steps.

Gastón panicked. He felt the stares. His neck felt hot. He realized he was still wearing his priest collar, the white tab obvious. He was afraid. He quickened his pace back the way he came. This was no place for a priest and certainly, Gastón thought bitterly, no place for a young man with such insecurities.


In the shadow of a tree, Daniel wondered what a priest was doing on the campus. He had also seen the first man this priest had been following. It was hard for Daniel to tell much in the darkness, but there was something strangely familiar in the first man's features. Daniel couldn't place it.

Keeping his distance and his head down, Daniel followed the priest to the *subte* station and boarded the same car to get a better look at him in the light. After he tracked the man to the Jesuit apartments, Daniel stood on the street trying to piece it all together. It didn't make sense. He couldn't see a connection.

He spent the night at a cheap hotel across the street from the small Jesuit compound, insisting on a room that overlooked the walls into the courtyard.

The next day was Friday. At midmorning, Daniel followed

the priest as he ran errands, learning the nervous and gangly cleric's name was Father Gastón.

That evening, he followed Father Gastón to evening mass where he listened to a priest – a Father Brizzio – and his impassioned words. "Take heart in the Apostle Paul's words. Put on the full armor of God, take up the sword of the Spirit. For our struggle is against the rulers, against the authorities, against the powers of this dark world."

Daniel watched the pulsating throng fall under the trance of this Nazarite with his long black hair and beard, and his pale face.

*Yes, that face, a familiar face.*

And suddenly everything clicked together.

# CHAPTER 37 – LA CONFESIÓN

## *The Confession*

"Welcome, my child. May the Lord bless you and keep you."

Through the screen partition, Daniel saw Father Gastón make the sign of the cross.

"May the Lord make his face to shine upon you and be gracious to you," the priest continued. "May the Lord lift up his countenance upon you and give you peace."

The confessional booth was musty and rank, the old wood fouled by the innumerable sins exposed in the aged cabinet.

"Bless me, Father, for I have sinned," said Daniel. "My last confession was four years ago."

The thick walls of the church dulled the sound of the city outside.

"I confess lying," he continued. "My whole life is a lie. The more I lie, the easier it gets." It felt strangely satisfying to say it. It wasn't why he came, but here, in the anonymity of this place, it felt good to be honest and truthful.

"I confess much anger," said Daniel, warming to his sins. "I've caused much pain and suffering to others."

"Are these mortal sins?"

"I've brought on death, Father, so I think yes."

The seat squeaked on the other side of the screen.

"The Lord God will not be mocked, my son. Mortal sin is a horrible offense against God. It can destroy the life of grace in the soul."

Daniel could see Father Gastón trying to see him through

242

the screen. Daniel kept his face in the shadow.

"Did you know what you were doing, my child? Did you know this would cause pain and suffering, even…death?"

"Yes."

"Did you do it of your own free will? Not coerced in some manner? Not under any extreme physical or emotional pressure?"

The question made Daniel think. *Hadn't he chosen this path?*

"Are you truly sorry for these sins and all of your sins?" said Father Gastón.

"I'm going to hell, Father." There was no bravado and no bitterness in Daniel's voice. He remembered when his mother died. He was ten years old. He had told the priest he wouldn't serve as an altar boy anymore.

"That is only for our Holy Father to decide," said Father Gastón. "He alone knows the condition of your heart. He extends his love and forgiveness to the undeserving."

"You don't know what I have done, Father."

"Do not think too highly of your sin, my son. No sin is too great for Christ's blood."

"You don't know who I am," said Daniel. The words hung in the air, unable to escape the constricted wood booth. The musty smell was stronger now.

"You must be truly sorry, and you must resolve to amend your life," said the priest. "If you do not desire to stop sinning, then you are not truly sorrowful, and I cannot offer you absolution."

"I did not come here to seek forgiveness," said Daniel. "I know it's impossible. I've betrayed everyone I know. I've betrayed myself."

He reached his hand to feel the smooth varnished panel, his fingers lingering on the dimpled imperfections and the peeling paint. He thought of his father and Cacho. Of Fede. He thought of Eva, smiling at him in the car on the way to Boca and when she reached up and kissed him on the lips.

"Christ calls us to Him as we are, not as we ought to be," said the priest. "God has saved us not because of the good things we have done but because of his mercy."

A parishioner shuffled past.

"Do I know you?" asked the priest. "Are you from this parish? Perhaps you would let me or the padres speak with you. To guide you."

"I have heard Father Brizzio speak at mass," said Daniel, focusing. "He's a gifted speaker. Do you also believe, Father Gastón, that violence is justified?"

The priest coughed.

"I know his sister," continued Daniel. "She's a student. Father Brizzio visits her at the university. But you know that already, don't you, Father Gastón?"

The seat across the screen squeaked, and Daniel saw the priest again trying to peer at him through the latticework.

"Whether violence is justified or not makes no difference," said Daniel. "It's out there, beyond these walls, Father, where God can't protect you."

"This is not a conversation to be had in this holy place," said Gastón. "May we speak privately? May I ask, what is your name?"

It was time for Daniel to leave. He bolted from the booth. The cool stone floor absorbed his hurried steps. He pushed open the heavy wooden door and returned to the loud traffic and the suffocating weight of his unabsolved sins.

# CHAPTER 38 – TIGRE

## *Tigre*

It was a rare day off for both Daniel and Cacho. Unsure of what to do, they sat around the apartment for most of the day until Daniel suggested a visit to Tigre. They took the train to the last stop and found a sidewalk table by the river's edge. The morning was dull and gray, but the cloud cover burned off and it turned out to be a pleasant afternoon on the delta.

Children played under the proud gaze of their parents. Lovers lounged in the treelined parks. Beyond the grassy lawns, motorboats trolled the lazy Río Luján. Daniel thought of the happy times he had come here as a child, and it seemed to him now a world lost forever by the hardening of innocence into a crystallization of discontent.

"Do you think we're doing right?" Daniel said as he sat with Cacho at the café.

*"¿Que decís?"* Cacho said. "What did you say?"

"I'm just wondering if we're doing good," Daniel repeated.

Cacho looked at his roommate and took a last drag of his cigarette. He flicked the butt beyond the sidewalk tables and onto the street. The smoke curled out from his nostrils.

"I can tell you one thing," Cacho said, tapping his side holster. "I can do a lot of good with this gun."

Cacho lit another cigarette. "Maybe, Inglés, when enough men have been killed, perhaps then we'll know if we've done good."

Across from the restaurant a father kicked a ball with his

son. The wife sat on a bench nearby, a cooing baby on her lap. Near the agents, a young couple sat at a table holding hands and in close conversation.

"That mole in the department," Daniel said, "the one I told you about. He's dead. Shot himself after I found him."

"No shit!" said Cacho. "I see. You're feeling bad about the bastard, no? Let me ask you. Did he deserve it?"

"Yeah," said Daniel. He tapped his empty beer glass at the waiter. "He deserved it."

"There you have it, *¿viste?* Your problem is that you think too much," said Cacho. "Who do you think these *subversivos* are? Don't forget they're trying to kill us."

The waiter brought more beers, and Daniel took a big swig. He leaned back and let the alcohol buzz detatch him from his worries and permit their consideration from afar.

"We spend so much time fighting against something," Daniel said, "maybe we don't know what we're fighting *for.*"

"Look at all this," said Cacho, sweeping his arm about the park. "And this too," he continued, pointing at the amorous couple, who noticed the attention. "This is what we're fighting for." Cacho twisted himself in his chair so that he faced the staring couple.

"What we do every day, it's to let this couple come here and kiss and hold hands, and to let this *pibe* take his *zorra* back to his crappy apartment and..."

*"Pará, imbécil,"* said Daniel.

Cacho winked at the couple and turned back around. The young man behind him stood, red-faced, but the woman pulled on his arm and they left.

"I was born to do this," said Cacho. "And you were too. You're good at it. My father was a cop. Your uncle too, no? This is what we've always wanted."

"My father once told me," said Daniel, "that my uncle was

a great cop but a lousy man. My cousins didn't even show up to his funeral. Neither did his two ex-wives. His life was one big mess. A violent drunk. Maybe *he* was the problem. Maybe *we* are the problem."

He paused and shook his beer at Daniel. "I know I'm a little drunk right now. *Pero escuchá.* Listen. We're in a war, Inglés. We're not the problem. We're the solution. The foreign minister, Picozzi, he said it the other day, *¿viste?* I've kept a copy of the article."

Cacho checked the pockets of his jacket and extracted a page from *La Nación.* He smoothed it on the flimsy table. "This is what our foreign minister said at the United Nations last week." He tapped the newsprint with his finger and read. "When the social body of the country has been contaminated by a disease that eats away at its entrails, it forms antibodies. These antibodies cannot be considered in the same way as the microbes."

Cacho refolded the paper. "You see, you're not the only doctor here. I'm one too." He flashed his police badge inside his jacket. "Says so right here. And besides," he continued, grinning and laying his Browning on the table, "I fight diseases with this. What do we care?"

*"Sos loco,"* said Daniel, grinning now too. "You're crazy."

"And you think too much, Inglés. You're better when you don't think."

They smoked a while longer. They ate empanadas.

Daniel closed his eyes, his stomach comfortably full. Cacho was right. Maybe he *did* think too much. They spent so much time fighting evil that it was easy to lose sight of good.

The wind picked up, and the loose napkins blew off their table and fluttered against the tangle of chair and table legs on the sidewalk. White caps formed out on the water.

By the time they left the café, the boats were all gone.

# CHAPTER 39 – EL ALVEAR PALACE HOTEL
## *The Alvear Palace Hotel*

President Villalobos's Christmas ball was extravagant and the security tight. Against the wishes of the Admiral and his advisors, it was held at the Alvear Palace Hotel. In the end, they contented themselves with having dissuaded Villalobos from hosting the party at the Casa Rosada, which would have drawn unwanted attention to his dubious claims on the nation's presidential palace.

"Spare no expense!" the Admiral recalled Villalobos commanding his advisors in a moment of uncharacteristic giddiness. And no one could put on a bacchanalia like the Alvear.

Located just three blocks from Recoleta Cemetery, the Alvear Palace was the most luxurious hotel in all of Argentina, perhaps even in South America. Inaugurated in 1932, the Belle Époque hotel was graced by Louis XVI style furniture and giant crystal chandeliers. Gold leaf and famous works of art decorated its walls. It had seen pass through its Italian Botticino-marbled columns the rich and famous, the flauntings and the secret trysts, and Evita Perón in a dazzling Dior gown.

Admiral Bertotti arrived at the ball in his starched dress whites, conscious that the stares were not for him, but for his wife María Soledad. He stole a sideways glance. She did look rather stunning in that full-length green gown, he admitted. The effect would wear thin as soon as she opened her mouth.

He snorted and searched for the welcome champagne.

Through the bottom of his glass, the Admiral's eye took in the gilded ceiling. Yes, he thought, Villalobos certainly had settled on a fine choice in the Alvear. And why not? Things were looking up for the president and the regime. The people clamored for him. When he came to power, the country was on the brink of civil war and the economy in shambles. Hyperinflation now was mostly tamed. Wage earners no longer rushed to cash their paychecks to stay ahead of the grocer repricing the shelves behind them.

There were indications, too, that the police and military were getting the upper hand on the subversives. Assassinations of policemen were down for the first time last month. Kidnappings too. Pride coursed through the Admiral's veins and mixed with the alcohol hurrying to his brain. His SIDE agents were doing their part. Fighting terror with terror was working. Arrests and torture were proving brilliant tools of economic stimulus.

Wasn't the president now an important world figure in the fight against the communist threat? Hadn't he taken his place alongside Pinochet, Stroessner, and others? Hadn't he the support of the United States? Secretary of State Kissinger had given foreign minister Picozzi the green light to move aggressively against the leftist threat. Not since the 1930s had Argentina enjoyed such attentions from the world. These were heady times for a man with such reckless disregard for the dangers and pathologies of an authoritarian regime. The Admiral frowned. *I should be closer to the president.*

Admiral Bertotti watched the arrivals. As head of intelligence, he had the final say in the carefully culled guest list for the great Christmas ball. Invitations had been sent to the preeminent families and the pillars of society, to wealthy businessmen and the industrialists. With few exceptions, the literary and arts luminaries were conspicuously absent.

But the military elite were all present, striking in their olive dress uniforms and resplendent in their collections of medals, wives, and mistresses.

Cardinal Archbishop José Carlos Aburuzaga was invited too, and lacking a wife stunning or otherwise, had settled for the joyless secretary Ignacio. They arrived at the carriage entrance in his gleaming black Mercedes-Benz, a short ten-minute chauffeured drive from his palatial archbishopric.

"Pompous ass," the Admiral muttered as the pontiff was announced. He knew that despite the Cardinal's stern demeanor, the pontiff loved parties. The Cardinal could count on being a person of note, greeting the powerful and the connected, people whom he might almost consider peers. The Admiral knew the Cardinal was proud of the swish of his gorgeous red robes and the attentions they drew, and of the heavy gold chain and diamond-encrusted cross that was his burden to bear on behalf of the people. His glinting signet ring given to him by the pope himself. These were the vestments befitting such a highly decorated soldier of Christ. No, the Cardinal would not be outdone by the military officers with their gold braids and their multicolored ribbons and their quivering medals. Mere men who operated in the temporal while he served in the sphere of the eternal.

It was indeed the season to remember the Christ Child, and the Cardinal would see to it that none would forget how far his holy institution had progressed from its origin in the lowly manger.

Last to arrive at the Christmas ball was President Villalobos himself. The Admiral watched him come in wearing his dour expression, his Hitleresque mustache, and the presidential albiceleste sash. He had on a dark green military uniform with three gold stars on the epaulets, and marking this special occasion, he had replaced the usual olive-green tie with a black one. As they entered the ballroom, Villalobos and his wife clasped their hands and acknowledged the cheers and applause.

The president had but one formal task that evening and not an unpleasant one at that. A short speech to be delivered, thanking everyone for their continued support as the country moved ahead toward a bright future. El Proceso was working. *Feliz Navidad* to all.

There were a few unpleasant tasks to be done that evening, but these had been left to underlings. One of these underlings, of course, was the Admiral himself. Bertotti sniffed airily and continued greeting friends and acquaintances, his wife María Soledad smiling at his side.

"Sole," said the Admiral, grabbing his wife's arm, "meet my good friend and colleague Capitán Oscar Maldonado and his wife. Alicia, isn't it? Yes, that's it!"

Soledad stepped forward and kissed the cheek of the captain, who seemed shocked not so much by the presence of such a lovely creature, but that Admiral Bertotti would call him a good friend. How could the Admiral possibly have remembered his wife's name? The captain's eyes widened at his brightening career trajectory. He must be thinking what a superb party this is, thought the Admiral.

*The poor bastard. I wonder if he knows I'm fucking his wife.*

Soledad and Alicia embraced.

*"Encantada."*

*"Un gusto."*

*"Un verdadero placer."*

Soledad paused. She must have sensed something, thought the Admiral. A flash of familiarity. She had smelled that perfume before.

*"Disculpá,"* Soledad stammered. "Excuse me."

The Admiral smiled wanly at the couple. "It must be the champagne," he said. He tried to help Soledad find a place to sit down, but she pushed his hand away.

The Admiral went to find the Cardinal, whom he found flanked by several congressmen.

*"Su Eminencia,"* he greeted with a bow.

"Admiral," said the Cardinal, uninterested.

"May we speak privately for a few minutes?" said Bertotti. *"Con su permiso,"* he said with a nod to the politicians.

The Admiral led the Cardinal through a marbled hallway and into a wood-paneled library. The Cardinal settled into an overstuffed leather chair and fussily arranged his skirts.

"Don't ever get old," he advised the Admiral. "Everything hurts, and what doesn't hurt doesn't work."

"I'll be sure to avoid it," said Bertotti. "I have a joke of my own to share with you if you permit me, Your Eminence."

The Admiral sat in a chair opposite the Cardinal and leaned back, placing both elbows on the armrests and folding his hands together under his chin. The Cardinal looked annoyed.

"It's quite funny, I just heard it the other day," said the Admiral, smiling, and with that he began.

> *One day in a country church, during*
> *the middle of mass, Satan himself*
> *suddenly burst through the doors. The*
> *parishioners instantly were in an*
> *uproar. The Devil was in the church!*
> *Everyone screamed and ran for the*
> *exits, pushing and trampling each other*
> *to get out.*
> *Everyone, that is, except one old man.*
> *He sat just quietly in his church pew,*
> *hands in his lap, looking forward.*

*Satan smiled to himself, quite content at*
*the commotion he had caused until he*
*spotted the old man sitting unperturbed*
*in his seat. Approaching the old*
*parishioner, the Devil thundered at*
*him, "Don't you know who I am?"*
*"Yep," said the old man, staring straight ahead.*
*"I sure do."*
*"Well, aren't you scared of me?" demanded the*
*exasperated Devil.*
*"Nope, I sure ain't," said the old man.*
*With true wonder now, Satan asked,*
*"And why aren't you scared of me?"*
*"Well," replied the old man, "because*
*I've been married to your sister for*
*forty-eight years!"*

The Admiral finished and chuckled at his own joke, but while the Admiral's heart was gladdened, it was obvious the pontiff's was hardened. He glared at Bertotti, his steely eyes magnified through his horn-rimmed glasses.

*"Su Eminencia,"* said the Admiral, "I understand your inability to find amusement at my story. Undoubtedly it is sacrilegious on the one hand. On the other hand, you, as a man of the cloth, cannot possibly understand the sufferings accompanying the institution of marriage. I rather envy you on that score."

The Cardinal frowned.

The Admiral continued. "I'm not an old man, Cardinal, yet I've seen much. Little surprises me now. I remain calm when others cannot. But you have a serious problem that is stirring the waters."

The Admiral paused to ensure he had the pontiff's

undivided, if petulant, attention.

"It has not gone away despite your assurances," Bertotti continued. "The devil still roams freely within your parish churches. The people are confused and scared. They need guidance. Listen to me very carefully, my dear Cardinal. If you cannot control these radical priests, these priests stirring up the people and spreading subversive sympathies. If you can't control them, then the government will not be able to protect them."

Cardinal Aburuzaga sucked his teeth with a loud smacking sound. The Admiral knew the pontiff was not used to being lectured or threatened, especially by someone he considered an impudent attack dog of President Villalobos. The Cardinal, red-faced, stood and towered over the Admiral, glaring at this inferior being.

The Admiral smiled.

"Look, Juan Pablo," hissed the Cardinal, all formalities now cast aside. "We are doing everything we can, but we have many priests. Many of them are young and inexperienced, easily influenced by outside forces. I should mention that you, too, have a problem within. Do you think I'm not fully aware of the abuses your government commits against innocent people? I hear the stories every day. And it's not just aberrant cops. Your problem is systemic. It's you people, the military, the government. You are the ones that are stirring up the people and agitating our priests. You are fueling this fire."

The Cardinal wasn't done. He shook a bony finger at the Admiral. "And you tell Villalobos that if he has something to say to me, next time he should tell me himself!"

With that, the Cardinal stormed toward the double doors, but with his hand on the handle, he stopped and turned. "Yes, let's do this," he said, more to himself than to the Admiral.

"It's the one thing that will put an end to this. Yes. Let some of these errant priests serve as an example to others. Perhaps, for once, Juan Pablo, your violent hammer could be put to good use and help straighten the ways of the crooked."

The Cardinal swished down the hallway as the Admiral absorbed these parting words, understanding the implications and appreciating them. A smile broke across the Admiral's face. The Cardinal was a team player after all.

The Admiral got up from his seat and closed the large doors to the library with a satisfying click. He turned around and sighed contentedly at the walls of books resting on their Honduran mahogany shelves.

Books were so much more enjoyable than people.

# CHAPTER 40 – EL RUBICÓN
## *The Rubicon*

Dressed in a black cassock and cape, Rector Alejandro boarded a bus for the twenty-minute ride to downtown. He took a window seat and fingered the red wax seal of the Cardinal's summons. The drizzling rain slid down the glass in long streaks. The wind shifted and the rain fell harder, and the rector listened to the drumming on the bus roof.

He felt uneasy. Two years ago, he had received a similar letter, but he had expected it. He had been honored for his innovative peer mentoring program which had improved the performance and retention of young priests.

By the time Alejandro got off on Corrientes, the rain had stopped, and the sun peeked from between the dissipating clouds. It was a short walk to the walled residence of the Archbishopric of Buenos Aires. The heavy brass knocker thudded dully.

He was ushered through the courtyard and into the marbled entry hall where he surrendered his cape. At his last visit, he had been received in the expansive offices at the end of the hall, but now he was led to the Cardinal's private rooms upstairs. He picked at the edges of his robe.

Opening a door, the butler motioned Alejandro into an octagonal sitting room. Green velvet couches and chairs lay atop an exquisite gold Persian rug covering the polished wood floor. Floor-to-ceiling bookcases occupied the entirety of the walls. Two tall curtained windows were on one end.

Alejandro stood and waited, his hands folded behind his back.

It was fifteen minutes before Cardinal Aburuzaga swished into the sitting room, his reading glasses perched high on his forehead.

*"Buen día,* Alejandro. Bothersome bright sun in this room, no? Please, sit. *Café?"* The Cardinal said all this in a single, monotone ejaculation. He extended a hand to Alejandro who held it and kissed the signet ring.

*"Muchas gracias, Su Eminencia."*

The Cardinal motioned for Alejandro to take a seat on the couch while he settled himself on an opposite chair.

A uniformed waiter poured coffee. Aburuzaga waved an irritated hand, and the server shuffled backwards and closed the doors behind him.

"My predecessor, Archbishop Antonio Califano, was a Nazi sympathizer," said the Cardinal. "At the close of the war, he facilitated the safe passage to this country of a number of senior Nazi officials. The question is, why did he do this?"

*The Cardinal is confiding in me.* But rather than feeling encouraged, Alejandro sensed a hidden danger lurking between the pontiff's words. He folded his arms across his chest.

The Cardinal sipped his coffee. "Califano hated the Jews because they killed our Lord Jesus Christ, and he also despised the godless Soviets and their oppressive Communist system. By then, being short on hate, perhaps he had nothing to offer the Nazis but sympathy. Those were complicated times, wouldn't you say, Rector? Perhaps not unlike today?"

*"Sí, Su Eminencia,"* said Alejandro, "I feel the pressures every day."

"Pressures?" the Cardinal said, his upper lip curling ever so slightly. "You don't know pressure. You see, Alejandro, those of us in senior church leadership, we are not permitted the joys of a simple life. Our authority does not allow us to be meek, and the scope of our responsibilities makes it impractical to be pure in heart. These are blessings given to you and to the faithful, but not to us."

The Cardinal fingered the gold cross dangling from his neck and gazed out the windows at the manicured gardens below. "I wish sometimes I could return to that, when the fruits of the spirit were sufficient nourishment for the body and soul."

He rang a bell impatiently. The waiter emerged with more coffee.

"You should be thankful for where you are," said the Cardinal. "The position in which I have been placed in service of our Holy Father, things are not black and white, but treacherous shades of gray."

The pontiff crossed his legs and smoothed an invisible crease in his cassock.

"Over the centuries, the Church has built influence all over the world. It takes leadership to maintain our influence. We need future leaders who can take up this banner. This burden. To make difficult decisions in the interests of the Church."

The Cardinal leaned forward and cocked his head. "Are you prepared, Rector, to make such decisions? To make *sacrifices* for the sake of the Church?"

*What sacrifices?* Alejandro heard but didn't understand. *"No entiendo, Su Eminencia,"* he said, and his eyes drifted to a painting on the wall above the pontiff's head, Caravaggio's *The Sacrifice of Isaac.*

The Cardinal drained his coffee and leaned back in his chair, steepling his hands. "Do you know why I've called you here?"

"No, Your Eminence."

"Alejandro, you have much potential," said the Cardinal.

"You are talked about in circles where it counts. But this potential could vanish very quickly." The Cardinal snapped his fingers and waved them through the air as if chasing a vapor.

"In the careers of those whose lives really matter," he continued grandly, "there appear a few critical career moments where important choices are made. A decisional crossroad if you will. You, my dear Rector, are at such a crossroad now. *Tenés una oportunidad.*"

Alejandro's mind whirled trying to see where the archbishop was going with all this. He felt anger at the Cardinal's quibbling words and a fear of comprehending what he was truly saying. Then he knew. *This is about Brizzio.* Alejandro sucked in his breath. He was conscious of the Cardinal watching him closely.

"I need not remind you," said the Cardinal, "of the dangers of the Marxist tendencies within liberation theology. Frankly, I worry you are ignoring – perhaps even encouraging – this heresy within your parishes."

"Your Eminence, I never..." protested Alejandro, but the Cardinal was transformed by a sudden flash of fury, and he snatched his glasses from his forehead and shook them at Alejandro.

"This could end your career, young Rector."

In a sudden frightful instant, everything fell into place for Alejandro. A chill ran up his spine as he grasped the awful sacrifice he was being asked to make. And yet, in the same moment, he was more horrified by knowing he would not hesitate to make it if it would save his career.

The Cardinal seemed to sense all this too, and his eyes narrowed with a glint of triumph. Alejandro sank into the velvet couch.

"Your Eminence," Alejandro began, trying to find a way to

rationalize the predetermined outcome and assuage his prickling conscience. "It is true our Jesuit parishes are in the poor neighborhoods and slums of the city where socialism offers an attractive alternative to a system they believe has failed them. And it's true, Your Eminence, our priests lend a sympathetic ear to the poor, especially when they see no improvement in their lot, and when they experience..." Alejandro paused to choose his words with care, "...heavy-handed government interventions in their neighborhoods."

"The only interventions," snapped the Cardinal, "are directed toward those involved in subversive activities. And some of your priests are doing much worse than lending a sympathetic ear to the poor. We both know this."

"Your Eminence, I do not support it. I've warned them many times. Christian ideals do not support armed revolution, particularly when inspired by tyranny and atheism, which are the very definition of Communism."

The Cardinal raised his eyebrows and chewed on one end of the glasses dangling in his hand. "Well said, Rector. Very well said."

The Cardinal smiled and leaned back in his chair once again. "I knew I could count on you. We must stamp this out. Make a few examples. You have several priests I wish to discuss." He looked at Alejandro and smoothed his slicked-back hair with a hand. "I'm sure you know of whom I speak."

Alejandro did indeed know. It was the right thing to do, he told himself. Yes. He would show he was capable of making difficult decisions to protect the Church and preserve doctrinal purity. After all, who was he to question the Archbishop Cardinal?

And in that bright room with the billowing, sun-blazed white curtains, facts were transfigured into conjectures. Dark rumors were spread and fates sealed, futures were secured and others jeopardized.

# CHAPTER 41 – LA EXPOSICIÓN

## *The Exposure*

"I have two surprises for you tonight, Gorila," Bagre whispered to Daniel when they loaded into the cars.

It was 2 a.m. and a warm breeze blew west, picking up moisture as it traveled over the wide river so the whole city smelled like wet, rotten leaves. The fake operation had been Daniel's idea, but the cell group leader was hijacking it.

"The first surprise," Bagre continued, "is this won't be another *operación falso* to uncover our mole. We're going to kidnap this businessman. We need the attention and the ransom money. Besides, you're wrong about El Turco. He's not our mole, so I don't expect the police to have been tipped off. I'll bet my life on that. We both know El Turco is not our problem, don't we?"

The terrorist patted Daniel on the shoulder and he flinched, unable to hide his aversion to Bagre's touch. He cursed himself for what signal he might have given away. *Does Bagre know? Did Lunati somehow manage to give him my name after all?*

The two cars raced north on the Pan-American toward Martínez. Daniel sat in the passenger seat, unable to blink. He mustered his courage.

"What's the second surprise?" he said.

Bagre gripped the steering wheel. "I can't tell you," he said. "It's a surprise." His yellow teeth flashed.

The cars exited the freeway and made their way up

Avenida Libertador. Daniel felt claustrophobic. He toyed with the trigger of the FAL. *How would the police react? How many would be there?* Daniel had assured Sebastian the police needed only a show of force, that it was a fake operation and the terrorists would drive by when they saw the cops outside the mansion. The police certainly would not be expecting seven well-armed men. For their part, the terrorists were not expecting any confrontation either. A knot formed in Daniel's stomach.

In the cramped passenger's seat, Daniel found his mask and pulled it on. The others behind him did the same. The terrorists didn't always cover their faces, especially at night, but Daniel couldn't take any chances. His need to hide his face was rather different from theirs. It was Sebastian's job to ensure the policemen came from other units, ones who wouldn't recognize him. But the possibility always worried Daniel.

Calle Paraná was dark and quiet as the cars passed the walled manse overlooking the black River Plate. Bagre pulled to the curb and shut off the engine. He grinned at Daniel. *"¿Viste?* You see?" he said. "Nothing. No one's compromised our operation."

The men stepped out of the two vehicles. Bagre whispered final instructions. Daniel saw him pause before leaving his mask on the driver's seat.

A dog barked.

The neighborhood watchman appeared around the corner. The unarmed guard was quickly subdued and left hogtied and frightened inside his flimsy Formica booth.

*Where were the police?* Adrenaline coursed through Daniel's veins.

The police were supposed to have an obvious presence outside the house. Maybe the message hadn't gotten through or was deprioritized. *Damned Bagre and his last-minute change in the plan. Damn the police too.* But perhaps it was better this way, Daniel thought, and the realization brought a sense of relief. If the police had been warned of a serious attack, it could have gotten ugly.

Headlights appeared from Libertador. The terrorists pressed into the shadows of the overhanging bougainvillea. The car passed, and the men relaxed.

At Bagre's signal, the men broke down the metal front gate. More dogs barked now. Another set of headlights appeared, and Daniel quickly followed the terrorists into the courtyard. Sticking to the plan, he skirted along the wall toward the back of the house to cover the rear escapes.

It would be an unpleasant night for the businessman and his family, Daniel considered. The simple drive-by had morphed into a kidnapping – or worse. There was nothing Daniel could do.

Suddenly, shots rang out behind him, back toward the front entrance. *What the hell?* Daniel drew his gun and retraced his steps toward the gunfire. The body of one of the terrorists laid awkwardly across the front gate. Gunfire erupted inside the house.

Daniel hesitated and then edged toward the light spilling from the doors of the grand foyer. He felt a violent shock to his head, and his knees crumpled. A searing pain shot across his right temple, and he wondered how badly he'd been injured. On his side now, he tried to spin around to return fire, but he couldn't see. Blood streamed down the right side of his face and fouled up his mask. He picked himself up and stumbled toward the house, tripping up the front steps and trying to find cover. Ripping off his mask, he dove into the foyer and scrambled into the first room he found.

Daniel gingerly touched his wet forehead. It stung like hell.

A bullet graze. He wiped his eye with his sleeve.

"Hey, Gorila! Thank God you're here. There's cops everywhere." It was El Turco. "Watch my back. Watch the door. Che, what happened to your face?" He crouched over a policeman who was gutshot. "I've got this pig, Gorila," El Turco said, sticking his gun into his belt. "Shot him." The terrorist drew a knife. "I thought I'd just help him along."

The injured policeman on the floor rolled his eyes toward Daniel, and there was a flicker of recognition. The policeman lifted a weak hand.

"Inglés! Help me!" His voice was raspy. *"Ayudá, Inglés."*

A look of confusion crossed El Turco's face. He whirled to look at Daniel. "How does he...?" Dropping his knife, El Turco reached for his gun, but Daniel squeezed off two rounds. The terrorist crumpled to the floor.

*"Ayudá."* The policeman moaned. He was bleeding out.

Daniel knew him. *Dammit!*

"Shut up!" Daniel hissed as he crouched over him.

There was a sound behind Daniel, and he whirled around. Bagre stood in the doorway, his machine gun levelled at Daniel.

"So it wasn't El Turco after all, was it, Gorila? Now we know our mole is *El Inglés*, don't we?"

Daniel opened his mouth, but there was nothing to say. Slowly he stood and wiped his face with his sleeve.

"See you in hell, *hijo de puta*," said Bagre, and Daniel tensed for the impact that would tear him apart.

The wounded policeman on the floor made a sudden movement for a gun, and the distraction was all Daniel needed. He rolled to the side and fired a quick burst from his FAL.

Bagre tottered forward and collapsed onto Daniel. Groping with a bloody fist, he clutched Daniel's jacket and pulled him close. "The night the courier...," he struggled, spitting red, "he didn't show up. I knew it was you. Eva...Eva defended you. Said, 'don't be ridiculous, Bag...re, Daniel wants to find this mole as badly as we do."

Bagre choked and gurgled. "I tracked down the courier, Gorila," he wheezed. A bloodstained smile broke across his face. "He told me how you insisted...he gave the folder to you."

Bagre's body stiffened and shuddered.

Daniel tore the clenched hand from his jacket and stepped back from Bagre's staring eyes. He pushed the lifeless body from him and let it drop to the floor.

Daniel trembled uncontrollably. He dabbed at his injured temple. It smarted like hell. The policeman was dead now. The room smelled sharply of iron, and the sight of all the blood on the floor made his stomach heave.

Daniel bent over and retched.

# CHAPTER 42 – LA GARANTÍA

## *The Guarantee*

Gastón learned of the news when one of the brothers burst into his room early that morning.

He dressed quickly and bounded up the stairs to the third floor where he hesitated by the rector's office near the church sacristy. The door was closed but the light was visible under the door. Gastón knocked.

*"¿Sí?"*

*"Disculpá,"* said Gastón. "I'm sorry to interrupt you at this early hour, Father."

Gastón stepped inside.

"What is it?" said Alejandro, his voice clipped.

"The brothers," said Gastón. "They say two priests have been killed. That the military is responsible, and I…"

"Yes, yes, I've heard the rumors too," said Alejandro. "Late last night. I've heard a Jesuit priest has been killed, and a priest in La Rioja was a victim of a car bombing."

"Father, was it the military who did this? Is this true, what we're hearing?"

Gastón leaned against the doorframe, shifting his weight.

"I don't know," Alejandro said, folding his arms. "You shouldn't jump to conclusions."

"But who would do this?" asked Gastón, his voice cracking, and he suddenly felt a sinking sensation that the rector was not sympathetic and, even worse, was not on his side at all.

"For the love of God, Gastón, we're practically in a civil war! People are dying every day. It's not a time for fanning the flames."

"But these are *priests*, Father!" said Gastón. "They're just doing their jobs." But even as the words tumbled out of his mouth, Gastón knew he himself didn't fully believe it. He thought of Brizzio. A mixed feeling of doubt and fear crept up from Gastón's gut and lodged in his throat.

Alejandro leaned back in his chair, his face a crimson red. "I know this Jesuit priest," he said. "He has not been careful. He drew unwanted attention to himself."

"Father," Gastón choked, "they've been murdered!" He knew he was pushing things too far.

"Let me make something very clear to you," said Alejandro. "This priest was a vocal critic of the government and a known sympathizer of subversives. When a priest strays from religion and into politics, he no longer answers to God but to man. Let this serve as a warning to you too. To all of us," the rector quickly added.

"But, Father, we have no political inclinations here. We don't collaborate with subversives or guerillas." Gastón was scared. *What did the rector know about Brizzio?* His roommate was drawing attention to himself. He was doing the things the rector was warning against. Gastón thought about the disturbing person in the confessional booth. This person seemed to know something even darker about Brizzio. Something Gastón didn't know.

"Father," Gastón said slowly, still wrestling with the decision to say it, "I wish to share with you my concern about Brizzio. I believe he..." and Gastón paused, "he may be running risks with what he's saying at mass. I thought you should know. So that you can keep him out of trouble. Perhaps you already know this."

"What I know may not matter," the rector said, his voice cold and flat.

Gastón stopped breathing and an awful silence settled in the room. He opened his mouth to gulp air, but his lungs and throat didn't respond.

"What do you mean, Father? Should we be worried?" Gastón said. *Should I be worried? Am I in danger too?* And he came to the sick realization he *was* in danger, and that he was guilty by association. Brizzio was his roommate, and he assisted him at mass. His mouth went dry. Alejandro stared blankly.

Gastón needed to say something, anything that might help. He struggled to get the words out.

"I think we're being followed," Gastón said, his voice quavering. "A few weeks ago, at Friday's mass, it was full of people. Someone was there, watching. I just know it. And just last week, a man came for confession. He seemed to know things. Secrets. I feel that this was some sort of threat against Brizzio or against me."

"Brizzio has been unwise," said Alejandro. "He's allowed his passion to confuse his thinking."

"Father, are you implying..." Gastón could not bring himself to say it out loud, and he fell back against the doorpost. "You must stop these rumors. You must protect us!"

"I can't protect you!" Alejandro shouted. "I'm only a priest. Like you."

The moment passed and Alejandro's face softened, but Gastón sensed something false in the rector's changed demeanor, and it scared him more than the shouting.

"We're all in God's hands," the rector said, his eyes now shut as if willing Gastón to leave his office quickly.

# CHAPTER 43 – LA OPERACIÓN

## *The Operation*

Gastón was at his desk writing a letter when he heard a loud bang in the courtyard below and then a commotion downstairs. It was past 10 p.m. Without warning, his door was kicked open and he was thrown to the floor. His glasses skidded across the tile. His cheek was pressed against the cold floor, and his heart was beating its way out of his chest.

A policeman in assault gear frisked him and bound his hands tightly behind his back. One of them jerked Gastón's face toward him and compared it to a photograph he fished from his pocket.

They pulled a hood over his head, and a rope tightened around his neck. He gasped for air. He was shoved into the hallway where he bumped into someone. "Father Brizzio?" he cried out.

Gastón was pushed down the stairs and into the back seat of a car. He heard other vehicles start up. His own car began to move. The rope around his neck hurt. He was going to vomit. He worried about the mess in the hood, and he panicked. He might drown. And suddenly he was six years old at the lake, his tip toes slipping off the submerged sand dune where he could touch and the sparkling water closing over him, flailing and understanding this was how he would die.

*"Por amor de Dios*, please loosen the ropes."

For that he received a cuff to the head.

A bit later, Gastón sensed a change. The car slowed and stopped. More voices. The car made a sharp left-hand turn and stopped again. The driver spoke in a low voice to someone outside the car.

A heavy chain dropped. The vehicle bumped, and the chain rattled and chinked. The car continued, slowly now, and stopped once more.

Gastón was pulled out and taken into a building. He was led down a flight of stairs. A basement, it seemed. It frightened him to be shoved forward with his hands tied behind him and a hood over his head, not knowing what was coming.

At that moment his head struck a low beam. He heard the guards laugh, *"¡La viga!* Gets them every time!"

His vision narrowed and everything turned black.

Gastón awoke, groggy, to the sound of the cell door opening. His hands were bound behind him and the hood was drawn tight. A sharp prick stung his arm. *A needle?* He thought about his glasses and wondered if they were broken and if anyone had found them. He wondered about Brizzio. He felt very tired.

A woman whispered to him, *My son's been detained. He's at the ESMA. Will you visit him?* It was one of his parishioners. He recognized the voice. He reached out to touch her, but he felt only empty space.

Now Gastón was floating high in the air, looking down over this active naval academy within the city, over this forty-two-acre oasis of manicured lawns and shady treelined streets, and the orderly whitewashed and red-brick-accented buildings.

He closed his eyes and imagined the jacarandas were here,

too, glowing purple in the spring and fall, their fallen blossoms crushed by the marching feet of the naval cadets and by the tires of the unmarked Ford Falcons with their hooded occupants.

Gastón heard the clunk of the heavy metal chain and the bump of the car passing over it, and he pictured the chain marks still visible decades later on the concrete road inside, just past the guardhouse.

He felt himself now drifting down, toward one building in particular, one building out of twenty-nine, and not the biggest one. *The Casino de los Oficiales*. In its basement, the torture happened, and in its attic, under the green-painted metal trestles, the madness lived.

Gastón screamed.

# CHAPTER 44 – UN BRINDIS

## *A Toast*

"Whiskey."

The bartender poured Daniel another shot.

Eva was late. He checked his wristwatch for the hundredth time. He swiveled his barstool to look at the back table where they had sat the first time. That was months ago. She hadn't been so pregnant then. *Maybe she's feeling sick and couldn't come?* Daniel rubbed his temples, remembering too late that one of them was still sore and bandaged.

The clock ticked above the neat rows of liquor. A quiet foursome played cards in the corner. She will be here. He was sure of it. He had been very clear. *Come tomorrow to El Planeta. Right after your evening class. You will promise me? Eight o'clock sharp. ¿Entendés?*

She had understood. She had promised.

He was going to tell her everything. To warn her and help her disappear.

Daniel drained his glass and glanced at his watch again. He still had thirty minutes. It was okay. He could make it there in ten minutes if he needed to.

He rubbed his sweaty palms on his thighs. A new fear crossed his mind. S*he knows who I am. She thinks this is a setup to have her detained.* He pushed the thoughts away. It can't be, he told himself. It's something else.

His temple throbbed.

Daniel slid off the barstool and found a payphone in the

back. He slotted a coin and dialed but hung up before the call went through. He paid and stood outside the bar. He paced the sidewalk and returned inside to dial again. No answer.

It was time to leave. He couldn't wait any longer.

It took Daniel eight minutes to arrive at SIDE's headquarters on the Plaza de Mayo. Sebastian met him in the foyer, a slight smile breaking across his face.

Daniel paused. Sebastian never smiled. *What did he know?* Daniel's fear melted by a sudden anger that things were no longer in his control, and that Sebastian was keeping things from him.

"You're a piece of shit," said Daniel. He jabbed a finger into Sebastian's chest. "You hung me out to dry. That shootout at the mansion was a real screw-up."

Sebastian swatted Daniel's hand away. "You think you're the only operation I'm running? You don't think we have other factors to consider?"

"I almost died because you didn't do your job."

"You know how many agents I've lost?" Sebastian shook his head. "*Mirá, vos.* You're still here."

"You almost blew my cover and the entire operation at the UBA. Everyone's clammed up now that Bagre's gone."

"This is where you are wrong, Inglés," said Sebastian. Another smile creased his face, and Daniel felt uneasy all over again. "When you killed that terrorist," said the Admiral's aide, "it accelerated our timetable. You gave us forward momentum."

Sebastian motioned toward the stairs. "The Admiral is waiting."

They climbed to the third floor. Daniel's feet felt like lead. *They know something about Eva.*

He had a basic script for what he planned to say to the Admiral, but things had changed now, and Daniel hesitated. His apprehension slowed his steps. Sebastian looked back. "*Apurá,*" he said, waving him forward.

In the corner office, the Admiral sat behind his oversized desk. A bottle of Johnnie Walker lay within reach.

"Ah, Inglés," said the Admiral, twirling his pen. "Good, good. Please, sit."

It was late, and the heavy office curtains were drawn as if to contain the many secrets within and shut the prying eyes out. A heavy weight settled onto Daniel's shoulders, pressing him into the sofa's soft leather, and he wished very much to be swallowed up and disappeared.

Admiral Bertotti crossed the floor and plopped into an armchair opposite Daniel. It seemed that the Admiral's cocksure attitude had an added element of being pleased with himself.

"How about a drink?" said the Admiral, rubbing his hands.

"*No, gracias,*" Daniel said, disconcerted by the Admiral's friendliness and wishing he hadn't had that second shot at the bar. He needed all his faculties.

The Admiral let out a deep sigh as if disappointed his offer was not accepted. "Now what do you know about a priest connected to the UBA terrorist cell?"

"A priest?" Daniel said, and as soon as the words left his mouth, he regretted them. They would suspect he was hiding something. *What do they know?* Daniel shifted his body and crossed his legs.

"Let's not play games," said the Admiral. "Sebastian tells me you've been following this priest." The Admiral snapped his fingers at his aide. "What's his name?"

"Nicolás Brizzio," said Sebastian. Daniel noticed a leather briefcase beside him.

"Yes," said the Admiral, "and that you made this connection between the priest and the university terrorist cell. That he may be involved with Judge Calva's assassination."

The Admiral clapped his hands. "It's so far-fetched, I'm inclined to believe it. And you see, my young spy, your lead delightfully coincides with an operation we executed last night. We have this priest now, Brizzio. Detained last night with his roommate. Part of an operation to scare misguided priests from dabbling where they shouldn't. A little arrangement I had with the Cardinal," said the Admiral, chuckling. "And if this priest indeed *is* the judge's killer – oh the fun! To see the Cardinal's reaction, to see him cut down to size."

Daniel's head reeled. *They are way far ahead of me.* They wouldn't be satisfied with him dribbling out information. They would want hard facts, and they would want them now. *Will it be possible for me to keep Eva out of this? Do they know about her?* They *had* to know. They would miss nothing. Daniel's mouth went dry.

"So," said the Admiral, wiggling his fingers in Daniel's direction, "what do you have that can help us extract this priest's confession? What can you tell us?"

Daniel tried to reassure himself. He could still get the upper hand.

"You are correct, sir," Daniel said. "This Jesuit priest, Brizzio. He's the assassin that killed Judge Calva."

"How can you be sure?" said the Admiral, cocking his head. "Maybe when we put some pressure on him, he'll tell us he was just the terrorist cell's personal priest. That he was only giving them confession and communion. The one they call to deliver last rites. Nothing to do with the judge at all."

The Admiral leaned his handsome face forward. Sebastian loosened his jaw for improved listening.

"Brizzio's an activist, sir," said Daniel. "Militant social justice type. His father was kidnapped and killed by the government when he was a boy. His mother went crazy and was committed to a psych ward. It was Judge Calva, in fact, that turned him into a ward of the state. Declared their mother unfit and sent him off to a Catholic orphanage school. This was motive."

Sweat trickled down Daniel's back. He knew these details brought Eva uncomfortably close to the conversation. But even if they knew about Brizzio's sister, they wouldn't suspect anything about her. *Would they?* He glanced at Sebastian at the other end of the sofa. He seemed to be staring at some unknown point beyond the walls of the office, making connections in his mind. It made Daniel nervous.

*Where the hell was Eva?*

"None of the cell group told me outright," said Daniel, trying to steer the conversation away from Brizzio's personal life, "but from the way they talk, it's clear everyone knows he's the killer. And I tracked the priest to several secret meetings at the *Facultad de Filosofía y Letras*. They've been planning more assassinations."

The Admiral let out another loud sigh as if he'd been holding his breath for a long time. He leaned back in his chair and ran his hands through his hair, the shock of gray above his forehead disappearing and reappearing again.

"This will certainly help the interrogation tomorrow," said the Admiral. He turned his attention to his aide. "What else do we have?"

"We have the sister," Sebastian said, looking at Daniel.

Daniel's heart stopped. He reeled and put out a hand to steady himself. Sebastian squared up on him from the other end of the sofa.

"The sister," said the Admiral as if remembering. "So you

found her, yes?"

"We picked her up this morning," said the aide. "She claimed she was on her way to classes."

"*Excelente*," said the Admiral, clapping his hands together. "You see, Inglés, more pressure to get this priest to talk. We can find out what she knows too."

Daniel's blood boiled. He no longer feared them. He rubbed his left leg against the hidden holster on his other leg, wondering if he could get two shots off before these bastards could stop him. *But maybe they don't know anything about Eva.*

Sebastian riffled through his briefcase and extracted a sheet of paper. He walked over to the Admiral and whispered in his ear. Bertotti raised his eyebrows and whispered something back to his aide. Daniel's injured temple pounded.

"Tell him what we have," said the Admiral, snapping his finger at his aide.

Sebastian looked at the ceiling as if recalling the facts in his briefcase. "This priest's sister, Eva Brizzio, arrested this morning. She was a suspect anyway and not just because of her close relation to the priest. You will recall, Inglés," said Sebastian, dropping his eyes from the ceiling and settling them onto Daniel, "that this young woman, this university student, caught our attention when she was arrested a few months ago at a student protest. The big one at Avenida Córdoba, when you were arrested too. Part of your undercover work, you said. You helped get her released, remember?"

"You see, Inglés," said the Admiral, getting back into the conversation, "*you* are the one who brought this woman to our attention in the first place. Bravo! What do you know about her, this Eva Brizzio? She was part of this terrorist cell, no? Maybe the driver of that white Fiat? No matter. We'll soon know everything."

Daniel's entire body suddenly went numb. He'd been played.

"She's not involved," Daniel choked out, trying desperately to find some way to save Eva.

"Not involved, you say?" said the Admiral, his eyes squinting at Daniel. "That's not what our sources say. Isn't that right, Sebastian? They say you know quite a bit about her involvement, Inglés. I understand she carries your involvement right here," and the Admiral grinned and cupped his hands about his belly.

Sebastian smirked, and the two of them made crude jokes about Daniel's *infiltration*, but he was no longer listening. His head spun.

"Wasn't there another boyfriend involved too?" said the Admiral. "This is just too good."

"Yes," said Sebastian. "Eva's boyfriend, Federico Ibañez. We picked him up this morning."

"Yes. Federico," said the Admiral, scratching his head. "Old schoolboy friend of yours, I understand. *¿No, Inglés?* All very curious. This threesome. Very curious indeed, wouldn't you agree?"

Daniel squirmed. He had betrayed his friend, Fede. He had betrayed Eva. The guilt wrapped around him like the coils of a giant snake and tightened about his throat. He wanted to scream. *They've done nothing!* But the words wouldn't come. He resisted the desire to bury his head in his hands.

The Admiral stood and grinned. "Inglés, I don't know whether you are right or wrong, whether your methods have been sound or not. But it's the best lead we have, and we have you to thank. So for now, let's have a toast."

Admiral Bertotti waved his hand toward the bottle on the desk. "Sebastian, fill us up with a round of scotch."

Sebastian muttered under his breath as he crossed the floor.

He found three tumblers and poured a splash of the amber liquid into each.

"You're a tightwad, Sebastian!" said Bertotti. "Your social faux pas never cease to amaze me. Give us a proper drink!" commanded the Admiral, and he chuckled and winked at Daniel. Sebastian filled two glasses to the brim.

The Admiral took the drink and extended one to Daniel, who pulled himself out of the sofa. "Here's to your success in busting this campus terrorist cell, Inglés. And here's to this improbable lead you've brought us. Maybe, finally, I can get this albatross off from around my neck. ¡*Salud!*"

Not knowing what else to do, Daniel raised a shaking glass to the Admiral, who had already drained his. Daniel held his tumbler with both hands to steady it and gulped it down. He wanted another, and he eyed Sebastian's untouched drink on the coffee table.

"Fill us up again, Sebastian," said the Admiral, tapping his empty glass toward his aide. This time Sebastian ignored him, but the small insubordination passed unnoticed because the Admiral already had the bottle in his hand.

"To the success of our interrogators tomorrow!" said the Admiral. "If you are correct, Inglés, we'll know very soon. And who knows," said the Admiral, his face suddenly darkening and tilting his head at Daniel, "we may start investigating you too."

Daniel's legs suddenly went wobbly, and he groped for the bookshelf behind him. He pushed off the bookshelf and made for the door.

"Wait," said the Admiral, chuckling. "Stay and have another drink with us."

Daniel could hear the laughter long after he fled down the hall, down the flight of stairs, and out onto the Plaza de Mayo.

# CHAPTER 45 – LA INTERROGACIÓN
## The Interrogation

Gastón awoke thirsty. His whole body ached from laying on the hard floor. The hood's burlap fibers made him gag and forget the rawness of his cuffed wrists and ankles.

"*Agua,*" he called. "*Agua, por favor.*"

His thirst was unbearable. He had urinated on himself and his damp pants chafed at his legs.

He heard distant sounds from other parts of the building.

Gastón didn't know how long it had been. Days maybe? He prayed, crying out from his soul to God. He prayed for strength and deliverance.

He heard footsteps and the door rattled open. A needle pricked his arm. The rope at the base of his hood was loosened. Thank God for the relief of pressure on his windpipe. His neck felt raw and his throat ached.

"*Agua. Por amor de Dios.*"

A bottle was slipped under his hood and bumped against his lips. He gagged and choked.

"*Gracias.*"

"*¡Idiota!*"

Gastón was yanked to his feet, and he swayed against his captors' arms. Removing his cuffs, they pulled him from the cell. His mind wandered, and he tried to bring it back to something that made sense. His body felt like it belonged to someone else.

His feet dragged along until he was pushed into a chair. It

was the most wonderful thing in the world to be seated. Something was in his front pocket. His eyeglasses! He tried to put them on but forgot about the hood. His hands were slapped away.

"You are Father Gastón?"

Someone was speaking to him. Gastón's mind couldn't focus.

"Father Gastón!"

"¿Sí?"

"You are here because you are a subversive."

"Yes. What?"

"Tell us when you became a collaborator with the guerillas. Was this before working with Father Brizzio or after?"

Gastón's mind wouldn't compute. *Why isn't my mind working?*

"You are innocent are you, Father Gastón? Father Brizzio is a killer."

"Yes. Of course. May I please have some water?"

"We understand you've been having sexual relations with a female catechist. Is this not a grave sin?"

"Yes. Would you please say that again?"

"Father Brizzio has already told us everything. You've been collaborating with the subversives."

If he could just wake up.


Gastón knew he had been moved to the fourth floor of the building because he counted the stairs and landings. The L-shaped fourth floor was the attic. Triangular metal trestles supported the roofline and eaves. It was stifling hot as the summer seemed reluctant to cede to fall. Gastón imagined the cold of this uninsulated space in the winter.

*Will I still be here?*

He no longer was in a cell, but in a small partition open to the hallway. The hood was always required, but it was kept loose, and by moving his head he could see the space about his feet between the folds of the cloth.

He learned there were many other prisoners too. Speaking or removing their hoods for any reason was cause for a severe beating. He did his necessities in a bucket, a process difficult and humiliating with his hood on and his hands tied behind his back.

But the worst was when they came to get him.

At the sound of approaching footsteps, Gastón's heart raced, and his breath came in quick shallow bursts. He would back up against the wall, praying they weren't coming to take him down the four flights of tiled stairs, past the floors housing naval officers and their families, and to the basement to be tortured. Sometimes he was hauled from his cell only to be taken back up, then down again and finally beaten. At times he was told simply to *wait his turn*, and so he would wait on the cold floor and listen to Deep Purple and AC/DC played full blast to hide the screaming.

Gastón was given paper and pen and made to write confessions. Torture, he found, had a way of unleashing creative energy.

One day a guard pulled him aside. "The situation is very grave, Father Gastón," the guard said. "Aguirre has decided to kill you. He says it's because you have not been rehabilitated."

Gastón was convinced he would never leave this place, and he wrestled with God to try to accept it. He lay in his cell, listening to the sounds within the ESMA and the traffic on the busy street nearby. His hearing sharpened on account of the hood, and in the forced silence, his ears tuned to the hissing of the rats. Once he thought he heard the voice of Brizzio.

Gastón prayed constantly. He recited all the Psalms of David he could remember. He sang hymns. And in that dark place, he poured out his anguish to God.

*Why, Lord, do you stand far off?*
*Why do you hide yourself in times of trouble?*
*Look on me and answer me, Lord my God.*
*Give light to my eyes, or I will sleep in death.*
*May those who seek my life be disgraced and put to shame;*
*May their path be dark and slippery.*

# CHAPTER 46 – LOS VUELOS
# DE LA MUERTE
## *The Death Flights*

Daniel was listless. He ambled to the *tabacalera* to buy his Jockey Clubs. He lingered at a bar on Suipacha, one of the narrow streets downtown that digested sunlight like a black hole so the shadows here were much darker than anywhere else.

Every evening, he sat at the same barstool, his back to the windowed entrance where pedestrians hurried to the broader avenues of Corrientes and Córdoba. It was proving all but impossible to find where Eva was being held. Sebastian wouldn't tell him, and no one else seemed to know.

"I know you from somewhere, no?" The man sat several seats down. Daniel had seen him before, drinking alone.

"I was here yesterday," Daniel said.

*"Sí, debe ser."*

He slid his glass down and sat beside Daniel. "Let me buy the next round," the man said.

Daniel drained his beer. To be honest, he didn't mind the conversation, especially since the man appeared willing to do most of the talking.

"I grew up in La Plata," the man said. "You know it?"

Daniel shook his head, and it provided an opening for his new drinking companion to explain the wonders of La Plata.

"You're a lot like me," the man said finally, after a lull in the conversation. "A man of secrets. I have secrets too."

"You say you're a military pilot?" Daniel said.

"*Was* a pilot," said the man. "I quit."

The man glanced about and leaned toward Daniel. "*Los vuelos*," he said quietly, and Daniel felt a tingling rise from the base of his spine.

"I told them I wouldn't do it anymore," the man continued. "They said they would take away my pension. *Hijos de puta.* They threatened my family. I'm telling you because you're my friend. Because I can see you've had enough too, no?"

The man sighed deeply, his breath rank in the small space between them. The man's eyes glistened, and he put a tentative hand on Daniel's shoulder. Daniel felt a sudden pity for the man who had probably once believed in what he was doing too. And something stirred within Daniel's soul, a deep longing for justice in the world, and yet an even more powerful longing for mercy.

"I've just been doing what they tell me to do, *¿viste?*" the man said.

"*Contá tu historia,*" Daniel urged. "Tell your story."

The man swiveled in his chair, looking past Daniel and out at the narrow street to gather his thoughts.

"The flights originate from Aeroparque, El Palomar, and El Morón," the man said quietly. "My crew and I fly for the air force, but others fly for the navy. My crew, they're good people, I swear to you. Julio, Enrique, Mario, and Alejandro. We fly the British twin turboprop Skyvan. We call it the Flying Shoebox because it has a convenient, giant cargo door. Sometimes we use the U.S.-made Lockheed L-188 Electra because it's good on short runways and maritime patrolling."

"One of the servicemen, Alejandro," the man said with a forced laugh. "Just a kid. He's newer to these duties and unsure, and he keeps asking if the Church has sanctioned these methods, and we tell him yes. The bastard desperately wishes to believe it. We tell him these are honorable murders. The Church has said so."

The man shook his head.

"The subversives. They are guerillas, students, and journalists, and they are professors, unionists, and priests, and often several things at once. But all of them are accused of terrorist activities against the state, and for most of them, it's true. They really are bastards. I believe it. But when you see them in person, you know…" The man's voice trailed off.

"They are so young," he continued. He coughed. "It's both men and women, and they have normal names like anyone else. Like Óscar, Elena, Ricardo, and Juan. We tell them they are being transferred to a work camp, and that the injections of sodium pentothal are a vaccine against the diseases in the south. It's all a lie of course."

The man paused and his eyes seemed to settle on some point on the ceiling.

"Their hands and feet are tied, and they say things like *please* and *no* before being loaded onto the planes. And they cry."

Daniel's nostrils flared. He thought about Eva. He fought an urge to smash the man's face.

"Do you want me to stop?" said the man. "I'm not sure I can go on, to tell you the truth. But somehow it helps me to tell this story."

Daniel shook his head. He *wanted* to hear the details. He *had* to hear the details.

"They are stripped and sometimes put into bags weighted with rocks," the man continued. "Like anyone about to face certain death, they refuse to believe this is happening to them, that they indeed are going to die at this time, in this way."

"It's a short flight out over the bay of the Río de la Plata," the man said. "We pilots know just where the deepest parts are, and we know the secrets of the tides, and where the ocean currents are most favorable. But sometimes the river rejects the offerings, and it returns the bodies up onto the beaches south of Buenos Aires and the coast of Uruguay, and sometimes they are caught in the vast network of inlets of the Delta del Tigre."

"I've heard," the man said, "that the fishermen in the delta are quiet folk, but the beachgoers at the resorts are not, but none of them want to cause any problems, so they politely inform the authorities when they find the bodies and when they find the bags. The police come quickly. They bury some in secret shallow graves, and others are sent to the morgue where the forensic pathologists determine the cause of death is not drowning but high velocity impact with something hard. Most have signs of torture and the women of violation."

The man chewed a fingernail. "Do you have a cigarette?" he asked, but Daniel wasn't listening anymore. Daniel rubbed his hands in his face, and with each pass, he rubbed harder and harder and harder.

"You bastard," Daniel said softly, "you *maldito bastardo*."

# CHAPTER 47 – DESAPARECIDA

## *Disappeared*

"I knew it was you. It was always you, wasn't it, Daniel?"

Eva's pale face glowed from out of the shadow of her cell. She reached through the bars, her hands scabbed and covered with black marks, and placed them over his. Her eyes no longer burned brightly. Her belly no longer bulged.

It had taken Daniel a lot of work to find her, almost two weeks. She had been at the Hospital Militar and transferred here. He had heard the rumors, what they did to pregnant subversives.

He had called on a lot of personal favors to be here in front of her. His pleadings to get her released had been met with laughter. *What are you talking about, Inglés? She's a cop killer. All mixed up with the cafeteria bomber. ¿Sos loco, che? She's a chupada and deserves what's coming to her. You unmasked her! You're a hero, Inglés.*

Shame washed over him. He fought a rising panic. He wanted to rip the bars off. To get her out.

"Why didn't you kill me?" Daniel said, his voice anguished. "Why?" He stroked her disfigured hands.

"Because I had no more hate left for you, Daniel. There was already so much of it. I hated a lot of things we did. Maybe I wanted it all to end."

Eva's lip suddenly quivered, and she pulled back and buried her face in her hands. "I never made time for love, to love my baby," she sobbed, and her breath came in great gasps that whistled through her fingers. "She's a girl. Did you know that? Tell Fede. Will you tell him?"

Eva dried her face and looked into Daniel's eyes. "At the Hospital Militar, what they did to me…They took my baby. They took everything and left me only emptiness."

Great tears welled up and rolled down Daniel's cheeks and into his thin beard. His body shook. He gripped the bars of her cell to steady himself.

"My hate is all gone," Eva said, "and I have nothing. I will die and have nothing to die for."

The prison echoed with unnatural sounds.

"They say I am to be transferred to a work camp in the south," Eva said. "That I'll need a vaccine."

Daniel gave a start. His mouth turned dry.

"I'm afraid," Eva said, and her legs buckled, and she put out an arm to let herself down gently onto the cold concrete.

It took four guards to pry Daniel's hands loose and drag him away. He knew he would never see her again.

*Desaparecida.*

# CHAPTER 48 – EL TIBURÓN

## *The Shark*

It was a whiff of perfume that made Daniel stop walking. He glanced back at the pedestrians. It was the same hair. It had to be her. A loud bus startled Daniel, and he shut his eyes tight, trying to make his head stop hurting. His mind drifted and transported him onto the bus.

Daniel could smell his mother's perfume from the back where the engine vibrated up through his boots. The bus traveled faster and faster, and the city became a blur of gray before turning into blackness.

They lurched into a turn, and he fell into the passengers across the aisle. El Oso's fleshy face grinned down at him, sweat pouring from the torturer's forehead. Daniel jerked back into the aisle in horror only to find it was no longer El Oso but Lieutenant Cazorla. *"Solo nos dejan con la mierda,"* said Cazorla, and he saluted Daniel.

Above Cazorla's head, the blades of ceiling fans spun wildly. With a loud bang, one of them careened off its screw and struck several passengers. Everyone screamed.

Daniel caught a glimpse of his mother up front again. She turned toward him, her hand outstretched, pleading. He clawed his way toward her. He *must* save her.

The aisle was clogged. *Where was she?* He could no longer see her, but he could still smell her perfume. Daniel, frantic now, bounded over the seats. *There!* His mother wore her red scarf. Daniel touched her shoulder, and she turned. But it was the face of Eva, a grotesque, horrible face. An eye had been pecked out and her nose eaten away. Eva extended her blackened palms, and Daniel recoiled and braced against a seat behind him.

A sudden gust of wind whooshed from the open bus door, and Eva was sucked out, screaming into the dark abyss.

Daniel awoke on his bed drenched in sweat, staring at the wobbly fan and the peeling paint on the ceiling. The nightmares had become so vivid now.

The orange glow of the streetlights shone through the curtains. He felt so tired. He couldn't remember when he had slept more than a few hours. The clock read 10 p.m.

Daniel sat up and reached for his Brownings, tucking one into his belt and strapping the other to his right leg. He found two beers, ripped off the tabs and drained them.

A note by the front door from Cacho caught his eye. His roommate had been trying to meet him for drinks for some time. "Just to talk, Inglés," Cacho would say. "We never talk. Come on, meet me there. I'll invite Luis. Meet us there."

The bar was near the downtown station, popular with policemen and the kind Daniel avoided. He arrived feeling buzzed. Cacho was not there. Daniel ordered a beer and sat by himself.

A laugh caught his attention and grated on his ears. The man was loud and boisterous. Daniel knew him. A bully whose fawning underlings orbited his macho universe.

Daniel heard the snide comment and the laughter erupting across the bar. The men looked in his direction. Daniel rubbed his face. He slid off his barstool.

"Ah, here he comes to join us now," said the policeman, winking at his buddies, "the hero who fingered that *puta* terrorist girl." He wiggled his middle finger and thrust his pelvis back and forth.

They all laughed.

"Come on over and teach us a few things, Inglés," the cop said loudly.

Daniel smiled before he sucker-punched the man, felling him in a clattering of chairs and scraping tables. A rage surged within Daniel as if someone else was controlling his body. He turned his attention to the stunned companions.

A burly cop whose mouth was turning from surprise to anger caught a right hook to his jaw that sent him crashing to the floor on top of the bully. The bar erupted in loud cheers and whistles. Everyone pressed in to watch the fight. Daniel swung his elbow back to catch a third man in the face, breaking his nose and splattering blood on the tiled floor. Two remaining men shrank back, and Daniel picked up a bar stool and began clubbing the bully on the floor. There was a sickening crunch on the man's back, and people began backing away.

"*Pará.* Stop," someone yelled.

The shout came from the front of the bar. Cacho and Luis broke through the wall of onlookers to restrain Daniel. "It's okay, Inglés. It's okay. Come on," said Cacho. "We're taking you home. Out of the way, everyone. Move!"


Daniel lay sprawled on the sofa, his eyes closed, and a rag wrapped around his fist. He listened to them whisper. It was spoiling his rest.

"He's getting worse," Luis said to Cacho. "He wears the same things over and over. Mónica didn't recognize him. Scared her and the kids. I tried to talk to him, but he got really angry."

Daniel heard a pot clank on the stove. There was a whoosh of the propane burner. The garlicky smell of phosphorus smarted in his nostrils.

"The super talked to me the other day," continued Luis. "Says Inglés works all the time, even when he's supposed to be off. That he pistol-whipped some cadet for being too slow. Says he's changed. He asked if I would talk to him."

"You think I can't hear?" said Daniel suddenly, his eyes flashing open.

Luis jumped. *"Disculpá, Inglés,"* he said. "I thought you were sleeping."

"And sit the hell down," Daniel said. "Stop hovering. *Por Dios.*"

Luis pulled a chair from the table and sat, rubbing his hands on his pants.

Daniel swung his feet to the floor. He felt the blood course hot through his veins as if picking up where it left off at the bar.

"You want to discuss how I've changed? Is that it?" Daniel said. "How violent I am? About my dark streak? I'm a goddamned violent person."

Luis licked his lips and looked back at Cacho, who leaned against the kitchen counter. Cacho had a finger to his lips and was shaking his head knowingly at Daniel.

"I see," said Daniel. "Cacho wants me to shut up. He doesn't want me to tell you about SIDE, Luis."

Luis's eyes widened.

Cacho turned away and busied himself with a *mate* gourd and tea leaves.

"That's right," said Daniel. "Now you know."

"Shut up, Inglés," said Cacho. "The super's right, you know. You need some time off. You've been working too much."

"You see, Luis," said Daniel, pointing at his roommate, "Cacho here thinks I can just stop. That he can stop too. Just like that," and Daniel snapped his fingers. "But SIDE's not like your crappy job at the Guardia where you go home to your family every night. No. We're so caught up in this shit, in the lies we're told every day. This goddamned military regime. And to tell you the truth, me and Cacho, we *need* the lies. Yeah, that's right, isn't it, Cacho? We *need* these lies. They keep us one step ahead of everything unraveling. You know what we're like? We're like sharks. You know about *el tiburón*, Luis? It has to keep swimming. It has to keep swimming or it will drown."

The pot burbled on the stove.

"That's what I am," Daniel said, slumping back into the sofa. "*El tiburón.*"

Luis had a pained look on his face, like the look of Daniel's father many years ago when Daniel told him he would no longer serve as an altar boy because he preferred to be a sinner.

"Come on, Inglés, share a *mate* with us," said Cacho, bringing the tea gourd to the sofa and holding it out to him.

Daniel bit at his fingernails and looked away. Cacho gave the tea to Luis.

"You're both agents?" said Luis. "I had no idea."

"Don't pay Inglés any attention," said Cacho. "He's under a lot of stress, Luis. You might as well know he's been doing some undercover stuff. Doesn't say much about it either. Something happened though. I just know it. Messed him up real good too."

He took the gourd from Luis and refilled it with hot water.

"Do you hear me, Inglés?" Cacho shouted to Daniel from the kitchenette. "You shouldn't blame yourself."

Cacho came back sipping the *mate*. He pulled out a chair and sat across from Daniel.

"I'm worried about you too, Inglés. You *do* smell. You

don't talk to me. I hardly ever see you. You rarely come home. I don't blame you. Hell, I don't even blame you for fucking my girlfriend. Right here in the apartment. That's how much I care about you, you bastard."

"Wait, what?" said Luis.

Daniel's ears flushed hot. He pushed back the shame and chose instead to treat his friend's overture as a painful stab wound. ,

"Right here, in the apartment?" said Luis, looking around with the vicarious imaginations of a married man.

Cacho waved an annoyed hand. "*Olvídalo*. Forget it. She was a *puta* anyway."

"Inglés, I'm going to help you, *¿viste?*" said Cacho. "I'm going to talk to the super. I'm going to speak with Sebastian. I don't want you going rogue on me, you hear? I've seen too much of that. *¿Entendés?*"

"*Dejáme en paz,*" Daniel said. "Just leave me alone." He shut his eyes. His temple throbbed from the bullet graze. His hand slid down his pants leg and felt the hard comforting handle of the Browning.

He just needed a little rest.

# CHAPTER 49 – EL PSIQUIATRA

## *The Psychiatrist*

Daniel was arrested late at night walking the empty Avenida Corrientes. After a few tense moments, the police relieved him of his weapons and handcuffed him. They took him to the station and left him in a cell overnight.

The next morning, he was plopped in a chair before his supervisor.

"You look terrible, Inglés," said the supervisor.

"I spent the night in jail."

"You smell." The super fanned a hand in front of his face. "Maybe you'd like me to say I'm sorry we arrested you last night, but it was for your own protection. You're out of control."

"You treat us like *mierda*."

The supervisor stood and kicked his chair back from the desk, his face flushed, and neck muscles strained. "No, Inglés," he said, jabbing a finger in Daniel's chest. "*You* are the one that's treating your colleagues like shit. For God's sake, you threatened them. Last week you beat up three police officers. You're drunk. You have crazy energy one day and then you disappear. Show up a few days later like nothing's happened."

The supervisor poked his head out his office door and yelled for coffee.

"I'll be straight with you," he continued. "Some believe you're involved with some assaults and robberies.

Unauthorized *grupos de tarea*. Is this what you're doing? Because I personally don't believe it. You hear what I'm saying? You've had some tough assignments, and I've been able to count on you. I know you're SIDE too. Doesn't surprise me. But, *mirá*, we've all seen a lot of shit. Most are handling it fine, but sometimes it gets to a person. I understand. You've had a rough spot of it."

There was a knock on the door and an elderly waiter set down two coffees.

"Your partner Cacho came to see me. Argued on your behalf," the supervisor continued. He stirred in two packets of sugar. Daniel gulped his coffee.

"I'm putting you on temporary administrative leave," said the supervisor. "I want you to see the police shrink. He'll probably put you on some reduced schedule. Just until you're able to pull yourself together."

"What about my weapons and badge?" said Daniel. "They took them from me last night."

The supervisor shook his head. "The doctor will make that decision. And I don't want any more problems. You got that? Pull your shit together."


The next afternoon Daniel found himself in the office of Dr. Longoria at the military hospital. He had a personal weapon strapped to a leg holster that security hadn't found. He felt for it now as he sat before the psychiatrist.

Longoria was a small, yellow-pallored man with drooping shoulders. His shifty eyes were closely cropped around a hooked Roman nose. Daniel disliked him immediately.

"*¿Cigarrillo?*" the doctor offered. Daniel could feel the man sizing him up, drawing conclusions from behind the round glasses.

Dr. Longoria slid a brown glass ashtray to the middle of his desk. He leaned across and lit Daniel's cigarette. His breath smelled like lung cancer. The doctor laid his white Bic lighter carefully on the desk, perpendicular to the edge.

"Can you tell me why you are here, Señor Romandini?" said the doctor, pushing back from his desk and gingerly crossing a leg.

"My super sent me."

"Are you sick?"

"No."

"I hear you've had a few problems recently," continued the psychiatrist. "You want to tell me about these?"

"No."

"What happened last Thursday, at the bar?"

"I got into a fight with some policemen."

"Some of your colleagues report that you are too violent sometimes." The doctor dabbed his forehead and the back of his neck with the handkerchief. "Do you agree with them?"

Daniel shrugged.

"Can you tell me what you feel when you get angry? When you get violent?"

Daniel hadn't planned on speaking at all or at least as little as possible. What the hell, he thought. Maybe this man could help. Maybe he could get some pills to help him sleep. Some pills to make him feel really good and forget everything.

"I mean, that's what they want us to do, right?" said Daniel. "To be violent? Feels sort of good when I get angry, to tell you the truth. Like it's helping in some way. It helps me forget that I'm so tired. That I'm not sleeping."

Daniel flicked his ash onto the floor. Dr. Longoria's eyes followed it, and he frowned.

"You really want to know, Doctor?" said Daniel. "I'll tell you. A couple of days ago, I was on the bus, sitting in the back. I always sit in the back. There was this man across the aisle from me. A subversive. A terrorist. I had my 9mm laid across my lap, hidden under the newspaper and pointed at the man's belly, like this. You see, Doctor, they're waiting for me."

Dr. Longoria leaned forward in his chair. "I see quite a few policemen these days, SIDE agents, too, like yourself. What you are experiencing is normal. It takes its toll, doesn't it?

Daniel wondered how much he knew.

"What can you do for me?" asked Daniel, tiring of the conversation and issuing it more as a challenge than a question. Now he doubted this weaselly man could do any good at all. He thought about the convenience store next door and the bottles arranged neatly behind the counter.

The therapist looked at him. "The first thing is to give you some time off. Then I'm placing you on a reduced schedule."

Dr. Longoria paused and switched his crossed legs, arranging the creases of his pants. "There's one more thing, Señor Romandini. You won't be authorized to carry your weapons or badge."

"You can't take my weapons. I'll be killed. You don't understand." Daniel's hand slid down his leg and felt his gun.

The small man brought his hands together and held them under his chin. "I'm sorry. You'll need to give them up."

Daniel jumped to his feet.

*"Calma, mi estimado Señor Romandini,"* and the doctor's delicate hand pulled on Daniel's muscular arm, urging him to sit back down. *"Mirá.* There are ways to work this out," he said. "If you are interested, that is."

Daniel was interested.

"If you want to keep your badge and weapons," the psychiatrist continued, "there's a processing fee to be paid. It makes a lot of work for me as I'm sure you can understand."

Daniel did understand, and an hour later he returned with an envelope of cash, which Dr. Longoria put it in the top drawer of his desk. The doctor took out a pad of paper.

"You see, as I said, this requires a lot of extra paperwork for me," he said, checking a few boxes on a form. He signed it with a flourish and tore it off from the well-used pad. He handed it to Daniel.

"One more thing, Señor Romandini." Dr. Longoria wrote out a prescription. "These are to help you sleep, and here's another one for some pills that will calm you down and get you feeling better again. I'll need to see you every week to monitor your progress. And to process your fees, ¿viste?"

Dr. Longoria stood and extended a pallid hand. "Go relax. Take some time off. Go see your family."

As Daniel passed the waiting room, he recognized a colleague from the Guardias. El Pato acknowledged him with a grin. It didn't surprise Daniel that Pato was under Dr. Longoria's care too. He remembered Pato once showing off a collection of stolen watches, three or four on each wrist and others in a case he kept in his police locker.

"I see you're here for the same thing," laughed Pato, and he shook his near-empty bottle of pills in front of Daniel's face.

Daniel used the first paper Longoria had given him to reclaim his weapon at security on his way out of the military hospital. He used the second slip to fill the prescription at the pharmacy next door. Before catching a bus back to police headquarters, he stopped at the convenience store where he pointed to a bottle on the shelf behind the counter.

Daniel stood on the street and tried to collect his thoughts. Dr. Longoria had suggested he go see his family.

It sounded like a good idea.

It was dark when Daniel got off the bus in Flores. It was gusty, and the wind whipped the brittle leaves of the ceibas and tore at the loose bark of the sycamores. He stood on the corner confused, suddenly unsure why he was there. He thought of the pills he had swallowed and the empty eighth of whiskey he'd left on the bus.

Daniel's mind raced. He hadn't been to these familiar streets in a long time. He felt angry and then suddenly fearful. He backed against a wall and felt its cold hardness. A bushy bougainvillea half hid him from the street, and he paused, holding the Browning in his trembling hand.

He stood across from his childhood home and watched his father Emilio reading a newspaper at the kitchen table. The back bedroom light was on. The two remises were parked in front of the house. Daniel sighted his father down the barrel, his hand steady now. His brother Antonio entered the kitchen and exchanged words with his father. Antonio disappeared down the hall. How easy it would be, thought Daniel, to kill his father. It had been *his* fault after all. *He* had been the one driving the car when his mother was killed. Daniel ground his teeth. He imagined the surprised look of his brother in his room. *His* room!

A car rattled on the street and Daniel's heart pounded in his chest. He felt nauseous. What was happening to him? Something was wrong. Something was terribly wrong. He turned and ran.

He boarded a bus and dozed.

A snake's hard head squeezed through the crack between the seats, its forked tongue flicking in and out. The body disgorged slowly, mottled and thick. It twisted and turned, its lidless eyes a sin-stained black. Daniel hurled himself backward, but now he found himself in a musty confessional booth. He scrambled onto the bench seat. It was stuffy and airless. Sweat dripped from his forehead and his clothes clung to him. He was frantic and clawed at the wood walls, trying to get higher.

The small screen partition flung open and the beast on the other side laughed. "What is happening? Where are we going?" it said. The beast laughed harder. With a loud bang the cabinet tore away, and a dark abyss yawned before Daniel.

"*¡Dios, salve!*" he cried out, "God, save me!"

He jerked awake. The bus was almost at his stop. He pulled the rope and got off.

# CHAPTER 50 – EL PATO

## *The Duck*

Daniel woke at noon and his head hurt. It hurt more when he reached for the bottle and found it empty. He hurled it against the wall and went out.

The streets were unusually quiet. When he got to the liquor store and found its steel shutters down, he decided it must be Sunday. He cursed and returned to the apartment. After searching it top to bottom, he slumped in a plastic chair. His knee bounced until he lit a cigarette.

A key turned in the lock. Daniel grabbed his Browning and sprang to the front door.

*"¿Que hacés, Inglés?* It's me, you imbecile," said Cacho with Daniel's hard barrel pressed against his temple. Cacho brushed past Daniel into the apartment.

"I heard you come in late last night," Cacho said, "making all kinds of noise. You look like shit."

"Do you have any alcohol?"

"I wouldn't give you any if I did. You drink too much."

"What do you care what I do, *idiota?*"

"Because I do. That's why," said Cacho, and then he caught sight of the broken bottle pieces. "What the hell happened?"

"You know exactly what happened, Cacho." Daniel tightened his hand around the grip of the 9mm. "You told the cops to arrest me. You told them where I was."

"You're going crazy," said Cacho, pointing a finger at his

own head and making circles. *"Sos loco."*

Daniel stepped toward him and jabbed his forefinger in his chest. He was furious. "I will never, never forgive you for this. You betrayed me."

"That's bullshit, Inglés. I don't betray my friends."

His roommate's stare pierced him. He thought of Cacho's girlfriend when he had found her alone in the apartment. She had a thing for him, and he had taken advantage of it. How he had moved his hands over her hips and pulled her close.

Daniel felt a sudden vulnerability, and he leaned against the front door.

"Did you see the shrink?" said Cacho. "I see cops referred all the time. There's no shame in it."

"Shut up," Daniel said. The anger rushed back. "I don't need your lectures and I don't need your help." He yanked on the front door and left.

A light rain fell. Daniel walked the city streets and stopped before a tired apartment building. He paused, trying to remember.

The policeman's wife opened the door of the second-floor apartment. A small child clutched her leg and peered up at Daniel. "Tuerto!" the woman yelled back into the house.

Tuerto pushed his way forward.

*"¿Qué querés, Inglés?"*

"El Pato Romero. You know where he lives?"

"Yeah. He's on Calle Asunción, the apartment building next to Bar El Oasis. *¿Por qué?"*

But Daniel was already halfway down the stairs. The address was only a few blocks away, and he soon stood outside Pato's door.

El Pato was a strange bird indeed. His splayed, flatfooted gait earned him his duck moniker. It was no surprise to Daniel that Pato, too, was under the care of Dr. Longoria, weapons and badge intact.

Pato lived in a run-down section of Devoto with two or three other policemen. To describe their apartment as messy was a gross understatement. It went well beyond the natural aversion young men have to cleanliness when they live without women. Empty beer and whiskey bottles lay strewn about. Stolen TVs were stacked to the ceiling against one wall. In the corners, the carpet's original pea green color was lost under a layer of dust, and the trafficked areas were a grimy black and sticky. The toilet was broken.

Pato's apartment suited Daniel and he stayed there. Here no one told him he was out of control, or that he needed to take it easy. No one pointed out he smelled. It was precisely the sort of place where a disturbed mind could flourish, and an unstable person might reach his full potential. And in this environment, Daniel found kindred spirits.

"Come with us tonight," Pato said. "*Vení.* We're going to have some fun."

Daniel spent the next hour helping Pato glue paper squares onto tennis balls and painting them dark green. "People are unimpressed by real military grenades," his new friend explained, "they're just too small. They like these a whole lot more," Pato said, inspecting a completed specimen and placing it on the floor to dry.

During that first drug- and alcohol-fueled night, the four new roommates assaulted several groups of people downtown, robbing them and leaving them bloodied.

It began a new pattern for Daniel. He met policemen and military types who shared a fondness for violence, men who operated on the outer fringes and had become part of the human backwash left by the strong tide of the authoritarian regime, flotsam set adrift by the relentless swell of events.

"*¡Inglés! ¿Qué hacés, che?* How are you?"

Daniel turned from the row of bottles in the convenience store. Luis held a can of Pepsi and a bag of chips.

"It's good to see you," Luis said. He took a step forward and stopped as if unsure. The bag of chips crinkled and grated on Daniel's ears. "Is everything okay? I mean if you don't mind my saying it."

Daniel blinked. He tried to process what Luis was saying.

"I'm on a break from work," said Luis, shifting his weight to the other leg. "I should get back."

Daniel thought about the Jack Daniels bottles lined up behind him. He tried to remember how much money he had and if it would be enough. He fingered the coins in his pocket. One bottle would get him through today. His other hand felt for the pills in his opposite pocket. He would mash them and stir them in. He thought suddenly he could ask Luis for money, but Luis was speaking again.

"I really should be getting back," said Luis. "I'm still working as a security guard at the hospital payment center, just here on Córdoba. You know, trying to make ends meet." He smiled weakly. "A wife and kids are expensive on a cop's salary."

"Payment center?" Daniel said. He struggled to pull this detail from his memory.

"I normally work Tuesdays and Thursdays," Luis said. "I'm trying to get some hours on Fridays, but they don't usually staff any security on Fridays for some reason."

Daniel digested this information with interest.

"I really need to go," said Luis. "It's good to see you." He exited the store.

Daniel's eyes fixed on the closing door, and a serpentine idea twisted in his mind.

The morning of the planned robbery, Daniel hailed a taxi near the Chacarita train station and headed toward downtown through the Friday rush-hour traffic. Since there was a chance someone might recognize him, Pato would commit the robbery while Daniel handled the getaway.

A block from the target, Daniel tapped the cabbie on the shoulder. Pato exited while Daniel and the driver continued and parked across the street from the payment center to wait. Sitting in the back of the taxi, Daniel watched Pato waddle toward the payment center entrance.

Shots rang out from inside the building. Pato emerged, firing wildly back into the building. Daniel stepped onto the busy street and fired his gun twice in the air to stop the traffic. The frightened driver tried to pull away, but Daniel dove back into the cab.

"Pick him up!" Daniel screamed, pointing his gun at the cabbie's head.

They peeled across the lanes and Pato jumped in.

"*¡Lo maté! ¡Lo maté!* I killed him!"

"What?" said Daniel. "What did you do?"

Daniel turned his attention to the shaking driver. "To the Chacarita train station!" he yelled. "*¡Apurá!*"

The day after the botched robbery, Daniel went back to work at the police department. "What son of a bitch did this?" the policemen heatedly discussed. "He will pay," they said.

He visited Luis in the hospital every day, holding his hand, watching his friend's life ebb away. Luis's wife trembled when Daniel gave her an embrace.

"He wasn't even supposed to be there," said Mónica. She dabbed her eyes with a tissue. "Did you know? He was sick on his regular day, on Thursday. He begged them to let him work on Friday to make up the hours."

She sobbed into Daniel's shoulder, and he held her. She smelled clean and feminine. He remembered the afternoon he and Cacho spent with their family.

The tiramisu.

Luis died at the hospital ten days later. Daniel walked twenty-five blocks to the military hospital. He ignored the receptionist's protests and barged into the psychiatrist's office, startling the doctor and a client.

"Help me!" said Daniel. *"Ayudá."*

"I'll help you as soon as you help me by respecting me and my client," said Dr. Longoria, straightening his tie and sitting up in his chair. "I'll be with you shortly."

Daniel paced in the waiting room until his help finally came in the form of another prescription.


The nightmares grew worse, now visiting Daniel during the day and coming on suddenly. He saw things that weren't there. He heard voices in his head. *¡Lo maté! ¡Lo maté!*

He saw the bus coming and almost stepped off the curb. He thought about Luis and about Fede. He remembered the girl Mercedes sobbing, and Eva on the floor of her cell. *I'm afraid, Daniel.* He would blow his brains out with both guns stuck in his mouth.

Daniel avoided Pato's apartment. He roamed the streets and slept in the alleys and doorways south of downtown with the drug addicts and prostitutes. He sought out women because he craved intimacy if only for those few moments. One late night he thrust and thrust inside a woman, her legs wrapped tight above his hips, but he couldn't reach climax and he cried out from somewhere in the depths of his soul. At a run-down San Telmo hotel within stumbling distance of the bar in which they met, a woman accepted his urgent advances, but Daniel found he couldn't get it up at all. The woman laughed and he stood over her, his fist clenched and shaking.

# CHAPTER 51 – UNA ESPERANZA EMBORRACHADA

## *A Drunken Hope*

Daniel woke up with a start. He blinked, trying to make sense of where he was. It took several minutes of hard thinking, the end of which left him with an overwhelming weight of despair and loneliness.

A desire gripped him to be somewhere, to be with someone. Someone connected to what he used to be before he had become like this.

*What have I become?*

It took him two buses and forty-five minutes before he stood in front of Valentina's apartment building in Villa Crespo.

*"¿Quién es?"* Valentina's familiar voice squawked through the intercom. Daniel's heart leaped inside him. He realized how much he missed friends. How much he missed her.

"It's Ingl…it's Daniel," he said.

*"¿Dani? ¡Dani! ¡Subí!"*

The lobby door buzzed.

In the elevator, Daniel watched the slow climb to the third floor. He saw a familiar stain on the passing shaft wall. How many times had he seen it? He remembered the taste of her full lips and the softness of her breasts.

He couldn't remember why they had agreed to just be friends. That was a long time ago.

Valentina was waiting for him and she smothered him in an embrace.

"Dani, we've been so worried about you! You disappeared."

She stopped and crinkled her nose. "You smell terrible." She pushed away from him and looked him up and down. "Are you okay? Fede said you…oh, *entrá*, come in," she said, pulling him by the arm into the living room and toward the sofa. "Oh, you poor thing. What's wrong?"

Valentina, in jeans and a sweater, sat cross-legged beside him. "I'm so worried about you," she said, rubbing his shoulder. "Can I get you anything?"

Daniel leaned over and kissed her on the mouth. He pulled her toward him, and his hand cupped her breast.

*"¿Qué hacés, Dani?"* Valentina said, pushing on him, but Daniel kissed her harder and fumbled with the button of her jeans.

"Get off me!" Valentina said. She slapped him hard across the face. "What are you doing? You're scaring me, Dani."

He gripped her harder and rolled on top of her. Valentina shrieked and twisted away from him and tumbled off the sofa. She scrambled up and stood by the window, shaking.

"Get out," she said, and her lips trembled. She hid her face in her hands.

"I'm sorry. I'm so sorry," said Daniel, and he fell on his knees in front of her. "I need help, Vale. *Por favor. Ayudáme.*"

He felt a terrible panic of having ruined something of great value that could never be replaced, like when he secretly played with his *abuelo's* pocket watch and left it out in the rain.

"Get out!" Valentina screamed and ran at Daniel, flailing at his head and face.

Daniel pulled himself to his feet, stumbling as Valentina pushed him out of the apartment and slammed the door.

# CHAPTER 52 – LAS CONDESAS

## *The Condesas*

Admiral Bertotti had a problem, and he knew it. "Have Sebastian meet me at Las Condesas," he instructed his secretary.

At 1 p.m. sharp, the Admiral was seated as his regular table and swirling his wine glass. Out the window he saw Sebastian cross Plaza San Martín and turn onto Calle Reconquista. With a nod to the bodyguards, his aide entered the restaurant and took a seat across from his boss.

Las Condesas was a downtown tradition. The midweek lunch catered to bureaucrats and executives from the office towers overlooking Retiro Park. It was a place where people lingered, and business got done. Slabs of meat hung on skewers around an open spit just inside the front windows, beckoning to all but welcoming few. Lapacho walnut beams supported the whitewashed walls, and a bar extended across the right side of the restaurant.

The menu was meat. The handful of pasta and fish options were included as a courtesy but generally ignored by diners and discouraged by the scowling waiters in their black vests and bow ties.

The Admiral looked up from his papers. Sebastian, he knew, was of humble origins and ill at ease in such restaurants. While the cuts of meat and sweetbreads would be familiar to him, the quality and prices would not. Sebastian would be unused to the impeccable wait staff attuned to such social class subtleties, and whose careers depended on worthier clients who appreciated their discernments.

"Have you read *Frankenstein*?" asked the Admiral, finally addressing his lunch companion.

"No, sir."

"Did you see the movie?"

"No."

The Admiral contemplated Sebastian across the table. "You have no imagination."

"I have no imagination."

"No imagination and no ambition either," said the Admiral. "That's why you work for me. It's what makes you so useful." It was the highest compliment he had ever paid his aide, and the Admiral felt an odd feeling of warmth inside him that he attributed to the wine.

The Admiral put his elbows on the table. "You see, Victor Frankenstein reanimates a dead body that he's assembled from various parts, and this grotesque monster gets out of control and goes on a rampage of violence and destruction. But what happens is the monster recognizes his freakish nature, and he cries out to his maker." The Admiral tilted his head back and closed his eyes, enjoying the pleasant lightheaded rush of the alcohol to his brain.

*"I ought to be thy Adam; but I am rather the fallen angel."*

The Admiral opened his eyes. "In the end, you see, Victor is sorry for creating this monster. It begs for forgiveness, and Victor is sorry *for* the monster, but it must be destroyed."

A waiter arrived at the table with menus. He handed the wine list to the Admiral, who waved it away. "Get us another bottle of the Rutini. Bring us the *chinchulines* and two *bifes de lomo*. Rare."

"I'll have the raviolis instead," said Sebastian quietly. "And no wine for me, thank you."

The Admiral looked at him, appreciating that his aide's literary shortcomings extended to the culinary arts as well. The waiter seemed unhappy too, and he snapped up the menus and turned on his heel.

"I need you to do something," said the Admiral. "We have a situation. *Vos entendés.* These rogue elements, they must be controlled."

Sebastian said nothing.

"These policemen are an embarrassment," continued the Admiral, "to me and to my boss. To our entire nation. It's a complication with the Church too. I don't give a damn about the fear they're spreading. Keeps the subversives off balance. It's the embarrassment I care about."

A waiter brought the wine. Another brought the sweetbreads and a dish of chimichurri.

"Give me your report from this morning," said Bertotti.

Sebastian had the folder in his hands. "First of all, sir, another assault. In Martínez, they broke into the house of a nephew of Forchieri, beat him up in front of his wife and kids. Stole some cash and valuables. The man is in the hospital. These were policemen and didn't even attempt to hide it. Yesterday evening, just before closing, a bank robbery. Banco Galicia, in Olivos. They had masks, but several people recognized the police-issued guns. And in Córdoba, a bar fight. Three policemen shot a civilian in the stomach. The owner called police headquarters to complain, and that night his establishment was broken into and smashed."

"Dammit," said the Admiral.

"What do you want me to do?" said Sebastian.

"What should you *do?*" cried the Admiral, pounding the table. "Haven't you been listening? Frankenstein, you Cretan, Frankenstein! Our monsters must be destroyed. I'll tell you what you should do. I want you to stop this. I want a list of our problems. Find out who they are. And about the Córdoba thing. Call Commander Menéndez. You tell him I said he needs to get his people under control."

The entrées arrived. The bife de lomo was served with a flourish while the plate of raviolis was plunked down in front of Sebastian.

"You know," the Admiral said, waving his thick steak knife over the spread, "a fine cut of beef and a superb Malbec, these are the things that remind us of what we are fighting for. Of what really matters. It's what separates us from the subversives."

They ate in silence until the plates were cleared and the coffee served.

"One more thing," said the Admiral. "We need to manage public opinion on this. Let's announce this crackdown on these rascals within the police force. Make some showy arrests. Tell the communications minister to prepare an article for the morning papers. Tell Picozzi too. I know he's anxious to smooth things out with the foreign press, especially with all those bastards about to arrive for the FIFA World Cup."


It was 5:30 a.m. and the Admiral was at the office. It was his favorite time of day, well before anyone else arrived, when he could work uninterrupted and when he thought most clearly. He had to make his own coffee or wait for Sebastian to arrive later.

The Admiral read the press release in the morning paper and tossed it onto his desk. He opened a drawer and reached for the bottle of Johnnie Walker. It was almost empty, and he poured the last of it into a tumbler and gulped it down. He leaned back in his chair and let the alcohol clear his mind.

He needed to focus on the issue at hand and to be

circumspect about it. It was one of the things he was good at. Looking at the bigger picture.

Yes, it was true, he thought. Many of the policemen, and even some of his own agents, were unbalanced. But in every war, the Admiral mused expansively, there was a progressive degradation that couldn't be helped. And now, here, a certain kind of lawlessness had settled in. It hadn't been there at the beginning. No. In the beginning, it was merely collateral damage that occurred in the process of executing operations against the subversives. Smashed doors, busted furniture, and broken bodies. Unavoidable byproducts in the business of creating destroyed lives.

Yet the business was changing, and the change deserved study. The government was winning this war against the communists. There was more demand for subversives now than supply. With legitimate targets becoming scarcer and the testosterone pump fully primed, the byproduct was becoming the object itself. The young men just had too much enthusiasm. *Yes, that was it.* The sheer pleasure of unbridled hooliganism. The young men spoiled for a fight, and the officers and supervisors encouraged it because it achieved more results. The Admiral smiled. Certainly no one could fault him for lack of results, especially not President Villalobos.

We just need to rein these men in, thought the Admiral, these rogue *grupos de tarea.* He wasn't about to let a few bad apples ruin the progress he'd made. *It can be handled.* The Admiral found himself thinking about one of his rogue agents. This Inglés – Romandini, he was a special case, but he too was done. He'd cracked. He's no more use to me now, he reflected. Sebastian would handle it.

The Admiral reviewed some paperwork and then checked his wristwatch. It was 6:25 a.m. *Sebastian better not be damned late*. It was bad enough that he refused to come into the office before 6:30.

Picking up the empty whiskey bottle, the Admiral walked down the hall and into Sebastian's small office where he placed it in the middle of the neat desk to remind his aide to procure him another. He couldn't recall if he had ever been in here before. A picture frame caught his eye, a smiling woman with two shy boys clutching her skirt. Strange, thought the Admiral. Sebastian had never mentioned them before. *Of course he has children. Everyone does. Everyone except me. Damn Soledad.* Another problem that needs my fixing, he thought. This too could be handled. He was good at these things.

He sighed and returned to his corner office where he tilted his head back to collect the last drops from the tumbler. He wanted coffee.

# CHAPTER 53 – EL CHUPADO

## *The Unregistered Detainee*

Daniel stood across the street from his old apartment and wavered. The late afternoon sun on his back brought no warmth. He just wanted a hot shower and a short rest. Maybe there would be something he could eat.

But something was not right. He sensed the apartment was being watched.

Daniel backtracked and made his way to Pato's apartment, but the police activity there was obvious. Panicked now, he boarded a train in the direction of his father's house. It was an instinctive move. And in the steady rhythms of the tracks and the gentle swaying of the car, Daniel comprehended his desperate need of family like a deep ache in his bones. He knew his father would overlook all wrongs. His father was waiting for him, not judging. His father would help him.

But as the train clattered past his childhood home and toward the station just beyond it, Danie's heart sank. Cop cars were parked in front and policemen milled about. It wasn't supposed to be like this. He was supposed to return home a hero, not a hunted criminal. His father would know his son was a thief and a murderer.

That's what he was.

He felt a deadness inside like a cold lump of resignation.

Daniel got off at the next station and found a pay phone. He unhooked the receiver and slumped against the side of the booth. He set the phone back in its cradle but picked it back up and punched the numbers. An unfamiliar voice picked up.

"*Sí.*"

"I want to speak with Emilio."

"Is that you, Inglés? Why don't you come here so you can speak with your father in person? He misses you a lot. In fact, we all miss you."

"Put my father on the line."

"Like I said," came the voice on the other end, "Emilio can't speak right now. He says not to worry. The police are here now, and everything will be okay. He wants you to come home."

*What are they doing to my father?* Daniel knew the tricks they would play. They would try to get him to talk and give up information, to figure out what his mental state was.

The policeman on the other end continued. "We know *everything*. It's best if you give yourself up."

*What do they know?* Daniel's breath came in short gasps, and he covered the mouthpiece with his hand.

"Pato's been talking to us. He told us it was all your idea," said the policeman. "That *you* are the one who pulled the trigger at the payment center. Don't you want to come in and clear this up, Inglés? Give us your story of what really happened?"

Daniel braced himself against the phone booth. He knew at that moment it was all over. The word was out, and he would have no allies. He was vulnerable and he knew it. The police knew it. He tried to stay calm, but he felt trapped, the walls closing in on him.

"You have nothing to say?" said the policeman on the other end, the annoyance audible. Daniel thought of escape. It was his only option.

"Do you know why we are here? At your father's house? We're taking him in to be interrogated. We're taking him now. This is your fault, you understand, Inglés."

"You bastards," Daniel said, spitting into the mouthpiece. He thought of El Oso and imagined his father tied naked to the bedframe. And suddenly Daniel's anger turned into a cold sweat as he realized escape was now impossible.

"No, *you* are the bastard, you cop killer. Traitor! Turn yourself in and you'll be treated fairly. We'll let your father go. We'll catch you anyway sooner or later, Inglés. It will be much worse for you."

Daniel pounded the receiver against his head.

"Inglés? Are you there?"

Daniel hung up and vomited on the floor of the booth.

He was the only attorney Daniel knew. The office was on Calle Viamonte, and Daniel had been there three times before, always with his father. The first time, his parents had come to sign a will, and Daniel remembered playing hide and seek with his brother Antonio in the cramped office. When his mother died, his father had hired the attorney to pursue the settlement from the company that had operated the truck with the faulty brakes.

The third time, Daniel had signed papers too. His father had added a second remis and registered his service as a family company in the hopes that the fleet would expand.

The office lights were on, and Daniel climbed the wooden stairs to the second floor.

At *Arballos y Asociados*, Esteban Arballo was the only attorney and notary, and his wife served as secretary, bookkeeper, and paralegal. There were no associates and never had been. The sign's aspirational power had been lost many years before.

The attorney didn't immediately recognize Daniel, but he

ushered him into the small and cluttered office as the connection was made.

"Ah, yes, the Romandini family." Arballo sat in a chair next to Daniel. "How is your father Emilio? It's been a long time."

Daniel attempted to answer but a welt grew in his throat. It was the memories of being in this office before, and it was the kindness of Arballo, who sensed Daniel's fragile state and patted his arm and told Daniel everything was going to be okay.

But Daniel knew things weren't okay. *How did I end up here?* He tried to tell Arballo everything, and several times he started but realized he wasn't beginning at the right spot. Then he would go back and try again only to have his voice trail off. He simply couldn't make sense of his own story. It was a jumbled mess.

The attorney's eyes grew wider and wider as he put the bits together and comprehended the full horror before him. Arballo wrung his hands and beads of sweat appeared on his brow. "I'm sorry, *mi hijo,*" he said, "there's nothing I can do for you. I don't practice criminal law, *viste?*"

Arballo stood and looked at his watch. "I have another appointment, I'm sure you understand. I can refer you," he said, and his face suddenly brightened. "Yes, there's a law practice nearby on Corrientes. I'm sure I have the address." He riffled through a drawer. "Yes, yes, here."

Arballo wrote on a slip of paper and pressed it into Daniel's hand. "It won't take you but a few minutes to walk there."

"I shouldn't have come, *abogado,*" said Daniel, standing and pacing the small office. "I didn't know what to do."

The attorney scratched at his chin, and Daniel could tell his presence was making him very nervous.

"I'm turning myself in," Daniel said, and saying it out loud seemed to settle it for him. It was his only option. "Yes, I'll do it tonight."

Arballo took Daniel by the shoulders. "I think you should consider leaving the country." The attorney lowered his voice and looked past Daniel as if perhaps there were someone else in the office. "Others have done that. You must know. You, with your story, you're not safe. Not in South America. Maybe Mexico. Many young people – *subversivos,*" Arballo whispered emphatically, "they're going to Spain."

"No," Daniel said, shaking his head. "What would they do to my father? I deserve what's coming to me."

Arballo blinked and licked his lips. He put his hand on Daniel's shoulder and nudged him toward the door. "Daniel, maybe you should see a priest. It would do you good right now."

Daniel laughed, and it sounded to him like the laugh of the beast from his dream, the beast in the confessional booth. "Jesus Christ himself couldn't help me now, *abogado*. I'm beyond the reaches of anything good. I'm at the gates of hell, and I don't need a priest to tell me that. No, it's all over." And Daniel bounded down the creaking stairs two at a time.


The Plaza San José Flores was intended as a rare break in the concrete neighborhood, but its rusted swing sets and misshapen trees created instead a grotesque interruption. The leaves from the previous fall lay scattered in small piles where the wind and passing feet had pushed them under benches and around the fountain and into the depressions by the walkways.

It was past midnight, and from his vantage point, Daniel counted fifteen policemen staked around the plaza and the Estación Flores beside it. A single bar on the plaza was still open. Music and laughter spilled from its tables within the clear plastic sheets that protected the patrons from the wind and rain.

After leaving the attorney's office, Daniel had worked up the courage to call the police and arrange this meeting where he would turn himself in. But now he felt fearful again. He doubted they would honor the promise to release his father. He thought about what Arballo had said about fleeing the country.

Daniel didn't trust the police. They would kill him and arrange it to look like a shootout, or maybe his body would be placed at the scene of a gun battle with terrorists. He knew about that. How easily he could be disappeared. Another *chupado*.

He didn't blame the police for wanting him dead, but he didn't want to die. He felt a sudden fear of dying forgotten and alone. He slipped behind a tree and lit a cigarette with unsteady hands. He recalled a story from his grandfather's friend, a German immigrant who had fought at the Battle of Verdun. The unrelenting bombing had pinned him for three days, alone with the corpses of his comrades, their chests splayed open and intestines spilled out, and all he could think of was how he would die without anyone knowing what had happened to him.

Daniel crushed the cigarette butt beneath his boot and thought bitterly of how little a life was worth, but yet how desperately he wanted his own to count for something.

It was time.

Daniel walked to Calle Rivadavia and entered the Plaza Flores. He thrust his hands into his worn leather jacket and thought of how many times he had used it to commit robberies, its large pockets perfect for hiding his weapons.

Daniel saw the cops around the plaza as he headed to the

steps to the train station. On the platform, a man pretended to read a newspaper under the lamplight. There were several other policemen on the platform, and beyond it, a half-dozen cop cars were parked in a cul-de-sac, their lights off.

Daniel stopped and held out his hands, palms outstretched. "I'm turning myself in," Daniel cried out. The cops swarmed in with their weapons drawn. "I'm turning myself in. You are witnesses!"

He was thrown to the platform and felt the weight of bodies pile on top of him. His breath came in gasps. He knew they would take no chances with him, a dangerous traitor. They relieved him of his jacket and weapons. He was handcuffed and a hood thrown over his head. The burlap smelled of sweat and fear.

# CHAPTER 54 – LA CÁRCEL DE DEVOTO
## *The Devoto Prison*

Inaugurated in 1927, the Cárcel de Devoto covered an entire city block in the Buenos Aires neighborhood by the same name. Despite its fairy castle appearance, the prison had a long history of problems with sanitation, ventilation, and safety. Fifty years later, overcrowding was added to the prison's many problems as the military regime had an insatiable demand for these dilapidated buildings.

Daniel was taken to Unit 2 at the prison, a place he knew as one of the largest clandestine detention centers. *How many subversives have I brought here?* He tried to remember any of the faces or a detail about any of them, but he couldn't recall anything at all, and for some reason, it filled him with panic. He would be forgotten too.

*Unidad 2* was one of the strange new names entered into the annals of this dirty war, taking its place beside others such as El Olimpo, Automotores Orletti, El Campito, La ESMA, La Mansión Seré – places later seared into the fragile social conscience but, for now, simply centers in the capital city where subversives could be rounded up and conveniently tortured and shot.

Getting into Unidad 2 at the Cárcel was a violent affair, one that began upon entering its gates. Daniel heard the angry voices and sharp sounds. Hands grabbed at him, stripping him naked and leaving only the hood. He steeled himself for what was coming. He knew about the gauntlets and sensed one forming before him. On previous visits, he had seen guards lining the pathway just inside, each carrying a meter-long baton, the *bastón largo*. The guards were eager tonight. They knew who was coming, and they were ready for this special *chupado*.

Daniel was kicked forward, and the blows from the *bastones* rained down with particular cruelty. It hurt so much that his body went numb. He cried out not from the pain but from an utter feeling of despair. He desperately wished for his penance to matter, to make up in some small way for all the bad he had done.

Daniel collapsed at the end of the line. Arms pulled him up, trying to make him stand. He was dragged and thrown into a solitary cell.

It seemed like hours later when Daniel heard the tramp of boots. He turned his head but found one eye was swollen shut and the other was no use on account of the hood. The lock clicked open.

"Get up, *hijo de puta*! *Levantá.*"

Daniel absorbed a kick to his ribs. He tried to get up but collapsed. Everything hurt. He couldn't get his body to do anything. His mind was foggy.

"*Dejálo que se muera.* Let him die."

He felt himself lifted and thrown. His head hit something hard.

He awoke again later, shivering and naked. The cell smelled of urine. It hurt to breathe.

A key turned and a door opened. Daniel knew what the loud voices were for, and he curled himself into a ball to protect himself from the blows.

Over the next days, instead of food he received beatings. After ten days, his hood was removed and the handcuffs switched to the front, allowing him to attend to his raw and bleeding wrists.

One bright afternoon, he was blindfolded and taken outside. "We're going to kill you," he was told, and a blow to the back of his legs forced him to kneel.

Daniel heard the rattle of someone handling a machine gun, and he felt the barrel press against his temple. He shut his eyes. *It will be a quick death.* He almost welcomed it. The pop of the weapon made his ears hurt. He felt a searing pain on his scalp. The bullet had been fired inches away.

One evening he was extracted and pushed into the back seat of a car. The vehicle wound its way through heavy traffic. A sixth sense told Daniel what was coming.

The car came to a stop and Daniel was ushered into a building and down two flights of stairs where the air was humid. Dampness clung to his body.

A door opened and his hood was pulled off. Daniel blinked in the light. El Oso stood shirtless in the middle of the room, grinning. The single overhead bulb cast stark shadows. Light shone off his glistening bald head and white belly. El Palito was there too, wringing his hands in the corner and shifting his weight from one foot to another.

The instruments of torture lay on a table next to the metal bedframe *parilla*. The electric prod and the length of cable. The gags and the telephone. The sharp smell of iron-tinged blood mixed with half-eaten empanadas on the floor.

*"¿Cerveza?"* offered El Oso, uncapping a beer and extending it toward Daniel, whose hands remained handcuffed behind him.

*"Hijo de puta,"* said Daniel.

El Oso grunted and took a swig of beer himself. "I was told to treat you with extra care."

He pushed Daniel onto the metal frame. Palito produced an extra set of handcuffs.

Daniel tensed. Adrenaline coursed through his body. Perhaps he still could be capable of doing some good.

In one quick movement, he arched his back on the bedframe and wrapped his legs around El Oso's knees and twisted. El Oso fell heavily, and Daniel leapt on top of his head, trying to crush it. El Oso howled with rage as he wriggled to get out from under him.

El Palito came in swinging the set of handcuffs at Daniel's head, but Daniel dodged them, and the blow fell onto his back. Daniel headbutted him and El Palito went down cold.

El Oso managed to get loose in the exchange, and he tackled Daniel. They both fell hard onto the concrete floor. Daniel bit down on the bulbous nose and ripped. Blood spurted onto both of them. El Oso screeched and jumped onto Daniel, pummeling his unprotected face with his fists. Daniel aimed a well-placed knee into El Oso's groin.

Guards rushed in.

Daniel was lashed spread-eagled to the parrilla and left waiting while El Oso had his nose treated. A short time later, bandaged and unhappy, the big man returned.

The electric shocks made Daniel feel as if his body parts were being ripped from him. He lost consciousness. When he came to, he found himself staring at the blood leaking from his nose and pooling on the edge of the bedframe before trickling onto the floor.

When the torture finally stopped, burn marks covered much of Daniel's body, and his testicles and feet were completely black.

He was unable to feel his feet for several days, and every day there were new layers of dead black skin to be peeled off. It was two weeks before he could walk again.

Daniel smelled the smoke before he heard the screaming. A fire had broken out in another pavilion of the Devoto Prison, and by the time it all ended, fifty-eight prisoners had died and sixty-two were injured.

The official report said it started with rioting prisoners who lit mattresses on fire, and the flames had spread out of control. Later, Daniel heard the filtered accounts by prisoners indicating a different story, one of criminal neglect and of murder. The firefighters had not been permitted to enter. The fire was under control, the prison officials had insisted, and besides, the dead couldn't be helped anymore.

In the weeks that followed, Daniel was beaten almost daily, and he felt himself barely hanging onto his sanity. During one such session, the tormentor leaned over Daniel's broken body as he gasped for breath.

"I was told to tell you your buddy Cacho is dead."

Daniel couldn't hold it together, and he sobbed, not knowing if it was pity for himself or sadness for Cacho. He remembered their day at the park at Tigre.

*"¿Muerto?"* said Daniel. "How?"

"Who the hell cares?" said the guard. "Probably was a cop killer just like you. I hope he rots in hell."

Hatred coursed through Daniel, and he imagined all the things he would do to this guard if he were given the chance – and if he weren't so hurt. *For Cacho.* He'd be fighting for Cacho.

After two months at Cárcel de Devoto, Daniel was moved to another location, a police station named Comisaría 50 on Avenida Gaona.

One day in his first week, there was a tap on the bars. Daniel roused himself, hobbling on damaged feet. A middle-aged woman held a pitcher of water and smiled.

*"Buen día,"* the woman said and smiled again, her face misshapen and scarred, and her large teeth crooked. "You are thirsty. Drink. Good, good."

It was the first human contact Daniel had had with anyone aside from the guards. Over the next few weeks, the woman visited on occasion, bringing water and sometimes food. Crackers, a hunk of cheese. An apple. She brought him ointments and bandages for his hands and feet.

He learned she was a prisoner from the women's wing. She had been a frequent visitor to the police commissaries for prostitution, and her unwillingness to give up her trade had landed her at Comisaría 50 for an extended period. She had a knack for making herself useful to both guards and prisoners and was given some freedom about the floor.

Daniel strained to hear her steps in the corridor. She spoke softly to him, like a mother, and reached her fingers through the bars to stroke his hands. She held his face. Her hands were warm and gentle. She smoothed his hair and patted his cheek.

Daniel couldn't remember the last time he'd felt a woman's touch. He wiped his eyes with his sleeve.

# CHAPTER 55 – EL ENCUENTRO

## *The Encounter*

"You are a priest, yes?" The guard stood outside Gastón's cell.

Gastón tried to process the question. It could only mean one thing. The thought filled him more with sadness than fear.

Things had been better since he'd been transferred from the ESMA to this new prison. No hood or handcuffs. Even his own private cell. He should have known it wouldn't last. It was stupid to hope there would be no more torture.

The guard let out a deep sigh. "Well, are you a priest or not?"

"I'm Father Gastón, yes."

"Come," the guard said, and beckoned Gastón out to the hallway. The guard led the way to another prison wing until he stopped before a cell.

"A man says he needs a priest. Won't stop asking for one. His problems are beyond our capabilities. Perhaps a word from a priest will do him some good. Make him more receptive to our rehabilitation." The guard smiled. "When you're done here, *Padre*, there are others. I'll come for you."

The guard put his hand on Gastón's shoulder. "Be careful what you say. *¿Entendés?"*

Gastón was marched to several cells that day. He took their confessions and offered what words of encouragement he could. Over the next days as word got out, demand for his services increased. Gastón found encouragement by ministering to others, and his own faith and hope were strengthened. He found himself clinging to the idea he could save these imprisoned men and that his reason for enduring depended on these priestly duties.

He met with prostitutes in the women's wing, many who owed their incarceration to other criminal activities too. He remembered his days at the downtown parish, and he thought of Old Ezequiel. He now felt very old himself.

One day a woman appeared at Gastón's cell. He had met her before, a middle-aged prostitute who seemed to always manage a smile. "Will you please visit my friend at the far end of the next wing?" she asked.

The guards, however, were unwilling. "He's a violent psychotic," they told Gastón. "The only help he needs is the *bastón*," and they rattled the priest's bars with their long batons.

Gastón's priestly duties were abruptly cancelled one day. Over the next week, he was subjected to occasional beatings and sleep deprivation. He grew despondent over the erratic mood swings of the guards, which vacillated between brutality and indifference. He begged them to let him resume his prisoner visits as if his very life depended upon it.

On a cold morning, Gastón was taken to the next wing and down the hallway to the last cell. "Don't get close to the bars," he was told.

The cell was dimly lit and Gastón made out an agitated figure sitting on the bed, crossing and uncrossing his legs.

"I'm a priest. I've come to visit you. May we talk?"

Leaping from the bed, the man emerged from the shadows and appeared suddenly at the bars, startling Gastón so that he jumped back. The man's eyes were large and wild, his thick dirty hair matted.

"I'm Father Gastón. May I pray for you?"

A horrified look crossed the man's face, and he lurched back from the bars into the dark recess.

"*¿Viste?* Didn't I tell you?" the guard said to Gastón. "A complete idiot."

Gastón turned his attention to the prisoner. He read him Psalms. He prayed for God's peace to descend on him, and for God's hope and courage in this dark time amidst those who can harm the body but not the eternal soul.

The poor light made it hard for Gastón to see, but the man seemed to be sitting still, listening.

"My brother," said Gastón, "you and I both are in a dark place. A very low place. But it's precisely at the bottom when most people discover God's grace and grandeur. What's glorious about the bottom is that God is here."

Two weeks passed before Gastón was asked again to visit the troubled detainee in the other wing. For whatever reason, the prison again had cracked down on the prisoners, and Gastón had not been spared. He limped painfully down the hallway, a reminder of a recent treatment. The worst part was never knowing when they would come for him. This time when they came for him it wasn't for a beating, but his heart still pounded in his chest as he followed. *How can I possibly help this crazy, violent man?* He wished Ezequiel were here. He would know what to say and what to do.

"He's stopped eating," said the guard as he left him in front of the cell. "I don't care one *carajo* if he dies, but the whore won't stop insisting you see him."

Gastón could see the figure in the corner, swaying.

"Daniel? They tell me you are Daniel. I'm Father Gastón. I came here before. A few weeks ago."

"I know who you are." The voice came from the shadows.

"You know me?" said Gastón, and he approached the bars, straining to see the face. "From the parish, perhaps?"

"If you knew who I was, you wouldn't be here to pray for me."

Gastón pressed his face against the bars, forgetting the guard's warning.

There was a quick movement and a strong grip pinned Gastón's hands. Daniel's face appeared inches away, his eyes no longer wild but sad and resigned.

"You tried to bless me once in your confessional booth. You offered me absolution, but I was unforgiveable then and even more so now. I've become a monster."

Gastón remembered the voice now, and the same unsettling feeling washed over him.

"I remember," Gastón said, recalling the experience. "You mocked God's forgiveness. You said you knew Father Brizzio too. Do you know where he is? Who are you?" Gastón blurted out, unable to contain his curiosity.

The hands gripped his more tightly. Daniel's face pressed against the bars.

"Will you forgive the man responsible for what's happened to you?" Daniel said. "The man who has the blood of Father Brizzio and his sister on his hands?"

Gastón recoiled.

The hands released him, and Gastón reeled backwards into the hallway.

"I'm a policeman, Father. I *was* anyway," said Daniel, still standing at the bars. "I once believed I was doing good, but things got confusing. Complicated. Perhaps just like your Father Brizzio. He's complicated too. A killer and a priest. Did you know that, Father? Is that what you are too?"

Gastón scrambled up from the floor, his face flushed. "No, I'm not," he shouted. *I'm innocent*, he wanted to scream. He knew Daniel was right about Brizzio, and Gastón felt a sudden anger at his roommate for dragging him into this mess.

He looked at the imprisoned man and he thought how easy it would be to hate him for what he had done, too. But this pitiful picture of brokenness before him was such a vision of God's preposterous reconciliation that Gastón buried his hands in his face and wept.

"You told me in the confessional," said Daniel, "that God extends his love and forgiveness to the undeserving. You said no sin is too great. Do you still believe that, Father?"

Gastón felt the sad eyes lock onto his. And the sadness seemed to peel the scales from Gastón's eyes and reveal the full complexity of this *dirty war*. Things were never black and white. Yet there still was right and wrong, and more importantly, there was God's love and forgiveness.

Time was up. As the guard took his arm to lead him away, Gastón realized he needed Daniel as much as Daniel needed him. *Perhaps more.*


One afternoon, a guard let the woman into Daniel's cell. She carried two pails of warm water, a towel, and clean clothes. Gently undressing Daniel, she gave him a sponge bath.

The woman rubbed and washed Daniel from head to toe. She scrubbed his matted hair and combed it out. When he was toweled dry, she helped him dress in clean clothes and she kissed him on the top of the head.

The guard let her out and the cell door clanged shut. She turned to Daniel. "I'll be released tomorrow. I've come to say goodbye."

Daniel stepped toward her. "You are the sweetest person I've ever known," he said, and he reached his hands out through the bars to trace the scars on her face. "You are a bouquet of lovely smelling flowers, my beautiful mami," he said, and the woman's eyes filled with tears and slid down her ugly face.

Daniel knew Father Gastón would be coming that day, and he was not surprised when the priest stood in front of his cell.

"It was difficult to get permission to see you again," said Gastón. "They say you are...not right in the head."

"You didn't need to trouble yourself, Father," said Daniel, coming forward and standing at the bars, his hair now combed out and his body no longer reeking. "I know your priestly duty requires you to come and forgive me. Isn't that why you came? To make yourself feel better?"

Daniel was glad for the visit, for someone to talk to, even this curious gangly priest. He hoped his words wouldn't scare the nervous man off.

"I did in fact come to forgive you," said the priest, pushing his wire-framed glasses higher onto his nose. "To forgive you for what you did. And I don't doubt that you are correct, what you said the other day about Brizzio being a...for doing those things."

"You are surprised," said Daniel. "I suppose as a priest you must expect to see goodness in the world. There is nothing but evil, and I am a part of it."

But even as the words fell out of his mouth, Daniel didn't believe them. They rang hollow as if they no longer described him. The rage living in the pit of his stomach was gone.

Gastón reached a hand through the bars and placed it on Daniel's shoulder. "You must not despair, Daniel," he said. "Remember that outside there is good, like all the good when we think of our mothers. There's beauty. Beauty like the purple blossoms of the jacaranda I can see from my cell if I stand on my tiptoes. And there is truth to combat all the lies of this dirty war. Somewhere, there is still *true* truth. All these things point us to our desire for God."

Gastón produced a small thick book. "I've brought you something," he said, and he pressed a Bible into Daniel's hands. "I pray it encourages you, like it does me. Psalm 35 says,

> *But I trust in your unfailing love;*
> *my heart rejoices in your salvation. "*

Daniel suddenly recalled the words from years ago as an altar boy. He chimed in with a surprised Father Gastón,

> *"I will sing the Lord's praise,*
> *for he has been good to me. "*

"You see," said Gastón, drawing Daniel's eyes into his own, "the Bible is not about how to be good people but rather to learn how good God has been to us. And in this confused world, *He* is the source of good and beauty and truth."

Daniel's mind turned to his home. A deep ache welled inside him. He thought of his mother, and he could smell her scent through her red scarf. He remembered the jacaranda across the street and the crunch of the purple blossoms under his feet.

He put his hands to his face and wept.

# CHAPTER 56 – EL TRASLADO
## *The Transfer*

The door to Gastón's cell opened and he was jerked to his feet, the hood over his head secured with a rope. His hands were bound behind him. He felt a sharp prick in his arm. As the guards dragged him down the hallway, Gastón tried to stay conscious. *Is it the middle of the night?* A grogginess settled over him that he couldn't shake.

"*Traslado,*" was all he could make out. *A transfer?* He'd been horrified of this place, and now he was afraid to leave. *How long have I been here?* It seemed like a lifetime although he knew likely it was only a few months.

He heard the heavy doors to the outside open. The cool night air enveloped him. Spring sweetness filled his nostrils from under the hood. Pushed from behind, he stumbled forward and was boosted into the back of a truck.

They were moving. The vehicle ground through the gears, and the hum of the engine lulled him to sleep.

The truck lurched to a stop. Gastón awoke. His eyes felt heavy and lethargic. He was pushed off the back of the truck and fell onto the hard pavement. It seemed a dream. His head spun. The lusty beat of helicopter propellers cut the night air. He was pulled up by two guards and made to stand. Were there other prisoners here too? He couldn't be sure. The whir of the screws was closer now, and a blast of wind pressed his cheeks and glued his clothes to his body. Gastón tried to breathe. His heart pounded in his chest. He tried to focus.

"Climb up. Hurry. ¡*Apurá!*" someone shouted in his ear.

Gastón was pushed into a seat. He panicked, hyperventilating under his hood. He had never flown in his life, and the thought of a helicopter terrified him. His stomach knotted into a ball, and he began to sweat. His feet trembled. He desperately wanted to see, and he tried with his elbows to remove the hood.

He felt a guard's hand on his knee. "We're heading out over the river. You'll like it there, trust me," the guard yelled. "Relax. It's a short flight."

Gastón heard laughter from other guards and some words he couldn't catch.

The door of the helicopter closed, and they left the ground and banked sharply. The cabin was loud, and the vibrations pulsed through his body. Gravity held him to his seat. He wanted to throw up. He felt tired again and just wanted to sink back and sleep. He fought against it. His eyes closed.

He dreamt that hands were groping him and ripping his clothes off. He leaned his head over his knees to try to get away from the hands. He squirmed in the cuffs behind him to get free. He realized now he was awake. The dream was true. His shirt had been ripped from him and someone was tugging at his pants.

"We're getting you into your swimsuit. You're going for a late-night skinny-dip, Padre!" The guards laughed and Gastón felt a blow on the back of his head. Hands grabbed his legs and tied them together.

"We lied to you, Padre. Forgive us. You're not being transferred. You didn't really believe that, did you?" Now another voice. "You've heard of these kinds of flights, right? Well, it's your turn. Guess who we took just yesterday? Your good friend Father Brizzio. Maybe you should pray now, Father!"

Gastón's head spun.

"Father Brizzio? What have you done with him? Tell me!"

"We told you. He deserved everything coming to him. Just like you. Now you'll get a chance to explain it to God too."

The helicopter door opened.

*Save me, O God, for the waters are come in unto my soul!*

Hands grabbed him and he was thrown out into the dark space.

Gastón immediately hit the ground, landing hard on his side. He heard faint laughter with the departing whir of the blades.

*Am I dead? I'm not dead.*

He curled himself into a ball in the dirt, his arms wrapped around his naked body. He shivered and rocked and cried.

*I'm alive!*

# CHAPTER 57 – EL BAUTISMO

## *The Baptism*

The baptism happened on the same day the Admiral's mastiff had escaped during the night. It was a cold Saturday morning at the house on Calle Aguilar, and Admiral Juan Pablo Bertotti had awoken in a foul mood. He screamed into the phone using such profanity as the house staff had only ever heard him direct toward his wife.

The phone slammed into its cradle, and the Admiral was heard shouting at his wife. Soledad's soft voice pleaded in the pauses.

The old butler was upstairs replacing a light bulb but had started back down to the main floor when the Admiral appeared at the top of the stairs fully dressed and in a hurry. Bounding down, he quickly caught up with the shuffling manservant making his way down the steps.

"Get your limping carcass out of the way!" growled the Admiral, and he gave him a vicious kick in the seat of his pants that narrowly avoided tumbling the old man down the stairs.

And with that act, the Admiral finally succeeded in winning the last enmity of the entire household.

After Juan Pablo left, the house grew quiet. Soledad held her new baby in the sitting room upstairs, rocking slowly. She marveled at the tiny hands and fingers, and she gently squeezed the miniature toes. She giggled at the small mouth pursed into a scowl, fussing at the dry nipple offered to her.

"Where did you come from, *mi chiquita*? How could anyone not have wanted you, *preciosa*? We don't believe your mean old papá, now do we? He says someone left you on the steps of the Clínica Suizo Argentina. *No, mi nenita.*"

She fingered the downy black hair and gazed into the small porcelain face. "You are so beautiful, my little bunny rabbit. Your mami loves you so much."

Soledad closed her eyes and rocked her baby, and the white baptismal dress lay on the bed neatly pressed.


The church bells at the Catedral Metropolitana took a full ten minutes to chime through the noon hour. Inside it was cold, and a modest crowd of distinguished guests had gathered for the private baptism of Admiral Bertotti's new baby girl. The Cardinal Archbishop himself had been invited to administer the sacrament, but regrettably he had another commitment and had declined the honor.

Soledad stood nervously at the front of the cathedral with her baby. The Admiral was beside her in his creased dress whites. A painting of Mother Mary holding the infant Jesus caught Soledad's eye, and she remembered her visit to the Parroquia de la Inmaculada Concepción in Belgrano. "Thank you, sweet Blessed Mary, for your miracle," she mouthed.

The bishop stood by the baptismal font and waited for the chimes to die down and the last guests to settle into their seats.

"Children are a gift from the Lord," the bishop began.

"They are a reward from him. My dear brothers and sisters, let us ask our Lord Jesus Christ to look lovingly on this child who is to be baptized, on her parents and godparents, and on all the baptized."

"Lord, hear our prayer," came the unison response from the pews.

"Make the lives of this child's parents and godparents be examples of faith to inspire this child."

"Lord, hear our prayer."

"By the mystery of your death and resurrection, bathe this child in light, give her the new life of baptism, and welcome her into your Holy Church."

"Lord, hear our prayer."

At that same hour, directly outside the Catedral Metropolitana, the Madres de Plaza de Mayo were gathered again as they did every week, their cause now bolstered by the international attention received during the hosting of the FIFA World Cup.

But today there was a new face among the silent crowd of white-scarved mothers, and there was a new picture attached to a wooden stick, a young woman with striking long black hair and a porcelain face staring straight into the camera. Her lips were pursed in a Mona Lisa smile. *Eva Brizzio Ruíz y Su Bebé*, the sign said, and it was lost amidst the white-capped sea of banners and scarves that filled the plaza.

# CHAPTER 58 – LA LIBERACIÓN
## *The Liberation*

*Fall 1982 – Four Years Later*

"Daniel! Daniel!"

He felt a hand shaking him, and he leaped instinctively out of bed.

"*Relajá*," said the asylum prison guard. "Take it easy."

Fully awake now, Daniel noticed from the window that it was still dark.

"*¿Qué pasa?*" Daniel said.

"It's over," said the guard. He smiled. "Get your things. You're being released."

"What's over?" Daniel said. "*¿Qué decís, Ignacio?*"

"Everything's over," said the guard. "The war, *los militares*. All of it. You're being released, Daniel. Don't you get it?"

Daniel stood by his bed and tried to absorb what Ignacio was saying to him. He had known the guard for four years. They talked about everything and laughed a lot. They had become close. But Ignacio had never talked like this. News from the outside was taboo. There was no contact from the outside. Even Ignacio would never bend those rules.

*Could it be true? Was it really true?*

"The war," said Daniel slowly, more to himself than to the guard. *La Guerra de las Malvinas*. It had to be that. A couple of months ago, the guards had gotten lax and were caught up in listening to the radio, not careful to prevent the listening ears of the prisoners. Word spread quickly.

Looking to distract attention from growing domestic problems, the military regime had launched a war against Great Britain to take back the Falkland Islands. The radio gushed with the tremendous successes of the Argentines. The guards were euphoric. The impending victory had a cathartic effect on the strict rules within the psychiatric prison hospital, a balm that softened the tight lips. Daniel once saw the guards crowded around a sticker book the military regime published so citizens could tally the daily number of British ships and tanks Argentina had destroyed.

But two weeks ago, something had changed.

Daniel heard the rumors. The radio had announced abruptly the war was over. Argentina had lost. It had been a disaster, and the whole country was in shock. The conflict had lasted seventy-four days and claimed 649 Argentine soldiers and 255 British military lives.

"Did you hear me?" said Ignacio. "*Los militares*. President Villalobos resigned. There's going to be new elections. *Democratic* elections. You've been released, Daniel."

Daniel sat on his bed to steady himself. He stretched out his hand to grasp Ignacio's.

"I want to thank you for your kindness," said Daniel. "May God repay you."

Fifteen minutes later, Daniel stood by the entrance to the *Cárcel Psiquiátrica de Hombres*. His small bag contained everything he owned. He embraced Ignacio, who pressed a few pesos into his hand.

Daniel took a few tentative steps onto the sidewalk. He looked back, still in shock. He had been held there for over four years with no contact with anyone from the outside.

There was only one place to go.

He boarded a bus. He had thought about this many times, and he had rehearsed what he would say. But now that it suddenly was here, he choked up. He forgot all his plans. He knew only that he wanted to see his father even if his father didn't want to see him.

It was stuffy in the *colectivo*. It was the smell of humanity. It was the smell of life.

Daniel slid open the window and inhaled the fresh air.

*Almost there.*

He pulled the rope and stood, clutching his bag. *"Disculpá,"* he said as he made his way through the crowded bus and got off.

Daniel strained his eyes up the street.

It was a brilliant morning. As Daniel neared the house, he saw his father emerge, shuffling onto the narrow front porch and blinking against the sun's brightness. Daniel's heart surged with joy. He felt as if a great weight had been lifted from his shoulders and replaced by the buoyancy of freedom.

His father started down the short steps to the street, but suddenly he paused.

*"Papi!"*

His father's eyes brightened, and a broad smile dissolved the wrinkles of his face.

*"¡Mi hijo!"* his father cried out. He hurried forward and threw his arms around Daniel and kissed him.

"Papi, I'm so sorry..."

*"Callá, hijo.* Quiet. You are home! We are going to celebrate. I thought you were...I thought you were..." and his father's voice cracked, and he cried into Daniel's shoulder.

And to Daniel, his father smelled of tobacco and home and love, and of all things reasonable and good.

# CHAPTER 59 – SUDACA DE MIERDA

## *Greaser*

*Winter 2008 – Twenty-six Years Later*
*Barcelona, Spain*

The rain fell steadily and when the wind gusted, it beat against the window of the apartment above the sycamores that lined Las Ramblas. It was an unusually cold morning, and Juan Pablo Bertotti stood bundled in two sweaters, but he still didn't feel warm. The old radiator heaters never kept up on days like these. The dampness seemed to rot the bones in his arms and legs and seep into his very soul.

On any other day, Juan Pablo would have called the building manager at his home. But not today. Today the manager would not need to make the apologies and the excuses and would not have to find a way to end the call with an understanding that nothing would be done. *Sudaca de mierda.*

Today something kept Juan Pablo staring at the grayness outside. He let his mind wander to another street with tall sycamores, of a grand house on Calle Aguilar, of a life so long ago when he had been an admiral.

When he had been a man.

The call had come early that morning, even before he had washed his face and smoothed his gray hair and the single white shock that lay above his forehead, and before he had walked down to the café for a cortado and *El País*. The judge

348

had approved the extradition. He had already decided long ago what he was going to do when this phone call came, but now he found himself wavering. It was another phone call that gave him pause. The conversation with his daughter two days ago.

"Tell me the truth, Papi," her voice had come through his mobile phone, her voice tinny and faint from across the Atlantic.

"The truth, *mi hija*, is that you are my daughter," he had said. He could hear her crying.

"No, Papi, you've lied to me all my life. Soon the entire world will know what you did, and the monster you really are. What did you do to my parents? My *real* parents?"

He had heard her sobbing. "I saved you, Gabriela, my sweet daughter. You don't understand," he had said.

"No," her voice had quavered. "I never want to hear from you again."

He walked to the bathroom and turned on the shower. Since Montse had left, there was nothing to break up the stark whiteness of the tiled bathroom. The emptiness of the medicine cabinet could not be ignored now that he had removed the broken mirrored door and after he had picked up the shards of bloody glass. She had left the next day, and he had never had a chance to apologize. It had been the same when Gemma had left.

Juan Pablo tested the water with his hand and peeled off the two sweaters, and he removed his slippers and pajama bottoms. He closed his eyes and let the hot water run over his head and down his back.

He had needed to leave, and Barcelona was so much like Buenos Aires. It had all been decided so quickly after the war ended, *La Guerra de las Malvinas*. It had been a bitter blow, especially when Soledad had divorced him and denied him custody of their daughter. In Barcelona, he had joined the shipping company by the port. He had done well for himself, but not well enough. The retirement party had been nine years ago when he had been sixty-two. He could have stayed a few more years, but he needed to get out. An Argentine could only rise so far. He had endured the stares and the whisperings behind his back.

The articles in the news media were more frequent now. There were more senior officials, and he knew many of them. The damned Peronists had come back to haunt Argentina one more time, handing out indictments and locking up old men for war crimes. He took a deep breath to stem his surging anger. His only comforts now were his books and the picture of his little girl, Gabriela, her dark eyes lit up by a mischievous smile across her pale face. It was the only way he ever wanted to remember her.

Juan Pablo kept his eyes closed as he shaved, his hands expertly guiding the sharp blade across the familiar contours of his face. He stopped shaving and dropped the razor. He sobbed.

*I never want to hear from you again.*

He picked up the razor. His hand shook now, and he steadied it with the other as he finished.

He knew where it was, where it had been resting for almost thirty years. He toweled off and applied deodorant and aftershave. Padding down the hall, he entered the closet but returned to the hallway to get a chair. He stood on it to test his balance, and then eased the chest from the top shelf and somehow brought the awkward load down safely. He carried it to the bedroom and set it on the bench at the end of the bed.

The starched white uniform was neatly folded. The white cap rested on top and the polished shoes underneath. The gold stars and the braids and ribbons were pinned to a black-felted board beside the uniform. Beneath the board was his 9mm Browning, still resting in its white patent leather holster, now yellow-tinged and brittle.

Juan Pablo dressed slowly, putting each piece on with care. The pants were baggy, and he no longer filled out the chest. He cinched the belt a little tighter and smoothed down the front of his jacket. He adjusted the cap in front of the mirror.

Returning to the chest, he took out the holster and the sidearm and clipped in the magazine. He belted on the holster and again adjusted his uniform in front of the mirror. He unbuttoned the flap and took the Browning in his grip. Juan Pablo's hand shook, and he fumbled to fasten the button again on the empty case. The shaking stopped only when the muzzle rested firmly against his temple.

"I'm sorry, Gabriela," he said. "I'm so sorry for everything." He stood in front of the mirror for a long time before he took his finger off the trigger and holstered his weapon.

Juan Pablo walked down the stairs of his apartment and out onto Las Ramblas. The rain pelted his white uniform, which contrasted with the dark colors of the passersby, all bundled up and hidden under black umbrellas, scarcely noticing him at all. He arrived at the café and sat at his usual table. The conversations stopped. He felt the stares.

*"Com de costum, Jordi, amic meu,"* the Admiral called out to the waiter in a commanding voice. His medals jangled against his breast.

He would face his accusers. He'd stood up to the Peronists before, and he'd do it again. *Damned cowards, hiding behind their laws and capricious judges.* He'd take the stand and point out the good he had done. He bristled. *We saved the country. And look at Argentina now.* The ruinous leftist policies and pandering to the populist masses. Their deep-seated corruption. The country a bankrupt, indebted mess. *Who are they to accuse me?*

The Admiral pulled out his mobile phone and punched in the number for the Spanish justice department. "I'm here at the café. I'm ready to go back to Buenos Aires. Come quickly before I change my mind."

# CHAPTER 60 – HOSPITAL EL BORDA

## El Borda Hospital

*May 2016*
*Buenos Aires, Argentina*

Daniel lowered his window at the corner of Avenida Libertador and Bullrich, revealing his salt-and-pepper hair. He held out a one hundred peso note.

The panhandler sauntered to the car and grasped the money, but Daniel did not release it. Bending down, the man found himself peering into a pair of large sad eyes. Eyes that had seen much and had chosen compassion over resentment.

"You've been in prison, haven't you?" Daniel's voice from inside the vehicle was fatherly, soft and gentle.

"Yes. Yes, I have."

"God bless you. Know that God loves you very much."

The light turned and Daniel clasped the panhandler's palm. "Go in peace, *hijo*."

Daniel looked straight ahead as he merged into the traffic.

"You can always tell those that have been in prison," Daniel said to Father Gastón in the passenger seat. "Something about them. It changes a person. It changed me, but in a way most never experience. It was there I met God. I met you there too." Daniel smiled. "I'm glad you agreed to come today."

"Of course," said Gastón, removing his glasses to dab a handkerchief across his perspiring face and bald head.

353

"You've told me so much about them. Especially about *him*."

The car pulled up to Hospital El Borda, the psychiatric prison hospital for men. Daniel fished in the glove compartment for his chaplain credentials.

"I can't undo what I've done," Daniel said. "The hurt will always be there. I depend every day on God's forgiveness and healing. That's why I'm here. It's why I do this today."

Daniel opened the car door and swung his legs out stiffly. He stopped and turned to Father Gastón. "I think it's important for you to know," he said, "very few have told these stories. There are many stories from the other side. But from the side I've told you about, most of those who were involved are now dead. Violent deaths, homicides. Drug overdoses and suicides. Lots of suicides. And those who haven't died are in here, in places like these."

Daniel got out and limped past the gate toward the dilapidated buildings.

"They call him The Admiral in here. He insists on it. The nurses and patients, they tease him, and he gets all worked up about it. Juan Pablo's not right in the head, of course. He'll be glad to see you though. He likes meeting new friends."

Daniel paused on the steps to the entrance. He seemed to speak more to himself than to Father Gastón.

"One can still find here a remnant of men society desperately wants to forget. Men who did their duty in a confusing world they didn't understand. Who stood in the way of the terrorist's bullet. Men who served their country and men who committed atrocities. Yes, within these dilapidated walls, a wasted manhood with untold stories and dying secrets and unfulfilled dreams."

THE END

# AFTERWORD

The military regime ended in 1983 following the disastrous Falklands War and immense international pressure against the government repression. To this day, the period between 1976 and 1983 remains a delicate and painful topic in Argentina. Much has been written about Argentina's Dirty War with many half-truths, exaggerations, and accusations from both the left and the right. Yet from the documented accounts and research, reasonably reliable figures can be deduced:

- 10,000 Argentines were killed at the hands of left-wing terrorists. This includes approximately 5,500 members of the police and armed forces killed by guerillas.
- 15,000 to 20,000 Argentines died or disappeared at the hands of the military dictatorship. This includes 10,000 guerilla fighters killed that were self-reported by the two principal guerilla groups, the ERP and the Montoneros.
- 11,000 Argentines have applied for and received up to $200,000 each as monetary compensation for actions against them by the military dictatorship. Included in this figure are some guerillas who died fighting military forces. No compensation ever has been offered for civilians or policemen killed by terrorists.
- 200 to 350 babies were stolen from detained mothers during the Dirty War after giving birth in places like the Hospital Militar. Their identities were hidden, and oftentimes they were given to senior military officers for

adoption.

- A memorial in the Plaza de Mayo was set up for the disappeared. The cremated remains of Azucena Villaflor are buried at the memorial. The Mothers of the Plaza de Mayo still meet monthly at the same plaza in Buenos Aires, their work now focused on addressing human rights issues all over the world.

- In the early 2000s, the Argentine government brought to trial a number of former military officials for human rights abuses during the seven-year dictatorship. Some were extradited from other countries, principally Spain.

- U.S. documents declassified and released in 2009 reveal then-Secretary of State Henry Kissinger and other top administration officials at first supported what Argentine dictators branded "a war against Communism." But the papers also reveal Washington knew people were being kidnapped, drugged, tortured with electrical prods, and some murdered. The Carter and Reagan administrations walked a delicate balancing act between pressuring the Argentine government on human rights abuses and maintaining an ally against the global threat of Communism.

- The Catholic Church struggled to contain Marxist leanings among some of their priests. There is evidence that the Church turned a blind eye to the military regime's arrest and torture of a number of such Jesuit priests.

# ACKNOWLEDGMENTS

I am grateful to my dear friend Daniel for entrusting me with his astonishing and heart-wrenching story. His life is a testament to human dignity, personal responsibility and forgiveness that finds a way to break through the darkness of a brutal and morally challenging world.

Thank you to my beta readers who patiently read early versions of my manuscript – Mickey Konson, Jonathan Whittle, Lauren Shannon, Tanya Klitch, Ricardo Czikk, Dan Smith, Grant Wishard, and Christian Whittle.

I am indebted to Reston Writers' Review who welcomed me in and taught me so much about the craft of writing. Thank you especially to Bill Krieger, Gordon McFarland, Jeffrey C. Jacobs, Jennifer Johnson, Jen Loizeaux, Jessica Johnson, Jon Payne, Liz Hayes, Micah Abresch, R. Gatwood, and Stephanie Siebert. You believed in my story and in my storytelling abilities. Your critiques were invaluable.

Thank you to my editor, formatter, and cover designer. Your professionalism and responsiveness made working with you a pleasure.

Thank you to my wife Laura for your patience in putting up with my time-consuming project and your constant support.

Finally, thank you most of all to God who is the source of all hope, and truth, and goodness.

# ABOUT THE AUTHOR

 **MARK WHITTLE** has a BA from Claremont McKenna College and an MBA from the University of California at Los Angeles (UCLA). He is originally from Southern California but grew up in Spain. He has lived in Buenos Aires, Argentina and has traveled and worked extensively throughout Latin America. He currently lives in the Washington, D.C. area with his wife and three sons. *The Jacarandas* is his first novel.

Did this book help you in some way? If so, Mark would love to hear about it. You can connect with Mark at linkedin.com/in/mark-whittle-4b03172 and twitter.com/MWhittleDC.

Made in the USA
Middletown, DE
23 December 2021